Nothing Ever Breaks
Except the Heart

Books by Kay Boyle

NOVELS

GENERATION WITHOUT
    FAREWELL
THE SEAGULL ON THE STEP
HIS HUMAN MAJESTY
"1939"
A FRENCHMAN MUST DIE
AVALANCHE
PRIMER FOR COMBAT

MONDAY NIGHT
DEATH OF A MAN
MY NEXT BRIDE
GENTLEMEN, I ADDRESS YOU
    PRIVATELY
YEAR BEFORE LAST
PLAGUED BY THE NIGHTINGALE

STORIES AND NOVELETTES

NOTHING EVER BREAKS EXCEPT
    THE HEART
THREE SHORT NOVELS
THE SMOKING MOUNTAIN
THIRTY STORIES

THE CRAZY HUNTER
THE WHITE HORSES OF VIENNA
THE FIRST LOVER
WEDDING DAY

POETRY

COLLECTED POEMS
AMERICAN CITIZEN

A GLAD DAY

FOR CHILDREN

THE YOUNGEST CAMEL

PINKY, THE CAT WHO LIKED TO
    SLEEP

KAY BOYLE

Nothing Ever Breaks Except the Heart

1966
Doubleday & Company, Inc., Garden City, New York

*All of the characters in this book
are fictitious, and any resemblance
to actual persons, living or dead,
is purely coincidental.*

From *The New Yorker:* "Nothing Ever Breaks Except the Heart," "Army of Occupation," and "Evening at Home" Copyright © 1941, 1947, 1948, respectively, by The New Yorker Magazine, Inc.

From *Tomorrow:* "French Harvest" Copyright 1948 by Garrett Publications, Inc.

LIBRARY OF CONGRESS CATALOG CARD NUMBER 66–15667
COPYRIGHT © 1939, 1942, 1943, 1945, 1950, 1953, 1955,
1963, 1964, 1965, 1966 BY KAY BOYLE
ALL RIGHTS RESERVED
PRINTED IN THE UNITED STATES OF AMERICA

For Ann Watkins Burlingame
with my devotion

Contents

PEACE

Seven Say You Can Hear Corn Grow

DAN Minos was a boy who collected all kinds of odd information from the newspapers he read, bits and pieces of things that had already taken place, or were still taking place, here and there in the world; such as the report that an octopus in the zoo in Berlin, Germany, was devouring itself at the rate of a half inch of tentacle per day. One of the aquarium officials had stated that the octopus was suffering from some emotional upset, and that by the end of the month, if the situation continued, it would certainly be dead. The boy read this and looked at his own gnawed fingernails, and then looked quickly at something else.

Once he read about how scientists are trying to dilute the venom in the stings of jellyfish that drift along the eastern seaboard like fringed umbrellas (as the paper put it), pulsing in and out among the bathers with limp curved handles hanging under them, while the tide, or some unseen hand, opens and closes them continuously. This poison, went the story, is stored in cups along the umbrella handles, and it acts in the same way as the stuff South American Indians tip their arrowheads with, causing paralysis, failure of the respiratory organs, and death in the case of small sea animals. Another time there was a half-page report on the remarkable navigating abilities of the green turtle, saying that the U.S. Navy was financing a study of how this large seafarer finds the pinpoint island of his birth.

When Dan's mother came back to their Brooklyn apartment at night, she would bring some newspaper or other with her that a customer had left behind on a table in the restaurant where she worked. One night it might be the *Herald Tribune* or maybe the *New York Times* that she carried with her handbag into the kitchen, and other nights it might be the *Journal-American* or the *Daily News*. But whatever paper it was, Dan would go through the pages of it in his room before he went to sleep, not noticing the name of the paper or the date, but reading the columns eagerly, as if in search of some final communiqué that would tell him how either beast or man had coped with the predicament of circumstances; as if seeking, in the silent doom of animals without precisely knowing what he sought, some indication of what his own vocabulary might one day be.

If you came to the conclusion that Dan Minos speculated on these things he read because the world of newsprint was the only world he functioned in, you would be wrong; for he had as well the daily world of high school, and he had major league baseball to follow, and television to present to him as reality the myths of power by which America lives. It was more that he carried the news items he read like a kind of shield between himself and others, a shield that was never emblazoned with any likeness of himself, but with that of aquarium official, or of scientist isolating the sting of jellyfish, or naval experimenter tagging green turtles at Ascension Island. Once it was the likeness of a German priest he carried, a priest who had been sitting in the front row of the circus when the lion tamer in the enclosed arena clutched at his heart and fell to the floor. The wild beasts had slunk down from their perches, the newspaper item said, and moved stealthily toward the fallen lion tamer while the spectators watched with bated breath for what was absolutely certain to take place. And then the priest had jumped up, pulled open the door of the caged arena, warded off the lions with a chair, and dragged the stricken man to safety. (Whether or not the lion tamer died of his heart attack in the end, the newspaper did not say).

It was only the story of the harness racing horse that went berserk in an airfreighter eight thousand feet above the ocean that Dan couldn't put to any immediate use.

"Sometimes I've thought of being a pilot, a commercial pilot," Dan said to his mother that evening when she came home, "but then I read this thing about the horse in the airplane, and maybe I don't feel the same about pilots any more."

"If my opinion was to be asked," his mother said, "I'd say go ahead and be a commercial pilot and forget about the horse." She worked as a waitress, and she never gave him any real trouble except when he came in so late at night that for hours she'd have been walking her high heels sideways up and down outside on the street. Sometimes it was three o'clock when he'd come home, and she'd be walking back and forth on the Brooklyn street without so much as a Kleenex to stop her crying, complaining about him to anyone passing by. "He doesn't know five o'clock in the afternoon from midnight," she'd say to anyone at all. "I don't know how he gets along. He can't tell good from bad." Or she'd give a description of him in case someone had seen him, saying: "He's nearly six foot tall, and his shoulders are broad, and he's nicely built, the way his father was. He'd be good-looking if he went and got his hair cut every now and then." She got up now from the kitchen table, and crossed the room, and took a can of beer out of the refrigerator, and she swore under her breath as the new-type, built-in-the-can opener tore a piece out of her nail. "But my opinion isn't worth anything to anybody, living or dead," she said.

Dan looked at her dark orange hair, and her face bleached smooth as a china cup, with the various features painted carefully on it.

"There were six horses in the plane," he said, thinking of this thing that had taken place maybe yesterday or the day before, "and this one, this champion, he panicked. He'd been winning harness races everywhere, Australia, New Zealand, all over, the paper said. He was worth seventy-five thousand dollars, and he was kicking and rearing like at a rodeo."

"All they had to do was turn around," the mother said, drinking exquisitely from the can. "Planes can always turn around and go back the way cars can't. You get yourself on a throughway in a car and if you're heading west you have to go to Chicago whether you want to go there or not."

"This plane was going to Montreal," Dan said. "They couldn't go back."

"What's so special about Montreal?" the mother asked, her small, cherry lip mustached with foam.

"The freight engineer, he said they'd tried cutting the sling around his ribs so they could get him to lie down," the boy said. "There were three of them trying to quiet him, but he threw them off, and his front legs were hanging out over the side of the stall. He was smashing against the cockpit, like trying to get to the controls. The other five horses had started acting up, so that's when the pilot told them what to do."

"I don't want to hear what they did," the mother said, taking another swig of beer.

"You can't change it by not listening," Dan said. "It happened. You can't make things different by just looking the other way."

"If you drank a can of beer every now and then, things would look different to you whether they were or not," his mother said. "It would relax you. It would do you good."

"The pilot of the airfreighter said the horse had to be destroyed," Dan said, perhaps not even having heard her speak. "That's the word they use," he explained. "But they didn't have a gun."

"They could have pushed the horse out the hatch," the mother said. She got up from her chair and carried the empty beer can across the kitchen to where it had to go. "For a horse worth seventy-five thousand dollars, they could have afforded a parachute," she said, daintily pressing her foot in a bedroom slipper trimmed with gilded ostrich feathers on the pedal of the garbage pail. When the white lid gaped open, she dropped the beer can inside. "Can't you see that horse parachuting out of the plane, pulling the rip cord and everything?" she said, and she gave a little scream of laughter. Then she took another can of beer from the refrigerator, and walked carefully on her wedge-soled slippers back to the table, and sat down. "So this time maybe you'll open it for me," she said, as she had said it on so many other evenings; and Dan took the can in his narrow fingers and twisted the flat metal tongue from its misted top. "I bought another pair of eyelashes today. Better quality," she went on saying. "Real dark long ones, with a new kind of stickum on them. If I go to the show tomorrow night, maybe you'll help me put them on."

"So when the freight engineer got the word from the pilot about what to do, he grabbed a fire ax," Dan said, and she still might not have spoken. He was seeing it exactly as it must have been.

"Stop it!" his mother cried out in sudden ferocity. "I don't have to hear it! I have a hard enough time working myself to death on my feet all day!"

"You have to hear it," Dan said. He looked at her small bright trembling mouth and her quivering chin, but he did not seem to see her. "If you don't know whether you're on the side of the horse they killed or on the side of the pilot, there's no sense trying to work out your life. You have to decide that first," he said.

"On the side of the horse or the side of the pilot? You're

crazy!" she cried out in fury, her hand too agitated now to lift the can of beer.

And then, two nights later, on Christopher Street, in the city itself, Dan made the acquaintance of the girl. It could have been any month and any Saturday, with no extremes of any kind, and only the first beginning of chill in the bluish New York air. It had not yet begun to go dark when Dan saw the old man lying across the curb near the corner of Seventh Avenue, lying flat on his thin back with his legs sticking out into the street so that the passing traffic had to swing around them. His ancient trousers were slashed across as if by a knife, and his shoes were split by the bunions and corns he had carried around with him for half a century or more. His small head lay in a semblance of ease and comfort on the sidewalk paving, economically crowned with a crew cut of the purest white. The same white bristled without hostility along his jaws, and his cheekbones were bright as apples on either side of his short, scarlet nose. Beside him, in a turtle-neck sweater and slacks, the girl squatted, her face masked by a swinging curtain of long, straight, almost tinsel-colored hair. She was trying to raise the old man by his shoulders, and she was trying to push her bracelets and the black sweater sleeves back on her forearms, to get these encumbrances out of the way. "Repeatedly striking with force between the horse's eyes," the newspaper line kept going, for no good reason, through Dan's mind as he stooped down, "the flight engineer brought the frenzied pacer to its knees, and the ordeal of terror for man and beast was over."

"He looks as though he'd been here a week," the girl was saying.

"I'll get his shoulders," Dan said, and the girl shifted on the heels of her loafers out of his way.

The mottled-tweed jacket the man wore was soft and expensive to the touch; but however good it had once been, and whatever tall and elegant stranger had worn it once with grace, frayed wool now hung like feathers from the cuffs and from the jaunty lapels. As Dan drew him up onto the sidewalk, the girl moved on her heels beside them, her knees in the tight black slacks almost touching her chin, her bracelets ringing musically when she laid her palms beneath the old man's head. The three of them might have been quite alone in the crowded street. No one slackened his pace, no one turned to look in their direction, perhaps because of the sad sharp odor of grieving dreams and rotted teeth that lay in an aura around the sleeping man. Dan knew it well. It was there winter and summer, in snow or in rain, in the gutters and alleyways of the downtown streets he wandered. It lay in stupor under the park benches in the early mornings when drunks sobbed aloud to stone and grass the furious accusations of their pain.

"You'd better get that pint out of his hip pocket," Dan said to the silky lengths of the girl's hair, knowing, too, the exact size and shape the flask would be. "Sometimes when they fall, it cuts them up right through their clothes."

"You're sharp, aren't you, kid?" the girl said. For the first time now she looked up at him, and he saw that her eyes were wide and dark and stormy, and her brows and lashes were smudged like charcoal across her face. "I happen to live in this city," she said. "I happen to live right on this street." Dan held the little man under the armpits still, and as he looked down at the girl he thought of the things that might be of interest to say. He might tell her that in Japan a drunk is called *o-tora-san*, which means "Honorable Mr. Tiger," and that there are over a hundred and fifty sobering-up stations over there called "Tiger Boxes." He could give her the statistics even, saying that just last year one hundred and twenty-eight thousand and ninety-seven drunks had been taken to "Tiger Boxes" by the police to sleep it off. But he had got the little old man in a sitting position, with his neat skull fallen forward on his breast, and it did not seem the moment to speak. The girl reached into the little man's back pocket and took out the gold-and-red lettered bottle that had clung so perilously to his hip. "Two houses up there's an alley where he can lie down, where the fuzz won't see him," she said. She slipped the half-empty flask into the depths of her black shoulder bag, her bracelets ringing like sleigh bells as she moved.

They were walking now, the little old man held upright between them, and Dan thought of the Potawatomi Indians on Michigan's Upper Peninsula drinking for solace, as one newspaper had said. The professor who made the report had been drinking two years with them, and he said that alcohol now substituted for the tribal customs and rituals that had disappeared from their lives. Alcohol, the professor stated to the press, had given them the illusion that their ancestral rights had restored to them the high status that Potawatomi men had held until the white man had come upon the scene. "This professor said drinking was a way for them of asking for pity," Dan wanted to say to the girl, but he didn't say it. Nor did he tell her that in Brazil the police let sleeping drunks lie as long as they didn't block the sidewalk. With the little man propelled between them, they had come to the alleyway now, and there seemed no reason to speak of things that were taking place so far away.

"Get him to the end, back there behind the garbage cans," the girl said, and the pigeons who had been pecking at the paving stones hurried aside to let them pass.

The girl lowered her half of the little man to the ground, and Dan could not see the back of her neck because of the window shade of her hair drawn down across her shoulders. But he saw her slender, tightly belted waist, and her narrow hips, and the long, slim tapering legs in the black slacks, and he could not look away.

"I'll put my jacket under his head," he said, once the little man lay flat on his back in comfort.

The girl waited until he had folded it under the neat, impervious head, and then she drew the old man's right hand free of the elegant frayed sleeve and laid it, palm down, on his breast.

"Give me the other one," she said to Dan. It lay as if cast off, as if forgotten, on the alley stone, and Dan lifted it while she took the whiskey flask out of her bag. Then she bent the old man's will-less arm so that his two hands lay upon his heart, and she closed his fingers around the flask so that he, this ancient, malodorous infant in his asphalt crib, would find it there in solace when he awoke. "Regulations," the girl said. "Orders from the top." She stood up now, and Dan saw she was not tall, and that her hair was parted in the middle, and that she had no lipstick on her mouth. "This is my job. I get paid for it," she was saying, and a look of singular shrewdness was in her stormy eyes. "I've got quite an important position. I get paid by the city," she said.

"If they're hiring people, I'd be free to work every night," Dan said. They walked down the alley together, past the last of the pigeons hastening back and forth in the beginning of dusk, their eyes cocked sharply in their smooth, gray-feathered skulls. And every word that he and the girl exchanged seemed as reasonable to him as the story of that other, foreign pigeon who had hopped a hundred and sixty miles across Denmark with its wings bound. The newspaper had said that it crossed two rivers, nobody knew how, to get back to where it came from in the end. "I'd like a job like that," he said.

"You have to be twenty to work for the city," the girl said. "You look too young." As they entered Christopher Street again, the street lights came on in the early evening, and she shifted her black bag higher on her shoulder, walking now with that sort of frenzied dedication that takes people across deserts, across prairies, not caring about food, or drink, or sleep, driven toward some final destination that has no geography or name. "You have to know Spanish and French and Puerto Rican, and a lot about history," she said.

"I know about things like that," Dan said, keeping step beside her. "I read a lot." He thought of the green turtles' knowledge of the currents of the sea, and the Caribbean beaches they came back to, not every year, but whenever they could make it, navigating sometimes more than a thousand miles to reach the hot white sands where they were born. "The green turtles' lives are something like history," he said. "Anyway, Columbus left written records about them. I read about how they come swimming in to these beaches, and dig their holes, and lay their eggs. Columbus and the other explorers, like Leif Ericson and everyone, they used to eat their eggs."

"Did they eat them fried or boiled?" the girl asked sternly. "These are the things you have to know."

"That wasn't in the paper," Dan said, and his voice was troubled. They had come to the corner of Seventh Avenue, and the girl turned left without any hesitation, and Dan followed where she led. "They have something like a compass inside them, the turtles," he went on saying. He and the girl were moving through the electric blue and yellow and red of the café lights, and through the spaces of city dark, and his head was turned to watch the side of her face changing as the lights and the diluted darkness changed. "I think I have something like that, too," Dan said. "I bet I could find New York wherever I was. I could come straight back across the country without needing maps or roads or anything like that."

"What country?" the girl asked, with the sharp edge of something different in her voice. "What country are you talking about?"

"Well, this country. The United States. I mean, America," Dan said, as if not quite certain of the name.

"You're pretty weak on geography," the girl said. She was stepping down from the curb, over rotting orange peels, over onion tails that had once been green, and flattened grapefruit rinds. "We haven't got a country. Wise up, kid. We've got New York," she said.

They crossed this side street as they had crossed the others, moving through the altering sections of dark and light. Wherever the girl was taking him was of no importance, and the impatience of the words she spoke was transformed to gentleness by the curve of her cheekbone below his shoulder, and the delicacy of her temple and brow when she swung back her hair. They were entering warehouse territory now, and high above the traffic hung the perpendicular letters of a sign not written in neon, but only faintly alight with the dying glow of bulbs set in its frame. "Volunteers of America," the sign read, and Dan knew that a queue of men would be standing beneath it, standing night or day, crippled or upright, sober or drunk, and no matter what time of year it was, waiting to pass through the double doors.

"They're waiting for something to eat," Dan said, and the girl did not take the trouble to turn her head and look at him. But she said:

"They're waiting for me. I make a report on them every night. I'm the only one in the field the city trusts." And even this Dan did not question, believing as he did that everything she said was true. Just this side of the slowly moving queue of men, she slipped without warning into the shadows of a warehouse doorway, and flattened her shoulders and her narrow hips against the wall. "Don't let them see you," she whispered, and Dan stepped in beside her. "If they start running after me, don't move. Stay out of sight. Some of them are still very strong even though they're old. If they once get hold of you, they squeeze you terribly in their arms," she said, her voice still hushed, "and they push their chins into your face."

"About us not having a country," Dan said. He was standing so close to her in the darkness that he could hear the breath running in and out of her mouth. "Did you read that in the paper, that we only have New York?"

"Oh, the paper!" she said in irritation.

"Sometimes there're interesting things in the paper," he said. "Last night I read about the artichoke war they're having in France."

"Do you speak French?" the girl asked quickly. "Sometimes I need it. Some nights there're Frenchmen standing in line, sailors who jumped their ships, and haven't any place to go. I have to get their names. I have to make an official report on them."

Dan waited a moment, thinking of this, and then he said: "Do you report back on these men? Is that the kind of work you do?"

"You're very handsome," the girl said softly, her breath running gently in the darkness, her voice turned tender and low. "I like your hair, and the way you talk, and everything, but you don't seem to understand things very well. I'm paid by the city to call them back from where they are. I'm the only one that can do it." And this might have been the whispered password, the valid signal given, that would cause the sentries to lower their guns and let the trusted through; for now the girl stepped out of the doorway, and her bracelets rang as she made a megaphone of her hands through which to call the words to the waiting men. "Oh, Daddy, Daddy, Daddy!" she cried out in almost unbearable and strident despair, and some in the slowly advancing queue turned their heads, as if aroused from sleep, and some did not. "Oh, Papa, Papa, Papa!" she cried as a daughter from a foreign country might have cried from the sucking undertow before the final music for the drowning played. "Oh, Daddy, Daddy, Daddy, help me!" she cried. "Oh, Popio, Popio, here I am! I'm here!" And now that she had summoned them four times, a wail of anguish rose from the throats of those who had broken from the line, and stumbled back through the darkness to where she was.

Brenda, or Shirley, or Mary, or Barbara, were the names they called out as they tried to run in other men's castoff shoes, in the outsized bags of other men's trousers, and could not. Jean, or Amy, or Pat, or Ann, the muffled voices sobbed like foghorns, and the men in whose throats the hoarse names rose fumbled their way past utility poles and fire hydrants, felt their way like blind men along the warehouse walls toward the sound and the flesh of all they had mislaid in the desert of their lives.

"We'd better get going," the girl said to Dan. She was standing beside him again in the shelter of the doorway, her breath coming fast. "Just run, just run," she whispered, and she pulled him out onto the sidewalk, her fingers closed tightly around his hand.

They did not stop until they had reached the flight of subway steps, and there she let Dan's hand drop. As she threw back her head to look up at him in the wash of the street light, she shook her bracelets savagely.

"You were faster than any of them," Dan said; and, without warning, the vision of the racing horse gone berserk plunged through his thoughts again. As it reared in terror, hammering the cockpit of the airfreighter with its frantic hoofs, Dan touched the girl's silver hair with uncertain fingers, saying: "But you'll have to stop running soon, before you get too tired."

"No, no!" the girl said, whispering it quickly. She stood close to him, looking up at him with her wild, stormy eyes. "You have to get somewhere, don't you?" she said; and then she did not say anything, but she put her arms in the black sweater sleeves tightly, tightly, around Dan's hips, tightly, as if forever, with her head pressed fiercely against the beating of his heart.

It was only for a minute, and then she was gone, running like crazy across Seventh Avenue. The green light turned to red as Dan got to the curb, and the beams of headlights poured between them, and he waited, understanding now with singular clarity the urgency of the choice to be made between horse and pilot, man and man. He could see the white of the harness pacer's eye, and the features of the airfreighter pilot's face, and he knew what should have been done in that interval when the election of either life or death hung in the balance eight thousand feet above the sea. He could not hear the pilot's voice saying *quiet, quiet,* to the stampeding terror. He could not hear it naming the destination to which they were, man and horse, committed, as the course of turtle and pigeon with its wings bound named it louder and clearer than catastrophe. Instead, the pilot's voice, not only heard but visible as are the words contained in comic-strip balloons, pronounced *destroy,* thus summoning death as witness to his fear. *We are not turning back. We shall complete this flight as scheduled,* he might have said, but he did not say it; and, standing waiting at the curb, Dan felt the failure of all men in the pilot's failure, and he whispered "Quiet, now, quiet," to the horse or the girl or the traffic passing by. When the light changed again and the cars halted, he crossed, running, in the direction the girl had fled.

But she was not in the alley off Christopher Street. The little old man was gone, and only his empty flask and the garbage pails were there. At the "Volunteers of America" the sign had gone dark and for once the street was empty. There was no queue of derelict men waiting at the door. It was growing cold, but Dan did not think of this as he walked up one street and down another, searching among the faces that passed in twos or threes through the lights from the cafés, and searching among the solitary others that lingered in the intervals of dark. If he did not find her tonight, still it would not be the end, he kept saying to himself, for he could come back to the city every night, whatever the weather, and on one of the streets, around one of the corners, he would hear her bracelets ringing or see her tinsel hair. If it was not tonight, it would be the night after, or maybe three nights later, or else at the end of the week; and after they had put the drunks to sleep, they would sit down on a curbstone together, and he would say, or try to say, "Don't call the lost men back from where they are. Don't make them remember. Just let them go." He would tell her about things that were taking place in other parts of America, beyond New York; about the Middle West, for instance, where seven university professors had made a tape-recording proving that you can hear corn grow.

It was three o'clock in the morning when he got back to Brooklyn, and his mother was walking up and down outside, complaining loudly enough about him for any neighbors who were awake to hear.

"Your jacket!" she cried out when she saw him coming up the street. "You had your good jacket on when you left the house! Oh, God, oh, God!" she wept.

Above them, as they went into the apartment house together, the one big planet was fading from the sky.

You Don't Have to Be a
Member of the Congregation

FOR a long time I didn't know how to begin this story, or how I'd manage to keep it going if ever I got the opening sentences down. It is a story about a man sitting on the floor of a Brooklyn church in the dark, and that statement is not only the climax of the situation, but it happens to be the entire story. But whatever is recounted to others must be transmuted by the various processes of the heart, or by anger, if necessary, or even by the valediction of despair, into something beyond mere statement. So for weeks I kept trying to get someone into the church in Brooklyn where he was so that the dialogue between stranger and stranger could take over. But those who at different moments appeared to be the ideal postulants slipped from under before I could get them as far as the church door.

"You don't have to be a member of the congregation," I would say, accosting these figments of my own or a higher power's imagination as they came down the quiet Brooklyn street. "If you'll just step inside, nothing will be asked of you except to sit down and talk with him for maybe five minutes. You won't have any trouble finding him. He's sitting on the floor."

One of those whom I sought to wrench from a flight of fancy into reality was a fair young woman with a white mantilla laid over her hair, and a diamond ring on her engagement finger. I could see exactly how it might work out. She would enter the church quite shyly, with her head lowered and a prayer book clasped in her gloved hands (gloves that she would have, just before entering, worked her pretty fingers into), and she would kneel down in the inner gloom to pray for guidance in the new life she was about to undertake. So lost would she be in her devotions that for a while she would not perceive that there, in the farthest corner of the chapel, was this little wisp of a man sitting on the floor with his legs crossed under him. And then, as the darkness thinned, she would see him there, almost within hand's reach, with his lids drawn down across his eyes. He would be wearing the long black cotton gown of the Asiatic scholar, and a black skull cap, and the shaded light beside him would cast its sorry illumination not on his face, but on the papers and scrolls that were laid out before him with the greatest care. After a moment of wonder, she would rise curiously and quietly from the pew where she had been kneeling, and move to where he was, and she would sit down on the floor beside him, for that was the only way that a conversation with him could take place. And in the absolute silence of the church she would begin the story by whispering: "Why are you here?"

"If you would just go in for a minute or two, you wouldn't be under any obligation of any kind," I said to this particular figment, and I laid my hand on her arm so that she would not, like all the others, start moving the other way. "It would be a great service to me. All you would have to do would be to draw him out about himself so that I can get the story down."

"I don't think it would be convincing," she murmured to me. "I would have to be going into a confessional church, to make it logical. It would be quite natural for me to be going in to see a priest, for instance, so this church wouldn't do."

"Well, it's Unitarian," I admitted. "We can't compromise with that aspect of reality. But if you went in, perhaps just to sit down for a moment, just to be alone in the dark and quiet, and then suddenly you would see him, and the conversation could begin."

"Oh, no," she said, smiling at me, but shaking her head under the white mantilla's lace.

"He might make your whole life different for you," I urged. Now that I knew she too was about to fail me, there was a note of desperation in my voice.

"But I'm terribly happy with my life," she said. "I'm going to be married. I'm really terribly happy"; and with these words she moved on into another story and left me standing in the street.

The next one that came to sight or mind was a boy in a great hurry, a kid all skin and bones and furtiveness. Over his shoulder was slung a green book bag, and his hair was hacked unevenly across his forehead and hung long in his neck in back. When he saw me looking in his direction, he began to walk faster in his shabby desert boots, but by running I caught up with him before he reached the corner of the street.

"If you'll walk back half a block with me, as far as the church," I said in a low voice to him, "I'll make a deal with you. I'll tell the cops you went in the other direction." It was essential to the role I wanted him to play that in the book bag there should be something contraband, or at least something stolen perhaps no more than half an hour before. "Whatever you've got there, you can stash away in a corner of the chapel," I said, "and after nightfall I'll help you get away."

"I don't know what you're talking about," he said, but his Adam's apple jerked in his throat.

"I want you to go into the church and talk with a man who's sitting on the floor," I said. "It'll change the look of everything for you."

"What am I supposed to talk to him about?" the boy asked uneasily.

"Just draw him out about himself. Find out why he's sitting there," I said. "I can't start the story until I get some dialogue." There was that sound of appeal, of urgency, in my voice now that the young have every reason to mistrust. "You don't have to be a member of the congregation to go inside," I said. "The place is wide open to everyone, even to kids like you who are on the run."

"If I was looking for cover, I wouldn't go into a church," the boy said; but at least he had turned and was walking back with me. For a moment it seemed to me that the plan this time just might go through. "I'd try to get out of the neighborhood first of all," the boy was saying.

"If you talked to this man, you'd forget about neighborhoods," I said. If everything went the way I wanted it to, he would go into the church, and glance around in the unaccustomed obscurity, and I could even hear now the ring of the stolen silver (if that's what it was), or the rattling of Leica cameras, as he slipped the book bag down between the pews. And after a little while, when his breathing had quieted, he would be able to see the man in the black scholar's robe sitting cross-legged, with the dim light touching the scrolls and papers laid out before him, touching the writing brush in its bamboo stem, touching the small glass jar of India ink as well. "You wouldn't have to stay any longer than you wanted to," I said with a certain cunning, for I knew once the man sitting on the floor began to speak, the boy would be held by the purity, the tranquillity, the alien delicacy, of the things that he said, and, like a knight of the Holy Grail, he would drop on one knee before the scholar, and the conversion, like the conversation, would have instantly begun.

We were going up the church steps now, brown stone they were, the boy keeping a step below me in caution, his face knotting and unknotting with his uncertainty. At the closed double doors, we both came to a halt, and it should have been clear to me then that he could not, whatever the recompense, go any farther.

"You've got hold of the wrong person," he said, his eyes

searching up one side of the street and down the other. "I don't need to talk about anything to anybody. I don't have to hear what that man inside has got to say."

The blaze of the afternoon was hammering and clamoring for entrance at the church doors, but they did not open. Behind them was sealed the impenetrable darkness of sanctuary, and it was this, this crossing from light into obscurity, from all that he knew to all that he did not know, this voyage beyond the familiar limits of himself, that the boy could not undertake.

"I'll go in with you," I said, my voice very quiet. "It's something that doesn't happen every day, that you find someone who is the feeble but enduring pulse of every nation and every race on every continent. If you listen, you can hear his heartbeat through the door."

"I've got a heartbeat of my own," the kid said impatiently, and he shifted the book bag from one shoulder to the other. "And I've got a biology class in fifteen minutes. I got to go."

This is the way it went on day after day, week after week, and it was only when I had come finally to believe there was no way of writing the story that the fife and drum of the military began to play. I saw him coming down the Brooklyn street, wearing the uniform of the U.S. Army, a lieutenant, according to the insignia, of medium height and stocky, as solid in build as a commercial airlines' pilot, knowing exactly where he was going and what he wanted to do. He came up the brown stone steps to where I was sitting in some kind of painful lethargy in the sun, and he made no bones about anything. If he had to face a firing squad, I knew at once he would do it in this same unerring way.

"Do I have to be a member of the congregation to go inside the church?" he asked, looking straight at the muzzles of the guns with his forthright, blue, rather quizzical gaze.

I told him he didn't have to be a member, but when he put his hand against the door, I got suddenly to my feet.

"Did you have some particular reason for coming here?" I asked.

"Yes, I did," he said in his pleasant voice. "I read in the paper that there's a professor from Saigon on hunger strike to the death in the chapel here. I wanted to see him. The piece said he's a professor of Oriental culture, and I thought I'd have a little talk with him."

I looked at his solid healthy cheeks, and his sandy brows, and his straight blue gaze, and such an unreasoning fear took hold of me that my hands began to shake.

"This is the ninth week that he hasn't eaten. Visitors tire him," I said. "He says that fasting enables him to pray with more fervor and constancy for the awakening of the human moral conscience . . ."

"Yes, I read that in the newspaper account," the lieutenant said, his young voice still very pleasant, his hand still on the door. And I knew what I was afraid of now. I was afraid of what this man in uniform had come to do.

"He might not be strong enough to tell you that his fasting is in accord with the traditional customs of his country," I went on saying, speaking hurriedly as if the time left in which to save him was running out. "It's like an act of personal purification, you know, an act of penitence and meditation. That's how he describes it, anyway."

"Yes," said the lieutenant, and he stood looking at me, his mouth half smiling. "Yes," he said. "I know."

"It may be difficult for him today, because of his increasing weakness, to talk about the destruction of the wild and brilliant jungles of his country," I said, the words sounding as if I read them in stage fright from a prepared script. "You see, he's not political. You understand that, don't you?" And now the young lieutenant, so smartly accoutered, his face unperturbed above the uniform, was actually on the point of pulling open the church door. "He's neither Communist nor anti-Communist, neither Catholic nor Buddhist," I said, seeking for other things to say that would keep the lieutenant where he was. "He's very humble. He leaves politics to others. He just believes that the Vietnamese people are able to choose for themselves the side of righteousness. Those are his words," I said. "He says he's ashamed of himself for being so helpless in the mission he has set himself." I could hear the sound of panic in my voice, for I knew now that the lieutenant was going to do what he had come to do. "I'll go in with you," I said, speaking almost inaudibly.

"I think maybe I came here to say it alone to him," the lieutenant said. "I just wanted to tell him, to let him know, while I still can." He stopped and gave an abrupt, soft laugh. "I wanted to say I've told them I won't fight in Vietnam," he said, and he went inside; and I knew this was where the story began, and that I could finally write it down.

The Ballet of Central Park

THIS is a story about children, and about what happened to two or three of them in New York one summer. It is a story that has to be written quickly before it is too late. "Too late for what?" may be asked at once, and to that there is no answer. It would be dramatic, but scarcely true to say: "Before something happens to all the children in the world." But if you think back far enough, you will remember Dostoyevski saying that whatever pain or martyrdom adults endure is of negligible importance because they have already been granted a certain expanse of life. They have had the time to accumulate courage and wisdom, if those were the qualities they put value on, while children have not yet had their chance. Children are still trying to feel their way, Dostoyevski said (or else are shouldering or elbowing their way, or perhaps shouting or stamping or weeping their way), toward what they want to be if everything turns out right in the end. And there is another writer, the gentlest and most misconstrued of men, a man called Freud, who said that psychoanalysis could be at its best a hand reaching out to children in the dark rooms of their confusion, as a hand had never reached out to them before. To those children who cry themselves blind because they cannot bear the vision of the adult world, it could give their childhood the clarity of mountain water, he said.

The story that must be told as quickly as possible is about a little girl who was baptized Hilary by a mother and father who had no other children. They treated this isolate one as though she were a poet of distinction, an actress of international renown, and a musician as gifted and precocious as Mozart. This kind of acknowledgment had been given her since the day of her birth, and in appreciation of it, she had never ceased trying to become these things. Since the time she was six she wrote ballets and danced them out, and she put on puppet shows of her own invention, in which she spoke in four different voices. At twelve, she composed a number of small and agreeable concertos for strings and winds that the school orchestra played. At her home, somewhere in the far reaches of suburbia, she had ridden for years standing upright on a horse's back, around and around in a grassy paddock, her light hair open like a silk fan on the air behind her, her bare feet holding flexibly to the horse's rippling hide.

It should be stated here that I am no relation to Hilary,

except inasmuch as every adult is related to all children. I am as casual and, at the same time, as committed, a stranger to her as any passer-by in Central Park, where Hilary ate her lunch between classes, sitting on a bench, two days a week that summer. I am perhaps that idle lady, twisted out of shape by the foundation undergarment she has chosen to trap the look of youth for a little longer, her feet crippled by the high-heeled sandals that grip her toes like a handful of cocktail sausages, who has strayed over from Fifth Avenue, leading an evil-faced poodle, gray as a wasps' nest and as nervous, on an expensive string. And I am equally the lady with bright orange hair and muscles knotted high in the calves of her shapely, still agile legs, who taught Hilary ballet that summer she was fourteen, or thought she taught her, for actually Hilary needed to be taught nothing, having learned it all sometime, somewhere, before. I am also, being adult, the police officer who apprehended Hilary, except Hilary could never be apprehended. She was beyond arrest or incarceration, for the walls of any prison would disappear if she laid the palm of her hand against the stone.

The story begins on a Thursday, the second day of the summer ballet course, when a wealth of sunshine was poured out hot over the trees and lawns and the asphalt bowers of the playgrounds. Hilary had eaten her sandwich and drunk her milk, and before the ballet would begin again she wanted to get to where the flotillas of sailboats and schooners would be blowing across the waters of the lake. She wore a short blue dress over the black legs of her leotard, and her pink satin toe shoes were slung across her shoulder by their knotted strings. Her light hair was wrenched away from her scalp into a glossy ponytail, and her eyebrows were jet black and seemingly as perishable as the markings on a night-flying moth.

As she ran across the slope below those benches where the

old men bend over their chessboards in the sun, the violent and unexpected battle began. Balloons of every color, swollen with water, sped from the bushes toward the benches, and smacked wide open on the players, drenching their clothes, their hair, and their crumpled faces. Under this multicolored barrage, they leapt to their feet, and knights, castles, kings, queens, bishops, and pawns rolled to the sidewalk or were flung into the sewer opening of the inner avenue. The old men shook their fists and whimpered imprecations.

"Where are they? Where are they?" one old man cried out as he spun around, but there was no one to answer.

"You never know when they're going to strike! They make fools even out of the police!" cried out another, kneeling to retrieve the chess pieces with his veined and faltering hands.

Except for the old men and the passing traffic and the stirring of squirrels, there was no sign of life. Even Hilary was gone, having seen the bare legs fleeing from ambush, and running with them in surprise. When they had scattered in a dozen different directions, she found herself standing with three boys in the circle of the zoo, and for a moment none of them could speak because of the wild beating of their hearts. They had halted before the bars of the elephants' yard, and Hilary saw that the clothes the boys wore had been worn too long, and their shirts were torn like paper. The three of them were as thin as deer, and the backs of their necks were stained brown either by the sun or by the climate of the place their people had come from. The tallest carried a bootblack box on a strap across one shoulder, and the smallest had longish black hair, and the side of his face was of great delicacy and beauty. It might have been carved from the ivory tusk that man had relieved the elephants of some time before, giving them nothing in recompense except this small enclosure of captivity. Beyond the bars, the elephant hides appeared coarser and drabber than ever in contrast with the smallest boy's pure face.

"Do you prefer elephants to zebras or zebras to elephants?" Hilary asked the three of them when her heart had quieted. But it was only the tallest boy who turned his head to look at her, his chest rising and falling, rising and falling, with the laboring of his breath. He said hooded cobras were better than zebras or elephants, and his accent turned to music these words he spoke. The other two had cautiously locked the doors of themselves and drawn the blinds down as they stood looking through the bars. "I like armadillos best," Hilary went on saying. "I saw a lot in Mexico last summer."

"I don't know what that animal is," said the tallest boy; and the middle-sized boy, fragile as a wasp, with dark, narrow shoulders hunched up around his ears, gave Hilary a quick, sly glance.

"It's a mail-clad mammal. It has a coat of armor all over it," she was explaining, her curved hands shaping the way the armor fitted on.

"That would be good," the tallest boy said. He shifted the strap of the bootblack box on his shoulder. "It would be good to be like that," he said.

"You'd have to feed on roots and reptiles to preserve your armor," Hilary said. Because of the mask of wariness he wore, the features of his face were difficult to determine. His hair was like a thick black cap pulled down to join his eyebrows, and the narrow space left between scalp and brows was deeply engraved with the lines of his concern. It went through Hilary's mind then that he was perhaps twelve years old, and the others younger, but he had been so many things for such a long time that his face would have great trouble being young again. "Would you want to live on nothing but worms and carrion?" she asked him, as if speaking to a child.

"I wouldn't mind what I ate if I could be armored," he

said, his voice low, the accent altering the sound of the words on the summer air.

"Let's go look at the camels," Hilary said. She was suddenly uneasy, for there were his eyes, two mortally stricken and savage beasts, crouching in pain in the darkness of their lairs.

They set off together, two by two, passing the fox and the coyote cages, and when they came to the peanut and popcorn stand, the two who had not yet spoken abruptly took on their separate identities.

"This here's Giuseppe!" cried the delicate-boned and beautiful boy, pushing the other one into Hilary's arms as he danced up and down. "He wants peanuts, nothing but peanuts!" His teeth were white in the ivory mask of his face, and his eyes were thickly lashed. "He's got a big hole inside him and all the peanuts in the world can't fill it up!"

"Maybe two bags would, just maybe!" Giuseppe said. He had swollen, golden eyes set far to the sides of his skull, and his voice was high and wasplike when he spoke. "Jorge, he likes popcorn. He steals it from the pigeons! I seen him stealing it yesterday!" he said, his teeth grown long and venomous.

Hilary took her wallet from the pocket of her dress, and she bought them what they wanted. The seals were barking hoarsely behind them in the pool, and the boy with the shoeshine box walked up the macadamized path alone.

"Are you brothers? Are any of you brothers?" Hilary asked, catching up with him.

"We're none of us brothers," he said. They could smell the camels, like bad butter, on the air ahead. "Jorge there, he's from Puerto Rico. Giuseppe's people, they're from Italy. My father and mother, they were born in Spain." Whatever he said, it was as if he carried within him a small harp on which the sun, and the breeze, and his own sorrow played.

"My name's Federico. They named me after a Spanish poet the cops killed back in Spain," he said.

"If you'd like some popcorn," Hilary said, holding the waxed bag out to him, "I haven't touched it yet." But he shook his head.

"I only eat reptiles and carrion," he said.

There was no time left even for the camels, for in twenty minutes the ballet would begin again. The smell of them, and the sound of the seals' voices, grew fainter and fainter as Hilary and Federico climbed the steps toward the traffic of the avenue. Federico shifted the strap of his bootblack box higher on his shoulder, and he might have been speaking of something as casual as the way the grass grew between the trees, or of the tunnel of sidewalk shade that was waiting at the top. But what he was saying was that Giuseppe's brother had drowned in the Bronx two weeks ago. It was a kind of reservoir that he'd fallen into, he said, with a big fence around it, and nobody could get over the fence in time.

"There was a cop there, and even the cop couldn't get off his horse quick enough and get over the fence," Federico said, his voice low, the words he spoke playing like music in the beginning of the leafy shade.

"So what?" Jorge, the beautiful, said, coming behind them up the steps.

"He kept on crying for help for a long time, but nobody could get over the fence," Federico said. "People just stood there looking at him."

"Sometimes people are like an audience," Hilary said, not wanting to hear Giuseppe's brother crying out. "You keep on waiting, and sometimes they don't even applaud," she said, her pale mouth chewing the popcorn fast.

"So what?" Jorge said again.

"And what do you do if they don't applaud?" Federico asked.

But it was Jorge, the delicate-featured, the jet-black-lashed, who answered.

"Then they pull the curtain down on you—quick, like that," he said. He stood beside them on the sidewalk now, making a baseball out of his popcorn bag, and aiming it at a pigeon strolling by. "I saw a kid killed yesterday. A horse was running away with her up near 72nd Street, and she fell off and cracked her head wide open on a rock. She was dead like that," he said, and he snapped his fingers. "I got real close. I touched her hand. It was cold like stone."

"That's nothing," said Giuseppe, his long teeth slyly smiling. He had come so quietly among them that they had not known he was there. The cars passed before them on the avenue, and Hilary waited at the curb, waited either for the light to change from red to green, or else for the terrible story to be told. "There was a kid downstairs from us," he was saying, the waspish shoulders hunched up to his ears. "I guess she was something like six months old. And this man—maybe he was her father, except her name was Angela Talleferico, and he had another, different name—he used to get drunk, and he'd beat her when she cried. And one night she kept on crying, and he picked her up by her feet and smashed her a couple of times against the wall. They had his picture in the paper, resisting arrest."

"They kill rabbits like that where I come from in Puerto Rico," Jorge said, and he did a step or two of his casual, gypsy dance. "It's a quick way to die," he said, and Hilary suddenly cried out:

"Stop saying these things! Stop saying them!" Her face was white, and her teeth were clenched. "I don't want all the children in the world to die!" she cried out above the sound of the heedless traffic.

"Well, they have to just the same," Giuseppe said quietly, and he smiled his venomous, slow smile.

"All of them," Jorge said, walking on the edge of the curb as if balancing on a tightrope. "All of them, except for me," he said.

"The poet they named me after, he died, but they never found his body," said Federico. He did not look at Hilary, as if not to see the tears coming down her face. "He wrote a poem telling he was going to be killed. He said they would never find his body. And it was true," he said.

"Maybe God took it," said Giuseppe, the wasp. With his thin crooked arms, he made the motion of great wings flapping across Fifth Avenue.

"You didn't say what your name is," said Federico after a moment.

When she told him, he said the letters of it over twice. And then the light changed, and she lifted one hand and pointed to where the ballet-school sign hung, halfway up the side street, partly in shadow and partly in sun.

"I have to go there and dance," she said, and she crossed the avenue alone, without looking back at them, wanting never to see any one of them again. Her head was down, and her heart was filled with grief, and the taste of tears was salty in her mouth.

That was Thursday, and on the next Tuesday Hilary came back to the city again to work on the *pas de chat* and the *entrechat* and the *arabesque*, and the rest of the rigmarole that the lady with bright orange hair tried to teach the young. When Hilary walked out of the ballet school for the noon-time recess, Federico and Jorge and Giuseppe were waiting there beneath the canopy. In spite of the heat, she wore the tight black leotard, and carried over her shoulder on their knotted strings were the same pink toe slippers, somewhat soiled and frayed. But this time her dress was yellow, and her hair fell open across her shoulders to her waist, and she held her lunch in a small brown paper bag.

"Isn't your hair hot?" was the first thing Jorge said. He was even more delicate-boned, more gazelle-eyed, more ebony-hoofed, than he had been before.

"No, it isn't," Hilary said, and she swung the length of it sideways, as if out of the reach of his hand. She did this without thought or intention, not knowing that the outcry of children who had died by violence would be there forever between them, only not to be mentioned aloud again or acknowledged in any way. If Federico had spoken in warning then, telling her that a shadow hung over the streets, the parks, the avenues, the reservoirs, the bridle paths, even in clearest sunlight, if he could have said this to her in musical words, she might have taken them dancing elsewhere, perhaps back on a train into suburbia, where the grass springs green and fresh in the horse's paddock, and the cricket voices are as bright and separate as stars. But Federico did not speak. So instead Hilary went on saying: "If we're going to talk, let's think of the most interesting possible things to say, not about the weather."

Giuseppe began at once by saying there were coins in the fountain across from the Plaza. Jorge was dancing backward down the street before them as they walked, and he said that people made wishes when they threw the coins in the water, so you could make wishes the same way when you took them out. He said that he and Giuseppe had made two dollars and ninety-five cents that morning in the subway; saying they could walk through maybe ten or twelve subway cars on their hands when it wasn't the rush hour; saying they carried the nickels and dimes and quarters that people gave them in their mouths so they wouldn't fall out of their pockets. He said they stood on their heads on the express-stop platforms, because that way you covered two trains at a time,

while they played their mouth organs upside down; saying
that when they learned to juggle they'd be in big-time money.

"Where do you keep the nickels and dimes and quarters
when you're playing the mouth organs upside down?" Hilary
asked.

"In our ears," Jorge said; and how they could laugh with
all that lay behind them and all that still lay ahead, it is
difficult to say; but, except for Federico, they laughed out
loud. Even Hilary laughed as Jorge danced backward down
the street, speaking to her of rain and shine, and now and
yesterday, and what they did winter and summer. "In winter
we keep them in our earmuffs, and in summer in our snor-
kels," he said.

"We went every day except Sunday to the door of the ballet
school and waited," Giuseppe said, his shoulders hunched to
his golden ears, his face scarred by his furtive, insect-smiling.

"That's not very interesting. That's like talking about
your hair being hot," said Jorge, the supple. But Federico did
not speak.

"There's going to be a competition at the ballet school,"
Hilary said suddenly. "They told us that today."

"For dancing the best?" Jorge asked, and he spun himself
three times into the air.

"For the best ballet a student writes," said Hilary. She
looked at the side of Federico's face, at the lowered head,
and the hair jerked down in a black iron helmet to his brows.
He carried the bootblack box on a strap over his shoulder
as he had carried it before, but today he seemed a little taller.
He might be thirteen, or even fourteen, she thought, and
she liked it better that way. "I want to do something like
Petrouchka. I want to have organ-grinders, and monkeys, and
things like that in it, ordinary things, not swans or angels,"
she said.

Jorge skipped to the right and then to the left in his backward dance to avoid the people passing by.

And now Federico spoke. "Did you ever make up a ballet before?" he said.

"I made one out of a miracle play once," she said, and she wanted to tell him then that she had made up a dance of the forest-trees. Each tree was exactly like the others, swaying and murmuring with leaves, she wanted to say to him, until it stepped out from the others and danced in the spotlight alone. And then you could see that one tree had birds' nests in its hair, and the boughs of another were filled with fruit, and another had honeycombs packed in its trunk, and another had mistletoe at its crest, like a lighted chandelier. "I made it up for first graders to dance," she said.

"I don't know what is a miracle play," Federico said.

"It has something to do with religion," said Hilary, "and it has to have magic come to pass in the end."

Being a prisoner bound hand and foot by his own silence, Federico could not tell her that whoever had come close to the Spanish poet whose name he bore had been baptized in the dark waters of his magic. These were the words in which his father had described him.

"Wherever he went, that poet always found a piano," Federico said. "Even when he was running from the cops, he played."

They had come to the traffic light, and Jorge turned himself the right way around to cross Fifth Avenue. The four of them walked clear of the trees together, past the open carriages halted in a row. The long, bony faces of the horses between the shafts were masked to the eye sockets in their feed bags, and pigeons walked in and out beneath them, pecking swiftly at the grains that fell. The cushioned seats of the carriages were older than time, but neatly brushed and mended, and shiny-handled whips stood upright at the dashboards, alert as antennae for any promises that might be on the air.

"Someday we're going to cut all the horses loose and race them up to 110th Street," Jorge said. "We'll go faster than cars, faster than jets. There's big-time money in horse racing."

They crossed through the surf of heat to the shoreline of the little square, and the shimmering waves ran liquid to the curb with them, but came no farther, for here the trees made their own cool grove of shade, and the fountain waited. Hilary sat down on the curved edge at the brink, and took the squat milk carton and straw and the sandwich from her paper bag. Federico slipped the strap of the bootblack box from his shoulder, and set the box down on the pavings, and he stooped to look into the water held in the crescent of stone.

"I thought of writing a shoeshine ballet," Hilary said, beginning to eat. "We'd have to have ten or twelve more shoeshine boys."

"I could get them," Federico said, looking up quickly. "I have friends. I have enemies, too," he said with pride. "The poet had many friends. One of his friends was a matador. He got killed in the bull ring." For the moment he said this, the javelins were laid aside, and the armor was unbuckled. "He wrote a poem about the death of his friend. My father said the poem many times in Spanish to me. My father said it was the best poem he wrote because it had the most *duende*. The *duende* does not come to a poet unless it knows that death is there." If he could have remembered the exact words his father had said, he would have put them into English for her, saying that all one knows of the *duende* is that it burns the blood like powdered glass. He would have told her that Spaniards have said that the *duende* is not in the fingers, not in the throat, but that it surges up from the soles of the feet. He would have whispered across the trembling water: "For those who have *duende*, it is easier to love and to understand,

and also one is certain to be loved and understood." But he could not manage to say these things. "If you put *duende* into the shoeshine ballet, then it would be good. It would not be an ordinary dance," was all he was able to say.

Jorge had already sprung on his dark quick legs into the fountain, and his toes sought out the coins at the bottom and flipped them up into his open palm. Giuseppe, striped yellow and black by sunshine and shade, and drained now of his venom, hovered above the surface like a dragonfly. If there were any adults passing, they did not see them, for their eyes, concerned with the vision of something else, had wiped the sight of children away.

"I wish for all the elephants and foxes and coyotes and camels to get out of their cages, and the eagles and ostriches," Jorge said, with the wishing-coins held in his hand.

"I wish for all the cops and the cops' horses to be turned to stone, and everybody not standing in the fountain," Giuseppe said, his mouth stretched grinning in his face, his long teeth hanging out.

"Jump into the fountain quick and be saved!" Jorge cried to Hilary and Federico, but they gave no sign that they had heard. Federico was watching Hilary's finger trace the plan for the ballet up and down, and back and forth, across the stone.

"It could begin with the bombing of the old men playing chess," she was saying. "It could begin with a hundred balloons of every color being thrown across the stage."

"Maybe we ought to start practicing now," said Jorge, leaping from the fountain.

"That part doesn't need any rehearsal," Hilary said, "and there wouldn't be any water in the balloons, but the old men would shake their fists at us just the same. There'll be a dance for boys standing on their heads," she went on with it, "and a dance for boys walking on their hands through a subway train. We'll need eight or ten more acrobats for that."

"I'll get the acrobats, but they're rivals of the shoeshine boys," Giuseppe said.

"Thursday, I'll stay in town after my classes," said Hilary, "and we can begin to practice. The last dance of a ballet has to be like a climax. We'll find some very dramatic music for it. It will be the dance of the knives, the switch-blade knives," she said. "In the end every boy will lay his knife down on the grass."

As she finished speaking, a sudden hush fell on them, and after a moment Federico put the question softly to her.

"Our knives. What do you mean to say, our knives?" he asked.

"Don't all boys carry knives?" she cried a little wildly, not knowing how the thought had come to her. "You must admit that the ballet has to have some meaning. All ballets do. So the stage will get slowly darker and darker, until it is about like dusk, and the boys will kneel and lay their knives down on the grass."

None of them moved. They remained quite silent, looking at her face. And then a stranger's voice summoned them back from where they were.

"Hey, boy," it called out, "I want a shine!"

Federico got to his feet, and picked up his box by its canvas strap, and Giuseppe and Jorge stepped back into the fountain to get on with what they had to do. The stranger was leaning against a tree, and he fitted the sole of his shoe into the iron foothold as Federico kneeled before him. The top of the shoeshine box was open now, and from where she sat Hilary could see on the light wood of the inside of it, the name "Hilary" written in shoe polish black, ineffaceable, and strong.

Hilary was the first to get to the meeting place in the park on Thursday. It was five o'clock, and the members of the ballet troupe had not yet begun to assemble on the slope below the benches where the old men played. But after a moment they began to come up the path, or emerge from under the trees, or else come running down the slope. Some of them carried shoeshine boxes, and some were Negroes; some were olive-skinned, and some were white as grubs. Three or four of them turned themselves upside down at once and stood on their heads as they waited, and one of them played a harmonica, but not loud enough to attract the attention of anyone passing by. At first there were ten, and then fifteen, and at last there were twenty boys, some chasing each other across the grass on silent feet, some shadowboxing, some simply waiting. It was almost as if it were the wraiths of boys who had drifted, in the beginning of evening, to this appointed place. Even the old men at their chessboards did not interrupt their games to glance down to where they were. But Hilary was uneasy in their muted presence until Federico and Jorge and Giuseppe came up from the iron jungle of the playground, and then she knew there was no reason to fear.

"Have you got the balloons?" Jorge asked at once. His eyes were black-lashed, his delicate bones more pliable, his beauty even more eloquent than before.

"Have you got enough peanuts to go around?" Giuseppe said.

"I didn't bring anything for anyone," Hilary said. "It isn't going to be like that. First we decide on the different roles, and then we practice the ballet steps. In the end, if we win the competition, there'll be prizes and things to eat," she said.

But how to describe the rehearsal that now got under way is not an easy thing to do. However it came about, within a few minutes the lot of them were twisting and turning, and swinging and bopping, with Giuseppe playing on the harmonica the music of *Petrouchka*, playing it over and over as Hilary hummed it aloud. Jorge led the boys who walked on their hands, making them clap their feet together; and Federico danced the steps that a matador dances, his chest thrust out, his shoeshine box hanging from his shoulder, leading the bootblacks like him who, day after day, kneeled before men with shoes to be cleaned. As they followed the pattern he stamped in the grass, their tempers were running hot in their blood, but Hilary, the actress of international renown, the musical genius of sweet precocity, was not aware that this was taking place. That they had come to dance for peanuts, or the slap of water-filled balloons, or for some act of violence as reward, had nothing to do with the music of Mozart or Stravinsky, or with the *duende* of a Spanish poet whose last name Federico could not recall. It was six o'clock when the murmur of their discontent became an orchestration for bass violins, but still Hilary did not recognize the deep-voiced prophecy it made.

They had come to the moment for the final dance, for the climax of renunciation, and Hilary, her high, narrow cheekbones flushed, jumped up from where she had been kneeling on the grass. Her voice could scarcely be heard in the vast auditorium of the park as she called out to them in heedless pleasure:

"It was very good! It was better than any ballet I've ever seen! This is almost the end. This where I come in for the first time, and you must all stop dancing when I come on the stage!"

But they had already ceased to dance.

"Have you got the balloons with you?" one voice shouted out. "What are we getting out of this?" another asked, as if he had looked down in bewilderment and suddenly seen his empty hands. The sky, like a planetarium cleared for stars, was filled with the blue and lingering dying of the light. "We ain't jumping up and down here for our health!" cried another voice from the receding limbo where they stood, their features wiped away, and their color gone, in the slowly falling dusk.

"This is the final part!" Hilary said. "Don't be impatient! This is where you take your knives out, because the ballerina asks you to, and you lay them down, each making up a separate dance!"

And now the roar of their voices was like a tempest rising, and Federico pushed his way through the wild storm to where Hilary stood. He took the switchblade knife from the back pocket of his chinos, and whatever they may have thought he had in mind, he laid it down, with a sweep of his arm, before her. This was the last gesture he was to be permitted for all eternity, for the leaping, screaming mob closed in on them.

"So the Hooded Cobra dies!" they cried in fury. "The Hooded Cobra dies!"

The sirens of the police cars keened in pain, and the ambulance shrieked out like a mother for him, as his blood ran black across the trampled grass. The park was empty. The old men had folded their chessboards and gone home, and there were no children anywhere. He had been cast off by friend and enemy, by life itself, except for the little girl who sat with the iron helmet of his head held close against her heart. "The knife and the cartwheel, the razor and the prickly beards of shepherds, the bare moon . . . religious images covered with lace work," went the words of the poet whose name he had been given; "in Spain, all these have in them minute grass-blades of death." His knife lay there, with no blood on its blade, as the cops leaned over to take her hands away from him.

"Stop crying," said the one who apprehended her. "If you get mixed up in things like this, it has to end this way."

One Sunny Morning

HIS bicycle was home in Philadelphia, Pennsylvania, so he pedaled along on a borrowed one that was too big for him. From the eye of a caterpillar weaving its evil spell in the massacred trees, the land itself through which the boy rode might seem too big as well, but he knew it was not. As he bore his weight to the right or the left on the tarnished horns of the handle bars in order to follow the shade from one side of the road to the other, he could see in his mind the outline of it. It was no more than a narrow passage of land between two bays, known in geographies as the state of Delaware; but to him it was a lonely pathway leading from the far front stoop of home. The leaves of the roadside trees were shriveled to paper by drought, and their edges were scalloped by the grinding of a thousand insects' teeth. Beyond them lay cornfield and chicken-farming country, burned to a crisp, the air above it already shimmering and quivering. But he knew, pedaling in and out of the tattered areas of shade, that by noon it would be hotter; and yet this place had nothing to do with the real South. Philadelphia had twelve letters in its name, he was thinking, and he had been twelve days with his aunt and uncle, and they had the number 12 on the front door of their house. It might be another twelve days before they would put him on the train to go back home again.

He had been sent out on the bicycle like this to get the answer about the Chesapeake Bay retriever. You kept on going a mile and a half, maybe less, down the road, his uncle had said, and then, just around a turn where some trees stood in a little hump or clump ("hump," said his uncle, and

"clump," said his aunt), you came to three houses, and the
boards of them had been white once, but were not white any
more. There would be two on the left and one on the right,
with a stream running in a dip and a gully past the one house,
and on down through the trees. "Except the water'll have
dried up there like everywhere else," his uncle said. "But there
won't be any old sofas on the front porch, or any rusting
bedsprings, or an icebox without a door in the front yard, like
you might think. They're better than most. It'll be the house
on the right, and the kids'll have shoes on their feet, and if
Sam Ticer's home there'll be a Chevy standing in the driveway, if you want to call it that. You tell him you're Doctor
Edgeworth's nephew down visiting, and if Sam isn't there,
he'll have left word with his wife, and she'll let you know."

So the boy made the curve, pedaling slowly, thinking there
was never any comfort in visiting, and that this was the worst
day of all. It was the saddest of the whole string of days that
seemed like a season in themselves, longer than any long
summer in territory that he knew. There were the houses,
faded and worn, in a sudden oasis of shade, and in the middle
of the road stood an ancient Ford, a Model A, the boy knew
at once, leaning sideways there where it had no right to be.
He dragged the toes of his sneakers on the ground, and then
swung down from the bicycle. There was no Chevy anywhere, and there was no sign of any living thing. The great
brown coarse-haired dog his uncle wanted did not run out to
jump on him or lick his hand. Without raising his head, then,
he saw the woman come through the front door of the Ticer
house, pushing the screen door silently before her, and wait
on the threshold without making any sound. He could see
she was thin, and that two small children were enfolded in
the skirt of her violet-colored dress. He knew they were watching him set the bicycle against a tree. When he had come as

far as the porch steps with no sign being given, he looked up at the woman and said the whole thing wrong.

"I was to ask about the Chesapeake Pay receiver—the lady dog you want to sell. I'm Doctor Edgeworth's uncle. I mean, he's my nephew. I'm down visiting from Philadelphia."

"My, you're a long way from home," the woman said, her voice scarcely louder than a sigh. "A long, long way." She might have been referring in true sorrow to a place she too had left somewhere. She stepped onto the long, worn boards of the porch, and the screen door clapped behind her like the soft sound of a hand. The two children moved with her, so close in her skirts that it might have been a six-legged creature that advanced. "That Ford," she was saying. "My husband wanted to get it up into the yard before he left for work, but the engine got flooded. I told him I'd take care of it, but I guess I put no trust in myself. That's what my husband says. I can drive when I make up my mind to it, but I don't care too much for driving. When the engine's dried out real well, I'll have to try to get it in."

"It might be dangerous if anybody came around the corner," the boy said. He turned back from where he stood on the step to look at it again.

"Yes, it's dangerous, dangerous, dangerous," said the woman, in her soft, sighing voice, "but anyone careful could go around it if they wanted to."

"Once I backed my father's car around at home," the boy said. "He sat beside me and told me what to do."

"I could sit beside you, but I wouldn't be much good," the woman said. She and the children had halted at the top of the porch steps. "I have trouble keeping the gears straight in my head." Her voice drifted quietly back to what she wanted to say to him. "You surely are far, far from where your home is, and you're surely warm. You come in and cool off inside the house where there isn't any flies," she said.

There was no sense of shade in the kitchen, although Venetian blinds were hanging in the windows, for the yellow seats of the chromium-legged chairs were as bright as any sun. The little girl had come out from her mother's skirts, and the blue ribbons woven in and out of her short, erect braids of hair could be seen now; worked in and out as neatly as embroidery, and the braids too many to count. Between them, the little pathways of her scalp were as sharp as if they had been drawn with a pointed pencil. The brother had emerged in his own right, too, his face not as round and not as dark, and his hair placed high back from his sloping forehead in a small, elaborate crown. He sat down on one of the yellow-cushioned chairs and crossed his bare arms on the table. They were narrow, like laths of kindling, and the skin on them was a light tan.

"You take a chair like Ezra's done," the mother said. Against the dead alabaster of refrigerator and washing machine and stove, her face was pansy-black. "Would you prefer to have cream soda, or lemonade, or orange drink?" she asked, holding open the refrigerator door.

"I'll take a soda," the boy said, but he didn't sit down. He could feel the grit inside his sneakers as he shifted where he stood. He hadn't put on clean jeans that morning, because this was to be the worst day; and now it mattered that there was a button off his plaid shirt. "My uncle, Doctor Edgeworth, he wants to know the price of the dog, the lady dog," he said. ("Female," his aunt had specified; "bitch," his uncle had said.) "He sent me to ask because you didn't have a telephone."

"Yes, we just couldn't keep the telephone," the woman said, and the light behind her died as she closed the refrigerator door. She put the soda bottle and the glass pitcher of lemonade down on the gilt-speckled yellow of the tabletop. "It kept ringing so much at night, so after a while we just didn't answer it. Alice and Ezra here, they couldn't get their sleep."

"It was always wrong numbers," Ezra said in a high, clear voice as the mother took the glasses from the shelf.

"Always wrong numbers," the mother said, the words like the beginning and the ending of a song. "The children here, they're trying to get their growth still. Waking up every night, dreaming, and crying—this can stop you from growing." She opened the bottle of soda for the boy, and she poured lemonade for the other two. Ezra reached out his thin, tan arm and hand. "Alice and Ezra, they're four years old and eight years old. We've got other children," the mother said, speaking to the standing boy as if he were a man. "They're way too big for the elementary school. They're big like you."

"I'm twelve," the boy said.

"My, that's a wonderful age," said the mother. "That's a wonderful, wonderful age to be. Nowhere's too far to go, and nothing's too hard to do."

The boy sat down, and he saw the whitish hairs on his own arm as he took a swallow of the soda. And now the little girl pulled one of the bright chairs over close to his and knelt on it as she drank.

"Where are your bigger children now?" the boy asked this mother he had never laid eyes on before in his life, this mother who also sent her children away.

"They're visiting relatives," she said. She took an apron with great pale roses on it from a hook, and she tied the strings of it around her waist. "With school beginning soon now, we sent them up to New York to visit relatives. That way they can go to school with New York children, and they'll learn better. They'll be visiting relatives for a long, long time," she said.

"I don't like visiting very much," the boy said, drinking his soda. "My mother had another baby, so I came down here. I don't like visiting even relatives."

"Sometimes it's the loneliest thing anyone can do," the mother said. The little girl held a toy truck in her fingers now, the kind of truck that fits into a matchbox, and she ran its wheels up over the boy's bare arm with the light hairs on it, and over his shoulder, and up the back of his neck into his close-cropped hair. She did this over and over again, and each time the truck ran into his hair she laughed until she had to put her head down on the table, laughing and laughing, with the small jet braids erect as pine trees along the myriad pathways of her scalp. "We went visiting down to Mississippi last month," the mother said, her fingers touching the shining high crown on her son's head. "We took the children down to see my people, and visiting's visiting no matter if the same blood's running in your veins."

"I didn't like that trip to Mississippi," Ezra said. "We had to sleep in the car and eat in the car." His sister ran the truck over the bumps in the white boy's spine, laughing until she was weak from it, and then running the truck up and down his spine again.

"The children were kind of cramped on the trip," the mother said. "We didn't have time to stop much on the way. So we carried the milk and the water and the sandwiches right along with us. That way, we didn't make any trouble for anyone."

"Sometimes we stopped, but there wasn't never any room," Ezra said, looking straight ahead through his light tan mask. "You said we were going to sleep in a motel, but they told us there wasn't any room. And you said we'd stop when it was time to eat again, but you didn't stop. I wanted a hamburger, and Alice wanted one too," he said.

"Everything's crowded, crowded, in the summertime. Everyone's traveling every which way," the mother said. "This boy's going to have the best kind of life anyone could have," she went on saying, touching his hair, "without too many trials or tribulations to contend with. He's going on to university when he's grown. Maybe he'll go to the University of Pennsylvania, or anywhere he finds he wants to go."

"I might be going to the University of Pennsylvania too," the older boy said, and he drank the last of his soda.

"I don't want to go to Pennsylvania. I don't want to eat and sleep in the car," Ezra said, and he shook his mother's fingers away.

"There'd be more room in Pennsylvania. There'd be lots of room there," his mother said. She laid her long, dark hands on his thin shoulders. "Maybe someday you two might meet at the University of Pennsylvania," she said, looking over his head at the other boy. "And then you'll remember sitting down here with us, and you'll remember Ezra Ticer. He'll just be beginning when you're finishing, and you'll be able to show him around."

"I don't want to be shown around," Ezra said.

"You'll make him feel like he's at home, not visiting relatives," the mother went on saying. "You won't forget." Although it was not a question she asked, still the words beneath the sighing of her voice had their own urgency. But whatever answer was expected was never given because of the sharp death-scream of a truck horn on the road, and the thudding of a heavy motor, rhythmic and ominous as the beating of funeral drums. The mother's long-fingered hand fled to her heart. "That's what I thought might happen. That's what I was afraid of all the time," she said.

The two children were in her skirts again as she moved across the kitchen, and the boy followed behind as she gently pushed the screen door open and moved out onto the stoop. There was the truck, halted just short of the blunt-nosed Ford, its load of slipping gravel overflowing in rivulets down the

peeling red and the blistered green of the long-unpainted sid-
ing boards. The man behind the wheel leaned across the vacant seat to the truck window. Then his mouth stretched
open in his swollen, putty-white face, and he began shouting
out the words.

"Damned upstate double-dealers selling out!" he might
have been saying; or: "So you figure you own the highway
too!" But the boy could not be sure, for his mind, or his ears,
or what his life had been up to this moment, had not equipped
him to deal with the violence of this sound. The man's round
skull was inflating in the window, his neck expanding, the
muscles of it pushing his plump shoulders wider and wider on
either side of the blue bib of his overalls. "I could have you
run out of town, the lot of you!" he might have been shouting
from the height on which he sat, while the sliding gravel spat
like raindrops in the dust. His body had certainly grown too
big to pass through the opening of the truck door, but still his
bare arm struck it wide, and he squeezed past it and jumped
down on the road. And now, as he came toward them, he took
on the proportions of a carnival figure in a department-store
parade. The face had relinquished its resemblance to that of
any man the boy had known. The eyebrows sprang in whitish
bristles above the baby-blue, ballooning eyes, and the pink lids
had grown as big as tents as he advanced. He had reached the
path now, and he surged forward, inexorable as a tide, toward
the steps, toward the porch on which they stood. "There's four
trucks coming fast, so get that tin can out of the way before I
haul you in for murder!" he was shouting, the actual substance of his voice filling all space so now there was no air
left to breathe. *So we'll have to suffocate,* the boy thought in
reeling panic. Some act, some word, was being asked of him,
but he did not know what act or word it was. *We'll suffocate,*
he thought, *with our tongues rammed down our throats because there isn't anywhere else for them to go.* The truck of

gravel, the broken Ford, the rusted bicycle that leaned, no larger than a cricket, against the tree, were blotted out by the tower of flesh in the faded overalls. It had pushed aside the landscape until nothing but the fury of one man was there. The floating head seemed to be tangled in the top branches of the shade trees as he came, shouting aloud his abuse. So *we're going to die*, the boy thought doggedly; *Alice and Ezra and the lady and me, we're going to die.*

But that is not what took place. Instead, without any warning, the boy went running across the boards of the porch, and down the steps, and out onto the road.

"I backed the car around at home. In Philadelphia I did it," the boy said to the summer morning. He was sitting in the jalopy now, and his hands moved quickly, bringing it to shuddering life. As it gasped out its complaint, he backed it, jerking and bucking, into the Ticer driveway ("If you could call it that," said his uncle's voice from somewhere else), and stopped it in the fresh cavern of shade.

The truck driver had diminished. He sat, the size of ordinary man again, behind his wheel, ramming the truck into gear. It might have been that he had never moved from there, and never wrenched the breath out of their mouths. Then, just before the first of the four trucks made the curve, he swung the slipping, sliding, spattering load of gravel on its way.

"If you'll wait," the woman said from where she stood, six-legged because of the children in her dress; "if you could wait until noon, my husband will want to talk with you. I know that." The words that followed were lost for a moment as the second truck, and then the third, and then the fourth, came roaring through. "He'll want to talk to you about the dog. It might be he'd want to *give* the dog to Doctor Edgeworth," she said, the soft voice like a hammock rocking gently, gently, in the shade. "I don't know. I couldn't say for certain, but that's the way he might want it to be."

The boy did not speak. He sat on the cracked leather and the mildewed stuffing of the split-open seat, not hearing, and having forgotten it was not for this moment of pride that he had come, but for something else entirely.

Should Be Considered Extremely Dangerous

THERE was a boy named Tad Plover who was born in a Connecticut village on the left bank of a cove that had about it an air of true humility. One arm of the land that embraced the cove was wilder than the other, but on both sides there was a marsh of saber grasses, and these marshes were alive in the spring and the autumn with long-necked and long-legged transient birds. Sometimes swans, even, searched for food on the banks that were partly sand carried in from the sea, and partly soil from the bed of the stream that emptied its fresh creek waters into the brine. The village consisted of a firehouse, a drugstore, a seafood restaurant, and a half-dozen old-fashioned, shingled residences with wide piazzas, survivors of another epoch, standing back on their shady lawns with hedges marking the end of the soil and the beginning of the sand. In between these houses were the boatyards, with yachts and fishing yawls in dry dock, and boats turned keel up for calking, or painting, or debarnacling. Throughways might slash across the country, and trucks thunder night and day through territory where deer trails had passed in silence and mystery before, but the signs on the waterfront that said "Live Bait," or "Lobsters and Steamer Clams," or "Boat Livery," had never changed. All summer a motley fleet of boats was moored at the backdoor steps, and all year there was the taste of salt in the air and the smell of calking tar. These things gave the boy's life a certain rhythm and poetry, but there was something else that brought the drama of the outside world to him and gave his mind no rest.

His father was the postmaster of the town, and while the boy was still very young, he began to look at the leaflets the police hung over the ink-scarred writing desks. There was the assortment of glossy photographs, out of place in the rural post office that could be mistaken for a cottage, fashioned of brick as it was, with a vine growing up the white wooden pillars and across the cornice that framed the door. The faces he studied were shown from both the front and the side view, and below these likenesses of the hunted, the names and the violent records were printed out. *Has been convicted for burglary, larceny, theft of Government property, and felonious assault,* the story might go, and the boy would look into the men's bold, or sullen, or despairing eyes. *Reportedly will shoot anyone trying to apprehend him,* the legend might run, and Tad Plover would stand, transfixed, in the post-office room, reading the abridged, specific histories.

"What would you do if one of them walked into the post office, and you recognized him from the photographs?" the boy would say to his father in the evening, and, outside, the tide might be lapping in around the tall, spindly legs of the landing pier that teetered out from the back-stoop of their house.

"Well, I guess I'd just reach for the telephone," the father would answer, not looking away from the television screen. He was a heavy, small-featured man with tattooed forearms, who had once sailed far and wide as the member of a freighter's crew. "It wouldn't be a bad place to come to if you were trying to evade the law. It's pretty well off the beaten track," he'd say.

When the boy looked at him sitting there, heavy and quiet

in the lamplight, with the blue and the yellow of the tattooing showing on his forearms under the reddish, curly fuzz, he
felt the conviction of his father's life, and it gave him a sense
of certainty.

"Wouldn't you be afraid?" the boy would ask.

"Oh, I'd try to handle it casual-like," his father would say.
"I'd pick up the telephone, and when the cop at the other
end answered, I'd call him by his first name right away. 'Is
that you, Jim, or Sandy, or Bob?' I'd say, depending on who
it was at the desk at headquarters, and I'd tell him to come on
over. That's all. I'd say it like I was talking to a friend so the
guy who was standing there asking for stamps, or dropping a
letter into the slot on the other side of the wicket from me,
wouldn't get on to it at all."

"But they're pretty smart, aren't they?" the boy would ask,
in wonder of those who had no deference for authority.

"Sure, they're smart," the father would say. "You have to
play a waiting game with them. I'd just keep on talking about
the weather across the counter, or about fishing, maybe, making it kind of interesting, and hold him there until the police
came walking through the door."

It was the summer Tad Plover was eleven that the notice
about Bliss Mandry was put up in the post office, and the boy
couldn't get it out of his head. Bliss Mandry seemed different
from the others, for he did not have any aliases, and the year
of his birth was given as 1941, so that made him younger than
the rest of them hanging there. He was of medium height, the
description said, his weight was a hundred and forty pounds,
and his build was slim but muscular; his hair was brown, and
it might be worn in a crew cut. It was specified that his eyes
were green, and he had escaped from confinement three times.
There was a long, jagged scar in the palm of his right hand. His
occupations had been "waiter, caddy, and diner cook, mer-

chant seaman, and roustabout," and he had reportedly taken lessons in flying light aircraft. He had committed a dozen or more burglaries, was said to speak Spanish, and liked smoking small cigars.

But the face and the legend did not go together. Bliss Mandry's brows were heavy and handsomely arched, and, beneath them, his eyes established a communication as clear as speech, the way the eyes of movie or television actors did for the boy when he sat in the dark and watched them on the screen. The lips were narrow, and the left corner of the mouth was jerked just slightly to one side, and in this face there was a look of stubborn pride. The arbitrary story said that Bliss Mandry was reportedly adept at fighting with his fists, and on one occasion beat his victim with a blackjack; was highly proficient in the use of knives, and known to carry a switchblade knife and a .38 caliber revolver. He should be "considered extremely dangerous."

It was three o'clock of an August afternoon when Tad Plover came into the post office with the evening papers carried over his shoulder in a clean white canvas bag. Every weekday, the bundle of papers was tossed out of a truck before the drugstore. He would pick them up there, and straighten them into the canvas bag with *The Standard* lettered in red on it. Then he would go to the post office, and pass his father a copy under the wicket, below the sign saying: "Money Orders. Registry." After that, he would go out through the back, where his bicycle was, swing his leg over the saddle, and set out on his delivery route.

There was no one else in the post office that afternoon, and Tad Plover was thinking of fishing as he passed his father the paper under the wicket bars. He knew everything about the cove: that when the tide came in, the gulls came with it, their eyes peeled for the sight of fish flickering below. And when the tide ebbed, mallards with white rings feathered around their necks would leave the reeds and mud, and cross the main street on leathery feet, making their way through the grass on the other side to a barn where grain had once been stored. There they would go, and whatever cars might be coming down the meandering street would slacken their pace to let the ducks go past in single file. But now the tide would be running in, he knew, for he could hear the seagulls commenting harshly on what they saw. His father had opened the paper out to read, and he did not see the next thing that took place. The door from the street must have opened soundlessly, for when Tad Plover turned to go, the figure in dungarees was there. Whoever he was, he walked straight to the police flyers hanging on the wall, and he stood with his back turned to the boy, and one bare arm in the T-shirt leaning on the high, wood desk. The other hand was carelessly flipping the pages of a man's dishonor.

Tad Plover had not moved a step when he saw the lifted hand stop short, and the shoulders in the T-shirt jerk, perhaps with silent laughter, at the uproarious story of libel written out. Then the stranger picked up the pen that lay in the groove on the top of the desk, and he pressed the flyer against the wall, his palm flat on it, his fingers spread, and he began to write across it in a large and violent hand. When he was done, he dropped the pen on the desk again and turned, a young man of medium height, brown-haired and muscular, walking singularly erect. In that instant his face seemed to Tad Plover one he had seen before. He went out quickly, on soiled and dilapidated sneakers, and the door swung closed behind him without a sound.

When he was gone, Tad Plover crossed the small, square, empty room, and stopped before the sheaf of flyers. His heart trembled strangely as he read the words the man had written there. "Please hold my mail," went the careless, reckless message across the glossy surface of the printed page; "will be back tonight to pick it up," and the signature below was "Bliss." Just above these boldly written words were the static whirlpools of the fingerprints, and the caution: "Known to carry a switchblade knife and a .38 caliber revolver," and Bliss Mandry's eyes looked out of the photograph in stubborn pride. Tad Plover followed quickly out of the post-office door. Ahead, in the quivering veils of heat, he could see the figure in dungarees walking toward the boatyard lying opposite the barn that the mallards crossed to when the tide was low.

"Say, kid. I wanted to get hold of a boat," was the first thing the young man said to him, swinging around on his broken sneakers at the boatyard gate. "They got good boats here?" He jerked his head toward the signs that said "Lobster Pound" and "Boat Livery." His mouth was small, and his thin lips almost colorless. Tad Plover stood silently looking at the frail, high-cheekboned face.

"Her name's Mrs. Hopewell. She's got good boats," the boy said nervously. "It turned out to be a pretty hot day, after all, this afternoon," he said.

"I'm not worrying about the heat. I got other worries," the young man returned. "This isn't my territory. I'm just passing through."

"Sure. I know," said the boy, standing there, the bag of evening papers hanging by his side.

"What do you know?" the young man asked him quickly. His brows were dark and handsomely arched, but whether his eyes were gray or green, Tad Plover could not tell.

"Well, I mean that I always lived here, so I know everybody in the cove, so I knew you were a visitor," the boy said.

"Sure. That's it. A summer visitor, a tourist." The young man laughed without making any sound, and his teeth showed, small and white, with only the front ones a little crooked in his mouth. "I was thinking of getting a rowboat, and going out fishing, and asking someone to come along."

"I'd like to go fishing, but it's my newspapers," said the boy,
and he rubbed his palm on the canvas bag. He was thinking of
the photograph in the post office: the arch of the brows and
the width through the high cheekbones were the same, the
ears lying flat against the skull and placed a little low. But
the eyes of the man in dungarees seemed cold and silent to the
boy; or, rather, silenced. Their eloquence was muted, the reckless promise in them veiled by caution now. "I've got to deliver my papers. I go on my bike and it goes pretty fast," the
boy said. "It won't take me more than fifteen minutes, and
you could wait for me here." His father had said that you pick
up the telephone, and you tell the police, but he wasn't sure
yet. Until he saw the scar in the palm of the right hand, he
couldn't know.

"Oh no, you don't!" the young man said, and there was
something else in his face now. Under the tanned skin of his
forearms, the muscles were turned to stone. "You stick
around here. You forget about your papers," he said, and the
boy watched his hand move toward the pocket of his dungarees. "I can show you a lot of things you never knew before. If there was any helicopters lying around, I'd take you
up for a ride. I've been testing out hydroplanes in the Gulf of
Mexico."

They did not say any more, but walked through the boatyard together, the young man walking lightly in his ancient
sneakers, his head up, his shoulders pulled back as rigidly as
if his hands were tied behind his back. They passed the white
ribs and spines of boats laid bare to the sun, passed the upturned hulls, the gallon-sized varnish tins, walking through
the smell of paint and tar. In the office of the "Boat Livery"
there was a glass showcase and a counter where fishing rods
and nets, and the bright paraphernalia of fishing tackle were
on display. The lady who stood guard over it all was plump

and keen-eyed, and her hair as white as lilacs, without a trace of blue.

"Hi, Mrs. Hopewell," said the boy.

"Hello, Tad," Mrs. Hopewell said. The boy ran his tongue along his lip, and the young man took the conversation for his own.

"Hello, Mrs. Hopewell, I'm a summer visitor here," he said. "Me and Tad here, we thought we'd do some fishing. We want a boat for the afternoon."

"Well, that's just fine," said Mrs. Hopewell. "Where are you staying? I hadn't heard about any new folks taking a house in town."

"I'm staying with Tad," the young man said, and, like an eye winked in connivance, the muscles in his tanned, bare arms flicked quickly, furtively. "My folks couldn't get away from town just now. They're planning on coming up next month," he said.

Mrs. Hopewell said that would be two dollars down, and the young man put his right hand into the pocket of his dungarees, perhaps touching the blade or muzzle of violence there, and then he took it out.

"As long as I'm going to be around awhile, you could just mark it down on the books," he said.

"Well, I don't know," said Mrs. Hopewell slowly. "That makes for a lot of bookkeeping."

"Tad can tell you my credit's good," the young man said. "My dad, he's got a big garage in the Bronx. He's got a contract with the government, servicing post-office trucks. My dad and Tad's old man went to school together," he said, and the muscles in his smooth, bare arms seemed to jerk with a sly life of their own.

"You mean your father and Mr. Plover went to school together?" Mrs. Hopewell said.

"Yes, sure. Mr. Plover and my dad," the young man said.

So she let them have the boat on credit, but when the matter of fishing tackle was brought up, she did not seem to hear. The young man knew exactly what he wanted, and as he tested the weight of the rods by letting them dance and dip in his hand, his covetous eye was on the feathered hooks and the metal spinners under glass.

"You know, I got a lot of fishing tackle at home," the boy said.

"Of course you have," said Mrs. Hopewell.

"I could get it in a jiffy," he said, speaking wooingly, for this might be the last chance offered. "If you'd wait five minutes, I'd run and get my equipment," he said, but the young man, with a plastic rod as transparent as crystal in his hand, turned from the counter and looked down without pity into his uncertain eyes. "You could use my rod with the automatic reel," the boy went on with it.

"Who says we have to go fishing?" the young man said, and in the boy's heart all hope abruptly died. "First you say you got to deliver the papers, and then you start talking about going home to pick up your stuff. I thought you wanted to go out for a row?"

"I do. Sure I do," Tad Plover said, and he ran his tongue along his lip.

"I haven't been rowing this year yet. The fish can wait, *amigo mio*," the young man said. "That's Spanish. I picked it up from the Puerto Ricans we got swarming like lice all over where I live." He put the rod down on the counter again, and he dusted his hands off, as if ridding himself of the touch of a distasteful thing. It was then that the boy almost saw, but did not, the palm of his right hand. "Let's go," the young man said, and he jerked his head toward the open door. The cash register stood at the end of the counter, its metal burnished by the sun, and the young man ran his fingers lightly over its keyboard as they passed.

Once in the rowboat, he took the center cross seat, and settled the oars in place. Without lifting his eyes, he indicated the rudder seat with a jerk of his chin, and the boy moved obediently to the weathered, wooden triangle facing him, took the canvas bag from his shoulder, and set it down. There was an inch or two of water slipping back and forth on the boards of the floor, and, under the middle seat, an empty coffee tin. The young man kicked it with his broken sneaker toward the boy.

"Get busy, shrimp," he said. The tide was coming slowly, lazily, in from the Sound, and the young man who had begun to row lifted his head only once to look at the indolently flying gulls as he maneuvered the rowboat in and out among the moored ketches, the motorboats, and yawls. As the boy bailed the water over the side, the young man said: "I want to get out of this parking lot without scraping my fenders and having any questions asked." He was rowing carefully, a stroke or two with one oar and then the other, his palms, and whatever record of identity they held, closed out of sight around the handles of the oars. "When you go by water, it's like going by air. You don't leave any trail behind," he said.

"Where are we going?" the boy asked then.

"Oh, up the river," the young man said. He was looking over his shoulder at the river opening out ahead. "A long way up." They were free of the agglomeration of moored boats now, and they passed through the mouth of Two Ways River, and the young man rowing looked quizzically at the boy holding to the rudder cords. "I bet I know what you're thinking about. I can read your mind," he said. "You're thinking about that bagful of newspapers. Well, I'll tell you this: if you had any enterprise, you'd start a water delivery route. You'd row up the river every afternoon, and throw their papers into their backyards, and get some fishing while you went.

You got to combine one thing with another if you want to get anywhere in life," he said.

"Since I started, I haven't missed a day with the papers," Tad Plover said, and he tried to say it casually; "so perhaps if we didn't get back too late—"

But the young man interrupted it.

"We won't be going back," he said. "When we get up there where it's good and wild, I'm going to get out and cut through the woods, and you're going with me. I'm not taking the chance of you talking, and spilling everything you know."

The marshlands were lying on either side of them now, and, without turning his head, but merely riding there in the stern of the boat holding quietly to the cords, the boy knew every inch of the way. There were the five or six weathered cabins with their piers running out like boardwalks into the tide. Ahead, in the curve, the banks rose as the river narrowed, the debris of shells giving over to a carpet of reeds, and the taste of salt thinning out to nothing on the air. The boats in the cove lay far behind them, and, after a few more yards, he knew a tangle of tulip trees and weeping willows and juniper would move down to the edge. A quarter of a mile beyond would be the place called Revolution Crossing.

"When I don't turn up with the newspapers," said the boy, "they may phone the post office."

"Why the post office?" the young man asked, and his hoarse voice seemed a little wary, but he went on rowing steadily.

"Well, my dad works there, so they'll call to ask him where I am," Tad Plover said. "He'll say I was in with the papers earlier, and then he'll look out the back, and he'll see my bicycle's still there, and he'll begin asking around. He'll call Mrs. Hopewell, maybe, and she'll say she let us have a boat."

"If my old man'd ever interfered like that with me, I'd have told him where to go," the young man said.

The riverbanks were already turning wilder now, and the

boy remembered that here, just before the skeins of vine and underbrush and tree wove to the edge, two swans had nested in the spring. Sometimes the female had sat upon the eggs, and other times the male.

"Right there where you see that hump of twigs and mud, kind of high, like a throne," the boy said, pointing it out; "well, that was a swan's nest last spring."

"I bet swan's eggs would taste pretty good scrambled or fried," the young man said.

"They're different from ducks, swans are," Tad Plover said, still watching the empty tower of the nest. "A duck hen hatches maybe twelve or fifteen out, and they follow behind her in a string, but the drake never sails up and down with the rest of them the way swans do. The second day, there'll be maybe ten duck babies left, and the third day, maybe six or eight. I've seen crows get them, and water rats, or else the ones at the end of the string wander off after bugs, and they never catch up with their mother again. She's lucky if she raises one."

"Duck tastes pretty good. I ate it roasted once, with apple sauce," the young man said.

"But with swans, the father stays around," the boy continued, and he thought of big swans on the water at evening when the light turned blue. "The swans I saw in April, they hatched twelve, and they kept all twelve. I saw the father fighting a chicken hawk once when it came down. Even if the others had their heads under water, he'd keep turning his eye up sideways to see if any birds were coming down. He'd keep sailing around them so the wharf rats couldn't get near them. I've seen him hit the little swans with his beak so they wouldn't wander away."

"Are you trying to tell me swans are better than ducks?" the young man said savagely as he pulled at the oars.

"There's this that maybe you didn't think of," Tad Plover said: "if my dad starts asking around to find out why I didn't do my route, then Mrs. Hopewell may tell him about you saying your father had gone to school with him, and about you staying here with us, and he'll know it isn't true. If we went back now, before he had time to organize things and come out after us, you could wait in the boat while I went around with the papers. After that, when I'd finished delivering them, we could go out for a row."

"You're smart, wise guy," the young man said, "but you're not smart enough." Tad Plover watched him as he pulled first the right oar in, and then the left, until the full weight of them lay inside the boat. He watched him get to his feet, and keep his balance in the dipping boat by lifting his muscular, bare arms, his elbows thrust slightly out, as a boxer spars with space for a moment when the gong strikes and he leaves his corner of the ring. The boat was drifting into the curve, bearing them lazily on between the banks of trees, and the boy knew suddenly there was no roof, no window, no passing boat, no mallard cruising on the water, no white swan, to witness whatever might now take place. "You've been trying to give me the slip ever since we've been together," the young man said as he came toward the rudder seat.

Tad Plover could see the broken sneakers coming, and see the seeping water on the boards shifting place with the weight of the young man's advance.

"As long as the newspapers have been paid for by other people, I guess they're not exactly mine any more," he said, and his mouth was dry. "I guess they're more like somebody else's property."

"So what's wrong with getting rid of somebody else's property?" the young man said. He reached for the canvas bag on the floor, with *The Standard* lettered in red on it, and the veins lashed big and blue across his forearm, and the muscle in his upper arm rolled like a ball inside his skin.

And then the thing that seemed about to happen halted abruptly. The young man's hand did not close on the white canvas bag, and he did not fling it savagely over the side. Instead, the muscles ceased leaping with their own life in his skin, and even his breathing died upon the quiet air.

"Look!" he said in a whisper. He was leaning over the boy, staring down into the water, with one hand resting on the gunwale's weathered wood. Against his firm, sinewy shoulder in the T-shirt, his face looked too delicate, too perishable by far. "Look what's down there!" he was saying. The boy shifted on the rudder seat, and there, in the depths of fluctuating light and shade, he saw it, too. A man in a blue and gray seersucker suit lay, face down, on a bedding of reeds. Because of the two currents passing over him, he seemed to stir with life. The piece of his neck that showed above his collar, and his hands at the ends of the seersucker sleeves, were colorless, but the thin, gray strands of his hair did not lie quiet, and his shoulders seemed to lift and fall.

"He must be dead. He must be drowned," the young man whispered, as if denying the movement that he saw.

"We've got to get him out," Tad Plover whispered, and the blood was turned to water in his veins.

"Sure, we got to get him out," the young man mimicked it. "Sure, and then when they find him in the boat with us, they put the blame on me!" He stepped carefully back to the center seat, sat down and slipped the oars in place, and pulled on one and then the other of them to keep the boat from drifting off. "If we got him out, then maybe I could clear out before anyone came along and started asking questions," he said, and he glanced at the riverbanks where the trees came, thick as a jungle, down to the edge.

"Except they'd know I couldn't have got him out alone,"

the boy said, his hands as cold as if he had already touched the drowned man's flesh.

"What do we owe him, anyway?" the young man asked, his voice and his eye belligerent. Then he shifted to one side of the seat and looked down into the water again, keeping the rowboat where it was by a shallow, constant raking of the oars. "Sometimes when I see a drunk lying in the gutter, I get ideas. I got the same kind of an idea about this guy down there. I keep thinking it might be a relative of mine, and I wouldn't know. Put the anchor down," he said abruptly. "You can tell the police I was here and helped you get him out. You can tell them I didn't have time to wait and see them, because I had urgent business out to sea."

The boy left the rudder seat now, and he went the length of the boat to the prow, stepping over the handle of the right oar, and the plank of the cross seat. He took the anchor and its rope, and let it down with caution so as not to disturb the dead. The young man waited to see if they had ceased to drift, and then he settled the weight of the oars inside the boat and stood up.

"Maybe something's holding him there so he doesn't float. Maybe his clothes are caught on something," the boy said.

The young man pulled the T-shirt over his head, dropped it on the seat, and stood there a moment, naked to the waist, his chest deep and strong, the skin shading golden to his armpits, and drawn tight across his ribs.

"Sometimes I see an accident in the street," he said, "and I start getting the same idea. Some dope gets in front of a car, and they take him off in an ambulance, and I say to myself 'I bet that's him.' I keep thinking it might be my old man, and I wouldn't know. I don't know what kind of a guy he was," he said, "or even what he did."

He unbuckled the belt of his dungarees, and if there was still the shape of a switchblade knife or a firearm in the pockets, Tad Plover was not thinking of them now. He was thinking of the young man's father being dead, and of him fleeing from place to place.

"I bet that's the kind of thing he'd do, get hit by a car, or touch a live wire and get fried, or slip in the mud and get drowned," the young man went on, "I bet he was too dumb to learn to swim." He might have stooped then to undo the laces of his sneakers, and stood up again to pull his dungarees off and throw them on the seat, had not the soft, quick palpitation of a motor come downstream, downwind, and the young man raised his head. "Maybe that's somebody looking for this guy. Maybe we'd better clear out," he said, and his fingers moved quickly, fastening his belt again. "Get the anchor up. Don't stand there doing nothing," he muttered through his teeth, and he sat down on the cross-seat board, and jerked the oars in place.

Just as they turned the rowboat toward the cove, a trim white motor launch came around the curve, and the boy holding the rudder cords glanced back to watch it come. There were three men in it, their faces and their forearms flushed with sun. The badges on the visored caps of two of them might have been the official insignia of the law. The young man who faced them as he rowed pulled slowly, steadily, at the oars and gave no sign. The launch nosed its way back and forth, from one bank to the other of the river, while the three men watched over the side. They were still quite far when one of the men, cupping his mouth in his two hands, called out across the water to the rowboat:

"Hi, Tad! Caught any whales?"

"Hi, Dr. Matterson!" the boy called out in answer. He sat on the rudder seat, his head turned, watching the motor launch weaving back and forth behind them at the curve.

"Who are the other two?" the young man said, his lips not moving as he spoke.

"They might be the police from Northport Junction," said Tad Plover. "But I can't tell. They're still too far away."

"For me they couldn't be too far," said the young man, rowing steadily.

"Dr. Matterson took my tonsils out last year," the boy said. He did not turn his head again to watch the launch nosing back and forth across the stream.

"All right," said the young man, rowing; "in five minutes they'll see that guy lying at the bottom breathing in water instead of ozone for a change, and they'll ask us to do some explaining. They'll come after us fast to find out what we know."

As the rowboat descended the shining widening avenue, and the distance lengthened between them and the launch, the things to be said came urgently and clearly to the boy.

"If it didn't have to be like this, you always keeping one jump ahead of the police, you'd have the time to enjoy yourself," he said. He thought of the penal institutions, and the burglaries, and it was like the taste of dust on the water that they crossed. "You'd be able to go fishing and swimming, and do anything like that without having it always on your mind," he said.

"All right," the young man said, and his eyes were fixed, green as a cat's eyes, on the thing that was taking place on the river behind the boy. "They're circling the place where we put the anchor down. They're hanging over the side, looking into the water, all three of them. Now they're cutting the motor out," he said, and Tad Plover heard it die. "While they're having a powwow about how to get him up we'll give them the slip," the young man said.

The world had begun to be that of marshes, and boat cabins, and long-legged landing piers again, the fresh water of the river turning now to brine. In another ten minutes, the boatyards would open on the left, the sloops, the motorboats, the rowboats and yawls would ride at their moorings, and Mrs. Hopewell's boat livery would be before them. The boy knew he must say quickly whatever was to be said.

"Look," he said, keeping the rudder steady; "how long would you have to stay in prison if you served it out? I mean, maybe if they gave you two years or three it would pass pretty quick if you knew after that there wouldn't be any more need for you to keep on running away. You could come back here when you got out, and we could go fishing, we could do everything like that," he said. "If you needed a job, you could talk to my dad, and I bet he could fix it up in the boatyards for you. If you gave yourself up, instead of them catching you, I bet it would make a difference in what they did to you," he said.

"You mean, turn myself in to the cops?" the young man said. His hands ceased pulling at the oars, and his voice went high in incredulity.

"Yes," said Tad Plover. "Just tell them who you are."

"You want me to turn around now, and row back up there, and say: 'Take a good look, gentlemen, it's me!' And maybe hold out my wrists, just so they can slip the bracelets on easier?" The young man let go of the oars for a moment in order to act the farce of it out. "Is that what you're telling me to do?"

"Or you could maybe tell it to my dad," Tad Plover kept on. "We could go right to the post office, and you could tell him who you are. He's easy to say things to because he listens very well. If you went in to him, and gave yourself up, he'd go to court with you when you went. He's in the civil service, and that's like being in the government. He could even talk to the President."

The young man had begun to row again, and now the boy saw the look in his eye abruptly sharpen, and he too heard the rapid throbbing of the motor on the air.

"They must have left one man back there on the bank to keep watch," said the young man, rowing. "There're only two of them in the launch now, and they're coming fast." He glanced just once, and swiftly, over his shoulder at the cove, and, when he spoke, his eyes were on the launch again. "We'll put in here before they see us. We'll leave the boat under the landing pier, and cut through the backyards to your dad."

They did it quickly, keeping their heads down, their backs stooped like the backs of old and weary men as they tied the boat to the iron ring in the weather-blackened wood and made their way to shore. They did not risk climbing the ladder to the pier, but kept out of sight in the shadow it cast below. The boards of the pier made a roof over their heads as they slogged through the mud, their feet breaking the mosaic of clam and mussel and empty lobster shells. The young man led. He walked free of the water now, and up on to the bank, his broken sneakers crying with the wet. Tad Plover followed after him, the bag of newspapers on his shoulder again, with the white of its canvas strong and undefiled. Behind them could be heard the pulse of the launch's motor as it came downstream, a rhythmic tapping like the footsteps of someone running fast. They went through a break in the yew hedge, and into the yard of one of the shingled residences. Past the back stoop they went, past the bay window on the side, two boys, it might have been, come in from fishing, and making their way now toward the smell of supper through the summer light. And the sound of the motor came quickly, softly from the water, as if running on tiptoe after them. They could hear it still as they crossed the silent street.

"My dad's been around a lot himself," Tad Plover said. They had entered the tunnel of dusk made by the maple trees, and his voice sounded loud to him although he tried to keep it low. "He's been on a freighter to Singapore, and North Africa, and other places like that." On the other side of the street, the clock above the firehouse door said a quarter to six. It was time to eat, and no cars were passing, and nobody walked along the pavements under the trees. "He's been in a lot of countries, so I guess he understands things the way other people don't."

"Sure. That's what you think."

"So if you told him, then he'd be on your side," the boy said, keeping at it stubbornly. "Then you'd have two friends when you got out."

"Sometimes they teach you a trade while you're serving time," the young man said, with perhaps something faltering in him now.

Just before they went up the post-office steps, they both turned and looked back, as culprits might. But nothing was stirring on the cove side or the inland side, and the only sound was that of the motorboat, tapping its message lightly and steadily out. Mr. Plover was alone in the post office. He was standing behind the wicket taking the outgoing mail from the box below the letter drop, and when he saw the two of them walk in, he stopped with the letters in his hand.

"What's the matter with you, Tad, clearing out like that?" he said. He put the letters down on the counter on the other side of the bars, and the boy saw a nerve jumping in his cheek. "Mrs. Hopewell was in here raising Cain an hour ago. She wanted that boat of hers, and I told her she'd get her boat even if I had to close the post office and go out after it. What's got into you, going off like a vacationist, letting your newspaper customers down?"

"But it wasn't like that. It wasn't that way," said the boy.

"It wasn't that way?" the father said; his anger was rising now. "If somebody, anybody, comes along and says 'What about going for a ride?' are you just going to go? Wouldn't it come into your head to ask a few questions before going off in a boat you hadn't any right to take? I tell you it's criminal that way you've acted, Tad, and I'm not going to let you get away with it."

The boy knew then that things would not turn out exactly as he had planned.

"It was different from that," he said, and he ran his tongue along his lip.

Mr. Plover struck the counter with the flat of his hand, but whatever he was about to say was halted, for the young man stepped quickly toward the window and took over the conversation. His hands were thrust in the pockets of his dungarees, closed, it might be, on the weapons he carried, and he stood as erect as if before a firing squad.

"Quit picking on the kid," he said in his husky voice. His head was held high, and his mouth jerked a little crooked as he talked. "I wanted to go for a boat ride—city guy taking an outing," he said, and he gave a laugh. "Not having any dough on me, I fixed it up through him. He didn't have anything to say. You're too damned quick on the draw, every one of you, when kids come into the picture. Even you out here in the big open spaces, patrolling the place like every kid was guilty of murder, or arson, or larceny."

"I'm ready to hear his side of it," the father said.

"His side is my side," the young man said. "I got a gang in the Bronx. I'm the war counselor of the gang. Last night, some of the gang ran into trouble with the enemy, so I got out of town to give things time to quiet down. I stepped out on the parkway, and I got a ride. That's all. So what are you trying to pin on him and me? You've stacked the deck, and you've stacked it pretty, you cops, and you fathers, and the rest. You wouldn't give a kid a break--"

It was the telephone ringing that stopped the sound of it, and when Mr. Plover turned from the window to pick it up, the boy saw that the anger in his face had died.

"Hello. Hello, Doc Matterson," Mr. Plover said to the mouthpiece, and then there was silence as he listened to the voice they could not hear. "Sure, he's standing right here in front of me now, Tad is. Sure, they're both of them here," he said, and his eyes looked at them through the bars. "Sure, I'll keep them here until you come." There was silence in the post-office room as he listened again, and first a look of shock, and then concern, and then of weakness, came across his face. "That's a terrible thing, a terrible thing. I'm sorry to hear it," he said, as if confronted by a thing so final that there was nothing he, or any man, could do. "Sure, I'll keep them here, Doc," he was saying again when the young man jerked his right hand from the pocket of his jeans, and the boy sprang blindly forward, and flung himself between his father and the man. There he stood in this heroic posture, his eyes closed, his teeth clenched, his thin arms open, waiting to die.

"What did you think I was going to do?" the young man said, his voice scarcely louder than a whisper, and the boy jerked back to life again, and opened his eyes. The young man was holding his hand out, with the fingers spread, and it was empty. It was the right hand, and Tad Plover stood looking in silence and wonder at the callouses, embedded, as round and hard as coins, in the cushions below the fingers, but there was no scar across the palm.

"Listen, Tad," said his father's voice behind him, and the boy turned in bewilderment, certain of nothing now. It must have been then, he told himself afterward, that the young man walked across to the writing desk and ripped one flyer off from the others hanging on the wall. "There's been a suicide up at Revolution Crossing," said Mr. Plover, his voice shocked as he put the receiver down. "They've found his car parked in the woods, and they've got the note he left behind. A man from Northport Junction. They said you and your friend were up the river this afternoon, and they want to talk to you, so the two of you stick around."

"I haven't delivered my papers yet," the boy said.

"They've waited this long, they can wait a little longer," his father said. "Doc Matterson and the police will be coming in. You ask your friend to come home with us and have something to eat when they've got through."

But when the boy turned, the young man wasn't there any more. He must have gone quietly out the door while they talked. On the slope of the high, wood desk lay the leaflet, and the boy picked it up and looked at the photograph of a balding man with a sullen mouth, whose name was John Henderson, or else Jack Jameson, or sometimes Happy Jack. Under the picture had been written in ink that was still not dry the next line of the uproarious joke, or the bitter hoax, or the comedy.

"Please hold my mail. Will be back to go fishing sometime," the words were written in the reckless, careless hand, and the signature was: "Happy Jack."

The post-office room was so quiet that the boy could hear the gulls crying outside in the beginning of dusk. And there was nothing he could say.

Evening at Home

I am writing this in the hope that the young woman who told me her name was Mrs. Daisy Miller will read it and tell me why she never brought my two dollars back. I've waited three months, and because she hasn't come back, I'm going to tell it exactly the way it happened, so that if the girl who called herself Mrs. Daisy Miller reads it, she won't have any trouble recognizing the incident and the parts that both of us played. The place was New York and the time was a July evening, a weekend evening, when everyone who could get away from the city had got away. I was going to be alone for twenty-four hours in the brownstone house I rented in the East Seventies, and because of the work I had been doing all day, and because of the heat, I thought I would stay at home. I ate a cool supper in the garden behind the house, and then I came in, and, perhaps in loneliness, I wandered from room to room, as if seeking the people who were no longer there. It was then that I saw the earth in the window boxes of the front rooms had been parched to dust, and I got the green tin watering can in the butler's pantry and I filled it up with water. I might never have seen the girl, and all this might not have happened, if I had not begun to water the geraniums, which were begging for succor in the burning soil.

As I moved from window to window with the green tin can, the light and the heat were just beginning to fade. Below was the quiet street, and across the street stood a rather elegant little private hospital and, beside the hospital, a gabled, russet-colored church, left over from some other period of this century or forgotten from the century before.

But what had altered in the familiar scene was that on the steps, which shaped a crescent of russet stone around the church's portal, the young woman lay asleep. She was wearing a simple brown linen dress with a neat white collar at the modest neck and white cuffs at the elbows, and her slender legs were bare. On her feet were new-looking white sandals, strapped with a broad white band across the instep and fitted with platform soles. She lay quite naturally, there on the third step, her body relaxed, her face turned away from the street, her fingers loosely interlaced across her breasts. A small hat of glazed white straw, which she must have removed before lying down to sleep, was placed, as if with care, upon the step below her, and one could see the thick reddish hair, worn short, that fell with luxuriant carelessness back from her brow—the color of hair, I thought then, that means a chalk-white skin and freckles on the forearms, and on the shoulders, and on the probably upturned, short, wide-nostriled nose.

When I saw her, I stopped watering the geraniums, and I stood looking down across the street at her, but without any feeling of surprise. The evening was so warm, and the look of the church's stone so fresh, that to lie down there seemed a reasonable thing to do, and I wondered why she had been the first one to think of doing it. After a moment, I saw a trained nurse come out of the hospital next to the church and walk to where she lay. The nurse was handsome and young, and she had a silky knot of smooth black hair pinned just beneath the starched cap that rode high on her head. Her buttocks swung slowly back and forth inside her skirt as she moved with a singularly leisurely gait to where the girl lay stretched upon the stone. As I set my watering can down on the hardwood floor and wiped the drop from its chin, I saw the nurse place one foot, in its unsullied canvas shoe, on the first step of the church and lean above the girl, not in solicitude or gentleness, it seemed to me, but in distaste, perhaps even in disdain. She leaned there, almost startling in her immaculacy, and her hand did not touch the brown linen dress for the beating of a heart within it, and her fingers did not feel for the pulsing of life in the girl's wrist, but, instead, the hand of the professional picked up the hat of white transparent straw. It may have been that she was seeking a label inside it, and, perhaps because she found none, she dropped the hat onto the stone again. Then she straightened up and dusted her palms clean of whatever they had touched, and she moved back across the sidewalk to the hospital, her body moving slowly, consciously, the hips as eloquent as language in the clean white dress.

Now she'll get a couple of interns to help carry the girl in, I thought, and I waited, pinching off in my fingers the big lower leaves of the geraniums, which were scalloped with yellow and as dry as paper fans.

On evenings such as this, the hospital doors stood wide, sometimes until after midnight, and the windows of the rooms were open, with the tawny canvas awnings lowered, hollowing each room into a well of privacy and shade. And on evenings such as this, and whether one chose to or not, one participated in the life of the hospital, for the sound of the patients' radios could be heard across the street, and the patients' voices, or the nurses' voices, answering, like the voices of actors on a stage, the delicate summons of the telephone. But now a profound twilit quiet lay upon the hospital as well as on the street, and no bells sounded, no voices spoke behind the awnings. Everything was still; everything had ceased as the nurse went in through the open hospital door. Almost at once, she reappeared, in the ground-floor window to the left, and I saw her, the cap and uniform bluewhite in the dusk, lift the receiver and the mouthpiece from the switchboard and plug the connection in. She did not sit down to dial the numbers that she wanted, but she did it standing, selecting them casually with the end of the pencil she held in her hand.

I do not know why I remember all this so clearly, for I had not spoken to Mrs. Daisy Miller then, or given the two dollars to her, so there is no reason why I should remember the details of it at all. But I know that when the nurse's telephone conversation was done and she had taken her lipstick and pocket mirror out, I still stood waiting. Not having understood yet, I was waiting for the two interns, bearing the stretcher between them, to come down the hall and out the open door. It might be, I thought as the twilight deepened, that the girl had been struck by a car in the street and had dragged herself up across the curbstone and up the stone steps of the church and lain down there to die. I was glad that professional help was near, and I stood awhile watching the trained nurse shaping her nails at the open window by the switchboard, and there was only silence as the curtain of darkness jerked, instant by instant, lower on the scene. After a little, a man in a grayish suit, carrying his hat, came wandering from the direction of Third Avenue, his footsteps seeming to precede him through the silence and then he himself to come after, meandering, quiet, slow. At the sight of the girl lying on the steps, his aimlessness wavered toward intention for a moment, but only for a moment, and then he turned his head away, and he crossed the street, but still without haste, doing it casually, as if he had seen nothing, giving a wide berth to the church and the steps and to what was lying on them, and he wandered to the corner and was gone.

And then, standing there behind the geraniums, I knew, with a sudden sense of shock, that there were no interns hastening down the hospital hall with a stretcher between them, that there was no help coming, and that no one had any intention of doing anything at all. I ran to the desk and I opened the telephone directory, and I found the telephone number of the hospital across the street and I dialed it quickly. From where I stood, with the telephone in my hand, I could see the nurse put the nail file down and turn from the downstairs window to plug in the connection, her uniform in the still-unlighted office as blank and sharply edged as paper in the office's accumulated dark.

"Hello," she said, and I heard the word said twice, as if in double exposure, as I watched her. It was spoken first on the wire, and then the almost simultaneous echo of it followed across the evening air.

"Look," I said, "you know there's a young woman lying on the church steps next door to you. Aren't you going to take her in and find out what's wrong with her?"

"I know what's wrong with her," both the high, nasal voice on the wire and the high, nasal echo of it answered. "She's stinko," the trained nurse said. I could see her, in her blank white dress, lift her hand as if to jerk the connection out, and then stop the gesture in mid-air to study the nails on her lifted hand.

"So you're just going to let her lie out there all night?" I said.

"Listen, lady," said the double recording of the nurse's voice, "we're not running a home for alcoholics. I've put a call in to the police. I told them a woman had passed out on the church steps, and to come along and pick her up. And how did you get into this, anyway?" the two voices asked me sharply. "What's this woman got to do with you?"

Maybe I did not actually say the things I am under the impression I said then. Maybe I did not tell her, with my voice shaking like a weak and foolish woman's, to telephone the police again and tell them that they needn't come, because her heart had just thawed out beneath the starch of the uniform, and human blood was running in her veins. For a long time, I believed that I had said a great many fine and noble things to the nurse, but I could not remember the words I had used to say them. It may be that I simply put the telephone down without saying anything at all, but I don't like to believe this. I must have said quietly to her that to sleep in a police station all night might change a young woman's life forever, and alter the hearts of those who loved her, and turn the faith she had in herself to dust and ashes in her mouth. Perhaps I said no more than that if she did not take the girl into the hospital, then I would take her into my house. I must have said that much, at least, for I know that the two voices of the nurse cried out, "For God's sake, take her, lady," the echo more nasal and more impatient even than the voice itself, drawn high and thin across the wire.

"I'll be down at once," I said, and then I saw the nurse's hand jerk the switchboard connection savagely out, and she turned to the open window again, but she did not pick the nail file up. Instead, she raised her head and looked up at the windows of the brownstone house, and as I looked down at her across the geraniums, the white cap seemed to stiffen, and we looked with recognition across the space of the street, as evil as serpents, into each other's venomous eyes.

I went out through the basement door, taking the key of the iron gate with me, and when I stepped from the curb, I could feel the asphalt warm beneath my feet still, from the heat of the day. The evening had deepened, and the entrance hall of the hospital and the office where the switchboard stood were lighted, but beyond them the church had withdrawn even farther into the darkness and stillness of its own richly colored stone. And the girl had not moved from where she lay, with her head turned slightly on her slender neck, and the white fingers loosely interlaced across her breasts, rising and falling, rising and falling gently as she breathed. I planted my feet firmly on the first step of the church, and I leaned over and slipped one arm beneath her shoulders, and I raised her, but only a little, for at once her loosely clasped hands slid apart and her arms fell, lifeless and useless, by her sides. I tried holding her head in place with my other hand, but I could not keep it from rolling forward on her chest and swinging there.

I laid her carefully down again, and this time I began with her feet. I took the heels of the white platform-soled sandals in my hands, and I lowered them from the third step to the step below. Then I bent the knees, pulling the skirt of the brown linen dress down over them as I did it, and I brought the two feet down to rest between my own on the first step. Now, had she been aware of it, she was in a position to get up and walk away. But the thighs and the torso, and the arms and the head, would not be a party to it. They rested still in the deep, sweet dream that no stranger could disturb. I remembered the hat then, and I thought I would set it on her head in preparation for the journey we would undertake together, and when I had picked it up, I saw that it was a hat such as a bride might have been wearing, with minuscule orange blossoms, as frail as snowdrops, woven foolishly into the glazed-straw crown.

I lifted her head, and I set the hat as well as I could on it, and then I put her head gently down again upon the stone. I stood two steps below her now, holding her feet between my feet, and I took her hands in mine to pull the reclining portion of her into the sitting position that her lower legs alone maintained. And when I leaned above her to gather her hands up, I saw there were no rings on her fingers, and I saw that weariness and perhaps something like disappointment, only more moving, more profound, lay like a mask across her features, taking the look of beauty and the look of youth

away. But her skin was as white as the reddish hair had promised it would be, and there were freckles on her forearms, and
some scattered on her short, Irish-looking nose. I drew her up
by her long, pliant, ringless hands, and her helpless, seemingly
boneless arms followed after, and as her head lolled forward
on her breast again, the white straw hat slipped from it and
rolled down across the steps. As long as I held her strongly
by the hands, like this, she seemed to be a person sitting up,
except that the spine was water and the head, with the thick,
short reddish hair brushing soft as a veil across her cheeks and
forehead, swung lower and lower toward her knees.

"Look, my dear, this is very silly," I said, speaking severely
to her. "The police have been called, and they'll be arriving
any minute." I remembered reading that if you slapped a person's face, it would rouse him, but I could not bring myself
to do it. "You're going to try to walk now," I said. "We don't
want the police to find you here."

But, having no interest in anything that might be said,
she had begun now to tip slowly sidewise, and I sat quickly
down beside her, sitting close and putting one arm around
her to keep her from lying down again. Holding her like this,
I reached down with my free hand to retrieve the white straw
hat again, and as I leaned, the girl swayed perilously forward
with me, and when I sat up again, she swayed upward as
well. We sat quietly for a little while on the steps together,
and her head rolled, a detached and separate object, toward
my shoulder and came to rest, like a child's head, upon it, and
the tide of night lapped slowly up the steps across our feet.
And after a short time had passed, I placed the hat, with its
woven wreath of orange blossoms, on her head again, in
preparation for the journey on which we must embark together, and then I tightened my arm around her shoulders and
I got warily to my feet, and as I rose, I tried to lift her with
me, but she would not come.

"Now, listen," I said, sitting down beside her again. "Someone has put in a call for the police. They're on their way here." I hated to be persistent about this, but it seemed to me the only reality that might arouse her from the dream. "Besides, if you sleep out here all night, you'll be so stiff you won't be able to move tomorrow," I said, and I even thought of mentioning her hat to her. I thought of saying, "And you're absolutely ruining your new hat. It won't have any shape left any more."

But it didn't matter what I said, I knew by this time, for she had settled back in such comfort against my shoulder again that the hat slipped from her head before I could catch it, and I saw it jump the curb and float away on the surface of the dark. I knew that I must act with more decision now, and I got to my feet again and maneuvered myself up onto the step above her, holding her up by the force of my two hands placed underneath her arms. And, stooping behind her like this, I sought to lift her, but, instead of the girl's rising, her legs unfolded will-lessly beneath her, and her body slid, without life or protest, down the church steps and came to rest upon the sidewalk, but in a sitting position still, because of my hands, which held to her armpits and had not let her go. It was not until I had begun, in desperation, to wheel her, like a wheelbarrow with a loose, wavering wheel and no handles, across the quiet street that I saw the hat lying a little way beyond us, and I did not dare to set her down. Her legs and her heels were doing their part now in getting us to safety, and I couldn't risk breaking the movement of their advance, for it seemed to me then that I could hear the Black Maria purring down Lexington, its siren not quite wailing, its bell just preparing to ring. And in my distress it may be that I manipulated the girl forward too hastily, for her half-reclining body suddenly outstripped her automatically functioning feet, and her legs twisted under her like a cripple's, and she fell upon her knees. Even the strength of my hands beneath her armpits could not make her rise.

So then I tried the only method that remained, and I turned, holding her under the arms still, and I walked quickly backward, pulling her with effort, like a dead thing, the rest of the way across the street and up the curb and over the sidewalk to the basement gate. I was gasping from the effort as I propped her, sitting, against the brownstone of the house while I found the key and opened the gate. It was then, as I raised her again to drag her in across the threshold, that she suddenly began to laugh.

I could identify Mrs. Daisy Miller at any time and in any place by this singularly beautiful laugh, although it may have seemed to me at that moment a little loud. It was high and clear and, in spite of all we had been through together, marvelously untroubled as she lay there on the floor. After I had switched on the hall light, I half lifted, half pulled her across the downstairs hall to the foot of the stairs, and she kept right on laughing. Her eyes had remained closed, and now they were squeezed up with her laughter, and it seemed to me that they contemplated some extremely funny scene of which I was left in ignorance, that they were fixed on the hilarious action of an incident in which I did not share. I do not know how I got her up the steep flight of stairs or how long a time it took me. I only know that as I manipulated her up, step by step, I heard, through the sweet bursts and ripples of her laughter, the muted wailing of a police car's siren in the street outside, and the car must have stopped to seek for her, for after a while I heard the sound of its motor as it drove away.

I had planned to get her onto the divan in the sitting room, and this is what I finally managed to do. I lit the lamp on the table by her head, where the ash tray stood, and the volume of Henry James between the two blue leather bookends, and, even lying on the divan, the girl did not stop laughing at the truly funny, truly uproarious thing that she looked on or listened to in sleep. Her nose wrinkled up in delight as she laughed, and the mask of fatigue was gone, as if a hand had lifted it from her features, and however vulgar the joke might be that had been told her, or told on her, the laughter was pure, so wonderfully pure that I listened to it with longing, wanting to be included in its absurdity.

I undid the straps of her white sandals and took them off and stood them side by side upon the rug, and still she went on laughing, laughing without hysteria or strain, only breathlessly and foolishly. And as I sponged off her face and washed her long, pliant young hands, she kept on laughing, and I looked at her with envy, knowing that no matter how long I lived I would never be able to laugh like that again, because the time of finding circus clowns funny and finding slapstick funny was finished and done with a long time ago. I covered her over with a flowered cotton counterpane from one of the bedrooms upstairs, and I sat down in an armchair near her and for a while I watched the side of her face, and conjectured on her people and on her work and as to what sort of child or woman she might be.

There was something prim and yet arty about her that suggested she might sell books in a small, good bookshop, perhaps on Madison or Park, but the thick, careless reddish hair and the soft mouth would never have had the patience for it. And there was the hat, the white straw hat that I had not retrieved, and never would retrieve now, which might have come on a honeymoon from the sticks, seen first in the catalogue of a mail-order house. (And I thought in the morning, when I went out to look for it and did not find it, that it was perhaps to the sticks that it had, of its own volition, returned.) The sandals were as new as if bought for a young bride's trousseau, and they must have been chosen to match

the hat, and perhaps even the handbag that she wasn't carrying any more. And now, as I watched her, her laughter began
to subside into little gasps of childlike amusement, but her
eyes were closed in delight still upon the ludicrous spectacle
that I could not see.

When she had ceased entirely to laugh, I leaned forward in
the armchair, and when I spoke, my voice sounded strange and
lonely in the silent room.

"Listen, my child," I said, and I cleared my throat uneasily, "if you could tell me where you lived, I could take you
there. I could call a taxi and take you home."

But I might have been sitting alone in the room, talking
aloud to myself, for all the attention she paid me, and it made
me nervous. I didn't like the feel of things at all. I got up, and
I walked into the dining room, and I got out the bottle of
Scotch from the sideboard and poured not more than a finger
of it into a tall, clean glass that I took down from the shelf.
Beyond the dining room was the butler's pantry, and I went
quickly through the swinging door, not liking the almost human sigh of it behind me, and I held the glass under the cold-
water tap at the sink an instant and splashed some water in.
I could have gone down into the kitchen in the basement
and got some ice cubes and some soda, but the light was not
turned on there, and for some reason I had begun to feel uncertain of the dark.

When I went back into the sitting room, I glanced quickly
at the girl, and I saw that she was lying just as she had been
when I left the room. Her reddish hair was spread out on the
gray silk of the cushion that I had put beneath her head, and
her bare, slender arms, with the white cuffs at the elbows, were
lying outside on the counterpane. I sat down in the armchair
near her again, my glass in my hand, and I thought how dis-
turbing it was to know, as intimately as if she had been a
member of the family, the face and the arms and the legs and

the laughter of one who was an absolute stranger and with whom one had exchanged no words. I took my drink slowly, watching the side of this stranger's familiar face, watching the counterpane rise as her breath was drawn evenly, rhythmically in and fall as the breath was evenly, rhythmically relinquished, in the silence of the lamplit room. After a while, I got up, and I put my empty glass down on the table, and I crossed the room and picked out a record and placed it on the gramophone, and the red jewel glowed minutely as a spark on the panel when I turned on the switch.

"I'm going to play you a little music," I said, my voice unnaturally loud. I held the gramophone's metal arm above the record, as if giving her the time to speak, and I found I was smiling like a nervous, effusive hostess at the girl, who had not moved.

The first record was a Strauss waltz, and I knew that the strains of it must cross the street and drift through the hospital windows, and perhaps be heard above the sound of the radios. And when that record was done, I played two Bach jigs, and the movement of them filled the room with agility and life, but the girl on the divan did not stir and did not open her eyes. I would have played more, and perhaps it would have roused her, in the end, but now it was eleven o'clock, and I wanted to go to bed. I lingered awhile longer, not liking the idea of leaving her sleeping there, and then, having left the lamp lighted on the table near her, I went, humming one of the Bach jigs, perhaps for courage in the empty house, as I mounted the stairs.

By now, I felt an acute uneasiness, because of the presence of the girl and the uncertainty of when she might awake and start wandering from floor to floor. After I had undressed and washed and got into my bed, I could not sleep. I thought I should have perhaps called a doctor or perhaps roused her by violent means from the torpor in which she lay. The hands on the phosphorescent face of the leather-framed clock on my bureau had marked one o'clock the last time I lifted my head and looked at it, and after that I slept, for when I awoke, with a sense of shock in the darkness, and looked at it again, it was nearly four. And on the floor below I could hear the feet moving softly, warily, and I sat up in bed and felt for my dressing gown and pulled it around me, and my hands were shaking, for some reason I could not name. When I had found my slippers beside the bed and put my feet into them, I moved softly across the room to the lighted hallway, and there I crept to the banisters and closed my hands on the varnished wooden railing, and, clinging to it, I peered down the bright well of the stairs. There, on the landing just below me, the girl stood, her hair shining like copper, peering uncertainly into the darkness of the basement floor below.

"Were you looking for something?" I called down in a voice that startled me by its gay, shrill cordiality, and at the sound of it the girl jumped like a deer that the shot has just passed by. Then she turned, and she threw her head back, and the soft hair brushed across her shoulders as she looked up the well of the stairs to where I clung to the banisters.

"I'm looking for my hat and bag," she said, and the voice, in contrast to my own, was cool and composed, and pitched admirably low.

We did not say much more to each other, although there was a great deal more that might have been said. When I came down the stairs, she stood looking at me somewhat critically, and I saw that her eyes were a light sea green in color and that they were anxious and proud and shy. She said that her hat was a small white straw hat and that the bag was straw and white as well, and she didn't want to lose them. And because there was no way to explain how things had been, I could only say that the hat had blown off in the street, and that I had not seen the bag at all. And then, not having put her sandals on yet, and standing there barefoot but with dignity before me, she said, "I don't know what my husband must be thinking. I don't know how I got here at all."

And still it seemed impossible to tell her any of the story, for if I spoke of the police having been called, then I might just as well have let the police car come and take her—the bookshop girl, or the bride from the sticks, or whoever she might be. We had gone back into the sitting room now, and I asked her where she had eaten that evening, thinking perhaps she herself would be able to put it together up to a certain moment. She picked up one sandal from the rug, and she looked at it, considering how much she would say.

"I don't think I had any supper," she said, and she sat down on the divan and started to put her sandals on, but she had some difficulty with the straps. "I came out of work with a girl I know, and it was hot, and we went to a bar and had a drink together." Her voice was gentle, pleasant, low. "It was hot when we came out of the bar, and after we had walked for a while along Lexington Avenue, we went into another bar," she said, and perhaps because of the way she told it, without detail or conviction, I did not believe it had happened that way.

She had got her sandals on now, and she crossed to the mirror that hung above the mantel. She took a comb out of the pocket of her dress and stood there combing out her wavy reddish brush of hair. And as I watched her, the narrow fingers looked suddenly efficient, and strong and relentless, despite the delicacy of their bones.

"It's something that could happen to almost anyone," I said.

"What?" she said quickly, and she looked at me in the mirror, almost startled, and her hands stopped combing her hair.

"Why, just that," I said, trying to find the words not to say it. "Losing one's hat and bag like that."

"Yes," she said, and she jerked the comb through her hair again. "I know."

She did not ask me for the two dollars. It was I who made her take the money when she was ready to go. She said she knew exactly where she was going and that one dollar would be enough, and I said it was better to have the two. She suggested of her own accord that she bring it back about four o'clock the next afternoon. It was Sunday, and she would not be working, and it would be quite easy to come up with it, she said. She asked me to write my name and address down for her, and I got a pencil and paper from the desk and did this, and she folded it over in her supple hand.

"Look," I said, "would you tell me your name, too?"

And then I knew how impassable was the chasm of mistrust or fear or suspicion that lay between us, for now she seemed to be taken off her guard, and her green eyes looked wildly at the desk and the table and then at my face.

"My name is Daisy Miller, Mrs. Daisy Miller," she said, and even before I thought of the volume of Henry James standing between the bookends, I did not believe it was true.

At the door, I remembered how we had crossed the street and come through the basement gate together, and now there was nothing left of the thing that we had done together and the intimacy we had shared. I watched her go down the brownstone steps, walking carefully on her platform soles, as if she felt a weakness in her flesh, and I went back into the sitting room to put out the lamp on the table by the divan, where the counterpane still lay.

I am putting this down in the hope that the girl who told me her name was Daisy Miller will read it, because using the name that wasn't hers doesn't matter, and not bringing the two dollars back doesn't matter, but I just want her to know that, after all the rest of it, I hate the story's ending that way.

WAR YEARS

Anschluss

SHE had come out in July to Brenau for two years now, and come back twice at Christmas: Merrill, the fashion editor's assistant coming out from Paris for her vacation in Austria, stepping off the train into this other world of mountains, and seeing the shapes of the dark forests lying unaltered in the grass or snow. Fanni came to the station every time to meet her, the strong black silky braids pinned up high around her head, wearing her homemade dirndl and apron. It might have been Fanni that brought her back: they reached out their arms to each other and kissed each other's faces, but even while the slow, low American voice was saying: "Fanni, here I am again. Here I am back, Fanni," the travel-weary and fashion-weary eyes were looking for something else besides the scenery and the voice was waiting to say it. Fanni stood looking at her, the smile fixed on her mouth, seeing again not in desire or envy but with awe the mascara on the lashes, the hats that varied from summer to winter, from Descat to Schiaparelli, marveling at the undying scent of Chanel in the Paris clothes. "Is it possible, Fanni, I'm back?" the voice went on saying, the naïve youthfulness and blitheness masking for a little while the satiety and the concern, calling attention wildly for a moment to something fresher than the scars from thirty years of being gallant and bright. "Fanni, you're looking so this or that or the other thing. Or I simply *love* your dress or your shoes or your jacket—it's quilted, isn't it? You must tell me which shop it came from. I've got to have one to take back to Paris. They'd be crazy about it."

If the hotel porter didn't come at once, Fanni, being the

younger, stooped and without difficulty picked up one of the
pigskin bags. They would argue about it, one of them wearing high heels and the other broad hand-stitched soles, because Merrill said it was much too heavy for her; and then
when the porter came at last, the American woman began
laughing her soft, quick, youthful laughter. She couldn't
think of the German words to say any more—only *"Guten
Tag"* and that was as far as she could remember. Out of the
station the three of them went, the hotel porter carrying the
bags and laughing, and the two young women holding arms
and laughing, out into the unfailing miracle of the wintry
starlit world or into the stormy blue summer evening's light.

Outside in the square, Merrill knew all the horses and she
had saved sugar for them from the dining car. Sugar for
horses, said the eyes of the porters and eyes of all the drivers
on the boxes of the open carriages or sleighs, and even Fanni's
dark quiet eyes said it. It was a thing they never got used to
seeing: just one more of the lavish, unthinking gestures foreigners made over and over, like ordering whiskey in the
face of poverty. At one season, they would be carriage horses
when she came, drowsing there in the sun with their feed
bags on their noses; and the next time they would be wild
eager creatures with their breath white on the air before
them, shaking their harness bells and pawing at the thick-
packed snow.

Only when the two women got to the *Gasthaus* and sat
down at the long clean polished table in the public room did
Merrill say the words that had been there every instant, what
she had come across these countries alone to utter, had waited
mouth shut and eyes worn with despair over cocktail glasses,
manicure tables, typewriter keys, programs of couture openings, shorthand notes, to ask month after month: "Fanni,
how's Toni? How is he making out?"

She looked away when she said it, taking her gloves off or

her cigarettes out, or seeking for her lighter in her bag. Nothing was ever changed in the warm dim room except the seasons' changes: one time the tall, tiled stove hot to the hand and the next time cool, and hot red wine in the glasses instead of beer. Or else the changes in the waiters' faces: this one in jail for political agitation and another one moved on to somewhere else because he had worked his three months out of the year there and could go home and collect his dole in leisure for the months ahead. And Merrill drinking the beer or the wine and chewing at the big tough pretzels would look at something else and say:

"How's Toni, Fanni? I must say he's the most unsatisfactory letter writer! What's he doing now?"

Fanni would take a swallow from her glass and shake her head.

"Doing?" she'd say, wondering anew that this useless and uneasy thing must be asked. "Oh, nothing. You know the way it is here. There is nothing for anybody to do. He makes things out of wood, of course, a little, and he plays, you know. He plays the harmonica most of the time."

That was the sign for them to burst out laughing again, screaming, shrieking, rocking with laughter together, as if Toni were the name for half-wit, for village nut, for the queer white-headed boy; or as if this were a family joke they'd never get over if they lived to be a hundred, a pain in the side, an ache in the face season after season instead of the two syllables describing glory, naming at last the animal and golden-flanked Apollo toward whom their love turned, sistered by his power. Here they sat, summer or winter, laughing fearfully at it: Toni, my brother, said Fanni's slow, silent, loving tongue, and Merrill strangled in her nervous fingers Toni, Toni, my strange, wild, terrible love; the two women laughing and laughing as if the time would never come to wipe their eyes and speak coherently of him.

This year they had left it like this: whether there was the *Anschluss* or whether there wasn't, they would meet in Brenau toward the middle of the summer just the same. You can't change a people's ways or their faces overnight, Merrill said for two months to herself in Paris. Her right hand was free of its good glove and the silver-mounted pencil in her fingers flew at the paper while the mannequins in winter suits, fur wraps, ski ensembles, came down the carpeted floor toward the double row of seated women, hesitated, turned lingeringly, and mounted the salon's length again. "Really adorable fur buttons, leather-frogged," she jerked down, "like your very smartest Hussars."

Her left fingers took the cigarette from her lips and snuffed it out in the metal engraved dish while her right hand blocked quickly down in the still girlish American script: "Upper sleeves built to assist any filly beyond her first carefree youth to shoulder the responsibility of looking sixteen and spirited this winter." Outside was the Paris heat, July's, and Merrill thinking: Once this farce of the openings is through, I'll set my lovely profile toward the heights. Everyone, mannequins, sister journalists, salesladies, to be split into two categories if you caught them unawares: those who went upward out of choice and looked a mountain in the eye and those who took their clothes off at once and went to sleep on beaches. The Nordic and the Mediterranean blood, each manifestation of it going back to its source, like eels up out of the water with a flick of the tail and covering ground, field, thicket, swamp, wood, returning to their own latitude to breed. "Hats this winter," she wrote, "are likely to be taken by your little girl to put on her Dydee doll if you don't watch out." All the seas in the world could dry up and the beaches turn to oyster shells and I wouldn't care, she thought, noting that wimples were worth a word or two, as long as they left Austria and the mountains and the people exactly the way they were.

All because of one winter, and the depth of snow at Brenau that year, and the night air that stabbed you to the heart when you put your velvet parka on and stepped in fur boots onto the packed white road. Not the scenery or the ski jumps or the country making history, but one man's face and the muscles in his jaws flickering like breath in and out when he played the mouth organ, his fingers on the metal and the music held clear and steady in the palm of his thin tough hand.

That was the first year out, and the Englishman she'd talked with on the train came into the hotel dining room that night and sat down in his place at table with her, his jowls freshly shaved, his teeth Macleaned, the gray at the temples brushed back with oil and forethought. Outside the road, carving through the stiff pure drifts, led off toward St. Johann, and the moon and mountains halted in the vast icy paralytic light.

"By the way," said the Englishman, clearing his throat. "Have you looked out the window tonight? It's really stupendous. Full moon, you know. A night for—"

"Romance?" said Merrill wearily, and she lit a cigarette in the middle of the meal as any American would.

The ex-army officer's eyes turned rather fearfully on her, then bolted down the room's length while he laughed.

"Well, I don't know as I'd go quite that—I don't know as I actually—" he began, looking for help down at the thick black sauce and slices of the game. "I was thinking of tracking down a sleigh," he said, not daring to make it definitely an invitation yet. "Thought of taking a little run as far as the next village." He cleared the hesitation from his throat again and let his blue frightened eye rest on her face. Rather pretty, he might have been thinking; or damned pretty but a little worn; or thinking: chic, blond, I should say not over thirty. There might be something in it for a chap. "Would you—

would you be—would I be able to persuade you," he said, "to throw a few togs on and—"

The sleigh driver lifted the three rugs, like three long-locked gray shaggy animals with shape and life and obstinacy of their own, up off the floor and laid them across their legs, thrust them behind their feet, beat them into submission around them, and then he mounted to the seat and took the reins up and spoke the word the horses' ears were twitching in the moonlight for. The instant they moved, the bells they wore broke sharply into speech and then settled with the horses' gait into a high clear puny chatter which the silent indifference of the fields and the hills and the moon's marble eye neither awed nor subdued. Beneath the rug's uncombed hide, the Englishman's hand moved tentatively toward Merrill's and halted when she said:

"The human race might just as well die of its own insignificance on a night like this. But please give me a cigarette before you do."

So there was American wit at its best for you, she thought, the poor helpless American girl's defense, and there was the poor English army bloke, without his army and without his medals, shorn of his pith helmet and stripped of his crop and saber, sitting mortally wounded by her side. He was telling her about the French, holding the lighter to the cigarette's end for her; chap knew he was being done in as soon as he put his foot on French soil. The lighter's flame lit up his features for an instant, the packed rosy jowl, the graying temple under the Tirolean hat's brim, the bulging blue glazed eye. He'd seen all he wanted to of them in the war and the state they'd left their billets in for decent troops to move into after. He was saying this and other things like it to the aloof bright wastes of the night, and Merrill felt her blood moving wearily in her, wearily harking and hating, without hope or passion knowing: this is the way life goes on, just

like this, this is the way it will go on forever; when, without
warning, the harness, strap, trace, yoke, or whatever nameless
link of security it was, snapped or unbuckled and the left-
hand horse broke partially free. He skipped to one side on the
ends of his hoofs in panic, and the sleigh jerked halfway
into the drift as the second horse rose his full height in terror
into the sharp air.

There was nothing to do but climb out of the tipping
sleigh and undo the frightened beasts completely now, the
Englishman and the Austrian driver working together at it
while Merrill walked back and forth in the cold, stamping her
fur boots softly on the snow. The thing was not to be re-
paired; even with the handful of knotted cord out of the
driver's pocket, there was no way to lash the rotted leather
end to end. So they must set off on foot toward the lights of
the first houses which were St. Johann, the man leading
the two animals by their dark hanging heads while the bells at
their necks murmured in chastened complaint. The ex-army
man, in that intimacy born of peril, had put his arm through
Merrill's and they followed behind. Now and again the
horses' droppings fell before them on the moonlit road,
dropped and lay steaming in rich warm indecorum in the
heart of the night's icy austerity.

"Listen to the way our footsteps cry in the snow," she
said. "Listen, listen." His fingers were feeling down her arm
for her naked wrist, and if he touches me, she thought in quiet
fury, I'll strike his face, I'll kill him. Her blood and being
were filled with grief, weighted and numb with an inexplicable
sorrow as she watched the breath shaping white from her
mouth on the frosty air. This is the way life goes on, and now
I am old and nothing wonderful can ever happen. "Listen,"
she said, with the tears of weakness and pity ready to fall
from her eyes. "Listen to our footsteps crying," and then the
girl's voice could suddenly be heard singing, singing loud and

joyous from the house, shouting out of the dark walls and the small shut lighted windows the perfection of belief or youth or love in warbling wonder, the yip-ai-daidy-day, lari-liti-loe.

In a minute the Englishman had opened the inn's door before Merrill and the clear block of light fell yellow across her furs and her face and onto the road where the horses and man were turning toward the stables. Before them in the room, near to the high green stove, three people sat at a table: a young woman with black braids around her head, and the two others older, perhaps the woman and man who owned the place because they stood up and bowed when the strangers came in.

"God greet you," they said, and Merrill answered eagerly: "God greet you."

It was the first time she laid eyes on Fanni or heard her voice, Fanni sitting drinking hot wine with them, not friendly or unfriendly, but casually, insouciantly there. She would speak her slow, solemn English to them as much as they liked, her eyes black, bright, merry, like a peasant's with a craftiness and a conjecture hard and good as flint behind them. She lived in Brenau but she had driven down with her brother to see their aunt and uncle for the evening. Her brother's horse and sleigh were in the stable, she said. If their driver couldn't get the harness fixed, she and her brother would take them back to Brenau.

"I must say, that's awfully kind of you," said the Englishman.

"Order them more wine," said Merrill without looking at him but at Fanni's face. "That was you singing when we came along the road, wasn't it?" she said. "I know it was you. It was the most beautiful voice I've ever heard. I'd give my whole life, I'd give anything in the world to be able to sing like that." She looked at the plump, warm cheeks, and the

full neck, and the girl's bare hard white arms crossed on the
table, her own ringed, nervous hand with the painted nails
touching the glass of sweetened steaming wine. "It's wonderful to sing like that because it means you're *happy*. It's like
the mountains and the moonlight, like these wonderful old
houses that aren't like any other houses in the world. You
just can't help singing like that. That's what makes it so marvelous."

"Yes, I'm happy," Fanni said, speaking slowly, casually.
"They let my brother out of jail today. I'm happy," and now
that Merrill heard the word "brother" said again, she knew it
was this that had brought them out at night in the cold
and snapped the harness in the frost and wooed them like
the singing to this place. "My brother's horse and sleigh, my
brother's this, that, and the other thing, my brother's political work, my brother's sacred blood and bone," the song
was warbled high and low.

"What is his name?" Merrill asked. Now she had drunk,
she felt the color in her cheeks and her flesh was hot and
quick with promise: the fur hood tied still around her glowing face, her muff laid on the table in expectancy so that the
hands were free to seize on whatever was to come.

"Toni," Fanni said, and at once she began to sing.

"Order another carafe of wine," said Merrill without looking at the Englishman, and the old Austrian stood up from
the table with the empty pitcher hanging from his hand and
waited while the girl's voice rose and dipped and sprang with
grace and sinew about them, yodeling as clear as water falling
the ohs, the ahs, the lees, the lias, in silver beads of sound.

"Oh, lovely, how lovely!" Merrill cried out in sweet hysteria when it was done. Looking at Fanni's hard, bright,
merry eyes, she felt the brilliance, wild and unbearable, of her
own; the suddenly rekindled blaze of what animal beauty,
after years of fashion sketches, fashion notes, hints, cribs, boat

trains, special articles, the British royal family wardrobes, and decisions, still remained. In a minute the door may open, she thought, to what? to what? She held her breath, her eyes fixed in intoxication on Fanni's face. In just a minute the door may open and it may happen, even to me it may happen.

But it was merely the Englishman who cleared his throat and said to Fanni:

"Ah, just what is it you do, if I may ask? Are you a singer? That is, I was just wondering what it is you do—"

"Do?" said Fanni, looking up in surprise. "Do?" She bared her white small teeth, not laughing, perhaps not even smiling. "*Mein Gott*," she said, "what does anybody in Austria do?"

The innkeeper came back to the table with the pitcher of smoking wine and set it down, and the Englishman said "Ah!" cheerily and stretched out his hand for it. This movement and every other sound stopped short when the door from the back-room opened suddenly and quietly in.

"*Grüss Gott, die Herrschaften*," said the man who closed it behind him. He must have just come in from the cold for his face was fresh with it and his jacket was buttoned up close from his narrow hips to his chin. He was neither short nor tall, light or dark, heavy or lean, but his shoulders stood wide in the jacket's cut and the sides of his face were hollow. He took off his skier's peaked cap and slung it onto the peg by the door, and his hair was lighter than his sister's hair and even touched with yellow at the temples. He wore jumper's trousers, funneling to the ski boots' leather lip, and as he crossed the room to the table where the others sat he pulled off his gloves and unbuckled the strap of his jacket with one strong, quick hand.

That was the first night; that was the beginning. That was in 1936 when he drove her home on the seat beside him while Fanni and the Englishman rode behind. That was the winter he taught her to ski, and they climbed the mountains on skins at night and slept in huts and refuges together. Being young in a country where the young had no function because no occupation, they were none of them, none of the young Merrill met with them that year, either rich or poor, workers or idlers, either successful or not. The standards other countries knew were gone, slipped down the mountain like the avalanches that thundered their long way down in the spring. One season Toni was a ski teacher, and the next a guide on Sundays, a carpenter in the week, a harmonica player, a carver of small wooden monstrosities. Like this, one day was pieced onto the next as one schilling paid out by foreigners was added to another. The whole little town, the entire country perhaps, with no choice but to make shift with this way of doing: eating what was cheap and drinking only a little and dancing because dancing could be had for nothing, and all of it so casually accomplished, with such a fugitive, careless abandon, as if they all knew that something else was going to happen in a little while.

"What will you do this winter, Fanni darling?" Merrill would ask. She might be doing her nails or putting fresh mascara on her lashes, but when she thought of the future and put these questions to them there would be the intense American anxiety in her face to be enlightened, to have the thing arranged, to know. "What kind of work do you think you'll be able to do this winter, Fanni?"

Or climbing the hills in the night's dark with Toni, the uncertainty of what the end would be would smite her again and she'd say:

"Toni, my love, my love, what kind of work can you do when the snow's gone? How will you ever manage to live at all?"

"But I live," said Toni. "I live. I'm stronger than any man

in Paris. Sit down. By the tree there, sit down. I wish to tell you."

The snow had melted at the roots of the tree and they sat on the black pine needles that had fallen thickly there. He did not put his hand out towards her or draw her close in his arms, but here was his power, cold, marvelous, aloof, dismantling her, weakening her, leaving her no speech.

"I eat, I drink, I love a woman, this woman," he said, and he was looking down at the lights in the valley below.

"Yes, but what does it lead to? It doesn't lead to anything," she said, hearing her own voice weak and aimless in the night.

"Yes, it leads. It is being alive. It is being a man," he said, without turning his head.

"But it doesn't lead," she said. "I go back to Paris, the snow melts in the spring, you can't give any more ski lessons, you have no money. It doesn't lead to anything. It doesn't lead to marriage, for instance," she said.

Nowhere else in the world could it happen, she thought in irritation: the future depending on the amount of snow that fell or didn't fall. Nowhere else could one join that procession of women who went out from the church after midnight mass into the graveyard, carrying their little Christmas trees to the dead, crossing the snow with the ribbons and tinsel shining and the match-small candles flickering in the air. There the women kneeled down in the wintry midnight, shielding the candles' flames in their hands, and set their trees out in a lighted forest on the graves. Nowhere else could one share in this strange unnamable yearning, this sweet sad longing which spoke its own humble tongue to the lost and the bewildered who traveled from other countries to attend this miraculously staged performance of economic collapse.

In January, just before she must get back to Paris for the openings, they arrested Toni again and put him into jail. But there was no shame or even wonder to it as there would have been in any other place on earth. It was merely another part of the spectacle to see him at the high barred window, his ski jacket on because there was no heat inside those walls, and his harmonica playing fast and recklessly. Fanni and Merrill went down the back street at night and tried throwing a comb up the height of the *Rathaus* to him, and it struck three times against the bars and fell again before he got it, and each time he missed it he giggled like a girl. That's what I love, she thought wildly; that's what I love, that dark faceless shadow leaping like a fool for a comb to do his hair with, laughing like a nut when perhaps they'll hang him tomorrow, and she turned to Fanni with her voice shaking in her throat.

"Political agitation," she said fiercely, as if she had not said the same thing a hundred times before. "But what kind of political agitation? Why can't he have a lawyer and a room to himself if he's a political prisoner?"

"*Mein Gott,* it's nothing!" said Fanni. This softness, this female fury in the strange foreign woman was enough to take even the significance of truth away. She stood, a little shorter than Merrill, in the snow-covered back street, both of them held and hidden in the shadow of the *Rathaus'* wall. The street lamp was farther along, but even without its light Fanni could see or else remember the beauty of the other woman's face, fragile, nervous, balked, with the little lip trembling and the eyes painted blue and starry as a child's, and the child's hood fastened underneath her chin. There was the actual sight or else the photograph of it fixed indelibly in Fanni's dark, shrewd, merry eyes. "He'll be out again in three or four days," she said, wanting to touch Merrill's arm perhaps but not knowing how to make the move. "It's happened so often. It happens to them all if they go around lighting the fires. It's treason—Is that the word you said it was?—yes, treason, a small treason, very little, to light the swastika fires on the hills at night."

"Peaches!" Toni's voice called down to them. "Merrill, can you got me peaches?"

"Get, not *got!*" Fanni called up the call. "It's a joke," she said to Merrill. "He thinks that is very funny. He saw those pictures with colors on them about peaches in the American magazines you have."

"Fanni, I can't bear it," said Merrill in a low fierce voice. "I can't bear it. I'll get him diamonds. I'll buy his way out if they'll let me."

All the way back to the middle of town they could hear the harmonica playing, the little grief in it now nursed in the hollow of his hand and asking in warbling nostalgia for a homeland that had perhaps never been or for a hope without a recognizable or possible name to give it. Night after night he played until the evening he came out, and Fanni walked on ahead to let them kiss each other by the wall.

"Merrill, I like the perfume again," he said against the hood's fur.

"Toni, Toni," she said, holding to him, and she felt the tears running down her face. "Toni, we can do something together. You don't have to stay here. You could go to France with me—you could . . ."

"I've never been into a city," he said. In a minute he might begin laughing out loud at the thought of himself wearing city clothes. "I have to stay here in my country. I'm too poor a one for you."

"I'm old enough to take care of you, much older than you," she whispered, and he held her hard against him.

"You are my doll," he said, saying it savagely and hotly against the hood's white fur. "You smell good like a doll, and little small teeth like that. If I wanted to do it, I could break you like children do with a doll, pull your arms out and break all your little bones in your skin—"

He bit quickly at her cheek and chin and lip, soft, dry, nibbling bites at powder, scent, and rouge, and she looked up at him with the tears still on her face.

"Toni, I've put red all over your mouth and my mascara's running," she whispered.

"I'll keep your red like that," he said. "I'll keep it like that on my face. I'll never wash it away."

Then in 1938 it happened; it happened in the spring. The German troops went over the border without a word and there was the Anschluss, and *maybe he'll be singing a different tune about it now that he's got it,* thought Merrill. *Perhaps he'll want to get out of the country by hook or by crook now he's got what he's been wasting behind bars for. They won't be able to change his face or the shape of his hands or his mouth singing what words he did; not love ditties on top of a mountain, nor popular airs, nor things of classic pricelessness, but the pure loud clarion call of "Austria, Awake, Awake!" Awake and in your right mind by this time, I should hope,* thought Merrill, buying the ticket to go back; *united and awake and in her senses she can't cast the pearls of his teeth before swine, nor squander the fortune of his glance on one direction. His country nor no other can make a law-abiding man out of what he is. He'll go on rebelling, shouting the Nazis down as he shouted the Catholics and the Communists and Schuschnigg out of countenance, revolting now in the same cool careless way against what he's been wearing the flesh off his bones to get.*

For the first time, stepping off the train at Brenau, she could not fling her arms out to Fanni or kiss her face, nor draw that first deep draft of other air in before she said: "Fanni, it's like falling asleep again and finding the same

dream still waiting for you." This time she must stand
waiting on the platform alone, turning from the far sight of
snow on the mountaintops to the shady summery road leading off under the heavy boughs toward the first hotels where
the swastikas on the flagpoles folded and unfolded languidly
on the breeze. Fanni did not come running late down the
pathway worn along the rails, nor call her name out across
the picket fence. The sun shone hot in the waning afternoon,
thunder clouds were gathering on the rocky horns at the valley's end, and the horses sneezed in their feed bags on the
square outside. In a moment the hotel porter came through
the station door, took off his cap and said *"Heil Hitler"* and
shook her hand.

"Grüss Gott," said Merrill brightly, and then she started
laughing as usual because she couldn't think of the German
words to say. *"Und Fräulein Fanni—und—Fräulein Fanni?"*
She said it over several times to him, but he only shook his
head and stooped to pick her bags up. All he knew was that
the hotel had raised his wages and that the place was full of
Germans, full of them, just like the old days again before
the frontier was closed. And they'd put a new uniform on
him. He made her feel the cloth of the jacket. "Oh, *gut!"*
said Merrill, having forgotten the right word to say. "Perfectly lovely! *Très gut*, Hermann!"

At the *Gasthaus* the letter was waiting for her, and standing in the room where Fanni had always been, she read it once
quickly, and then reread it slowly. After she had folded it in
the envelope again, she took it out and stood reading it over.
You will forgive me for not being at the station, Merrill, or
words similar to this, it said. Now I am district nurse and I
cannot choose my own time. Today I must go on my bicycle to Kirenberg to arrange about the vacations for some
expecting mothers, and I shall then have to report what I
have done at the office when I get back. So, please, may I

come in this evening and see you? We are all very well organized now. Toni is Sports' Organizer at the lake, so if you go swimming this afternoon you will see him. He is also *Direktor* of the Austrian Youth Local. Of course he is very proud. If you do not see him swimming, he too will come in and visit you with me tonight. So until we meet, my dearest friend.

Even the little bathing cabins, set out in rows on the south side of the lake, were topped by swastika banners, small ones fluttering in dozens against the wide somber mountain waters. This place, where before so few people had come, was now singularly alive: the refreshment tables crowded and bathers lying on the wooden platform that slopes to the edge, swimmers basking on the floats, bathers stretched reading their newspapers and smoking on the summer grass. Enormous, thick-thighed, freckled-shouldered, great-bellied people, not Austrians but invading cohorts come across the border with heads shaved close to baldness, speaking the same tongue and bearing vacation money to a bankrupt land. The air was filled with their voices as they called across the echoing waters, the hullabaloo of monstrous jokers gurgling at the surface, the shower and impact as the great bodics dropped from the diving boards and smote the tranquil currents with their mighty flesh.

Their bathing dress was dark and plain, the women wearing skirted ones with modest backs and necks, and Merrill changed into her pale blue two-piece suit in the cabin and looked down at the strip of delicately tanned skin between the top and trunks, and wondered. I never minded wearing this before, she thought. Why do they make me know I'll look a queer fish among them: hair curled, mouth painted, thin as a rake and half-naked. With something almost like shame she stepped out of the cabin door into the strong cool mountain air. The storm was gathering quickly in the valley and in a little while the sun would be gone.

Once she looked up, she no longer saw the people: the heavy sloping shoulders, the shaved narrow pates, the folds of obscene hairy flesh at neck or chest, or cared for whatever insult or censure now stood in their eyes. Toni was on the springboard, ready to take the high dive, the heels lifted, the calves small as fists with muscle, the knees flat, the thighs golden and slightly swollen for the movement not made yet but just about to come. The throat, the lifted chin, the straight brown nose were set with cameo-clarity for an instant against the deepening sky, his arms thrown back and laying bare his breast as if for this once, just now, and this time forever, the shaft of love might pierce directly and the blood might flow at last.

"Toni," she said in silence, "Toni, Toni," watching his hands' one wing part the surface and the body slide perfectly into the water's place. Once he had risen, visible as light floating upward from the depths, and shaken the drops from his face and hair and thrust the locks back, she was at the edge, and kneeled there, waiting. "Toni," she said out loud, and immediately he turned his head, wiping the water from his mouth and chin, and treading water. He took the five long strokes that brought him to her and reached his fingers to the edge of rotted timber and hung there, the hands tanned yellowish, the square nails clean, his upper lip drawn back upon his teeth, and then he lifted himself out, dripping, and stood on the wood.

"*Mein Gott*, Merrill, you look like somebody from the theatre," he said quickly. For a minute she might not have heard him, sitting there mindless, heedless, watching his wet bare feet stain the boards beneath them with water as if a shadow were spreading imperviously across the weather-rotted and time-rotted wood. She looked at the small strong perfectly molded anklebones with the skin drawn over them like tight, sheer silk, and suddenly, as if at that instant she heard the quickly uttered words or just at that instant understood, she jerked her eyes up to his face.

"What time did you get in?" he said. "Fanni showed me the letter you wrote. I thought you said this week sometime—"

"No, today," said Merrill. She sat squinting up at him, trying to shade her eyes and face although no sun was shining, feeling in panic her half-nakedness, the thinness almost skeletonlike among these people, the strip of body between breast and navel obscene, infecund. "It's quite gay here, isn't it?" she said, making a gesture with her naked pale arm and hand. "Quite different, isn't it?"

"No, it is not gay," he said. He was smoothing his upper arms dry with the palms of his hands. "They are not like the English and American people who came here before. They know we are a country, not a playground. They respect us. They do not come to dress up for parts in a musical comedy the way the other people did."

She sat there at his feet, squinting up at him, watching him turn to pick the bath towel off the springboard's trellis and start rubbing his shoulders with it.

"It is very serious here now," he said. "You see how they dress? Fanni will tell you how things have changed for us." And then he said quickly: "The nails of your toes, Merrill," squatting down on his thighs to come nearer to her and so say it the more violently and brutally. Merrill looked startled the length of the legs curved under her to the ten dull red medallions varnishing their extremities. "Wear that in Paris. Wash it off before you come here to us," he said. "Now we're busy, we haven't time for people masquerading. We aren't the tourists' paradise any more. People can't come and pay to see us dance and roll over on our backs like bears with rings through the nose—"

"Toni, you got what you wanted, didn't you?" Merrill said in a low quiet voice, sitting there without movement, even the nervous hands lying still. "You got what you were working for, didn't you, Toni?"

"Yes," he said, "yes," and then he said, leaning again: "Merrill, don't go, but just put a bathrobe around you. Everyone here is looking at you like something out of the *Tiergarten*. Nobody's used to suits like that or paint like that on the mouth—"

That was the next to last time she saw him. The last time was when she took the train the day after at the station, and he was there on the platform with half a dozen others, all young, all neatly uniformed in gray and green and smartly belted at the waist. They were there to meet the Innsbruck train which must have been bringing officials on it, and when he saw her on the other side of the glass his face altered and he took a step forward as if he were about to speak, as if it were not too late to say it. But the movement of the car passed like a veil between them and he brought his heels sharply together and lifted his right hand and she saw his lips open as he spoke, either *"Heil Hitler"* or *"Auf Wiedersehen,"* and that was all.

Nothing Ever Breaks Except the Heart

PERHAPS you have been there, and you know the Avenida and the way the trees grow the length of it—palm trees and the foreign varieties of hawthorn and maple. Perhaps you've drunk iced coffee under a colored umbrella there, with your back turned to the traffic's noise and the sight of the horses and your face turned to the strips of green, fresh-watered grass. The trees make the long avenues of shade that flow like a dark stream through the city, and on the edges of them stagger the horses, knee-deep in burning, if imaginary, sands. Perhaps you've walked up the avenue through the leafy jungle-dark toward where the American flag hangs, heavy with summer, on its white pole in this foreign city's air. Either children or tropical mirages of them must have run barefoot and scrofulous after you, asking for something as cool as money, and if you were there this summer, you must have seen Miss Del Monte eating ice cream at one of the tiny tables under the trees.

Miss Del Monte used to buy all the American picture magazines there were, and she would sit there looking at them, so as not to think of the horses, with the carts they drew breaking their backs and crippling their limbs beneath them, nor of the lather frothing under the harness that bound them irrevocably to man. Something was always doing it to her, taking the heart out of her breast and tearing it apart, and now she had come to the end. The first day she arrived, she told this to Mr. McCloskey. She said, "You can have the horses and the children with pellagra. I'll take the mint juleps," and Mr. McCloskey stopped looking at the German and the Polish and the Czech and the Russian refugees for a moment and decided, without much interest in it, that she was probably the prettiest woman he had ever seen.

Perhaps you even know Mr. McCloskey—the set of his shoulders in his American businessman's suit, and the rather jaded look in his eyes, and the thick hair just beginning to go gray. He had a roll-top desk to himself, but he never sat down at it, because for eight hours a day he stood behind the elegant, glass-topped counter in the airways office and told the roomful of foreigners, and Americans even, that they wouldn't be able to board a plane and go where they wanted to go for at least another month or two. Miss Del Monte went into the office in June, the first day she got to the city, and spun the propeller of the miniature plane with one finger as she waited there. She had left her stockings at the hotel because of the heat, and her arms and legs and her head were bare and cool enough looking; her nails were long and immaculately done, and her mouth was far too brilliant. Once you'd seen her, you watched for her everywhere you went: at the Tivoli Bar before dinner, or at the Aquarium, dining on the balcony, and after that playing at the Casino, or dancing at the Palace or the Atlantico. But she was never anywhere like that. She was always in the airways office, talking to Mr. Mc-Closkey or waiting to talk to Mr. McCloskey, smoking one cigarette after another and putting fresh lip rouge on from time to time.

"I'd like to get over by Saturday," Miss Del Monte had said to him the first day, and when she said it all the refugees sitting on the benches along the wall stopped breathing for a moment and looked at something that wasn't bitterness and hopelessness at last.

"Look," said Mr. McCloskey, making a gesture. "Everyone in this country's trying to get over." His eyes were haggard and his face was a little gaunt from the heat and the amount of talking he had to do. There were three telephone calls waiting for him on three different desks and fifteen people at the counter where Miss Del Monte stood. "It's either the language that's driving them out, or else it's because they don't kill their bulls in the *corsos* here," he said.

"They broke my heart every Sunday afternoon in Spain," said Miss Del Monte. "They dragged it out with the horses, and now I'm not having any more." She took another cigarette and she said, "On account my show's opening up, I'd like to get over by Saturday."

"Saturday!" a little man in a pongee suit behind her cried

out, and for a moment Miss Del Monte thought he had been stabbed. "I've been three monce waiting here—three monce!" he said, and he held up that number of fingers. He didn't speak English very well, but he had diamonds on his hand.

That was the first day, and the second day, in the morning, they were standing three deep around the counter, so Miss Del Monte gave it up after an hour and came back in the afternoon. When she got opposite Mr. McCloskey at last, she lit a cigarette and looked at him carefully and evenly. He must have been just over thirty, in spite of the gray in his hair, and his shoulders would probably have looked too broad for any chair he sat in.

"I'm not prepared for summer," she said. "Monday's the latest I can wait. I haven't a single sharkskin to put on."

"Do you know Mr. Sumner Welles?" said Mr. McCloskey, and for the first time Miss Del Monte saw the madness in his eye. "Have you influential friends in Washington?" he asked, and Miss Del Monte shook her head. "Then perhaps I can help you out," he said, and he walked rather handsomely to his desk, passing Mr. Concachina at the counter on his way.

Mr. Concachina was native, and his head was bald, and his mind was going. "I'm just now speaking four different languages at the same time to five different parties, Mr. Mc-Closkey," he said, and there was sweat on his forehead. "I tell you, I can't do it much longer. I'm at the breaking point."

"You've been saying that for a year and a half," said Mr. McCloskey. He was looking among the other papers for the typewritten list of names. "But nothing ever breaks, nothing," he said, and he repeated it vaguely. "Nothing ever breaks," and he held the list in one hand while he said "Hello there" into one of the three telephones. When he came back to the counter, he looked at Miss Del Monte. "We have a very nice opening for the seventeenth of November," he said.

This went on for a week or more, and then, one Monday morning, Miss Del Monte felt she was getting somewhere at last. She was on her fourth cigarette, and she had combed back her hair and put fresh lipstick on her mouth, and she looked more beautiful than ever.

"Just a minute," said Mr. McCloskey, studying the list. "How old are you? How much do you weigh?"

"A hundred and fifteen," said Miss Del Monte quickly. "I'm twenty-four, but I feel a lot older."

Mr. McCloskey pondered for a moment, and then he said, "Did you ever think of trying a boat, Miss Del Monte?"

"A boat? Do you mean a boat?" she said.

"Yes," said Mr. McCloskey. He looked at her and moved his hand in a swaying motion. "You'd be surprised. You might like a boat."

Mr. Concachina, a little way down the counter, had a telephone receiver in one hand and a fountain pen in the other, and he was writing something down. But still he had time enough to look up at Miss Del Monte. "You know about Pola Negri?" he said, and then he spoke the other language into the mouthpiece. "Well, Pola Negri got fed up," he said, after a moment. "She went out of here in a huff this morning. She's going to take a boat."

"I'd just as soon go out of here in a huff as in what I have on," said Miss Del Monte, evenly. "I'm sure it would be cooler."

"It ought to be awfully cool on shipboard," Mr. McCloskey said.

It was never Mr. McCloskey's intention to start going out in the evening with Miss Del Monte, but by the second week he had got so accustomed to seeing her around that it seemed the natural thing to find her on the Avenida one evening after dinner and walk back and forth with her beneath the trees.

She carried a guidebook in one hand, with a cablegram marking a page in it, and she said she'd just had a double whiskey and soda.

"It breaks my heart to talk shop," she said, "but my show's opening on the first of September."

"It can't if you're not there," said Mr. McCloskey. Behind them, in the fountains, illuminated water lilies with iron stems and china petals floated monstrously through the night, and the bookstalls, each one shaped like a book, and the leather tooled across the back, were open.

"If I stay much longer, I'll be right in time for the summer season," said Miss Del Monte. "It says so in the guidebook on page twenty-three. It says there are always balls and processions, varinos exhibitions, gymkhanas, and firelarks. However they want to spell it, I'd give up the varinos exhibitions any day if I could see a gymkhana or a firelark."

"You probably will without a bit of trouble if you have another double whiskey," said Mr. McCloskey, but Miss Del Monte said she'd rather hear a *fado* sung.

Mr. McCloskey had never been to a *fado* café before, but Miss Del Monte seemed quite familiar with the back street where one was. The lights were still on when they walked in and took a table, and all the men in their pongee suits and their white silk shoes turned to watch Miss Del Monte go past. The only other women there were the female *fado* singers, with their Spanish-looking shawls on their shoulders, sitting there rather grimly at separate tables, some with their fathers keeping an eye on them and some with their entrepreneurs, either sitting silent or writing out *fados* while they waited for their turn to come. In a minute the lights went out, and two guitar players mounted a little platform and sat down on the chairs that were placed on opposite sides of it and tuned their instruments up. No one looked very pleased about it, not even when the *fado* singer himself ran quickly

up the steps in his patent-leather shoes and stood in the spotlight between the two guitarists on the platform's boards.
He was a short, evil-looking man in a black suit, and his hair
was wavy and very well greased, and he kept his hands in his
trousers' pockets all the time.

"If he takes his hands out of his pockets, he isn't a *fado*
singer," said Miss Del Monte, and although the man hadn't
yet started to sing, someone behind her hissed.

Presently the singer announced the title of the *fado* and
added that this was the first time it had been sung in public,
for it was about a stabbing that had occurred near the fish
market that day. But when he opened his mouth he might
just as well have been telling them all what he thought of
them, one minute facing half of the room with his neck going
red, and then one minute berating the other half with the
veins in his forehead beginning to swell. He said the same
words over and over to them, so that there could be no mistake, breaking the rhythm savagely and throwing it in their
faces while the throbbing of the guitars wove steadily and
systematically upward and, finding no foothold, wove steadily
and carefully down again.

When he was done, the lights sprang up all over, and the
applause scattered about him, and Miss Del Monte lit another cigarette.

"Did you find this in the guidebook?" Mr. McCloskey
asked. He removed the crockery jug from its pail of ice and
poured the green wine out.

"Don't be absurd," said Miss Del Monte. "This is neither a
bewildering panorama nor a rendezvous of the elite, nor is it
an imposing terrace overlooking the sea."

"It might be a gymkhana," said Mr. McCloskey, and he
took another drink of wine.

The second night they went out together, again to one of
the back-street cafés, Miss Del Monte explained to him fur-

ther about the *fados*. She said the better ones were either patriotic or heroic, and these had been handed down from generation to generation. The ones they sat writing out quickly at the tables were only the personal ones, she told him.

"You simply have to sense which kind it is," she said.

This time it was a girl who sang first, standing up on the platform between the two seated guitarists, with the fringe of the black Spanish shawl hanging just below her knees. Her throat was bare and broad, and her face was primitive under the *maquillage*, and it was only the feet that had nothing to do with the rest. She wore pink stockings, and her feet were as small as mice and twisted like mice in the traps of the open-toed, cork-soled shoes she had on. She began her statement of fact with her teeth showing white in her mouth, and her voice was husky. She said it beautifully, repeating it first to one side of the room and then to the other, with her hands clasped on her stomach, holding the shawl.

"This is a personal one," said Miss Del Monte in a whisper to Mr. McCloskey.

"I'd be interested to know," said Mr. McCloskey rather wearily, "if she makes any mention of Mr. Sumner Welles."

"It's something she read in the paper," said Miss Del Monte. "It's about a girl whose fiancé kills her sister because she takes the bracelets he'd given the other one and wears them to go out dancing with another man. He couldn't stand it."

Mr. McCloskey filled their glasses up again. "Miss Del Monte," he said, "I don't know how your public's getting on without you."

It may have been later in the summer, perhaps it was in July, that Mr. McCloskey took her across on the ferry to have dinner on the other shore. They were probably sitting on the open part of the ferry's deck when Mr. McCloskey said, "She's over there." He didn't look toward the city's delicately starred hills but off into the darkness. "The only thing in life I care about is over there," he said, and as he spoke the strung lights of the battleship and the cutter went running past.

He said it again, after they had left the ferry and left the taxi and were walking down through the grass to the river's edge. The moon had risen now, and everything was as brilliantly lit as if by daylight, and although no explanation had been asked for or given as to why they had come here, and why they went down through the night-drenched grass to where the bright stream of water lay, still it seemed, and singularly without question, the one thing left for them to do.

"She's out there, tethered on the water," Mr. McCloskey said. "The plane," he said, a little impatiently, because Miss Del Monte didn't seem to be able to understand English any more. "She's out there. You can see her just to the left of the jetty." They stood on a footpath at the water's edge, where a half-dozen dories, white-flanked and rocking empty on the tide, were chained up to the shore. "We can row out to her," he said, and Miss Del Monte stepped into the boat that he held steady with his foot and sat down on the cross seat, doing it slowly and without wonder, like one hypnotized.

Mr. McCloskey followed her in and fitted the oars in their rowlocks and then pushed off from shore. The water was smooth, and the light and the dark moved clearly in broken pieces on it, first light and then dark around them as the oars dipped softly in the night. Every now and then he turned part way in his seat and feathered the oars while he looked ahead at the suave, enormous body of the plane.

"I love her," he said. "I love her," and Miss Del Monte couldn't think of the right thing to say. As they drew nearer he pulled hard and in silence on one oar so as to bring them up against the wing.

"Have you ever piloted one?" Miss Del Monte asked, and Mr. McCloskey didn't say anything for a little while. They were riding close to the plane and he had pulled the oars in, and, until the water began drying on them, the splays of them looked as bright as glass.

"That's what's the matter with me," he said after a moment. "I used to be one. I used to fly them across." He did not move from his seat, but he raised one hand and ran it along the hard, sweet, sloping, metallic breast. "I didn't have what it takes," he said, and his voice was bitter to hear. "Or, rather, I gave away what it takes. I had it. I had it." The dory gyrated slowly and without direction near the marvelously still body of the plane. "One or two whiskeys too much every now and then, and jitters," he said. "Single whiskeys when I was tired and double ones to get me out of whatever trouble I happened to be in. Jitters," he said. "So now I'm just good enough to stand up all day behind a counter and tell them what day the company's going to let them fly."

When Miss Del Monte got to the airways office the next morning, there was one Frenchwoman talking faster and better than the others, leaning across to Mr. McCloskey, with her hand in the black fish-net glove closed sharply on his arm. She was telling him, in French, that she knew Mr. Sumner Welles and that she'd been to school with Eve Curie, and Mr. McCloskey was saying nothing in French or in any other language. He simply stood there looking at her with a rather faded, hopeless look around his eyes.

Luck for the Road

THERE was 1938—the summer of it—when Dennis Amboy and the boy called Malcolm White went out the bedroom window of the little house one night and left home together for a little while. They did not go up to Grandma Amboy's big house and take one of the cars from the garage, and they did not leave on their bicycles. It was Grandma who found the bicycles in the morning when they looked for the boys: the two wheels propped side by side against the boathouse, with the raccoon tails and the baseball pennants and the other trophies of manhood in prescriptive gala on the handle bars. They went on foot—at least for a part of the way —carrying their shoes, and by moonlight, although there was nothing except disdain for the lack of peril in it to have gainsaid their going by the light of day. They walked the three miles or more to what they wanted, and there—on John Hogarth's property—they broke the stables open and they got out the horses that their hearts were set on.

"So then what did you do?" Grandma Amboy asked young Dennis. It was the night his father brought him home, after the two days and nights that he had been away. "How much fence-clearing did you get before you broke his leg?" she asked, and she might have been speaking of anything excepting tragedy to him.

"We kept off the roads so they wouldn't get us," young Dennis said, "and we took 'em flying, every hedge and fence and stream. And then he fell, my horse fell, and I had to get the veterinary for him. I ran five miles to find him, and the veterinary drove me back with him, and he put the bullet through him right away." There was nothing like crying in his face, but when he spoke of the death the sound of his voice had altered. "The veterinary had seen our pictures in the paper, and he told us he was going to let the Danbury police know he had us." But in spite of the sleeplessness and hunger and the cut across his forehead, his eye met her eye.

"So you got as far as Danbury!" his grandmother said. "Blast it, I wish I'd been with you!"

But now it was her own son's turn to speak. He stood by the library table, his face haggard from the two days and nights of search, and he looked gravely at his mother.

"I think I'll handle things this time," he said. "Young Dennis has given us all a forty-eight hours we won't forget," he was saying—a good, kind, well-groomed man who spent his days on Wall Street because of the money he had to earn. "Now, this time Fran and I—after all, we're his parents—and this time we feel . . ."

"You're not fit to bring him up—neither of you!" said Mrs. Amboy. Her cheque book was there on the library desk, open before her, and she shook her fountain pen savagely before she began to write. "Old Hogarth's asking four hundred and fifty for the horse," she said, and she wrote the sum and the figures out and signed her name with a flourish. "Neither you nor Fran understand the boy. He's fifteen. You're middle-aged," she said.

Two years before, there had been something else. April had moved with singular tenderness up the Hudson Valley, and young Dennis learned to drive the station wagon that spring. That season the gardener was new to the place, and "blast him, blast him," thought Mrs. Amboy in irritation as she came down the kitchen-garden path and saw how he had set the lettuce in. The threadlike, white roots had been pressed in close enough to reach out and strangle one another, and the frail little pairs of leaves lay, row by row, fainting for succor in the soil. She was making, hard and grim, for the greenhouse when Fran came up the driveway from the little house and spoke across the currant bushes to her.

"Young Dennis is in trouble," she said, and the color had gone from around her mouth. "He telephoned from the police station," she said.

"He telephoned *you?*" said Mrs. Amboy from the kitchen garden. That was the first thought, as quick as anger in her heart. She held fast to the head of her cane in the April sunlight. "Well, what's happened to him? Lost your tongue?" she said to Fran.

"Speeding," said her daughter-in-law. "Thirteen years old and speeding! Oh, Mother Amboy," she cried out, and it might have been she was asking some leniency, some spark of pity of her. "He's too young to drive the car!"

Mrs. Amboy looked at Dennis's wife beyond the budding currant hedge—at the quivering lips, and the soft eyes bright with tears.

"Weaned, isn't he?" she said, and her grip on the cane head tightened. "Not a cripple, is he? I'll go down and get him out," she said.

Her house was big, with a gabled roof, set back among trees on a height above the river. When there was snow, young Dennis came up with his friends from school and played at skiing on the grounds. In summer, there was the pond—the wooded depository of the property's trout streams dammed and set dreamily with islands. It lay just below the pine trees in the hollow where chestnut and sassafras and birch ran fragrant and wild, and slipperwort hung stripped, immaculate as satin. There she put up the boathouse and the diving board so that young Dennis need not go to the seashore in the summer. If you wanted him here, you arranged the scenery for him. Summer and winter, you wanted him before your eyes because he was as handsome and sound as a nut, and because your own cooling, slaking blood ran quick and violent in his veins.

She saw to the work and the workmen on the place as a man might have done it—to the new garage being built for the town car, and the kennels being done over, and the boat-house that rose stone by stone by the pond. She'd stamp through the wet, rotting leaves and the tangled brush of the property, man enough and canny enough to say what was needed to them, showing them how and where with the point of her lifted cane. But whenever she thought of her husband lying dead in the churchyard, impatience would get the better of her. "Gave up, slid from under!" she thought. "Resigned from the bank, and died in retribution for it! Gave up at sixty!" she'd say in contempt. "Catch me being tricked by them into dying!"

"Is my grandfather dead?" young Dennis asked her on the day of it. He was six that summer, and his eyes the same dark, stormy blue that hers had always been.

"Yes, dead!" she said with a snort.

"I'm never going to die," said young Dennis, and she knew the taste of the pride that drew his shoulders straight as wire.

Those were the quiet, affluent years, the prewar years. Even in 1941, the war had not quite come. But in February, there was the broken plate-glass window on the main street of the college town one Saturday night, and there were three of them involved in it. The three of them had been drinking, but young Dennis said he was the first one to start picking up the bricks and start flinging them through the glass. Then he and the others had stepped inside the window and removed the hats from above the wooden, high cheekboned faces, and off the honey-colored ropes of hair of the models on display. Some of the hats had little veils on them, and some had fish-net filets hanging down behind, and they wore them all, the three young men: those with the cock feathers on them, and those with the flowers blooming on them, one on top of the other as they went down the main street, singing.

They were wearing them still when Dennis reached the court house. Young Dennis and the two other boys were seated on the prisoners' bench with their eyes unsteady and the ladies' millinery worn sideways on their heads, but the humor had somehow gone from it.

"This is his third offense," Dennis told Grandma Amboy in the afternoon. "Fran and I talked it over. We want him to take the consequences of it. I left him there. We want him to serve his ten-day sentence out," he said.

"You and Fran are a couple of fools," said his mother. "He's my grandson. Jail isn't the place for him." But she waited until Dennis had gone down to drive to the little house before she put on her astrakhan coat and picked up her alligator bag and called for the chauffeur. "What price would you put on a plate-glass window, a big one?" she said with a certain pride as she rode behind him in the town car. When they got there, she walked into the judge's room with her cheque book in her hand.

The next year, it was something else; and this—although it might have been taken as consummation of a kind, as the seal of solemnity set upon their lives at last—was outrage and bitterness to Mrs. Amboy. As quietly as Dennis Amboy and Malcolm White had gone as little boys out the window with their shoes carried in their hands, so they walked out and joined the Air Force together. Fran came up the gravel drive, and stood on the other side of the hedge, and her words came separately over the leaves. Mrs. Amboy turned on her cane, her old ear harking, and her blood was turned to stone. War was a thing outside them and alien to their pace of life, as a factory or a coal mine was outside them. It took ordinary people—took them permanently, perhaps. Only in error did it take away people who dressed for dinner and belonged to clubs. This thing that happened in 1942 had nothing of culmination in it for her; young Dennis in uniform was as outlandish as if he were wearing the ladies' hats from the broken window in the main street still, with the roses blooming on them and the veils hanging sideways across his nose.

The things that had gone before had merely been rehearsal —the speeding, the horse stealing, the window breaking had been part of the preparation for this that was to come. It was the actual drama now; the curtain was about to rise, and the lines of the cast were ready. Mrs. Amboy was seventy-four when she packed her overnight bag and called the town car and went down to Washington.

"You and I have known each other a good many years," she said as she sat down in old Hogarth's office.

"I won't deny it," Hogarth said, and he tried a smile, but she eyed him grimly.

"I heard you were messing around down here with the administration. Young Dennis is in a fix. That's why I'm here," she said.

"Whose horses has he been stealing now?" asked Hogarth.

"He's joined the Air Force," said Mrs. Amboy, and her mouth was bitter. "I want you to get him out."

It was when she began to talk about how much money it was worth to her that Hogarth told himself it was old age getting the best of her at last, or the shock of young Dennis being in it now that had touched her mind, and he grew a little wary. There she sat on the other side of the desk, the proud, belligerent carriage of her head and the stormy light in her eye familiar enough, but the words she spoke were senseless to him.

"I don't want my grandson in the war. He wasn't cut out for that kind of thing," she was saying.

Old Hogarth straightened the papers on his desk, and he

cleared his throat, and shook his cuffs and drew his coat sleeves down.

"I wouldn't mix money up with a thing like this, Mrs. Amboy," he said. "This has something to do with patriotism—national duty—things like that—"

"It's worth money to me, a lot of money. I haven't found anything yet that money didn't mix with," Mrs. Amboy said.

In spite of the nobility of the sentiments he expressed, he found it difficult to look at her now, and his eye moved uneasily from place to place in order to avoid her eyes. It took her an hour to see that with him there was nothing to be done. But he was simply one man in Washington, and this was merely the beginning. She had gone down with an overnight bag, but she stayed two months there—a well-dressed, elegant-looking old lady with a cane in her hand, tapping her way into government offices and tapping her way out, with the strange, far vision of the fanatic set now like a veil upon her features. She went home only because young Dennis was coming home on a pass.

When he and Malcolm White came back the weather was cold in the Hudson Valley, and they took their bicycles out. The spokes of the wheels had gone a little rusty, and the two young men—outsized, and their legs too long now for the bicycles they rode—pedaled up the drive from the little house, and past the kennels, and down the path to the pond, and around it, the raccoon tails and the baseball pennants, with the flannel of them faded, hanging on the handle bars still, and the front wheels wavering as they rode. It was part of the game to take it slowly: you had to pedal slowly, and if your foot once touched the ground, you had to go down the drive to the little house and start again from there.

"Sometimes it is said to fall a victim to the oyster," said young Dennis. The frost lay white in the shaded corners of the hedge, but where they cycled between the garden beds, the sun fell light as honey on their hair.

"What does?" asked Malcolm White, cycling just behind, and he lost his balance for an instant and teetered in peril on the edge, but his foot did not touch the frosted soil.

"The raccoon or mapach," said young Dennis. "Its oyster-eating propensities have frequently been questioned, but rac-coons—or mapachs—have been found held by the closing oyster shells, unable to extricate themselves, and have per-ished miserably in the rising tide."

"Of public opinion?" asked Malcolm White in mock con-cern.

"Of water, my fine fellow," said young Dennis as he turned into the footpath through the pines.

"I have heard it said," said Malcolm White, and slowly, painfully, standing upright from the saddle, he took the hill, "that it is for this precise moment beachcombers wait to wrench off the coveted tail—"

"A beachcomber," said young Dennis, wheeling slowly down the kitchen-garden path, "is, according to the Oxford dictionary, a white man on a Pacific island who lives by col-lecting jetsam. The tail of the raccoon is scarcely jetsam," he said, and he rode through the greenhouse door.

Grandma Amboy was at the other end, giving the gar-dener a piece of her mind in the greenhouse heat, but when young Dennis put his arm around her, she let the sound of it go.

"Flower pots aren't ornamental. They're intended to be filled with dirt," she was saying, but with young Dennis here she let it perish.

"Come on down to the pond with us," he said as he strad-dled the wheel. "We're going to open the sluices and watch the water go."

This they did every year: they opened the sluice gate of the pond, and once the water had poured from it, the bed lay drying and cracking a day or two in the sun or the wind. After the depths of it had hardened, they'd go in with their hip boots on and rake the leaves and the rotted boughs and the muck of the year away. There the pond would lie in the spring, so still, so somber, so untroubled, perhaps even with a frail cuff of ice along its banks; and then one human hand would loosen the bolt in the sluice gate by the diving board, and out the transformed, foaming waters would go. This was the ceremony every year, and every year for better than twelve years now, young Dennis had done it; and now he squatted down—a flier in uniform—ready to let the deep, still waters spill over the bracken and brush in fury and swell to a torrent the thread of stream below.

"Here she goes!" he said, and his hand went out, but Mrs. Amboy placed the tip of her cane on the sluice gate a moment.

"There are other branches of the service," she said, without any preparation for it. "I've been down in Washington. I've been investigating. If you took the trouble to ask, they'd transfer you," she said.

Young Dennis squatted there, looking up at her face, his hand out still, and for an instant he did not seem to understand.

"They'd do what?" he said then.

"They'd take you out of flying if you asked for it," his grandmother said.

Young Dennis stood up straight now, and, like hers, his mouth was grim.

"Out of what? Out of what did you say?" he asked her.

"Flying," said Malcolm White from the edge of the pond, and he raised his arms and made a fluttering movement.

"But I want to fly," said young Dennis. He said it slowly and exactly, and his eyes met hers. "You're not going to ruin the show, are you?" he said.

And then he saw what was happening to her face, and his hand went out, and he jerked the sluice gate open. The waters gave a low, quick gasp, like a sleeper stirring, and a shudder passed across the pond, like a hand across a dreamer's face. For a moment, the weight of water quivered at the brink, and then it arched, smooth and strong as the neck of a charger, and streamed marvelously away. The three people stood there a little while, dwarfed, extinguished, watching the pure white arch of water fall, and behind them the dark, mysterious volume of the pond ebbed slowly, leaving a widening band of wet marked black along its shore.

"You see, it's like this," said young Dennis in a troubled voice now that the thing was done. "You see, I want to fly, Grandma Amboy."

"So do little birds," snapped Mrs. Amboy, and she did not say any more.

Before they left that night, they took the raccoon tails from the handle bars of their bicycles.

"To hang in the cockpit for the look of the thing," said Malcolm.

"The appendage of the Procyon Lotor," said young Dennis, "is reputed to bring luck for the road."

Mrs. Amboy said nothing to her son and nothing to Fran in the weeks that followed after, but she talked to her lawyer. There was nothing in law to cover the case, he told her with the professional man's indulgence of the wealthy; there was no legal way to keep Dennis from piloting a bomber in the air. So she packed an overnight case in time and she went down to Tampa. The plan was her own, and she knew exactly what to do. She went by air, making use of the element almost in contempt now that she was going to get the better of it, and she taxied from the field to young Dennis's camp without stopping on the way. She asked for his captain at the provost marshal's desk, and as they made out the visitor's pass, she

settled her pure white ruffle at her neck, and pulled the gray
suède tighter on the back of her right hand.

"I've come to see you about my grandson," she said, and
she might have been any rich boy's grandmother walked into
the best prep school in the country to have it out with the
director about what he might be up to now. "I want him to
drop aviation," she said as if it were not a branch of the service, but Greek or Latin she was speaking of.

"Drop aviation?" said the captain. "You mean—drop aviation?"

His eyes had halted in concern on the elegantly dressed,
well-bred old lady who faced him sharply with her gloved
hands folded on her cane.

"Yes. Get out of it," said Mrs. Amboy. "He's had an education. He's not just anybody. I want to get him into something that will keep him from getting into trouble, getting
shot up or anything like that," she said.

The captain's mouth dropped open a little, and he sat there
in his well-cut uniform—a man in his forties with a piece of
one war won and shelved behind him and the start of another
in his blood already, not knowing what to say. It was only
after a little while that he saw he was not expected to speak,
that he had never been expected to speak. He was merely
there to listen in respect, in humility even—if he could sum-
mon it—to what young Dennis Amboy's grandmother had to
say.

"I don't want Dennis in it at all," she was saying to him.
"He's got a lot that these other boys haven't got—a background, education, temperament, forebears. There's no sense
in having Dennis killed off like the ordinary run of boys."

Even when she took the cheque book out of her bag, he
couldn't get hold of the words to meet it. He saw her undoing
the buttons of the gray kid on her right hand, and still he did
not speak. The fountain pen—the old-fashioned kind that

filled with a medicine dropper, he noted—was poised like a weapon as she watched his face.

"How do you spell your name?" she said.

"I don't understand," said the captain, and he sat there, stunned. "A cheque?" was what he said.

"Oh, not what you think! Not bribery!" said Mrs. Amboy with a snort as she wrote the date in. "Perhaps the camp here needs a garden, an officers' club—whatnot. I thought about fifty thousand would cover it," she said.

He stood up now behind his desk, and his knuckles showed white on its surface as he leaned his weight on the wood. Such a respectable, sane-looking old lady she had looked when she walked into the place, he thought, and she was talking this gibberish to him now.

"My dear lady," he began, seeking the words still. "Blood isn't bought cheaply—there are other values—other standards—"

"Very well, I'll make it seventy-five," Mrs. Amboy said.

The captain waited a moment before he spoke, and there was a singular, an unpredictable fluctuation in his eye.

"And then what?" he asked quietly as he leaned upon the desk.

"And then Dennis leaves. You discharge him. He comes home with me," she said.

"I like to believe that certain things peacetime made easy, made nearly normal for us," said the captain, and his voice was steady, "have come to their own conclusion." His knuckles were white as naked bone on the wood as he leaned his weight upon them. "Perhaps we are even through with class distinctions—"

"I'm not talking about class distinctions," said Mrs. Amboy in impatience. "I'm talking about my grandson," she said.

The captain came around from behind the desk now, his eyes sardonic, but he leaned above her as gallantly as if he were—at some purely social function—offering her a plate of sandwiches or a cup of tea.

"Aside from all that," he said, "we've got a pretty satisfactory setup here. We don't need an officers' club or a garden. The government's given us geraniums even—perhaps you noticed them outside. The only drawback is that we may not be here much longer to enjoy it." He was saying the words slowly, carefully to her, as if speaking them to a child, and he closed the cheque book gently in her fingers. "We shall probably be moving out one of these days," he said.

"Moving out?" said Mrs. Amboy, and her eye was sharp.

"You see, we've been preparing a good many months for the real thing here," said the captain. "We'll be going into action."

"Not with Dennis. I won't have it," Mrs. Amboy said.

This might, on the face of it, have been accepted as some sort of end, but to Mrs. Amboy it was little more than the beginning. If the captain had failed, there were other men in the place, smaller men, but men who might very well be made to serve, for the plan had become a shrewder one now.

On Friday night she gave the dinner party in the hotel for them—for eight of them: pilots, or gunners, or bombers, or whatever they happened to be. They took their places at table, and there she sat at the head of them, a handsomely dressed, sharp-eyed old lady, keeping the bite of her speech to herself for a wonder. What she was after, even young Dennis, seeing her sitting there with her mind on whether their plates and whether their glasses were kept filled, certainly did not know. She spoke to one side and then the other, asked the wives' names, and the children's, and talked of the states they came from, learning without guile, it seemed, what these men who were aviators now had done before the war. The war, thought young Dennis, and as he looked at her he wondered—

even for Grandma Amboy perhaps the miracle, the leveling of
the ranks . . .

"Rats," she said from the other end of the table. "Don't
refuse good things when they come to you. Have some more
turkey, Ellory—what did you say the first name was? Thomas
Ellory, have some more stuffing," she said.

Ellory had a delicate, weak face, long and narrow and almost bloodless. His neck was long, and the Adam's apple
jerked in it unhappily as he ate. His hands were as slender as
a poet's, or a woman's, and his hair dropped in a colorless
lock across his forehead. Who he was or where he had come
from, none of them had ever disturbed his reticence to find
out, and now young Dennis, looking the length of the table
in speculation at him, knew he had asked him to come here
with them not out of camaraderie but out of pity, perhaps
merely because of the uneasy, almost shamed look in his eye.

"Have some more of the lemon meringue, Ellory," Mrs.
Amboy was saying. In this way, through some unerring process of selection, she had chosen Ellory—as fatally as a knight
in armor might have been chosen—from among the others
there. But it was only as they had all risen to leave the dining
room that young Dennis heard them speaking of the other
things together.

"It was losing the baby like that, after everything else," said
Ellory in a low voice.

"She ought to have six months' rest, flat on her back, that
girl," Mrs. Amboy said with decision as they passed under the
arch of the dining-room door.

"I've made a kind of a mess of marriage, ma'am," said Ellory then, as if in apology to her.

"You certainly have," said Mrs. Amboy tartly, and then
Dennis did not hear any more. He did not hear because of
the other words that were being said to him in the hotel lobby.
The other man in khaki stood before him, not dim, not waver-

ing yet, but for a moment young Dennis did not understand the sense of what he said. He heard the name Malcolm spoken twice, and then the rest of it struck him a quick and terrible blow upon the heart.

"Crashed—on a routine flight—at six this evening, between here and—"

"Malcolm—Malcolm White!" cried young Dennis aloud, and he stood there blind before these strangers.

"Here, child, give me your hand, put it here on my cane," said Grandma Amboy, and hand in hand they crossed the rug to the elevator door together.

The appendage of the Procyon Lotor, said a voice they had never heard before, *is reputed to bring luck for the road.*

It was not that first night that Mrs. Amboy put the thing before Thomas Ellory. That first night at dinner was merely the laying of the ground. She had made the appointment for Sunday with him, and Sunday afternoon he came, and she ordered tea in the hotel lounge.

"What do you hear from Denver?" she asked as she passed the pastry to him.

"I had a letter yesterday. She's still in the hospital," he said.

"Who's paying the bills?" said Mrs. Amboy, and she watched—as a hawk will watch the calculated failing of its victim—the still unapprized and hopeless prospect of his face.

"I had to borrow," Ellory said, and the Adam's apple jerked in his throat.

"But that was the second time," said Mrs. Amboy. "You borrowed first for the house. Isn't that what you told me?" she said.

"Yes, I know," said Ellory in pain, and he brought his narrow hands together. "We should have started off in a couple of rooms somewhere, with what I was making. But that was two years ago, and I was proud, and I wouldn't have anything less than a house—"

"So that was fifteen hundred the first time?" said Mrs. Amboy.

"Three thousand in all," said Ellory, and his eyes were seeking for succor, running like trapped things from cup to teapot to pastry plate, fleeing over the silver and linen. And then, without warning, they halted for an instant on the diamonds on her hand. "That's why she took the defense job—trying to pay things off," he said, and his eyes were running again from pillar to post. "A fifty-four-hour week when you're nearly six months—"

"When your wife gets out of the hospital, she'll have to get busy," said Mrs. Amboy. "Three thousand. That's a lot of money," she said.

"Ah, don't you think I don't lie awake thinking about it at night!" Ellory cried out, twisting his hands between his knees. "I'm going crazy with it!" he said, and he set his teeth together to hold the trembling sound of it in.

"She'll have to get right to work," said Mrs. Amboy, squeezing the lemon over her cup. "She'll have to keep at it night and day, no matter what condition she's in."

"I know it—my God, I know it," Ellory said.

"Look here, young man. Have another cup of tea," she said, and she leaned forward and poured it. "You and I had better talk things over. We might strike a bargain," she said.

"What kind of a bargain, ma'am?" he asked, but there was nothing at all like hope, there was scarcely interest in his voice.

"Now listen to me," said Mrs. Amboy. "I never wanted Dennis in this war. I never approved of it, Ellory." If he saw the look of bright, mad exaltation in her eye, he gave no sign; the moment had not yet come for him to look around uneasily. "But now that he's got in it, I'm not going to have him killed.

I'm not going to have them do to him what they did to Malcolm White. I've made up my mind to that all right," she said, and she winked one eye in crafty decision across the pastry and the cups.

Ellory sat watching her face now, and he did not speak, but something had halted the desperate racing of his eyes and charmed the blood in his veins to stillness.

"I don't know how bombers work—that's not my business," she was saying to him. "That's part of the information you could give me, Ellory. You could tell me how the men are placed—in what relation—how close or far—and in what way they depend on one another. You could tell me how one man might be of service to another man in case the plane got into trouble. If one man wanted to save another man's life, you could tell me how it might be done. I mean, if he were paid well, and if he watched night and day for the chance to do it."

"The chance to do what?" said Ellory then.

"The chance to save the other man's life," said Mrs. Amboy, and her voice was crafty, low. "Suppose Dennis were piloting a bomber, and there was trouble—would there be any man near him, any man on his team—"

"Crew, Mrs. Amboy," Ellory said, and he ran his tongue along his lip.

"All right, crew," said Mrs. Amboy, and she had no patience with it. "Would there be any special man in his crew," she said across the tea things to him, "who could protect him—manage to keep him out of action—"

"You mean, dishonorably—even dishonorably?" said Ellory scarcely aloud, and his eyes were fleeing from corner to corner of the hotel lounge, seeking cover, it might be, from their own indecorous sight.

"I'm merely talking about life and death. Don't bring big words into it," Mrs. Amboy said. "I'm talking about money—

a lot of money—money I'd like to give away. I'd like to give ten thousand dollars, Ellory, to someone who would keep an eye on Dennis." And suddenly, as she talked, she was an old woman, she was a poor old woman asking to be fooled as a special favor to her. She sat with her old hands fumbling on the cane head. "Maybe we could strike a bargain," she said.

Ellory sat quiet a moment, and then he drew his tongue along his upper lip again, and his eyes were moving fast.

"There's the control officer—the control officer in the astro-hatch," he said, and his voice was scarcely audible. "He gives the orders to the pilot."

"All right! Now we're getting somewhere," said Mrs. Amboy. "The control officer gives the orders to the pilot."

"Yes, that's it," said Ellory.

"And this control officer—does he always go out with the same pilot? Is he always on the same pilot's crew?" asked Mrs. Amboy.

Ellory waited a moment, and then he ran his tongue along his lip.

"Yes," he said, and he cleared his throat. "That's the way it works. There's a kind of a crew set up for each ship, and it doesn't change."

"So that if a control officer wanted to alter a plane's course, he could give any orders he felt like to the pilot. He could tell him to take another direction—" said Mrs. Amboy, and she waited.

"Yes," said Ellory. He seemed to speak with difficulty now. "He could do that if he wanted to," he said.

"So a control officer—he could get a pilot out of combat even?" said Mrs. Amboy. She was leaning toward him over the residue of tea in the cups and the ends of pastry, her eye as shrewd as a hawk's eye on him.

"Yes," said Ellory, but he did not look at her face. "He could do whatever he had an interest to," he said.

"All right," said Mrs. Amboy cannily. "Just one more thing. Tell me who's the control officer on Dennis's crew?"

Ellory looked at her uneasily, and looked away before he spoke.

"I am, ma'am," he said in a moment, and he ran his nervous fingers through his hair.

In a month they shipped out, they were sent overseas, and Mrs. Amboy went back to the quietly moving Hudson. The corn was getting ripe, and the beets were ready for preserving, and she saved the orange rinds from breakfast and boiled them up with carrots for wartime marmalade. The first week in August, Fran came up the drive from the little house, and the card without any picture on it was in her hand.

"Young Dennis has got safely over," she said, and Mrs. Amboy stood up with the trowel gripped in the fingers of the worn kid glove, and she stared across the hedge at her. "Here's the APO address. He's got there safely," Fran said. In a moment, thought Mrs. Amboy in contempt, Fran's voice might break in two and clutter up the garden.

"Arrived safely?" Mrs. Amboy said. "Were you worrying about that?" She could see the card, with young Dennis's signature written on it, and she spoke her first thought in irritation. "So it came to you, did it?" she said.

"The War Department sends them out," said Fran.

"I've had some correspondence with them. They know my address as well as yours," she said.

There was something else that was on her mind, but she said nothing about it. Only when she went to her desk, she took the packet of canceled cheques from the drawer. She slipped the July bank statement from under the elastic band that bound them all, and she went through them slowly, carefully again, laying them one on the other, date by date before her. But the canceled cheque made out to Thomas Ellory's name in the sum of ten thousand dollars was not among the others there. She sat at the library desk, and the leaves moved softly at the window, and she took her glasses from her nose and tapped them against her hand. He had needed the money, and yet he had not cashed the cheque, she thought in speculation. She thought of the story, and she tried to compose some other ending for it. So for a little while it was not young Dennis's face or any possibility of his death that she saw before her. It was instead the face and figure of a young woman in a Denver hospital, a young woman with no money in the bank, and no baby to carry out in her arms.

A stretch of time went by before the wire from the War Department was brought up to the big house. It was an afternoon that Fran was at the Red Cross rolling bandages, and the boy on the bicycle found the door of the little house closed, so he followed on up the drive. There was the sound of the wheel on the gravel, like a whisper on the drowsy air, and Mrs. Amboy paused in the greenhouse and lifted her head. It might have been that the raccoon tails were swinging still on the handle bars outside, and that young Dennis's voice would say in a minute:

When engaged in this curious custom the mapach or raccoon grasps the edible matter in both forepaws and moves it rhythmically backwards and forwards.

And the voice of Malcolm White might say aloud as he teetered on the saddle:

I believe you were saying its oyster-eating propensities have frequently been questioned?

The War Department communication told Mrs. Amboy across the filtered sunlight that young Dennis Amboy was missing for three weeks in the Pacific area with all members of his crew. Missing might be the proper word for spectacles or a fountain pen you had put into another bag, thought Mrs. Amboy, laying the wire down on the watering can; it had

nothing to do with young men in a bomber. Young men
talked out loud, said where they were, rode bicycles up the
driveway. Missing! she thought, as if in contempt for the
vagueness and the inexcusable carelessness of it. The pilot,
the bombardier, the rear gunner, the control officer in the
astrohatch—they were men with parachutes, rubber boats,
they couldn't be dismissed like that. It was someone else
that she thought of now as she stood alone in the greenhouse's light—the face and the figure of someone for whom no
weapons had been provided, who had been assigned no paraphernalia of escape, given no ammunition, lying flat on a hospital bed and calculating the payments due on a house that
a fool named Ellory had decided not to live in any more.

She did not write at once, but when the August bank statement and the parcel of canceled cheques came in the first
week in September, she sat down and wrote the letter.
She addressed it to Mrs. Thomas Ellory on North Colfax
Avenue, Denver, and she made no mention of the cheque
made out to Thomas Ellory, because it was not among the
others there. The letter was not a long one. It said merely, in
Mrs. Amboy's sloping, regular hand:

> My dear Mrs. Ellory:
>   A few months back I had a couple of conversations with
> your husband. He was training with my grandson down at
> Drew Field at the time. I understand he is control officer in
> my grandson's bomber crew, and that the lot of them are re-
> ported "missing." I know my grandson, so I don't put any
> faith in the story. But your husband was worried about your
> health at the time, so I thought I'd take the trouble to in-
> quire about it.
>   Yours very truly,

At the end, she added a postscript.
"How did you make out with the payments on the house?"
she wrote.

In ten days the answer came to her, written from a hospital ward in a high schoolgirlish, backhand writing. It said:

> My dear Mrs. Amboy:
> It was kind of you to write and ask about me. I hope to be out of here and able to take on a defense job again in just a little while. It's been so long because of blood poisoning that set in. Then I'll be able to take care of the payments on the house. I'm not quite sure what you mean by Thomas being "control officer" of your grandson's bombing crew. Tom is a pilot himself—they only train pilots at Drew Field, you know. He's been listed missing since August the tenth. Perhaps they were out on the same mission together. But I know how you feel about your grandson, because I have the same kind of faith in Tom.

Mrs. Amboy walked suddenly out the door and down through the kitchen garden. Her gardening gloves hung just inside the greenhouse door's glass panes, and she jerked them off the hook in the sun and slipped them on her hands. Faith in him, faith in Thomas Ellory! she thought, and she seized the trowel up from the shallow pan of earth. Control officer in the astrohatch! Paying ten thousand dollars to be tricked! she thought in fury. She had come to the tomato beds now and she stopped and looked at them blindly, balefully. The plants were yellowing and spreading out in long, lacy, ineffectual boughs.

"So you tricked me, Ellory," she said, and now she was on her knees by the plants, and she stabbed the trowel's blade into the crumbling soil.

I suppose that's what you might call it, ma'am, said Ellory's drifting, spineless voice, or some memory of it, and she looked at the two small tight-fisted tomatoes that hung on the plant before her, fixing them in venom as if they were not fruit or vegetable but Ellory's pale, perfidious eyes.

"Very well then," said Mrs. Amboy. She dug savagely into

the earth at the roots of the plant and turned it over, baring to the September sun the underlayer of damp, fragrant soil. "And why did you do it?"

I suppose for the money. Because I wanted the money, he said.

Mrs. Amboy snorted as she moved to the next plant on her knees.

"Except you didn't cash the cheque," she said.

I was trying to make up my mind to that, Ellory's voice, or her calculation of it, answered. *I took it overseas with me. I thought I'd come to make up my mind about it better over there.*

"Oh, I see," said Mrs. Amboy. "So you preferred to leave her lying there, not knowing how to pay the bills!"

Yes, said Ellory as if in apology to her, *I suppose that's what I did. You see, I knew I couldn't do what I told you I'd do, because I had nothing to do with any other bomber. I never had anything to do with anybody else's bomber. I was just a pilot like anybody else,* he said.

"So that was part of the lie to get the money!" said Mrs. Amboy in fury to the tomato plants.

Yes, I guess that was part of it, ma'am, Ellory or some bitter recollection of him, answered.

And then you never cashed the cheque! After all that, you never cashed it! Mrs. Amboy said.

No, said Ellory, *but I always kept it on me. I don't know why, but I always kept it on me. Perhaps it made me feel I had something when I didn't have anything—a kind of power outside myself to turn to sometime—a kind of last resort, if I could bring myself to use it,* and as the breeze moved through the plants, it might have been that Ellory had lifted his narrow, nervous hand and run it through his hair.

"So you went traipsing around with that in your pocket, while she had nothing but blood poisoning, and debts, and a bed in a hospital ward to keep her company!" said Mrs. Amboy as she kneeled there in the path.

Yes, ma'am, said Ellory in a troubled voice, but, you see, I couldn't save Dennis. It was crazy, what I told you I could do. And as long as I couldn't do it, I didn't have the right to use it—

"A little bit late for honor," said Mrs. Amboy bitterly, and that night she made the decision: she telephoned Fran at the little house to say she was going away.

"I'm taking a trip," she said. "I'm going out to Denver."

"But, Mother Amboy," said Fran, "that's a long way for you to go!" She might as well have added: "You're seventy-five, remember, Mother Amboy."

"It's near enough by air," she snapped. And why couldn't the woman brace up, she thought in impatience? Why did she have to sit martyred there in the little house with her voice gone quiet and her eye gone dim, and the map of the Southwest Pacific area pinned up on the wall? "Wife of one of young Dennis's friends," she said. "I'm going down to see her. One of the pilots that he knew, listed as missing. She doesn't believe a word of it either. Got blood poisoning in a hospital," she said. That would fix her, she thought. It wasn't young men who took horses over hedges and broke plate-glass windows on Main Street who would slip from life like culprits! "Matter of spirit," she said, and she jammed the receiver back on the hook again.

Because she was traveling, then, she didn't see the War Department's second wire when it came. The first she knew of what had happened was when she walked into the Brown Palace in Denver, with her two neat air-weight suitcases following behind. She had put her cane aside, and snapped her glasses on her nose to sign in at the desk, and there was the evening paper lying on the counter. "Italy Surrenders" the headlines said, and somewhere on the page below it her eye found instantly: "Denver Flyer and Comrades Rescued after Twenty-Eight Days at Sea." So she did not go up to her room, but she went out on the sidewalk, motioning the doorman in braid aside, and she hailed a taxi with her lifted cane. As soon as the door of it was closed, she opened out the paper, and it might have been that Ellory sat down on the seat beside her and took off his aviator's helmet and ran his nervous fingers through his hair.

We were out on a scouting hop, he said, and she did not look up from the print of the newspaper before her. Line by line, in spite of him, she was going to read it through. *A bomber was flying just to the right of me,* was what Ellory said, *and I knew we two were off the course. We'd lost the others. There was a rain squall just before us, and I figured we'd find the others when we got through that squall. And then I saw that this plane off my right wing was having trouble . . .*

"Oh, he was, was he?" said Mrs. Amboy, and at the sound of her voice speaking out the taxi driver looked up into the windshield mirror in query at her. She was sitting there on the seat alone, and she quickly turned the page.

We didn't know who was piloting the plane, Ellory went on with it. *Because of the rain squall, we couldn't see the number on her. He was having engine trouble, but we didn't know that till later. We didn't know anything except that he was getting ready to bring her down, and setting a heavily armored war job down on water when she's been made to set down on land isn't a picnic for anybody . . .*

"But he did it," said Mrs. Amboy with a certain pride and grimness. "It says here that he did it—"

They sank at once, Ellory was saying. *They didn't have time for anything. They went right under.*

"It says here," said Mrs. Amboy, and she shook the folds of

the newspaper out as if for a better sight of the words "it says here that you were out of gas yourself—"

We'd been out on a flight that took us to the maximum range of our aircraft, Ellory said, the uneasy, apologetic sound of it familiar in her ears. *So even at that my gas was getting low. Add to it that we were off the course, and then when the other ship went down, I circled a time or two around where she went out of sight. And then we saw two men of her crew were swimming—two who'd got out of her were swimming. But they couldn't have lasted long,* he said.

"So then it came into your head to bring yours down on the water, too?" said Mrs. Amboy, and she did not take her eyes from the page.

I was just trying to get their position so as to send help back, Ellory went on with it, *but the sun had set. It was beginning to be evening, and I didn't like the idea of leaving those two men behind. And then—I guess it was just about then,* he said in his troubled, uneasy voice, *I saw there wasn't a chance of getting home on the gas we had, so there wasn't any choice left. I passed back word to stand by for a landing in the water, and I brought her down,* he said.

The taxi took the corner fast, and Mrs. Amboy felt herself swaying toward him with the paper in her hands.

"Very well," she said sharply, and she straightened up. "They say here that Bomber Pilot Ellory is up for a decoration. They say he saved Bomber Pilot Amboy's—"

We didn't go under at once. We had fifteen minutes to inflate the rafts and stow the emergency gear and get clear of the ship, Ellory said. *And then I saw for the first time who the other pilot was—he was swimming near us in the water. We'd done our training at Drew Field together—fellow named Dennis Amboy. There wasn't much room, but we pulled him and his tail gunner up with us in the rubber boats . . .*

"Look," Mrs. Amboy said, and for a minute she saw nothing now—not the print on the newspaper's page, or the hospital drive unwinding beyond the window—because of the weak and womanish thing that had happened to her eyes. "Look, Ellory, you fool," she said. "That cheque. You cash it—"

But Ellory seemed to be talking of something else entirely.

Funny what you'll find out on a trip like that, he said, and Mrs. Amboy had lifted the newspaper again as if to shield her face from what anyone might see. *Only one of us on those rafts had cigarettes—a package of them*, Ellory said. *They were wet all right at the start, but after a few days of the kind of weather we had, it didn't take them long to dry. We had cigarettes, the way it was, but we didn't have any matches.* She could hear him give the jerk of laughter. *But one of the fellows had a magnifying glass, and I happened to have a piece of paper. It was a piece of paper I'd set some store by, so I had it on me. It wasn't a love letter or anything like that*, he said, and she heard him jerk the laughter out again. *It was kind of a business matter, and I'd taken it with me, trying to make up my mind about it. But, you know, the sun's rays concentrated or deflected or whatever it is through glass like that will set fire to paper. So we lighted the cigarettes like that. We divided them up between the two rafts. There were enough to go twice around* . . .

"So that was the cheque?" said Mrs. Amboy to the silence. She had come to the end of the column of print, and the taxi had halted, and the steps of the hospital were there. "So that was the cheque?" she said, and for the instant that she sat there, an old woman in a taxicab alone fumbling the change out of her bag, she felt Ellory's eyes meet hers in apology, and he lifted one nervous hand and ran his fingers through his hair.

She paid the driver, and she walked up the steps and

through the hospital door, the evening paper under her arm, her cane grasped in her hand.

"The women's ward," she said to the girl behind the desk.

"Third floor, left, end of hall," the girl said without looking up.

"Thank you," said Mrs. Amboy in what might have been taken for humility.

The Little Distance

THE two men had never got on together, perhaps because of the disparity of the two sides of the maple tree that stood half in one man's yard and half in the other's—the half rooted in William Braddock's ground turned toward the north, and the leaves and branches of it sparse; the other half, rich with foliage, facing the south on the edge of John Pennant's garage drive. Or the antagonism between them may have begun in the slope of the suburban avenue on which their houses faced; because of it, John Pennant's land stood higher than Braddock's and thus shed its surplus wet upon the ground below. It was this, Braddock had been saying in thin-lipped censure for years now in the commuters' train, this damp and drainage from Pennant's side of the hedge that had blighted his garden for him. He had tried bulbiferous plants, and even as tough a weed as geranium, he would tell the other commuters, and none of them would flower; or else, in the time of Victory Gardens, it would be beet or cabbage or carrot that had rotted in the soil. While he talked, Pennant—sitting before him or behind him or across the aisle from him in the smoker—would turn to whatever stranger or acquaintance happened to share the seat with him, and he would speak out in testy derision. Anyone fool enough to dig up a good gravel driveway and try turning it into a garden plot deserved mildew and earth rot and general catastrophe, he would say as he rattled the morning or evening paper into shape in irritation. And from year to year there had been other things of bitterness to say.

There had been, for instance, the matter of the owl. It had taken place one autumn, when Braddock's son was seventeen or so. John Pennant had walked out the screen door onto his back porch one Saturday afternoon, and had stood there in his shirt sleeves, a flushed-faced, solid-jowled, seemingly constantly irate—or just about to be irate—and constantly winded, thick-set man, not yet fifty then, who wore even his spectacles with a kind of obstinate perversity. He had stood there a moment, looking with irascible pride at the things that were his—at the well-raked drive, and the newly redone garage standing side by side with Braddock's and identical in size, but not in need of paint and hinge and general repair as Braddock's was. He had even shot a look of appraisal at his half of the maple, and then he glanced over the sharp-twigged hedge at Braddock who was sitting playing chess with his son on the side porch of his own house. It was then that the first remark about the owl was made.

"What are you going to do about that owl of yours up there, Braddock?" Pennant had called out. "It wakes Mrs. Pennant and me up at the most infernal hours of the morning." His hand was tense with irritation as he adjusted the glasses on his nose.

Braddock studied the choice of moves offered on the board, and made one before he looked up and allowed his cold blue eyes to cut across the side-porch railing, the space of garden, and the hedge, and meet John Pennant's on the other side.

"That's your owl, Pennant," Braddock had said then. "I've

complained to the town authorities about it," and he looked back at the board. There he sat in his striped, collarless shirt in the autumn warmth, lean and long-legged, a widower twelve years now, nursing his naked, pointed elbows in his wiry hands. His hair was gray, and his eye was grim, and he clipped his words short on his tongue. "Donald, your play," he said to his son.

"That owl's hole, Braddock, is on your side of the tree," said Pennant. His fingers were twitching as if for murder, and he put his hands out of sight in his trousers' pockets to keep them quiet there. But Braddock was not inclined to speak again; he relinquished one elbow long enough to advance his king's rook two squares, and then he cradled it in his palm again, and Pennant went into his own house and slammed the kitchen door.

That was the day after Chamberlain and Daladier had flown back from Munich to their people, each with guilt and bewilderment in his heart, and a shame-faced story to tell. But whatever had been said at Munich meant nothing to Pennant or Braddock. What mattered was that Pennant left the office early the next Saturday and got home from the city before Braddock did, and he brought a ladder out of his garage and set it up against his side of the tree. The stories varied as to what he carried up the ladder with him: some said a tear-gas bomb, when they told about it after, and some said chloroform and a sponge, but they all agreed that whatever he carried, Mrs. Pennant had stood at the foot of the tree with one hand on the ladder—more to steady herself than to be of any actual support—and watched him as he climbed.

"John," she had said from time to time in a gentle and troubled voice up the height of it to him. "Do you think this is the right thing to do?"

"Don't make me nervous!" said Pennant from where he

was, shouting it almost savagely at her because of the trouble
he was having there above. He had climbed beyond the ladder
now, the thing he carried rendering one arm useless, seeking
footholds in the narrow forks of the tree. "Don't interfere!"
he shouted down, with the lenses of his spectacles blurred
and the sweat standing on his forehead; and Braddock's boy
heard the sound of it and came out onto the side porch, and
looked up in wonder at Mr. Pennant fumbling his desperate
way from bough to bough.

He was a tall boy, with dark eyes and a gentle mouth, and a
habit of running his fingers back through his soft, black hair.
For a while he did not speak and he did not move as he stood
there watching Pennant, but when he saw him grope around
the north side of the maple trunk with his paraphernalia for
destruction, the look in his face altered, and he went quickly
down the porch steps and ran across the yard to the foot of
the tree.

"Mr. Pennant, that's a squirrel's hole!" he called up to him.
He stood by the hedge, his hand on the maple's bark, speaking up to where Mr. Pennant was among the leaves. "If you're
looking for the owl's hole, that isn't it, honestly it isn't," he
said. "That hole on our side is a squirrel's hole, a white-bellied
squirrel's. She's been here for years now."

"Oh, dear," said Mrs. Pennant in an anxious voice.

"That's a white-bellied squirrel's hole," Donald said, looking across the hedge at Mrs. Pennant. "I've seen her taking
green apples down inside it. She brings them from across the
street. She's the only squirrel I've ever seen hoarding fruit
away like that."

"Keep quiet!" roared Mr. Pennant, and he slipped a full
foot down the gray bark of the maple's trunk and caught
himself by a miracle on the fork below. "I'll white-belly
squirrel you!" he shouted, and as Braddock walked up the

avenue and turned into his own yard, there Pennant clung, scarlet-faced and shaken, in the branches.

"Were you raising your voice like that to my son?" asked Braddock, and he came to a halt beneath the tree.

"I was," said Pennant, "and I'll raise it again if he keeps on interfering!"

"Then it'll be for the last time," said Braddock quietly, and as he walked toward the house he undid his necktie and his jacket and folded them across his arm.

A knot of people, of passers-by and neighbors, had gathered on the sidewalk now, and they saw it all take place. In two minutes' time, Braddock was out through the cellar door again, erect and gaunt and bearing his own ladder with him, and he crossed what had once been his garage drive, over the stubble of geraniums that had refused to grow, and he set his ladder up on his side of the maple. Whether it was an owl's hole or a squirrel's hollow was never made clear to anyone, perhaps not even to the two men fighting it out on either side of the tree. But when Braddock was at the top of his ladder, the people below saw him take the implement out—some of them said it was an automatic, and others called it a stiletto. It was only the incurably humorous who recognized it as a Flit pump, and who, standing among the awe-struck others, guffawed aloud as he sprayed it at John Pennant's face. It could never have been the premeditated weapon; it must merely have been the first thing Braddock's hand had fallen on as he went through the house five minutes before. But at the sight of it whipped out, Pennant had let his tear-gas bomb or his sponge and chloroform drop to the ground, and had started for his ladder.

"Oh, dear," said Mrs. Pennant, and she averted her eyes from the scene taking place above her, and looked in helplessness at Donald on the other side of the hedge. "Oh, dear," she murmured. "How do you feel about the owl?"

"I've never seen it, but I like the sound it makes," he said, and he ran his fingers back through his hair.

"I think it's a baby owl," said Mrs. Pennant in an uncertain voice. "I couldn't say which side of the tree it lives on," and still she did not dare to face what was taking place above. "I saw it perched up there as cute as anything one day," she said, and then her voice expired.

Just as she spoke, Braddock swung one long leg forward from the rung on which he stood, and before Pennant had the time to reach his own ladder and start down it, Braddock had kicked it clear of the tree. It stood upright for an instant, then lost equilibrium like a living thing, and fell across the Pennant driveway. And then Braddock had gone quietly down his own ladder, and removed it, leaving Pennant stranded like an ape in fury in the maple, his spectacle lenses blinded with Flit, his face showing hot and violent through the leaves.

One year it was one thing, and the next year another—either the bus-line matter, or the affair of the chain-store manager, or smaller things that no one remembered the details of after the time had passed. The bus-line affair took place while the Germans were walking through Holland and Belgium, but whatever was happening anywhere else was nothing to Pennant and Braddock. Pennant wrote letters to the local paper in favor of the bus line, and Braddock wrote letters in opposition to it, and they scarcely so much as turned on the radio to hear the news of international catastrophe. Pennant wanted the bus line because he lived six blocks from the station, and twice a day he had to walk that distance as long as Mrs. Pennant had never been able to collect herself sufficiently to learn to drive the car. Braddock didn't want it because he lived six blocks from the station, and he maintained in public declaration after declaration that he liked the walk to the station every morning, and the walk home in the evening. He had a car himself, he told the other commuters in the smoker, but he hadn't driven it in years because he believed in the natural expending of man's forces. He did not add that it was an early model Ford with its carburetor missing and its radiator cracked wide, and that you pushed it like a perambulator when you wanted it to go. But that year it was John Pennant's triumph. The bus line was established, and six days of the week, rain or shine, Pennant rode past Braddock who walked under an umbrella in winter and under a straw hat in the blaze of summer—who walked, whatever the weather was, and who made Donald walk, and who never, in the months that followed, so much as flickered an eyelash in acknowledgment of the fact that a vehicle bearing human beings was going by.

The chain-store manager business took place when Donald was twenty, and had a job as repairman with a radio concern. On his way home in the evenings he would stop in at the chain store for the things that he and his father needed, and there, every evening, was the girl behind the butter-and-egg-and-milk counter, and he would stop and talk to her awhile. There she stood in a short-sleeved, white dress—a smooth-throated, curly-headed, friendly faced girl with a singular quality of happiness about her. It was present as simply and warmly as the blood was present in her body, that look of dauntless and candid youth like a pledge made in her skin, and eyes, and hair. She was not beautiful, Donald decided the first time that he saw her; but once having looked at her, he felt a sudden sense of poverty and shame within himself because he had forgotten, or because he never had known, that the only thing of value is to bear that rich, sweet gusto for existence as bright as armor in the blood.

"Look," she said one evening across the counter to him. "You know O'Reilly," and she wrote the price of the stick of butter in red on the paper bag. "The manager of the store," she said, and she handed the package to him.

"I've talked once or twice to him," Donald said, but he wasn't thinking of O'Reilly. "I got a raise this afternoon. I wondered if I could take you one night to the theatre?" he said, and he ran his fingers back through his hair.

"I'd like it," she said, and then she went on with what she had to say to him, her bare arms as smooth as cream on the counter's glass, her eyebrows sweeping dark and glossy to the temples' delicate skin. "They fired him, they fired O'Reilly," she said. Her voice was low, but with nothing of stealth in it, merely the tranquil voice of uncorrupted justice stating: "The county inspector wanted a friend of his in here, so he turned in a bad report on O'Reilly. O'Reilly's a good man. I've worked a year here with him. He's got three children, and expecting a fourth. We're asking the customers to write to the head office, saying they want him back. We're not going to let them do that to O'Reilly," she said.

Donald Braddock went home and on the way he bought the theatre tickets for the New York show, and then he sat down to write the letter to the chain store's head office. "Dear Sir," he wrote. "As a daily customer at the Fourth Street branch of your store, I wish to protest against . . . ," and while he wrote he thought: *You look at her and you know that what you've been doing with your life isn't good enough, and will maybe never be good enough.*

"What are you writing?" asked Braddock, looking up from the game of solitaire he was playing under the lamp.

"A letter to the head office of the chain store," Donald said, and he went on writing.

But Dad, he was thinking; *my mother died a long time ago, and we've never talked much about her. There's this kind of silence between us, so I've never been able to ask you things. We can talk about Pennant next door, or baseball, or what we'll have for dinner, but I can't speak out to you about my mother. And now I want to ask you something. I want to know whether she made you feel the way I feel now about life.*

What way? said his father's silence over the cards.

That what you were doing wasn't nearly good enough, and maybe would never be good enough, Donald went on with it, while his pen worked carefully and steadily across the page. *I mean, that whatever you were couldn't be good enough until you were able to tie it up with something bigger, or until you found some other sort of meaning for it,* he did not say aloud.

What kind of meaning? asked Braddock's silence, and his face did not alter as he played the cards upon the table's cloth.

Well, when you looked at my mother's face or listened to her speaking did you feel that maybe something like honor, maybe something heroic was being asked of you? Donald was trying to say, but he couldn't say it. Instead, his pen went on writing across the letter paper: "I found Mr. O'Reilly at all times courteous and attentive, and it was always a pleasure to walk into a store where everything was arranged for the customer's . . ."

Abruptly, William Braddock stopped in his game and looked at his son, holding one card poised in the act of being played.

"Writing to the chain store's head office?" he said, and it might have been that the words had just made sense to him. "Has that got anything to do with what I heard Pennant talking about in the smoker tonight?" he said.

"It's about the manager being fired," said Donald, and he finished the sentence and put a full stop at the end.

"If you're writing about having O'Reilly reinstated," said Braddock quietly, and he played the card he held in his hand, "you can tear the letter up. Pennant was going around the smoker coming home tonight, asking people to write in."

"I'm not doing it for Pennant," said Donald. "I'm doing it for O'Reilly," and he put his name to the letter.

"O'Reilly's a friend of Pennant's. Tear it up, I tell you," said Braddock, but Donald had put the letter into an envelope and was writing the address across the face. And now Braddock got to his feet, and laid his little handful of cards down, and walked to Donald's chair. "You're not going to send that letter," he said evenly. "I won't have it. Give it here."

Donald looked up, and for a moment it seemed that he might be about to laugh, but once he had seen his father's eyes, he got to his feet too. He stood there holding the sealed letter in one hand, and the color was gone from his lips.

"I don't see where you and Pennant come into it," he said, and he could hear the tremulous sound of his own voice. "It's something between me and somebody else. It's a personal thing. I have to send it."

"A Braddock and a Pennant pleading the same cause!" said Braddock, quietly and bitterly.

"It's a good cause," said Donald, and Braddock stood there in mute, wounded outrage an instant before he lifted his hand and struck it, without warning, hard and quick across Donald's face.

Once it was done, Braddock looked down at his own hand, turning it slowly between them—first the lean, wiry, tired-looking back of it showing, and then the narrow, nervously lined palm—watching it move in grave astonishment. Then he walked back across the room again, his shoulders stooped and weary, and he laid his hand down, like an object he had no further use for, in the lamplight among the cards.

"I'm sorry, Donald," he said, and he did not turn his head. It was the first time he had ever used his hand to strike his son. "I'm sorry I did that," he said, and an awful weariness was in his voice.

"It's all right," said Donald, but his mouth and his chin

trembled when he spoke. He stood looking at his father. "There's something wrong with us if things like this are important to us," he said. "I mean, we must be crazy or something if things like this are the only ones that matter to us. We got started wrong in the first place, and we've gone on being wrong," he said, and he swallowed hard. "Maybe ever since my mother died, we've been wrong," he said. "I mean, like this, over on the other side, if you read the paper you know people are getting killed every day for something they believe in, or even if they don't believe in it, they're getting killed just the same. Maybe it hasn't anything to do with us, but sometimes I think all the big things are a part of the same kind of feeling, and all the small things are a part of the same kind of feeling, and when you know this then you can choose, and whether you choose the big things or the small things, that makes you what you are."

Because of the pain in his throat, he did not say any more. He went out of the house and through the front yard, and at the corner he mailed his letter to the head office of the chain store. It was a dark, autumn night, and there was a strange silence in the trees. As he walked on under them, the face of the girl who worked behind the counter became clear to him again, and he remembered words they had spoken together. *I am a young man,* he thought, *and the owl, or the bus line, or the chain-store conflict seemed to him now an old man's conflict in which he had no part. Other things have been demanded of young men in other generations,* he may have been thinking; or, *Is nothing to be demanded of me in my generation?* Except that the question was not given any shape, nor could any answer be spoken, but as he walked on under the silent maples in the dark, the girl's intrepid look was like a promise made him, and he heard the untranslatable speech of the young and the quickening playing pure and loud as music in his ears.

In less than a month after that, there was Pearl Harbor, and the face of everything changed. Donald wanted to fly, and he enlisted, and he went at once; he was among the first to go. He was sent south for training, and when he went he had a photograph of the girl behind the counter in the back of his watch, and he had the sound of her name to write his letters to. Mrs. Pennant made apple pie twice, and lemon-meringue three times, in the months that followed, and left the pie wrapped in a cloth on Braddock's doorstep; and Braddock ate it and returned the pie plate and the cloth, clean and exactly folded, to the back door the next day. Twice she made chocolate fudge and passed it across the hedge to Braddock.

"I thought maybe Donald would like a taste of something from home," she'd say uncertainly to him. Or she'd say: "I guess you keep on having good news of Donald . . ." scarcely daring to make a question of it.

If it hadn't been for the scrap-metal drive, the thing might have—month by month and week by week like this—been healed between them. Donald went overseas, and Pennant and Braddock had begun nodding to each other on the station platform in the mornings now. And then one Saturday afternoon in the autumn of 1942, the first actual conversation between them took place. Pennant had looked out through the screen door and seen Braddock standing, his back turned to him, in the vacant lot behind their garages, and he saw Braddock held a model airplane in his hand. It was a largish plane, colored blue and silver, with a wingspan, Pennant judged as he straightened his spectacles, of perhaps thirty inches. He had never seen Braddock with anything like this in his hands before, and he opened the screen door and stepped out onto the porch, and he stood there watching Braddock mount the rubber of the winding apparatus tight and hold it fast while he raised and poised the plane. When

Braddock released it, it took the air, nose upward, and soared to a height of close to fifty feet, and there it leveled off and glided across the back lot to the far street's line of trees. Pennant watched it pass, without losing altitude, between two maples, and then the life seemed suddenly to perish from it, and—reduced abruptly to the corporeity of mere wire and wood and silk—it nose-dived to the ground.

Pennant stood on the back porch and watched Braddock cross the lot, wade through the dry, drifted leaves, the clumps of shriveling ivy, marking a trail as he went through the faded, uncut grass. When he had retrieved the plane, he wound the strong, tough rubber of its motive power again, raised it and poised it, and set it gliding in flight toward home. As he watched it go now, he stood facing Pennant, gaunt-faced, erect, with his eyes not for an instant seeing Pennant but fixed on this thing that may have been vehicle at first for lonely curiosity, but which had become at once the exact miniature of hope, the flight made not once but over and over—as men made it—in puny, vulnerable advance.

"Nice ship you have there," said Pennant, for Braddock was near him now, stooping again to pick the plane up from where it lay.

"It's a Grumman Wildcat," said Braddock. "A Navy shipboard fighter," he said, and he drew his hand along one broad, sloped wing. Pennant came down the steps of the back porch and crossed the piece of yard to where Braddock stood in the lot, and for a moment they might have been two boys halted there appraising it, without even so much as envy standing between. Its fuselage was blue and silver, its nose was stubborn, and it carried the star insignia on its wings. Under the cockpit's celluloid dome, a dummy pilot sat at the controls, with the eye in his tanned, tin face set on a point in space ahead which neither Braddock nor Pennant had yet recognized as destination, or the steadfast focus of one man's unaltering probity. "Just started taking an interest in planes," Braddock was saying. "Looking into them a bit now, what with the war, and Donald, and one thing and another—"

He did not quite finish it, and neither of them lifted his eyes.

"Looks like business," said Pennant.

"Business!" said Braddock. "Do you know what its record is? In one single battle in the Pacific, Grumman Wildcats like this brought down sixteen Jap bombers—"

"Wouldn't mind having a shot at flying it," said Pennant, and Braddock showed him where to wind the band.

On Monday, Pennant brought a plane of his own home with him. He came up the suburban avenue with it under his arm, and when he saw that the side door of Braddock's house stood open, he stopped where he was in the driveway and called out to him across the hedge.

"Managed to pick up a Vultee Vengeance. Thought you might like to have a look at its performance," he said, trying to keep it casual, in spite of the exultation that glinted behind his spectacles' glass. Before he had his hat off, or laid the evening paper down, he started taking the string and wrapping from it, and Braddock came out onto the side porch and stood there looking across at the bold blue, and the black, and the yellow of its colors. "They call it America's answer to the Axis," Pennant was saying, holding the firm, svelte, pencil-shaped body. "They say it can fly higher than any ship like it that the enemy has."

"What's the length of it?" asked Braddock, studying from where he stood the marvelously upbroken wings.

"Fifteen and three-quarter inches from nose to tail," said Pennant modestly, and Braddock nodded.

"That beats the Wildcat by half an inch," he said, but there was no rancor in it. It was merely a statement of military fact, made by one man to another during maneuvers on the field.

"Might give them a workout in the lot together," Pennant said, and as Braddock went into the house for the Grumman Wildcat, the Vultee Vengeance was quivering, as if with life of its own, in Pennant's hand.

The light was not gone from the sky yet, and Pennant and Braddock went out into the lot behind the garages together, and they flew the planes as far as the other street, and when they had crashed, they retrieved them and flew them back again. The Vengeance held the air longer than the Wildcat did, but now that bitterness was tempered in the men themselves, the implements they handled were no longer the varying symbols of corivalry. Braddock said he had read somewhere that the Vultee Vengeance carried bigger bomb loads farther and faster than any other ship, farther and faster by actual test than Germany's Stuka even—as if the tools of victory were set beyond personal pride and personal ambition now, and were part of a national honor which they shared.

The next Wednesday, Braddock brought the Fleetwing home, carrying it in its paper up the avenue. Pennant was already in his shirt sleeves in the lot, flying the Vultee Vengeance in the heavy, autumn light, and watching the street for Braddock to come. Braddock brought it straight through the yard to the lot, and undid the wrappings from it on the grass.

"Takes off from the ground!" said Pennant, squatting down beside it, and he whistled long and loud.

"It makes a three-foot run, and then takes off and climbs at the rate of six hundred feet per minute," Braddock said quietly. It stood frail as a dragonfly between them—twenty-three inches and a half from tip to tail, and complete with three-point landing gear—its fuselage the pale silver stalk from which sprang, trembling, the delicate, transparent, pointed wings. "At an altitude of two hundred and fifty feet, it levels off and cruises from a thousand to five thousand feet," said Braddock.

"Seems impossible," said Pennant, his voice as tender as springtime across the fragile body of the plane.

And then the scrap-metal drive began, and the ancient thing came alive once more between them. Exactly how it happened, it was never quite possible to say. All one Saturday, a car with a loud-speaker funneling from its roof circulated through the suburban streets, exhorting the population to stack its scrap metal on the curb before the following morning. Municipal trucks, said the funnel loudly and clearly to the atmosphere, would start making the rounds at seven o'clock on Sunday; and little by little, piece by piece that Saturday, the piles of scrap began to grow. Braddock had got home early from town, and he put a tin garden table with its chairs, a wire basket from a bicycle, and a metal carrier for a garden hose out on the curb—both bicycle and hose having vanished, as outworn objects finally vanish, into their own particular limbo—some ten or fifteen years ago.

Pennant came home at two o'clock, and found Mrs. Pennant had carried the damaged saucepans as well as a punctured wash-tub out, and that she was waiting for him to bring the andirons down from the attic and the rusted grass mower up the cellar stairs. It may have been one thing and it may have been another that set the whole thing off; it may have been merely because the pile of scrap that lay before Braddock's house was larger than his own, or it may have been because that was the afternoon he brought the Ensign home. Pennant had gone without lunch in order to buy the Ensign at a downtown shop, and to get home the quicker with it, and it was perhaps the need for food that stirred the sudden anger in his heart. He had stood on the smoking-car platform of the commuters' train on the way out, so as not to risk the Ensign's wingspan, and its landing gear, and its motor mount in a luggage rack above his head. He had borne it as fervently as myrrh and incense might have been borne up the avenue to the vision of Braddock in the back lot already, flying the Fleetwing as far as the line of maples, and watching for him to come. And all the way in silence, the words to say about the Ensign were waiting to be said.

She's got a wing area of three hundred and seventy-two square inches, he was going to begin casually as he undid the string. *Super-streamlined model, the kind they're throwing into action out there. Thought I'd make it a gas model this time so we'd get some idea about how they're flying them, or how Donald's flying them, or how the real thing ought to look in flight . . ."* or however he would say it.

But Braddock was not in the vacant lot with the Grumman Wildcat or the Fleetwing. He was carrying an ancient umbrella stand, with pale metal iris flowers and their sword-shaped leaves embossed in high relief upon it, out through the garden to his scrap heap at the curb.

"Got an hour's start on you," Braddock said as he jerked the umbrella stand into place and dusted off his palms.

"So what?" said Pennant sharply, stopping short. Behind the monstrous shape of the Ensign, his eye lit suddenly in wrath.

"So nothing," said Braddock slowly, and he looked at the other man.

"Trying to give me a lesson in patriotism?" said Pennant, the color squeezed hot and violent in his face. "Is that what you're trying to do?"

He swung and turned into his own yard, carrying the outlandish package still, and mounted the piazza steps, and slammed the door on the sight of Braddock standing erect and gaunt at the curb by the tin garden table, and the hose carrier, and the embossed umbrella stand.

In not more than twenty minutes, Pennant's pile of scrap was as large as Braddock's. He had dragged the grass mower and the coal scuttle with the bottom missing up the cellar steps, and the andirons and a foot bath down the attic stairs—brought them savagely from the house, his coat and hat off now, but his stomach empty still, and flung them—without a glance toward Braddock—down among the dead leaves at the curb. And Braddock had stood on the side porch, dispassionate as a preacher in his pulpit, and watched the scene of fury being played. Only when Pennant's pile was as high as his own did he walk from the side porch into the sitting room. When he came through the front door an instant later, he had the tall, strong bronze of Atlas with him, the figure bowed beneath the invisible pillars of the universe borne down the front steps, and he set it, fixed in the fearful spasm of its posture still, in the middle of the pile.

Not five minutes later, Pennant came out his own front door and crossed the yard and the sidewalk with the mighty chandelier. The links of its four strong chains trailed on the ground behind him, and the dark metal of its fearful frame was bleached with dust. It may have been that he had brought it from the attic, for his shirt was soiled, and in the convulsion of his struggle at the curb, he lashed in frenzy at what might have been cobwebs in his hair. With superhuman strength, he raised the chandelier onto the foot bath, flashed a wild, canny eye at Braddock's pile, and walked back into the house in hot and winded pride. The door had scarcely closed behind him when Braddock came out of his own house with the bedsprings, carrying them upright like a carriage gate, and balanced them high upon his pile.

"Blast him!" roared Pennant from behind the window curtain. He spun on his heel in the sitting room, and his eye went rapidly past Mrs. Pennant, who stood with her handkerchief pressed to her lips in silence, and leapt from fire screen to table, from ornament to chair.

When he came out onto the porch, he was carrying the metal-stalked bridge lamp, the silk shade still quivering on it. As he crossed the doorstep, he stooped and picked the metal door mat up and bore it with him, swinging, in the other hand. Then he ran up the garage drive, jerked the door open, and brought the armful of license plates out, the accumulation of them stacked up from other years. He was on his way back for the kerosene stove when Braddock's cellar door opened, and Braddock rose step by step from the cellar's dark with the child's tub—perhaps what had been Donald's tub once, with the white paint peeling from it—and the chicken enclosure with its twisted yards of wire run.

And now the thing took on a steady and violent tempo; Pennant seized the largest ash bin at the back of his house, emptied it out, and kicked it savagely down the drive to the curb, while Braddock walked out of his front door with the curtain poles from the downstairs windows in his hands. Mrs. Pennant had watched him from the kitchen, mounting with dignity and decision upon a chair to remove them, one by one, and as the curtains slid from them to the floor the blankness of naked glass stared vacantly across the drive. At once, Pennant came out of the garage with two snow shovels, and a length of stovepipe, and set them upright on the kerosene stove. Braddock followed with a three-tier filing cabinet, and stood sorting the letters from the partitions of it once it was on his pile. Without an instant's hesitation, Pennant took the toolbox from his garage and went up the steps of the back porch with it. There, with the back of his neck gone scarlet, he set to work at unhinging the copper-screen door.

"Oh, John!" said Mrs. Pennant faintly through the handkerchief pressed trembling to her mouth. "Think of the flies!"

"Blast the flies!" said Pennant. "This is war!"

When the edge of the screw driver's blade snapped off, he threw it across the porch and wrenched the screen door free.

The thing had gone back and forth in almost absolute silence, and now there was nothing more that could conceivably be given or said. Nothing, that is, until the doors of Braddock's garage opened, and the ghost itself, the faint, high echo of what may have been a car once but could be called a car no longer, came, pilotless, in slow, tentative wonder, down what had once been Braddock's drive. It rode in round-wheeled, gentle amazement over the flower beds and the vegetable plot (in which neither flowers nor vegetables could be brought to grow) with Braddock's legs visible behind it as it advanced, creaking slightly—the Ford that would never run again pushed to the curbstone, and beyond it into the street, brought to its final parking place, where boys, seeing its height transcending all the other scrap would chalk on it before morning: "Last stop Tokio."

It was this, this drive for metal, that ended the interval of truce between Braddock and Pennant. And, in turn, it was a single line in the newspaper which, four days later, altered the set, bitter look of the new interim that had begun. Pennant was riding home in the smoker with the paper open before him, in spite of the headlines it carried not thinking of the Solomons, or the Aleutians, or the Nazis advancing inch by inch through the streets of Stalingrad. He was thinking of the Ensign, and that now with the weather fair and his spirit cooler in him, he would take it out and fly it that night when he got in. The battery was in place, and the power unit was mounted, and he would take the bus at the station and ride past Braddock up the avenue. The Ensign might be cruising, with her motor throbbing aloud in the evening, or she might be making her three-point landing as Braddock came up the side porch and into the house; and Pennant shook the paper open in the smoking car, and he could taste it, the actual flavor of vengeance, on his tongue. And then, without any kind of warning, the photograph was there, and the line written beneath it, and he sat without moving an instant, still not believing what he read. The dark eyes in the young man's face looked gravely, but without judgment or censure at him; in a moment, the arm in the aviator's sleeve might lift, and the fingers be run back through the hair. The picture was Donald's, but he did not believe the words that were written beneath it. He didn't believe them until he heard his own voice saying aloud to Mrs. Pennant:

"They got Donald. They got him," and he sat suddenly down at the kitchen table and looked blindly across the drive. Mrs. Pennant stood there with her handkerchief trembling in her hand, and neither of them spoke for another moment; and then Pennant said: "Look, that airplane. That new one. Get rid of it somehow. Smash it up, burn it, give it away. I don't want Braddock to see it." His voice was tight, stupefied, incredulous still. "Don't want him to think I went out like that and bought it just to get hold of something better than what he— Not now, not in times like this. Not when they're doing things like that to us."

He went out onto the back porch and stood there, blankeyed, seeming to look at his own garage, or at his side of the maple, but seeing none of these things now. Then he went down the steps and crossed the drive, and he passed around the end of the hedge, and went up Braddock's side porch and knocked on the door. A little time passed before Braddock came to open it, and when he stood bleakly there in the half foot of space, Pennant began to speak in a quick, low voice to him.

"Damn them, damn them, Braddock, damn them," he said,

and he kept on saying it. "Damn it, we'll make them pay for it, we'll see that they pay for it," he said. "Come over—come over and have a bite of something, or have a glass of something with us. Part of our responsibility too—share it together—"

"Yes," said Braddock quietly.

"Been fighting the wrong fight," said Pennant in the same quick, low voice. "Now we're in it together. Damn them, damn them," he kept on saying, and behind the spectacles he pretended not to see, or could not see, the wetness on Braddock's face.

"I was going to ask you," said Braddock, not looking up, "what time the bus runs in the mornings." After a moment their eyes bridged the little distance that lay between them. "Thought I might as well start taking it now winter'll be setting in."

Frenchman's Ship

THE story about the Frenchman began at the end of September, when the boarding school opened again and the girls started coming regularly to ride. There were perhaps half a dozen of them, slender young girls in jodhpurs, with ribbons tying back their hair, descending like a flock of smooth-throated, sweet-voiced birds upon the riding stables. Year after year they came like this at the changes of the seasons, calling names like Sylvia and Mary-Ann and Veronica after one another as they rode, with their soft hair flying, down the bridle paths of New Jersey in the autumn, and again in March and April and May. But this year the Frenchman was there, a man of thirty-four or five, with scars from the weather marked around his eyes and in the leather of his neck, and the look of romance on his flesh and in his eye.

All they knew of him was that a relief society had fitted him out with the shore clothes he wore and got him the job in the riding stables, and that his ship was being held for the duration on the Hudson's New York side. He did not belong to the stable as Manners and the other men who worked there did; he might simply have been passing through it in borrowed riding breeches, with a borrowed language on his tongue. Whenever it was he instead of the others who took the girls from the boarding school out and showed them how to slack the reins and take the fences, it seemed he was doing it for just this once, and in some furious spirit of resentment because of what he had been before and what he was this afternoon in autumn. They would turn in their saddles to watch him coming—dark-browed, tough-jawed, with a nameless, almost sullen power in him, his glove's worn leather turned back on his rein hand as he came.

"There's this Frenchman come to work up to the academy with us," Manners would say in slow, fumbling patience to the barman at the place next to the fire station. "I've tried to get onto his name, but I can't get it yet," he'd say, and his mouth would hang open in painful readiness for it, the Adam's apple jerking under the gray bristles in his neck, but none of the syllables would come.

"Well, call him Smith, call him anything," the barman would say as he wiped the counter dry, "but let's have the story."

But for a while there wasn't any story; all summer there were just these few phrases that Manners remembered the Frenchman saying, and he would repeat them slowly, in baffled stupefaction, to the barman or to the men drinking beer, and they would stop talking for a moment about the gas rationing or synthetic rubber or the draft.

"He says he never heard of a ship could dishonor you the way a woman can," Manners would say, as if seeking the sense of it across the bar. Or he'd say, "This Frenchman, he was saying to me that when a country loses sight of the north and starts acting like a horse or a woman, then you're better off at a distance from her," and for a minute or two the men standing there would see the foreigner or some portion of his past. They would see that if one part of the Frenchman's life was ships, then that must be the good part; and if the other side was horses, then horses were the wrong part, as frail and impermanent and vicious to him as women and his country must have been.

At first there was nothing said about the girl called Vivienne, because up until the end of September there wasn't much to say. Vivienne was sixteen that autumn, and this was her first year at the school. She had come down from Boston, where her people were good people, rich people, whose substance had somehow accomplished, out of generations of decorum, her beauty and her wild, sweet blood. It was in September, when the afternoon riding lesson was done and the other girls had gone up the road on foot with their little black ribbons tied in their hair and their riding crops swinging, that she began staying behind at the stable to watch the Frenchman water the horses or groom them down or lay the bedding in. She did not stay long—perhaps no more than a quarter of an hour at first—and afterward a little longer, saying only a word or two in a low quick voice across the crib's wood to him, with her hair hanging soft and dark to her shoulders, and her eyes moving gravely on his face. There she would linger on the edge of whatever he might be doing, the black, suèdelike jodhpurs she wore going a little too tight at the knees for her now, and her legs as long and giddy-looking

as a foal's. Sometimes she'd put red on her mouth, and sometimes she would forget to put it on, the way she'd forget to
put the links in the cuffs of her riding shirt, and then she'd
roll the silk sleeves of it up and let the slender, tanned arms
show.

"It must be funny with no poison ivy over there in France,"
she began the conversation the first or the second evening
with him, and the Frenchman did not look up from what he
was doing, but his voice was bitter when he spoke.

"There're other kinds of poisons over there, don't worry,"
he said, and the sound of his accent was music and mystery
in her ears.

"You mean poison sumac and poison oak—poisons like
that?" she said.

The Frenchman was taking the burrs from the horse's tail,
and for any sign he gave, the girl leaning on the tooth-nibbled
stall watching him in shyness and wonder might never have
spoken to him.

But after a little while he said, "I mean men—women and
men," and he stood erect for a moment and looked at her
with hot, impatient eyes.

Manners had seen from the start that the Frenchman
could handle horses; he could talk to the beasts in his own or
any language, and the skin of their shoulders would ripple
and quiver for him, whatever tongue he spoke. When the
door of the stable opened, the horses would turn their heads
on their shoulders and look for him coming, and it may have
been like this that the girls from the boarding school turned
their heads in impatience and watched for him coming, too.
The Frenchman would let them ride before him, letting them
play for a little with the fancy that it was they who led, but
whichever direction they took was merely rehearsal for the
way he would finally take them. When he spoke the word or
gave the sign, the girls' knees pressed in marvelous urgency

to their mounts' sides, their flesh as alive as the horses' to the sharp flick of his authority.

In the end, he would always take them up the Palisades path that ran high above the river, and he'd halt them there over the bright, clear avenue of water that lay motionless between the trunks of the trees. He never made any explanation to them; he never said, "Just down there you can see it," and he did not shield his eyes with his hand, seeking whatever it was that he had come that high to see. He merely sat there on his horse and looked down the river toward the city, and the spleen was wiped from his face for the time that he stopped there with them, looking through the haze of sun and distance to the other shore.

The explanation of why he came there might never have been given if the lame horse had not started to mend in October, and the Frenchman begun taking him out on the halter at the end of the day when the riding lessons were through. He would turn him back and forth in the yard at first, trotting him once or twice to see the leg's performance, and then he would cross the road with him and take him up the path through the birchwoods where the earth was gentle as moss beneath the foot. He went slowly, bending to see the horse's muscles flex in the hock, and as they walked up through the trees one late afternoon, the Frenchman saw that Vivienne, too, was walking there with them. She was coming along beside him in her black jodhpurs, her face averted a little in shyness from him, the throat's line pure in the open neck of the white silk shirt, and the riding crop she carried lashing softly at the underbrush they passed.

"When we come to a sassafras, I'll show it to you," she said, as if this was what they had been saying. All about them, as they walked, the woods were silent, filled with the drought and hush of summer's end. "There're three different leaves on it, one like a mitten with the thumb sticking out, and

one like a willow leaf, sort of, and one shaped like a bird—
you know, with its wings spread, flying. Maybe you've seen
the berries. They're blue, but you mustn't eat them," she
said. Only the soft step of the horse behind them broke the
quiet, and the girl shook her hair back, as if uneasily, from
her shoulders and tried the conversation again. "It's funny
sassafras doesn't grow over there in France. Do you have
lady's-slippers and dogwood? Do you have goldenrod?" she
said.

"There's nothing grows over there any more," he said with
the same impatience in his voice. "Not even the crops grow.
For two years the grain has rotted just lying in the soil."

"I'm majoring in French, you know," the girl said quickly,
and she lashed at the bush beside her with her crop. "I want
to learn to talk it."

"Talk it?" said the Frenchman. "Why talk it? It's the
language they asked for the armistice in," he said, his voice
hard, quick, contemptuous.

"Not all of them asked for it," the girl said, and she hit
stubbornly and steadily at the underbrush. "Lots of them are
fighting still."

"Sure, there're Frenchmen fighting," he said, and when he
halted in the path, the horse halted in obedience behind him.
He took the flat bottle from the pocket on his hip, and he did
not look at the girl as he drank. "Sure," he said in derision as
he lowered the bottle and wiped off his mouth. "Sure. You
can see their pictures in the paper every day. They got nice
uniforms on and they get invited all around New York. I
wouldn't speak their language," he said, and he held the flask
of liquid toward her. "Have a drink. It's brandy. It'll do you
good," he said.

"I don't like the smell of it," said the girl, and she was
thinking of the words he had said. Behind them, the horse
lipped the just-turning foliage and churned it, dripping and

fragrant in his mouth, to absinthe-colored foam. "But if it's your language," the girl said, and she stood looking in stubborn, soft-eyed tenderness at the Frenchman's face. "If it's your language, then you ought to go on talking it, so when you get back to your own people again you won't have forgotten how."

"My people!" the Frenchman said. "My people! I haven't any," he said, and he took another short, quick jerk from the bottle. "I'm through with my people. They laid down on me," he said.

"But if you have a home over there, it's still there for you," she said. "I mean, if you have a—a wife, or something like that," she said, and her breath came quickly, in trepidation that it might be true.

"A wife!" said the Frenchman, and he jammed the cork of the flask back with the cushion of his thumb. His mouth seemed ready to burst out laughing, the teeth showing white, the cheeks scarred in the exact facsimile of laughter, except that no sound of it came. He slipped the bottle back in his pocket, and the horse's head was suddenly jerked up on the halter strap as the Frenchman crossed the path to where the girl stood. "So you think a man goes back, do you?" he said, and his fingers closed on the flesh of her arm. "You think he goes back to a woman or a country?" he said, and the girl stood shaking her head in soft bewilderment at him.

"Yes," she said, scarcely aloud, but her eyes did not falter. The Frenchman was so close to her that she could feel his breath upon her face. "Yes," she said. "You go back. If you love them, you go back."

"Even if they walk out on him, you think he goes back to them?" he said, and he swung around and started savagely up the bridle path, drawing the girl by the arm and the horse on the halter strap in cold, explicit fury with him.

For five minutes or more he drew them like this up the

rising land in the woods with him, and when he had reached that place above the river to which he always led the way, he dropped her arm as if she had ceased to exist for him, and he let the horse go free. There he stood near the cliff's edge a little while in silence, his back against a tree trunk, looking down across the water to the other side.

"Look," he said, and his voice had altered. "There's my ship," he said. "You can see her funnels," and without taking his eyes from the sight of it down the river, he reached one arm out to the girl and his hand found her shoulder and he drew her quietly and strongly back against him, so that she might see. "There," he said. "You can see her. They haven't been able to get their hands on that much of France." He leaned against the tree, his arm holding the girl close, neither in tenderness nor passion, but merely as witness before the fact of what remained. "I'll go out of port when my ship goes," he said. "She's my country," and they did not speak for a little while, their flesh close but impersonal, their eyes fixed on this symbol of his honor set somewhere in the Hudson's deepening haze.

"But what will you do?" the girl said softly to him in a moment. "How will you bear all the time you have to wait? It's like being in school and waiting for Christmas or Easter to come," she said.

"Do?" said the Frenchman, and he dropped his arm from around her, and his hand fumbled on his hip and brought out the bottle again. "I'll have a drink," he said. "That makes the time pass." He lifted the bottle and took another swallow. "You take a drink and then you don't care much any more," he said, and he turned his head to see where the horse had wandered. "You take a drink, and then you're satisfied with the substitutes," he said, and he put out his hand again and touched her hair with his fingers. "A substitute for your country," he said, and he stood there grinning at her, "and a substitute for living, and even a substitute for what you just called 'love.' "

"When you're young, I don't think you want substitutes," the girl said, and her eyes moved in wonder on every piece of his face. "Because you were at the riding school, I haven't gone to the movies once. I mean, you were real, and nothing's ever been real before for me. This year I don't want holidays to come," she said. "I'll hate Christmas coming because I'll have to go away."

The Frenchman looked at her in indecision a moment, and then he tossed the empty flask away. He took her by the shoulder, holding her fiercely at arm's length an instant—breakable and slender and young in her white silk shirt, with her legs in the jodhpurs as foolish and helpless-looking as a foal's.

"I like you. I like the way you look. I like the way you talk," he said, and she did not falter or tremble beneath his hand.

"If you wanted to kiss me, I would like you to," she said, and the Frenchman stood holding her, with the thing beginning to alter in his face. "Nobody has ever kissed me," she said, and the Frenchman dropped his hand from her shoulder, and stepped back as abruptly from her as if some other presence had come up the path and stood between them there.

The first time Manners spoke about Vivienne to the barman and the men at the bar was after what took place on High Street one evening. He said the Frenchman had changed his ways and that, instead of sitting home at night, he'd started taking the bicycle out and riding into town.

"Every evening for the past three weeks," Manners said, "he'd come down Main Street on it and turn up High."

"Probably meeting a jane," the barman said, and Manners shook his head slowly.

"I started watching out for him," Manners said, "and he never did anything different. He'd just set the bike against the curb, and then he'd stand a long time looking into one of the windows of the stores." There weren't ships or anything like that in the window, Manners said, when the barman asked. The first night he saw him stop there, there were sweaters and skirts and colored handkerchiefs on show. "The things changed around quite a bit in the window," Manners said. "It looked like the folks who owned the place took a lot of trouble with it. They'd put underwear and nightgowns in it one night, and the next time it would be something else. The only thing that didn't change very much was the girl," he said, and he watched the foam swing slowly in his glass.

He said the Frenchman would get off the bicycle and stand it up against the curb, and walk over and start talking to her, and sometimes he'd seem to be talking quietly to her, and other times he'd talk short and quick, as if he were laying down the law. "Sometimes she'd be wearing a kind of red wool dress and a big red hat," Manners said, "and sometimes she'd have a party dress on, and sometimes she'd have trousers, and the nights when she'd be wearing something he hadn't seen before, he seemed to have more to say." Manners picked up his glass of beer and drank a little from it. "The night she was wearing nothing but the kind of white lace pants and the brasseer, he was pretty sore," he said.

"Now, wait a minute," said the barman. "Let's get this straight. You mean to say some girl comes right down High Street to meet this Frenchman and she's got nothing on but a brasseer and a pair of white lace—"

"No," said Manners slowly. "This girl, this model like, she's up there inside the window. She couldn't walk down the street. She's made out of wax, or wood, or something like that, to you and me; but to him she must be something different. Maybe she looks like somebody he used to know somewheres else," he said, and he stopped talking for a moment. "And then last night this thing happened," he said. "This girl they call Vivienne, this girl from the boarding school, she came walking up High Street with her brother, and the Frenchman was standing there the way he'd been doing every night in spite of the weather, and they stopped there and started in talking to him. And after a while," he said slowly, still trying to get to the heart of it, "him and this girl's brother, they started in to fight."

Vivienne's brother was up from camp on twenty-four-hours leave and he called for her at the boarding school on Saturday night, and he walked up High Street toward the movie house with her, wearing his khaki uniform, and his neat little cap on his head. It was dark, and the store windows were lit, and people were loitering a little because the night had moderated, and the girl opened her fur coat at the neck. She and her brother had come past the cut-rate drugstore, and they were passing the women's notion shop when the girl saw the Frenchman was halted there. He was wearing riding breeches, and his jacket collar was turned up, and even with his back turned to them there was something singularly dissolute in the set of his shoulders, and his hands thrust into his pockets, as if he alone were derelict and outcast among the safely and permanently established of the town.

"There's the Frenchman," the girl said, and she felt her heart beat swiftly in her throat. "There's the Frenchman we go riding with," she said.

In the window before which he stood were stockings on elegantly turned legs, and satin slips and colored bandannas on display, but they were less than nothing, they served scarcely as background even for the wax model in the lace-trimmed underthings who sat on a stool under the bright electric glare. Her limbs and her face were as smooth as marble and one hand was raised, and the delicate, pointed fingers

curved, as if to adjust the platinum wig that lay on her flaw-
less brow. Her scarlet lips were slightly parted, and between
them the teeth showed small and even as pearls; but her eyes
were a harlot's—they were fixed on the Frenchman in bold
blue insolence through the window's glass. It was only when
the girl and her brother stood beside him that they saw he
was talking to her under his breath, speaking in a fierce, bitter
voice, as if in reproach or anger, to the wax figure sitting
brazenly on show.

"Hello," said Vivienne's brother, and he stood before the
Frenchman and smiled his frank young smile. When he
spoke, the Frenchman turned his head and looked at him a
moment, looked slowly and uncertainly at him, as if returning a long and troubled way from wherever it was that he
had been. His hair was in disorder, and the weathered skin
of his neck was flushed, and his eyes moved beyond the
brother and found Vivienne's face, and he swayed a little.
"Well, what do you think of her?" he said, and he jerked his
chin toward the model in the window.

"I think she's beautiful," she said, and the Frenchman drew
his lips back, but still he did not smile.

"Lots of other people did too," he said. "That's what she
wanted. She needed it the way you might need a drink or
something. If I wasn't there, she'd get it from somebody else.
When I found out, I signed up and cleared out," he said. "I
knew when I was through."

"She's beautiful," the girl said again, *and because of her or
someone exactly like her*, she thought, *he didn't kiss me;
because he knew someone like that once, he's faithful still,
and he will always be.* "Perhaps if you're as beautiful as that,
it doesn't matter what you do," she said, and her brother
glanced uneasily at her.

"Look here," he said. "The show'll be beginning—"

"Yes," said Vivienne. "Yes, it will," she said, and she stood looking into the Frenchman's face as if she could never look away.

"Women," the Frenchman said, and he stood swaying a little and looking through the window at the model. "I know all about women I want to know," he said. He had his hands in his pockets still, and in the same low, almost lazy voice he began saying the words of abuse to her, pronouncing them in separate venom to the model seated in insolence on the other side of the glass. "Men putting on uniforms to fight for women, fighting for a woman or a country!" he said, and now he began laughing the way the girl had seen him laugh before —without any sound of it being heard. He stood there, his lips shaped in derision for it, his eyes turned in stupor on them, and Vivienne's brother in his neat little uniform squared back from him and his fist swung forward and caught the Frenchman swiftly on the jaw.

Everything seemed to halt in the instant that his head jerked back. The people in the street ceased walking, the breath ceased coming; even the Frenchman paused for a moment, as if suspended, before he took his hands from the pockets of his riding breeches and the color poured dark into his face. But Vivienne stood between them now.

"Don't," she said, "oh, don't," in a small, cold voice to the Frenchman, and her hand lay for an instant on the stuff of his open shirt, against the fury and venom of his breast. "Look at your hands; oh, look at them!" she said in a soft but terrible voice to him, and the tears were running down her face. "Look at the dirt on them! Look at your clothes, look at your shoes!" she said in grief to him. "Oh, look at yourself!" she cried. "You don't belong to any country!" The tears were coming fast, like a child's tears, and she closed her fists tight in the tan fur of her coat. "You can't fight. Don't try to," she said in a quick, cold whisper to him. "You haven't anything left to fight for," she said.

The people had pressed in on them now, and Vivienne's brother drew her back on his arm.

"He's drunk," he said, and the Frenchman made no move and gave no sign that he had heard. He lifted his two hands, as a reprimanded schoolboy might, and looked at the black-rimmed nails a little uncertainly. "He's drunk," Vivienne's brother said again, and the Frenchman fumbled his shirt in at the belt and smoothed his hands back on his hair. "Come on, Vivienne," her brother said, and the tears fell hotly down her face.

And then it was Manners who walked out from the people and who put his arm through the Frenchman's and led him quietly away.

The Christmas holidays came and went, and January passed, and nothing more about the Frenchman might ever have been said. Except that he walked into the bar with Manners one bleak February afternoon, and the two of them stood at the counter, a little apart from the others, and each had a glass of beer. The barman and the others had never laid eye on the Frenchman before, and it was only from the sound of the accent when he spoke that they knew this must be he. It may have been that there was some difference in him even then, for he didn't speak about women, as Manners had told them he did, and his hair seemed neatly done. If it hadn't been for the look of gravity that marked his face, thought the barman, he was giving and taking the talk about the possibility of gas rationing and the shortage of rubber not like a foreigner with his back up against them, but as easily as any native would.

"There isn't so much call for saddle horses this time of year," the barman said by way of conversation, and he wiped the rings of wet from the wood.

The Frenchman leaned on his folded arms on the bar, and

after a moment he said quietly, "I haven't been out for over a month with any of the boarding school girls."

"Well, first there was the holidays," Manners said, as if to save him from the implications of it. "And then there was the bad weather, and then the examinations beginning, and the war on top of that," he said, and he ordered the Frenchman another glass of beer.

But before the barman had time to set it down before him, the street door was pulled quickly, almost wildly open, and the girl came in and stopped short in confusion an instant just inside the dimly lighted room. She was wearing the tan fur coat they had heard about before, and as the door eased to behind her, they saw her legs, thin and impatient as a filly's, cut dark as paper against the afternoon's white light.

"Listen," she began saying through the anguish of having to take breath. "Something's happened, something's happened," she said. She was looking blindly toward the counter where they stood, and what she was saying might have been meant for any of them, and the young, despairing look given in supplication to any of them there. But they knew that she was speaking to the Frenchman and, as unequivocally as though she had spelled it out for them, they recognized the syllables of her name.

The Frenchman glanced at her once, and then he folded his arms and leaned on the bar again. "I'm drunk," he said in a quiet voice, and he looked straight at the beer before him. "I'm drunk again," he said in a quiet irony. "You'd better not come too near."

"If there's anything left you care about," the girl cried out from the door, "you've got to listen to me! If you're still a Frenchman or still a man, or if anything matters to you any more, you've got to come!" she cried, and her voice was shaking, and the tears were standing brilliant in her eyes. "Your ship's on fire. Your ship's burning," she said in desperation to

him, and the Frenchman's face went as white as paper, but
still he did not move. "I've got a taxi at the corner. We can get
there in twenty minutes," she said, and the Frenchman
pushed suddenly past the others and started toward the doorway. When he got to the girl he passed her, too, like a man
gone blind, and she caught the door as he let it go, and she ran
out after him up the street.

In the taxi she told him that an aunt of hers down from
Boston had telephoned from New York and asked her to come
in and have lunch with her one day. And they'd fixed the date
for Wednesday in the Chatham gardens. "I think it was
Wednesday we said we'd meet," she kept on saying softly
and breathlessly to him as they rode. And then when the telephone conversation was almost done, her aunt had said, "You
know, there's a ship burning on the Hudson. I can see the
smoke from the hotel window," or else she had said, "You
know, they turned in a thirty-five fire-alarm call this afternoon
because that big French ship's on fire. They say half the city's
population is down there looking on."

"And I went running out of the school as if I'd gone
crazy," Vivienne said, her voice still breathless and unsteady,
and the Frenchman rode on the seat beside her with his face
turned in the direction in which the water would be. "I ran
all the way to the riding academy, and you weren't there, and
the men there said you'd gone into town with Manners. So I
got a taxi, and I tried three bars—I knew you'd be in a bar," she
said in soft defiance to him, "but it wasn't until the third that
you were standing there."

"All right, I was in a bar," said the Frenchman, his face
turned in bitterness toward the window as they rode. "I was
in a bar, but I was sober. I've been staying sober ever since
then—ever since that night," he said. "I've learned that
much about substituting one thing for another. The next

time someone hits me, I'm going to be able to hit back," he said.

They were driving across the bridge now, and the Frenchman sat grim and tight-lipped, watching the smoke that lay along the farther shore. The taxi carried them as close to it as they could get, and the Frenchman jumped out and looked once at the crowd and at the ship beyond. In spite of the smoke and the people and the number of firemen working there, to the Frenchman it was nothing at all at first—it was a little mistake in the wiring, a breakdown in the insulation; it was something that would be adjusted in a minute or two. He ran across the street with that singular confidence in him. But once the girl and the Frenchman were as far as the ropes where the police and the reporters stood, they could see that the great, tall ship was grievously, perhaps fatally burning.

For the Frenchman it was just a matter of pausing there a moment before going on board. But once he had stooped and gone under the rope, a policeman stopped him.

"I'm one of the crew," the Frenchman said quickly, and because he thought at first that maybe it was his accent that kept the policeman from understanding, he kept repeating it to him. "I'm one of the men off the ship," he said, with a passion hot enough for anger. He said he'd worked nearly three years on her, and lame, halt or blind, he knew every inch of her, abovedecks and below. "They've never been on her before, they don't know their way around!" he said, and he kept on saying it, believing still that in a minute they would let him swing up the hanging ladder on her flank, breathe as his own the density of smoke on deck and smoke below, and pass, accredited at last, down the smoldering stairs and hallways to her blazing heart. "I'm one of the crew; I could do it in my sleep!" he said. "You can't keep me off her! I could do it with my eyes put out! I'm one of the crew; that's my ship!" he kept saying, and, "Ah, France, France," his despair may have found

the words for the first time to cry aloud. "You can't keep me
from getting on and helping them out," he said, but the policeman walked back to the ropes with him and, once there,
the Frenchman stooped as a man moving in a dream might
have stooped, and passed in among the spectators to exile and
banishment again.

When the crowd broke, the girl and the Frenchman
crossed the avenue together and, as inevitably as if no other
place of refuge offered, they went into the seamen's bar. The
Frenchman led the way past the tables where the sightseers,
come to the ship's demise as to a wake, sat drinking, leading
her to some measure of quiet and obscurity in the recessed
corner of the farthest wall. He did not speak after he had
ordered the two drinks, and when the waiter set the two
glasses down before them he did not start to drink. *And how
can I speak now of how poison ivy grows or the shape of the
sassafras leaves?* the girl thought, sitting in numb despair beside him. *For now there must be the words for a woman to
say, but I do not know what they are.*

In a moment the Frenchman lifted his glass and took a
swallow from it.

"My ship's gone," he said in a quiet voice, and his face was
bleak. "My ship's gone. I'm through."

The waiter came a step nearer and his eyes sharpened on
the Frenchman's face and then moved to the girl.

"He's French?" he said, and the girl looked up and nodded.

"That was his ship out there?" the waiter said, and when
he had the answer he walked away.

"Maybe you think I'm a coward; maybe you think I'm a
drunk, you and your brother," the Frenchman said when the
waiter was gone, and he looked without interest at the glass
the girl pushed from her place to his. "Maybe that's why I
started staying sober. I don't know. But it's not love!" he

cried out in impatience. "Don't get the idea I'm talking about love!"

"I know," said the girl, and she thought of the wax limbs and the platinum hair of the model in the window, and her voice was humble. "Please," she said. "I know."

"It was just you making me see myself, just once like that," he said, and he looked at the nails of his hand a minute. "They're clean," he said, "and my shirt's clean, and I'm sober, but my ship's gone and I'm through."

But listen, listen, the girl's heart cried out in silence to him; listen to the sound of love and the sound of reality speaking at last. Your ship's gone, and the model in the window, if you looked at her long enough, she would run to wax in the sun. But the other things are there, her heart cried out to him; they are there as clearly now as if nothing had ever stood between. Your country's there, and the woman with platinum hair, the wife or whatever she was, is somewhere.

And then the other man, whom they had not seen cross the room and stop beside the table, pulled out the third chair and sat down and faced them casually.

"*Salut,*" he said in a low, easy voice to the Frenchman, and he put out his hand. He was a youngish man, perhaps a sea-faring man, with his dark shirt open at the neck and his cap worn on the side of his head. "Frenchman to Frenchman, have a drink with me," he said, and the two men shook hands. The waiter was lingering near the table. "Bring us two brandies," the man with the cap on said, and then he looked at the other Frenchman. "Lost your ship?" he said quietly. "Lost her out there through accident or sabotage?"

"Yes," said the Frenchman, and they spoke their own language together.

"I've lost mine on purpose," said the stranger. "Docked from Marseille three days ago. I've skipped her. I'm going north tonight," he said.

"North?" said the Frenchman, and the girl sat watching him. "North?" he repeated, and nothing flickered in his face.

"You don't ask questions about it, you act," said the other man in the same low casual voice. The waiter put the glasses of brandy on the table before them. "That's all you're expected to do," the stranger said.

"And then what?" said the Frenchman. He was leaning forward on the table now, and his eyes did not leave the other man's face.

"You take part in the show," said the man with the cap. "You cross the frontier and get into it." He looked at the clock on the wall above them. "Stay around a half hour and we'll move out together," he said.

For a moment, no more words were spoken at the table, and then the two men—as if moved by an identical conviction or emotion—lifted their brandy glasses and touched them together as the simplest Frenchmen do before they drink, and each drank his hot little glass of brandy down.

That was the way it ended; it ended when the Frenchman turned to the girl beside him at the table and spoke, with the taste of English gone suddenly alien on his tongue.

"You'd better be starting back," he said, as if speaking to a child who had wandered this far from home with him. "We'll be clearing out soon, so you'd better not hang around."

"Yes," said the girl, and she stood up and looked at his face, but he and the stranger in the cap were talking together again. "Yes, I'll go back to school," she said; and Yes, yes, she said in silence, *this is the way I wanted it to finish, this is the way it had to be. Yes, yes, yes,* she said, and she set her teeth hard against any of the broken or whimpering sounds of sorrow as she walked out alone through the tables, her hair as long as a little girl's on her shoulders, her hands in the pockets of her schoolgirl coat; and she did not look back at the door.

Hotel Behind the Lines

I stood at the window of the hotel room and looked out across the stone balcony's balustrade, and beyond it across the square to where the river flowed, as clear and unbroken as peace itself, and marvelously impervious to demolition. A long way below, a dozen or more people stood waiting on the stones of the Arno's beach, faceless and sexless and scarcely human from the window's height, but more like the black, explicit letters of a caption saying: "Italian workers in blasted Florence waiting on the bank of the Arno to be ferried home at night." The rowboat for which they waited had no oars, but a cable had been strung across from the beach of shingle to the other bank, above which the cypresses stood, and the boatman's hands on the cable wove back and forth, back and forth, delivering the people who crossed with him into the brilliance of the sunset, and then weaving back across the shining surface of the water to the shingled beach again.

The front must be up there ahead, lost in the misty, bluish folds of the Apennines, but I did not believe in it yet. The roar of the airplane's motors had ceased in my ears just a little while before, and I believed now only in this pool of evening quiet that lay, unquivering, in the violent landscape of war. The front must be up there, with men I knew fighting on it; but here there was no echo, no whisper on the water. Outside there was the cable, strung, a delicate vein, through the stillness, and the boatman's hands on it drawing the people home. In the room, on the table behind me, were the daffodils Mario had sent, with a card saying to telephone him as soon as I got in. *In a moment I will call him,* I thought; *in just a moment, when I've stopped looking at Italy. I will call him, and see him tonight, and get the shape and the taste of things from him. He'll have grown up since 1937—he'll be twenty-three-or-four, and as free man and a poet he has somehow managed to survive.*

And then the telephone rang quickly on the little table by the bed and I went to it, and lifted the mouthpiece and receiver up.

"This is Colonel Sarett," said the Englishman's voice from the other end of the wire. "Stranger to you, I'm afraid. I just bumped into your name on the hotel list downstairs—"

"Oh, yes," I said, and there was silence for a moment.

"Once had a cousin from Dublin by the same name," said the Englishman's voice. "Occurred to me perhaps some member of the family. I thought I'd simply ask."

The family, my part of it, I said, left Ireland three generations back. I added that there wasn't much to say for it as a name, and the Englishman laughed.

"There was always Robert," he said. "Wintered here, you'll remember, studying the works of Galileo. I think it was 1642."

"They had a weakness for Italy," I said. "There was John, the Earl of Cork and Orrery. But probably we're none of us related."

"Oh, doubtless not," said Colonel Sarett. "Right you are. You'll forgive me for calling, won't you? I'm just down from the front for fifteen hours, covered with muck and grime." It might have been that he brushed at his blouse a little as he said it. "Awfully decent of you to have talked to me at all," he said.

After I had put the telephone down, I felt the singularly rebuking silence in the room. *You could have gone downstairs, sat five minutes at the bar with him, asked him what part of England he came from, not mentioned Greece, but spoken of the look of London ten days ago, and of England's inarticulated courage.* You could have done it for five minutes between the time of arriving here and having dinner with Mario. You could have done it for the sake of the muck and the grime and the fifteen hours he has of absolution. I stood looking out again over the roofs, and I thought of Eden in the House of Commons crying out like a petulant woman to the questions the Labor members put to him, but I laid the thought of that aside. There had been other Englishmen; there had been the quick, good words of the air marshal saying to me two weeks ago at lunch, "If the time has come when the common people of the world have found a party that can speak effectively for them, then, for God's sake, let the rest of us rid ourselves of our outdated prejudices—" and then the telephone rang sharply again.

"Damned cheek, I'm quite aware," said Colonel Sarett's voice, "but I've waited a decent interval, and I still want to say it. I want to ask you if you'd indulge in a spot of pity and come down and have a drink with me?"

I said I would. I told him I was in uniform; and in the lobby downstairs there was nothing but the military— the young, the middle-aged, the Americans, the British, the Scotch, the military without relief.

"It won't be easy to find you," I said.

"You'll know me at once," said Colonel Sarett from five flights below. "My hair is going thin—you know, receding from the temples. I'm definitely battle-worn, and there are bags under my eyes."

I said I would put a daffodil in the front of my blouse.

"You mean there are actually flowers blooming?" asked Colonel Sarett. I said there were lots of daffodils—cartloads of them in the streets. "Good God, flowers—flowers blooming in all this mud!" said Colonel Sarett. "I got in half an hour ago. I haven't had time to look around . . ."

The lobby of the hotel was marble-paved and built tall and dark for Italian summers. It was not made for the military at all. Yet here was the sharp, nervous weariness of men on pass drawn taut as a wire from pillar to pillar, and the nameless hunger, the nameless thirst of tired men and lonely men sunk in the split leather of the armchairs, or pacing back and forth on the marble flags, or grouped in nothing as absolute as hope by the revolving doors. But the man who stood quite alone, and a little nervous, by the central pillar, was watching over the heads of the others who passed him. He was watching the stairway that opened, fanwise, into the crowded place.

He was tall and rather slender, with a high, solid, broad chest—a man of forty-five it might be, standing there with the light, smooth hair receding from the peak of it on his forehead, and a clipped mustache on his lip. In spite of the wash of weariness across his face, his eyes were quick and sharp, and when he saw the daffodil, he came forward, pulling a little uneasily at his cuffs. He had not spoken of the campaign ribbons, the decorations, but they all were there.

"I say, this is sporting of you," he said at once. He must have washed his hands while he waited, for when he shook mine, the palm of it was fresh still. "We can have incredibly bad liquor in there, if you don't mind," he said, and he jerked his chin toward the door of the bar. We went in through the archway, past the uniforms standing, the uniforms seated, the great, featureless, khaki-clad army gathered in simulated ease, which turned its eyes to the sight of a woman coming, even though the look of the women loved and the women wanted had ebbed from the realm of possibility a long time back. We sat down on the only two seats that were left on the cracked, dark leather against the wainscoting. "You don't quite believe it at first—I mean, for the first few hours down from the front, you never quite believe you've got here," he said, and as he ordered the drinks of synthetic fruit juice and Italian

gin, his eyes were on me carefully. "You're just beginning to
get the feel of it when you have to turn around and go back
again. This isn't a complaint," he added quickly, and there
was the relentless military eye turned inward in self-interpel-
lation as unflinchingly as it would have censored anyone else.

"Fifteen hours isn't much time," I said, and the drinks came
then, and we lifted the short, thick-bottomed glasses, and
Colonel Sarett said:

"Cheers." The taste of the drink was bad, and he ran his
tongue in quick repugnance along his lip. His face was short-
nosed and neat, with none of the soft betrayals of indulgence
in it; the mouth was stubborn, exact, tenacious, above the
cleft chin. "I could, of course, stay down longer," he said, and
his eyes moved quickly to me again. "Twenty-four, thirty-six
hours, you know. But I can't bring myself to it. Vanity, possibly. Probably nothing more admirable than that. But I have
to get back," he said.

"You mean, the war is being won, and you're here—you're
out of it for fifteen hours?" I asked, and he turned his glass in
his fingers a moment.

"Lost causes," he said. "Damn it, they get under your
skin." He looked up; his eyes, with the drink beginning to fuse
in them, were brighter and less weary under his lightish brows.
"I remember watching the planes go out over Maidenhead in
the evenings—1940 that was," he said. "Old crates scarcely
able to make the hop and drop their load. And even if they
did get over—Norway and stuff—God knows how many managed to make it back. Isn't the smoke awfully thick in here?"
he said.

"After the mountains, it's like that. It always is," I said.
"You come down, and rooms seem smaller, and ceilings lower,
and you can't breathe the air."

"It's true," said Colonel Sarett, and he ordered the second
drinks. "That summer I'd watch them going out at night," he

went on saying, "and I'd listen for them to come back at dawn. I was convalescing from a wound I got in the Dunkirk show, and I'd lie there listening for them. When they'd begin to straggle back, I'd start counting the sound of their motors, and they'd be coughing their hearts out as they came. No recent models, no modern gear, just crates that spring and summer, but they kept on going over, and coming back when they could come back—coming back with their rudders out, and their landing gear gone, just to say that they hadn't cracked up in a foreign field—for God's sake, how did I get on to this?" said Colonel Sarett. "This isn't small talk, but I swear I've forgotten how it goes. I ought to be talking about your eyes, or the way you smile, but I've forgotten how to begin. I could tell you that the reason I telephoned the second time to your room was because of the sound of your voice, and that would be true. Or I could tell you that the sound of any woman's voice heard here is like a pain in the heart—not a sharp pain, but a really beastly, nagging pain, provided you have time for that kind of pain," he said. "Perhaps better to tell you about the mountain goats up there in the hills, just born you know, right in the middle of war, sticky as lilac buds. Rupert Brooke was awkward as hell with images—foreign fields and lilacs and all the rot. But still in 1940 those planes kept going out," he said, his stubborn voice jerking back to it again. "Theirs was the lost cause then, absolutely lost, there wasn't a chance. But we had faith in them. We had to, because there wasn't anything else, and, by God, they won—"

It was when the second drinks came that he began to say other things, looking straight down into the evil-tasting and evil-smelling liquor as if the revelation of all that he believed lay there. He said, speaking quickly, that he had his own army, the men of it his own men, his people, who bore their arms in personal loyalty. He had trained these men, he said, and he had armed them, and up there in the Apennines they were fighting their own individual and dogged war.

"Eighteen thousand of them," he said, and as he spoke the fire kindled slowly in his face, and the actual flesh of Lawrence of Arabia's legend seemed to come in its pride and passion to the table and take its place with us there. "They've fought their way up from southern Italy, because they want to be up there, they want to be in the show. They've kept the supply road through the snows open all winter, done it against all the odds the elements had to offer," he said, and his eyes were on me in unflinching estimate. "Two hundred and fifty more came up the pass yesterday, the survivors of a brigade of seven hundred operating in the northern Apennines," he said, "asking to sign up with me—tough, hard men who know there's a job of work to do, and who'll do it." He had been a soldier a long time, and there was nothing of forbearance in him, and the appraisals he made were perhaps nothing more than the soldier's assessment of what functioned adequately and what did not. "I'm talking about the Italians," he said. "Italian partisans."

He said he had begged, borrowed, lied, and stolen to get their paraphernalia for them. He had got them dark blue ski suits from American stock; he had got them shoes, signing chits for them that he had no authority to sign. He had kept them covered, and fed, and armed, and fighting up there all winter. As he talked, he took his drink quickly down. In a minute, he said, in a minute he'd have a hot bath and a change of clothes, but it was not this that mattered. What mattered was that the others, the eighteen thousand of them, were up there in the dark of the mountains without him, wearing the uniform and the shoes of no regulation army, keeping the road clear of landslides, and enemy destruction, and high mountain snow.

He was saying these things at the little table in the smoke-

filled crowded bar when the American major walked in and
paused beneath the arch for a moment. There he stood, looking, in something not nearly young enough or lost enough for
loneliness, for the sight of anyone he knew. When he saw
Colonel Sarett's face, the relief came swiftly across the broad,
square expanse of his own and lingered, the lines grew easy
about his mouth, and he made his way through the uniforms
toward us. Then he halted beside the colonel, and he nodded
to me, and he leaned over and stretched his arm across the
colonel's chair.

"I was thinking about you today, Colonel. A matter come
up that put me in mind of you," he said. The voice was
middle western, the features rugged, with wrinkles drawn
deep across his heavy brow.

"I say, sit down with us," said the colonel, coming abruptly
back from the front. "This is Miller, Major Miller," he said to
me. "A countryman of yours. An agricultural chap from the
AMG."

"Call it plain farming. That's what it is," said the major,
and he said, "Pleased t' meet-ya, ma'am," and he sat down.
He had narrow, bright, black eyes, and his ears were big, and
the hair sprang black and curly and lively on his head. "Ran a
farm journal back in Oklahoma. Doing something like it
here," he said.

"The major's draining the marshes out, getting flood walls
rebuilt from Marina di Pisa down," said Colonel Sarett, and
he raised his hand and snapped his fingers for the drinks.

"The colonel here's mustering an army of his own," said
the major. His mouth was wide, and when he smiled the
wrinkles scarred deep and crescent-shaped in the flesh of his
cheeks. "He speaks the lingo, and they listen to him as if
they liked it, the Italians do," said the major, and he sat there,
the jagged crescents of the smile in his face. "I've run into a
couple of Englishmen who don't like it quite so well," he said.

"All Lombard Street to a China orange," said the colonel, "but they'll take it. You can't dispense with a country's population, somehow, not even a liberated country's."

"Floods raising Cain all over the place," Major Miller said, and when he thought of the floods he stopped smiling. "You get floods, and no sewer systems, and then the epidemics get going. Our medics are up there shooting the people full of inoculations." The Italian barman brought the drinks and set them on the table, and the major raised his glass in his broad, clean hand and said, "Here's looking at you, ma'am," and he took a drink of it. "Jiminy crickets, that's lousy booze! I'm sure you're of the same opinion about it, ma'am," he said politely over his glass.

"There's a lot of future in it, my man," said Colonel Sarett. "It's keeping us here talking together. I think we might have another," he said.

"We'll drink it to Colonel Sarett's army," I said, and the major stopped smiling abruptly again, and the crescents were blanked out of his cheeks.

"I was coming to Colonel Sarett's army," he said, and he looked at the colonel. "I heard about thirty thousand Italian soldiers we're holding as prisoners of war. I just heard about them today," he said. "Question come up about disposing of them—thirty thousand of them that we took prisoner when we come in, and by the law of Acquisition, Retention, and Confusion, they're POWs still. Now maybe we'll conscript them into battle, and again maybe we won't," the flat middle western voice went on, and the bright black eyes watched Colonel Sarett in sanguine belief. "But if you put in a claim for them, I'll bet they're as good as yours," he said.

The colonel hesitated a moment, took a swallow of the synthetic juice and gin, and put his glass down. "There's no way of knowing what their politics might be," he said.

"There's nothing to keep you from making Englishmen, or

Americans, or even Russians out of them. Nothing on earth," said the major.

"Thirty thousand," the colonel said, musing on it. "I wouldn't know where to begin. I wouldn't know what to do with a lot of blokes who don't know by this time which way the wind is blowing. They wouldn't fit in with my blokes up there."

"Colonel, it could very well be that you're just not giving them a break," said the major, and he shook his head. "They've had twenty-five years of not acting like themselves, the Italians have, ma'am," he said in explanation, "and now they got to start learning how. You got to help them to get everything new, right from the inside out. It's like draining the marshes first and getting the crops in afterward. You can't do it quick, so you do it slow. And in the end you get it right," he said.

He lifted his glass to drink, but Colonel Sarett spoke almost sharply across the table, and the major put his glass down again.

"You've forgotten one thing," said Colonel Sarett. "The whole blooming lot of them in this country weren't in it, not by a long shot, Major." He chewed quickly, savagely, at his upper lip a moment, and then the vehemence died from his face. "Thirty thousand POWs," he said, musing on it again. Thirty thousand Italians out of prison, his men to clothe, to feed, to arm, to cherish. "Thirty thousand of them," he said, and the thought of them was alive now, moving up the mountain with him. "By Gad, who should I talk to about it?" he said, and the light of it was shining in his eye.

I remembered Mario then, and I got up from the table, and I gave my hand to Colonel Sarett.

"I have to telephone," I said. "I am having dinner with a man called Mario."

"Blast Mario," said Colonel Sarett, and he got up quickly

from his chair. He stood there, tall and straight, his thumbs hooked in his leather belt, his mouth twitching under his clipped mustache. "If I had a bath and a shave and that sort of thing—made a decent job of myself—would you dine with me instead of him?" he said.

We had dinner in the mess hall, meat and carrots and white American bread, and red Italian wine—the colonel, the major, and I. It was the major who had the jeep waiting at nine in the hotel's moonlit square, and he said good-by to us there. Colonel Sarett, with his cheeks shaven clean and his fresh clothes on, followed me in over the jeep's side and sat down beside me on the boards of the back seat. The doors and the sideflaps were buttoned on, for the night was cool, and our coats were belted around us. The address I gave the corporal at the wheel was not Mario's address; it was the name of the street and the villa where Mario would be.

"He said he would be there with his friend, the newspaper-man, tonight," I said to Colonel Sarett, and the jeep took the corner of the square and jerked into the narrow street. "A man called Valdarno," I said. "They can tell me exactly how things are in Italy."

"Who the devil would Mario be?" said the colonel.

Mario's mother was English, and his father had been Italian; I had known them in Florence eight years ago, I said. There had been an older brother then, a boy called Michele, who had played the mandolin and sung. He was nineteen when I knew him, and very beautiful—a good swimmer, a good runner—and he had gone to boarding school in England and liked it there.

"What school did he go to?" asked the colonel in spite of himself.

"That has nothing to do with it," I said in impatience.

"Very well," said the colonel as we rode, and he drew the skirts of his overcoat around him. "I merely wanted to know."

"They live up on the hill, in the same house still, Mario told me when I telephoned tonight," I said, and I could see it clearly. There were almond and mimosa and olive trees growing fresh on the slope below it, and two little stone-walled terraces baked hard by the sun, with the shade of the cypresses marked sharp and conical, as dark as if drawn in ink, upon the terraces' pure white. "It was in the autumn, early October, of 1937, and the English mother set off for a day or two in Rome. And Michele came to the door, and he was angry, he was in a rage. His mother wrote me all this afterward," I said. "He called out after his mother as she left not to forget to bring him back some tennis shoes from Rome. 'For the damned Fascist relay races—I have to have them for the relay races,' was what he said."

"The night of the day she left, Mario came down into Florence for a concert," I said, "and he left Michele alone in the house. And then he did it."

"He did what?" asked Colonel Sarett, and his voice was a little shocked, as though he knew exactly what was to come.

"He shot himself. He killed himself," I said. "Mario came home from the concert, and there was a letter on the table, with Michele's cameo ring lying on it. The letter just said that he had had trouble finding the gun, and after he'd found it, it was so rusty that he didn't know if it would work. But it did work."

We were out of the city now, and the jeep was moving tentatively along what was no longer street but road, as if feeling its way across the temporary planks of the bridges, and between the moon-blanched walls. Then it came to a stop before a gate.

The house lay close to the road beyond the garden wall, bright white and palace-like under the moon, the substance of it seemingly too lambent for stone. Colonel Sarett rang the bell, and as we waited the trees stood close around us, motionless, fragrant, and mysteriously leafed.

"In another month the nightingales will be singing," Colonel Sarett said. He had taken his cap off, and the moonlight lay in a sharp, metallic blade across his lightish hair. "The presence of a thought," he said in a low voice, "is like the presence of a woman we love. Schopenhauer and the moonlight making me eloquent again," he added in quick apology. Then the door opened, and I saw it was Mario, eight years older, standing hesitant in the dimly lit hall.

"I hope it wasn't too difficult to find the villa," Mario said, and he closed the door behind us. Inside it was colder than it had been outside in the evening air. Mario said that Valdarno was upstairs waiting; he said that if it had not been for the state of Valdarno's health, and the lack of transportation, they would have saved me the trip out and come in to the hotel themselves. "But there are no buses, and no way of getting from one place to another," he said, "and Valdarno is not well."

Mario seemed a shy man, and at first you believed that he was shy, this delicate, slightly stooping figure with the wealth of black hair on his Latin head. You believed it until he began to speak, with his large, dark, fearless eyes on you, and then you knew that it was something more admirable than timidity which marked his bearing and the features of his face.

"Valdarno was imprisoned, you know, because of the articles he wrote," he said, and he lowered his voice a little as we started up the stairs. "A friend has lent this place to Valdarno and his wife," he said. "When Florence was liberated, Valdarno was set free, but he was penniless and he had no house in which to live." At the top of the first cold, echoing flight, he turned to the door on the right of the hall, and laid his hand on the iron latch. "He is extremely eager to meet you," he said before he opened it, and his voice was low. "We want to know what is happening in other countries—in France, America," Mario said, and he turned his head and smiled at us, a quick, gentle, half-apologetic smile.

Valdarno sat alone in the room, seated by a table on which the lamp was lighted and shone dimly, and his wild black eyes were fixed upon the door. When we entered, he stood up, trembling a little, his chest concave behind the façade of the gray tweed jacket, and he shook our hands and spoke our names.

"Sit down, sit down, please," he said. He spoke in English to us, turning in agitation and uncertainty from empty chair to chair. "My wife, unfortunately, is not here. She works at the telephone company at night. Here is a chair, Signora," he said, and he leaned to it, and drew it forward in his trembling hands. "And for the officer—for the Colonel," he murmured, and he was turning like a swift, dark animal from side to side. There was a fine, black, silky mustache under his long, narrow nose, and his lips were thin-skinned and of a red so precarious that it seemed the blood might spring from them if he spoke his words too loud. "For the officer, the large chair here—"

"Please be seated, Signor Valdarno," Colonel Sarett said, and suddenly, at these words, the flurry of movement ceased in the room. Valdarno, his eyes fixed as if in fright on the colonel, sat slowly down in his chair. Colonel Sarett undid the belt of his trench coat, unbuttoned it without haste, and drew his arms from the sleeves. "I ask you please to forgive my coming here, Signor Valdarno," he said, and he spoke Italian to him, speaking it softly, and quickly, and well. He was leaning forward as he talked, his elbows on his knees, his fingers interlaced, as if in this bowed position he somehow discounted the breadth and the depth of his own chest as he faced Valdarno, and the display of ribbon on it. "I'm down for a few hours from the front," he said, "and I wish you would go on talking exactly as if I were not here. I came be-

cause I wished to be with the Signora, and because it is good
to be with men who are not in uniform for a little while."

He had made his explanation, he had offered his apology,
and I wondered a moment; and then, as Mario began speaking again, the thing became clear. Not to Valdarno, and not
to Mario, and not to himself was Colonel Sarett merely a man
come in from the moonlight to sit and hear them talk of
their country, or their country's shame, or to speak of their
country's future. He was not a man come casually, briefly in
of an evening as any visitor might have come. He was something else, and he did not like the role he had been given. He
was the Army, he was the British Army; he wore its uniform,
he wore its honors pinned on his breast, and nothing could
take the look of it away. To them, and even to himself sitting
there in the badly lighted, the unheated room, he was the
Army with its ear to the ground for the subterranean whispers; the Army with its machine guns leveled; the Army prepared to wipe out the weak and the hungry and the desperate
as they came.

"We can talk of nothing but Roatta's escape," Mario was
saying, quietly, evenly, as if with intention. "We can think of
nothing else just now—I suppose because of the symbol it
offers, the play within the play. The proceedings of Roatta's
trial would have stripped the story of all but its essential
drama and made it simple enough for everyone to have understood. The story, I mean," he said quietly, "of the criminal
policies which ravaged this country for more than twenty
years and brought her to disaster. We could have enacted in
that trial—the courtroom as stage, the people of the world as
spectators, and all the players perfectly cast—the history of
our shame and our atonement."

"It's been a match set to tinder, that rotter getting out,"
said Colonel Sarett. "Demonstrations in Rome, students
marching in protest—" *The kind of conflagration,* said the

silence when he had ceased to speak, *that we British have extinguished with such generous mercy*; and as his voice broke off, the colonel chewed nervously at his mustache an instant.

"Our government," Mario went on saying, "has created the climate for evasion. The accomplices in Roatta's flight are men who are still in high places, and who feared the revelations he would make—"

And *Hush*, said the furtive silence in Valdarno's face, *hush, hush now, Mario. These things are true, they are all true, but before the British uniform they cannot be said.* And Colonel Sarett sat, leaning forward, his fingers interlaced, his eyes on Mario.

"The farce we are enacting here in Italy—the farce, instead of serious, responsible theatre," Mario was saying, "the monstrous farce of purging ourselves clean! Do you know how many public figures southern Italy has executed?" he said, and he looked at us, half-smiling. "One, precisely one," he said, and he lifted the forefinger of his right hand. "Free Italy has executed one man of all those accused of specific crimes committed at a specific time. At his trial Roatta, former Italian Chief of Staff, head of the Military Intelligence Office, one of the most iniquitous and murderous organizations in the world, Lieutenant General Roatta testified that he had organized two Fascist brigades called the Black Arrows and the Blue Arrows to support Franco, but declared that he himself was neither Fascist nor anti-Fascist but an Italian general who obeyed his government whatever its color might be. He said that he had once helped many Polish soldiers and more than five thousand Jews who were wanted by the Nazis. Do you see how they are going to try to save their skins?" said Mario. "Now if our slate is to be sponged clean," he said, and his clear, dark, sober eyes were on me, "then one must begin at the top and wash down the slate, as we did when we were school children. Thus, we should begin with the King—only,

of course, that is absolutely unheard of. Too many Englishmen like our King—they are really devoted to our King. So,
obviously, we cannot begin at all."

Hush, said the unspoken anguish in Valdarno's face. *Do
not bare yourself like this before him. Do not betray us all
into his hands.* "And the King," Mario went on, "recognizing
himself in private as the perfect representation of our public
treason and shame, hastily retired, hoping that if he got out
of sight quickly enough the Italian people would not have the
time to get a really good look at what he was. He decided,
our little King, he decided very quaintly and humanly that it
would be very silly indeed to execute himself, and probably
quite unnecessary," Mario said, and then, abruptly, he ceased
speaking, and the humor was gone, and only the bitterness was
left to pull at the corners of his young mouth. *To execute
himself,* said the silence; *to execute himself,* and Mario sat
motionless, and he stared straight at the floor. And it might
have been that the figure of Michele lay there on the boards,
in the little lake of blood as he had found him eight years
before—lay there, eternally nineteen, eternally silent, the voice
no longer impatiently asking for tennis shoes for the Fascist
relay races, and the pistol lying near his hand.

"You know, here in Italy a great many good and brave
people have died," Mario said. "They died," he said, "and
their lives and their deaths have become the words of a kind
of vocabulary of violence for us, and now there is no other
vocabulary that men of honor can use—"

And *Hush, do not say it so loudly,* said Valdarno's eyes as
they moved in trepidation from Mario's to the colonel's face.
*We have come through prison, starvation, through torture
for it. Do not give it all away to him now, do not lay your
heart in his hand.*

"We speak the same language," Colonel Sarett said, and
because of the modest sound of petition in what he said, it

might have been he who wore the thin-soled, ancient shoes and the shabby coat. *Allow me,* he did not add, *to address you not as a unit, but as a man. Overlook the khaki and tin and the record,* his humility asked of them, but he did not say the words aloud.

"And yet one would scarcely say that it was English," said Mario bitterly. "Roatta's escape was a match set to tinder, as you said—Fascist riots in prison, buses turned over and burned. The police have been denying ever since the alleged mass escapes from the Soriano nel Cimino and the Vierbo prisons, and when a situation comes to the point of denials, it means that something is about to happen. It will have to happen—it will have to happen in spite of the English and because of the English, in order to save Italy from the fate of Greece—"

Hush, for God's sake, keep quiet, said Valdarno's agitated silence, and he turned one more look of desperation on Mario. Then he leaned toward me and spoke a few low, hurried words across the light. "And France?" he said. "In France how is the *épuration* going?"

I said there were trials, sentences passed, executions every week: prefects, mayors, journalists—the little men. The big men in France had not yet been touched—the industrialists were still to be taken into custody. And as I spoke, Valdarno watched the shape of the words on my lips and shaped them in silence with his own; watching eagerly, harking, waiting for the small, faint sound of promise or hope that might be in them, as a famished man might wait at a table for what crumbs of sustenance might fall.

"Puységur has been condemned to death," I said. "Stéphane Lauzanne has been given twenty years' hard labor. General Pinsard escaped capital punishment. No one quite knows why. Two of Mandel's murderers are to be executed—"

It was like a bar of music begun, the notes struck separately, precisely, but not completed, and as I ceased speaking, the rest of the tune hung curiously unplayed between us on the air. They ask for purity, the young men of Europe, I thought; they ask for the *épuration* of their countries and their souls.

Valdarno leaned one emaciated arm in the gray tweed jacket on the table beneath the light, and his long, fleshless fingers tapped quickly, nervously on the wood.

"Signora, we are not like the French," he said in a low voice, looking as if in entreaty at me. "We are less spirited, humbler, and we have been cripples for a quarter of a century now. We have been very ill," he said, and his bright red lips were trembling with intensity. "We still are not quite able to get up from bed and make our way across the room to the window where we know the light and air must be. Signora," he said, "we are just beginning to get well again, we are just learning now to get our pride back, but we are still unsteady when we try to stand alone. We need you, you Americans. Do not leave us yet. We need you until we can learn to do the mere physical things, like eating and drinking, for ourselves again. Signora," he said, and the wounds were there, unhealed still, the avowal of their pain marked in his eyes. "Do not leave us, you Americans. Do not leave us for a little while—"

"Blast it, there's no need to ask favors of any of us," Colonel Sarett cried out, and he jumped up from his chair. "The number of patriots fighting the Germans in northern Italy is twice that of the Italian regular army troops." He paced back and forth, impatient now with inaction, back and forth across the floor. "I tell you I've got an army up there on the front, an army that is fighting, damn it, bearing arms and fighting. We have camps set up where we're reclothing, re-equipping them as fast as they come. I'm talking of Italians, Italian partisans," he cried out. "They've established their own airfields at Cuneo and Pinerolo—behind the enemy lines. That's a resistance movement for you. More than two hundred and fifty thousand of them dead, resisting—"

"My sister and brother died with them," Valdarno said, and his pale hand on the table trembled, and the lamp's light shone dimly on his bloodless nails.

"Look here, Signor," said Colonel Sarett, and his voice was quieter now. He sat down on the chair again before Valdarno, leaning forward, the singular fire and vision in his eye. "There's a question on the boards now about a batch of Italian POWs interned down south. I want to get them, give them a battlefront, make men out of them," he said.

"What kind of men?" asked Valdarno, and his black, desperate eyes were halted as if in fear on the colonel.

"Men," said the colonel impatiently. "Men taking their part in this bloody show. Thirty thousand of them," he said, and he leaned forward, watching Valdarno eagerly. "I'm going to try through channels to get hold of them, fit them out, march them up here into the mountains with me—"

"And when the war is finished," said Mario's bitter voice; "when the north of Italy is liberated and they and the other free men come marching down on Rome to protest our decadent government, will British machine guns be turned on them as they were turned on the people of Greece?"

"If they turn their blasted machine guns on the partisans," said Colonel Sarett, and he had got to his feet again, "then they'll turn them on me as well, for I'll be marching with them. Out of thirty thousand," he went back to it as he paced in the room, "we can count on a third of them at least being rebels, and that leaves two-thirds of them fools, but rebels are far more eloquent than fools, and they'll do the job, a smashing job," he said.

"What job?" asked Valdarno, and his voice was cautious, and his eye was on the colonel warily.

"The job of saving a country, blast it. This country, Italy," the colonel cried out, and when I looked at Valdarno, I saw that the thing had happened to him: he had dropped his head forward on his hand, and the tears were running down his face.

MILITARY OCCUPATION

A *Christmas Carol for Harold Ross*

IT was four o'clock in the afternoon when the corporal stepped off the streetcar and into the organ music of the caroling. He was a slight, dark-eyed young man, with a tap dancer's quick, impatient action in his bones, and the singing bore down upon him in a solid wave that seemed to unfurl from heaven itself, having blasted the cast iron of the German sky. They were women's voices that sang, but so sublimated that they might have risen from the classical, stone throats of statues erected on the square, and the corporal took a cigarette out and lit it nervously, and threw the match away. The American shopping center was there before him, with neon lights spelling out the season's greetings over the portal of the Post Exchange, while behind him lay the city that was scarcely a city any more. It was a waste of excavations so long abandoned that no one could recall for what purpose they had originally been made: a city of gaping walls, and gutted churches, and cellars laid open to the elements. It was a boneyard of a place, and he didn't want to look at it. No one in his right mind would have chosen it as a site for Christmas, but the colossal voices warned him that this was where it was to be celebrated this year. The chorus of voices moved, as solid as carnival floats and as grotesque, over the carcasses of city blocks, and the debris of public gardens, and over the corporal himself, and he shook his head like a dog with a sore ear.

"It came upon a midnight clear," the voices stated.

"My God, I'd like to get into some other month!" the

corporal said to himself, for he was a poet and he prided himself on his alacrity.

He had seen a café a block or two back on the streetcar line, and he turned quickly and started for it, like a nimble dancer tattooing his way through the cold. But the singing not only swelled like organ music from the sky, but it rose as well, as dense as foliage from the rubble, pressing the breath out of the lungs, possessing the entire air. "Sleep in heavenly peace," advised the exalted voices with a power that would raise the dead, and the corporal knew they were at his heels.

"I'd like to get them by the throats!" he tried to say, but the sound was wiped from his mouth by the high wind of their caroling.

Last Christmas he had coasted with his sisters down the hill before their house, and stars were in the crystal sky. He knew exactly how the hair of younger sisters looked, pulled tight at the nape of the thin neck, the pure blond hair wrenched into braids, and the hair that was going darker yanked into a ponytail that wagged with each movement of the leaping, temperamental bones. He could almost count each separate hair at their temples, and see their ears fitted neatly to the sides of their heads, like matching ornaments, unlike the ears of men. Whether sisters or not, I believe in girls, in all girls, he thought with sudden emotion. If enough of them walked down the street at this moment, like marching in a St. Patrick's Day, New York, parade, he knew that even the caroling would cease. But the voices had no intention of retiring. Instead, as the corporal reached the café door, they adroitly changed sex and roared after him their mammoth yearning for white Christmases that had been known sometime, somewhere, before. And now he stopped in the twilit street and read the words that were lettered in black against a white ground on the café wall. "Off Limits," the brief message went. No more than that. But it meant he would not be allowed to evoke another time of year in a glass of schnapps at a table in the dark.

"So it's got to be December all day—and this December, not even last," he said, and then he saw the girl.

"Hello," she said as she stood with one hand raised to open the café door. Her heels were high, her legs slender, and her coat of billiard-table green was buttoned to the chin.

"You're late," the corporal said.

"You mus be a liddle bid grazy," the girl said, the words spoken slowly across the cold. Her hair was beautiful in color, and as heavy and cumbersome as a copper helmet resting on the small white brow and temple and clasping the hollow cheeks. "I neber see you before."

"All right. But I dreamed about you once," the corporal said.

"I'm gold," the girl said, and she shivered as if she already lay entombed in the iron earth and a dog in search of love had run across her grave. She had brown leather gloves on, worn through at the fingertips, and she rubbed her hands together as she stood before the door. "Wad aboud a liddle dring?" she said.

"I can't go in," said the corporal, and then the idea was there. "You go in and buy a bottle of schnapps, and bring it out." He had the D Marks already out of his pocket and in her hand, and his thoughts were jumping agilely. They could drink it in the seclusion of a rusted furnace, perhaps, in one of the cellars that war had taken the lid off of five years or more ago; or drink it before one of the handsome mantelpieces that hung by a thread from the shattered rafters; or drink it just cowering on a street corner as the voices of the carol singers shouldered them back against the wall. "What I'm interested in is peace and quiet," he said. The dusk of the December evening lay cold as concrete at their feet.

He shouldn't be seen standing there waiting for her to come

out again, or be seen walking in the street with her, so he set off as if he had another destination in mind. But the destination was nothing more than a sense of wonder that one man in history had fought a railway station for silence, had fought it singlehanded, and had won. It was perhaps this year, or the year before, that they had wanted to wire Grand Central Station, and fit it with amplifiers, so that words and music would drift up from its platforms, and wend their way out of the ticket windows, and twine like ivy around the commuters' ears. And one man had said, no, very loudly, for God's sake, no! He was an editor, and he had got up from his desk long enough to tell Grand Central that every man had the right to his own inspired, or uninspired, silence as he ran for his train, and the imponderable nature of this gave comfort to the corporal now. He swung in his tracks, alert for MPs, and moved tentatively back toward the café.

"I god id," the girl said, coming out the door. She was carrying it under one arm, wrapped in a copy of *The Stars and Stripes*, and they walked into the ruins together. When he saw that she had had the cork pulled out and just placed lightly in again, he said:

"Clever girl." But she may not have heard him, for the voices had muscled into the cellar with them, maintaining that all was still and all was bright as he eased the cork out with his thumb.

"Daystes gud," she said when the first drink had gone down her milk-white throat.

"Tastes damn good," said the corporal. "What did you do last Christmas?" he asked as the second drink warmed his veins.

"I hat a real nize dime," the girl said, and he raised the bottle for her, and she took another drink. "I vend do a danz ad de gasino, an Umerigan danz. I vasn't suppost do be dare, bekas off de fraderzation."

"I went coasting with my sisters," the corporal said, and it sounded so meaningless, stated this way, that he gave a laugh. "I wanted to say a word or two about silence, if you're interested," he said. When he had taken another quick swallow, he lowered the bottle and said: "I want to try to get hold of silence, but if you get hold of silence, then maybe you find you've got your hands closed around nothing at all. It hasn't any substance, silence, no matter how you look at it, and, anyway, you can't look at it. You can't touch silence the way I'm touching your hair, can you?" He had lifted one hand to feel with his frozen fingertips the rim of her copper helmet. "You can't braid it, and you can't make a ponytail out of it, so what the hell good is silence? You can't even hear it, so what's the use of fighting for something you can't hear?"

"Vell, no uze," said the girl. They each took another drink of the schnapps, and then she curled her fingers up in the split brown leather gloves, and breathed the warm air from her mouth on them.

"That's where you're wrong," said the corporal. The stones of the cellar wall were colder than charity at his back, and the furnace that had once heated a house that wasn't there any longer stood rusted and twisted in the rubble, its door swinging askew. "Once you've got silence, then you've got the beginning of everything. You've got the source. That's what you've got. It's the thing that Mozart used between concertos, instead of using schnapps," he said, while the outsized voices had their say about Nowell. "Shakespeare put big slabs of it before and after each sonnet, and in between the acts of plays, and El Greco used it like turpentine up in that hilltop on Toledo." The streetlight at the corner washed this area of the evening with blue, so that he saw with almost painful clarity how cumbersome was the helmet the girl wore, and how delicate, yet hard as ivory, her young face. He put the half-emptied bottle quickly down, and, seizing her shoulders in the green coat, he went on speaking rapidly. "It's like water to the gills of fish, and air in the lungs, that's what silence is. I can tell you from being in the army that the mind shrivels up and the heart breaks when there's none of it around. But they keep getting rid of it because it does something to the guilty, and everybody's guilty except the poets. It makes the guilty as uneasy as hell, maybe because it reminds them of the eternal hush that lies beyond the grave. And Christmas is the guiltiest season of all," he said. "It's the time when humanity faces the most colossal murder of all time, the most unspeakable crime it's ever done, and people rush out and spend a lot of money, trying to buy their way back to decency again. They cover the corpse up with mistletoe and holly, and they shout about shepherds and sheep," he said, and it seemed to him now that the caroling struck his chest, word after word of it, in separate, shuddering, nearly overpowering blows. "I'd like to cut the singers' throats," he said.

"You mus be a liddle bid grazy," the girl said again.

The corporal dropped his hands from her shoulders, and stooped, and nimbly picked the bottle up, and drank. His feet tattooed like a tap dancer's in the cold as he held the bottle out to her.

"If we did it together, we'd probably make it," he said. "I'd creep up on them from behind, and you'd be waiting at the door."

"You bedder vatch oud vor de MPs if you stard someding like dad," she said.

"We've got half an hour before the shopping center closes," the corporal said, tilting the face of his wrist watch toward the light. "So let's move fast. I want to get you something for Christmas. What'll be?" he asked.

"Me, I like a nylon zlip," the girl said, and the little dog ran across her grave again, and off into the night.

The bottle lay empty beside the furnace as they left the

ruins and started up the street toward the neon lights that jerked the season's greetings in three colors against the sky. Ahead, on the square, the world had come to life with shoppers, and the avenues that swung like spokes from its hub were fluid with the passage of cars. The girl walked fast on her ticking heels, and the corporal swayed a little as he walked, but he knew exactly what he had to do. No German national might cross the threshold of the shopping center, so he left the girl just outside the reach of the heat, with the warmth fanning on her through the revolving doors. And once he had passed inside, borne with the tide, a singular thing took place: the singing was abruptly muted, and the carol singers seemed to be merely humming their tunes above the crowded aisles.

"Amplifiers," the corporal decided, trying to keep the thoughts clear in his head. "That's how it's done. They're placed outside, all around the building, so that they cover a twenty-mile radius." He moved on with the others, steering no course until he saw Santa Claus leaning against the jewelry counter, and then he elbowed his way through the shoppers to where he was. "As the internuncio of Christmas, would you be kind enough to tell me where the carol singers are?" he said.

"Grismas ist von chopping day avay," said Santa Claus.

He was a lean man, but they had belted a paunch on him for the merry look of the thing, and below the hem of his long, red dress could be seen his cracked and broken shoes. The false face he wore was rosy and slightly indented with wear, and the white beard and eyebrows were as coarse in quality as a horse's mane. Out of the frayed, round perforations under the brows, he looked at the corporal with weary eyes.

"How much do they pay you for this, good saint?" the corporal asked, and even as he halted and spoke he knew this was delaying the thing he had to do. But still he lingered, for now two children moved out of the great, indifferent throng, wearing zipped snowsuits, and walking hand in hand, the hair damp on their foreheads from the indoor heat, their cheeks flushed from the outdoor cold. They did not speak as they stood before Santa Claus, but their eyes moved in speculation on the white cotton tufts that trimmed his dress, and on the split shoes, and on the scrawny throat that showed behind his beard.

"Vat you vant I brink you vor Grismas?" asked Santa Claus. When he leaned down to them, the children took a step backward, still holding each other's hands. And then one of them spoke.

"Are you a German?" said the high, sweet voice, the familiar, midwestern voice, shrill as a reed, of child or animal piping out of a Disney film as it passed in color on a screen.

The man in the red gown straightened up, endowed with a new dignity and honor. He stood erect before the jewelry counter, the cords in his neck drawn taut.

"Santa Claus vas alvays a Cherman," he said.

Then the corporal went quickly, nimbly up the stairs. He manipulated his way like an eel through the uniformed and through those in civilian dress, and by the time he reached the lingerie counter, the schnapps was burning even brighter in his veins. At intervals along the thick plate glass of the counter top, shapely legs were on display, composition legs with nylon stockings fitted on them, legs that seemed ready to kick on high as legs kick in a chorus, each with a sprig of holly embellishing the garter that clasped the brief, smooth stretch of amputated thigh. The corporal stopped and drew one finger down the lovely curve of calf to ankle of the nearest leg, and then he tap-danced lightly on, counting twelve legs as he passed. The muted voices of the singers had made full circuit, and now they were back where they had started, and they began their repertoire again. "Sleep in heavenly peace," they hummed under their breaths, and the corporal saw across the choppy, swaying tide of the guilty a record player revolving on a counter under the lighted Christmas tree. He halted beside it as the salesgirl took the next record up, and he laid his hand over her hand.

"Which one will it be now?" he asked as if in idle curiosity. He felt the grin stretched in his face, and his voice was intimate, caressing almost, as he took the record from the salesgirl's hand. "O Little Town of Bethlehem," he read aloud, seeming to muse upon it, and he turned the record over. ". . . Holy Night," he read. It took him only a moment to bend the record in two, and then he tossed the two pieces in the direction of the lingerie counter where the legs waited for the ballet music to begin. When he picked up the second record, the salesgirl cried out, but he pushed her small, thin hands away. "I'm a poet. I'm going to save what's left of Christmas," he said. He held the record high, out of her reach, and then he sent it spinning toward the chinaware. "So let's say about the fifteenth of December they give you three double-faced records, maybe four," he said, speaking quickly before the voice of authority would bawl its orders out; "and they stand you beside a machine, and they tell you to start the singing off at nine every morning and keep it going until closing time. And even if the holy beasts bolt from the stable, and the three kings abdicate in protest, still you're to keep on doing it."

He picked the third record up, but now the salesgirl was screaming, and he knew what would take place. He tossed the record toward the ceiling, and watched it hit, and then he slipped through the press of men and women and their children, and he descended, elusive as quicksilver, against the current that mounted the stairs. He passed the jewelry counter on the run, and through some trick of the eyesight or the pounding blood, he saw two Santa Clauses now; passed the

magazine stall, and the candy corner where GIs stood in line
for the cellophane-sealed boxes which had been labeled with
imperishable messages of holiday cheer six months before.
Outside, the singing had ceased, and, except for the gentle
sound of the passing traffic, the air was marvelously still.

The girl still waited, but the corporal did not seem to see
her, for his eyes had come to rest on a curious group that ob-
structed the going and coming of normal man's activity. Here
was a singular clot of men, its integral units not standing upright, and yet not sitting, but merely fixed in abbreviation,
like dwarfs, like freaks, waiting for some side show to open
so that they might cash in on their eccentricity. But they
were not dwarfs, he saw when he got near them. Down to
the hips, they were correctly, even handsomely, proportioned
men. He counted six of them, and they wore beaked, military
caps on the sides of their heads, and military blouses from
which the insignia, and the authorized buttons, and the
honor, had been deleted. But each bore the simple decoration of a tin mess cup hanging, empty for offerings, around
his neck on a knotted string.

"Dey're vederans, Cherman vederans," the girl said, shivering as she stood close to him on her high heels. Below the
hips, the rest of them was lacking, and the torso of each had
been strapped upright to a homemade, wooden platform,
mounted on wheels, which he could propel with his own
knuckles, bound with leather pads. "Dey're vederans of de
Afrika Korps. Id zez zo on der gups," she said.

"Do you smoke? Do you men smoke?" the corporal asked,
squatting down beside them, his mind swinging perilously in
widening rings. He took a crushed pack out of his pocket,
and he began dividing the cigarettes among the six of them.
"I'll go in and get more. Take them, take them," he said. The
men's faces were level with his as he squatted there, and he
held the flame of his lighter unsteadily for them while they

drew the sweet smoke in. "This is Christmas. I'd like to give you something. I'd like to give you all presents," he said, looking close at their strong, bitter faces under the beaks of their canvas caps. "I'd like to give you something you needed," he said, and he felt in his pockets for more cigarettes.

"Legs," said one of the freaks quite unexpectedly, speaking the word in English to him. "Legs," he repeated with gentle humor, and the others threw back their heads on their abbreviated bodies and began to laugh. They laughed so loud that men stepped out of the crowd that passed to stop and listen to them, and the smoke came out of the veterans' mouths, and the wheels beneath their platforms turned a little as their truncated bodies jerked with laughter in the cold. "*Ach, ya,* legs!" they roared, splitting their sides.

"Legs," whispered the corporal to himself, and he jumped up quickly. "Legs," he kept saying, and the whole thing seemed reasonable at last. "They've got legs inside!" he said. "You men wait here!"

And then he was gone through the revolving doors again, making for the stairway, not hearing the high, wild wailing of the siren as the MP jeep raced across the square.

The Kill

WHEN they first came to Germany with the Army of Occupation, the boy was six, and all through the first year, and the year that followed, the thought of going hunting was there, casting its shadows of longing like twilight across the bright hours of all that children have to do. He saw his father and the other men go off on Friday nights, or on the

eve of an American holiday, wearing their combat boots and
their field jackets, and he wanted to put the food he would
need, and the ammunition, into the rucksack his mother had
bought him to serve the puerile end of picnicking behind the
house, and go off with it riding his shoulders as he had seen
the others go.

"We get across a lot of country in one evening, John," his
father said all that first year to him, or else he said nothing
when the boy asked, but went on cleaning the long smooth
metal chambers of the rifle he had shot the wild pig or the
roebuck with the night before. He was partly American Indian, a small, strong, muscular man with black hair cut close
to his wide, long skull, and copper-colored skin drawn tight
across his cheekbones and the high bridge of his nose. "It's
tough on the legs," he would say, and he would fit a clean
white square of muslin into the eye of the steel cleaning rod,
and slip the rod neatly into the barrel of the gun, and manipulate it quickly in and out.

Or, "You'll have to wait until you're older, John," his
mother said in a dreamy voice to the boy, as if speaking of
something as far as love or combat to him, as she studied her
own young, prettily tinted face in the glass.

The father was a master sergeant, and toward six o'clock
on Friday evenings in the spring and summer, the other non-
coms he hunted with would begin coming to the house. They
would leave their Fords, or their Pontiacs, or their Chevrolets
parked in the lane, and they would come up the dirt path and
crowd into the narrow hallway, and set their musette bags
and their rifles against the wall. The boy knew all their faces,
and he knew some of the names as well, but he knew best the
tumult of their preparations, the stamping of feet from hall to
kitchen, and the talk of ammunition, and destination, and
what the weather might turn to before dawn. He would wait
in the hall, dark-browed, dark-eyed, and troubled, standing

close to the burnished wood and the metal of their rifles, brushed by the canvas of their jackets as they passed.

"Look at them," the boy's mother would say when the time came for them to go. She would stand at the dining-room window with him, watching them in their boots and khaki, their fatigue caps worn casually on the backs of their heads, as they loaded the two or three cars they would drive away in, leaving the others parked in the lane before the house. "All going off and leaving their wives as if they were sick and tired of them!" she would say, her glossy hair touching her shoulders, her small voice filled with grief.

"Maybe they're not all married," the boy would say, standing there in his blue jeans and his faded cowboy shirt, watching them go.

"Sure, they're married. But they don't care about that. They go off anyway," his mother would say in bitterness. It was not until after supper, when the stars were out and the cars stood locked and silent before the house, that she would begin to cry.

And then it was the second year, and he was seven, and one morning in June he and his mother walked down a cobbled street of the hillside town together, and he spoke of the boy's-size rifle that could be sent from a stateside store named Roebuck, if his mother would just sit down and write the order out.

"You'll have to wait awhile, John," his mother said. They had come to a toy store as they walked, and she stopped to look at the music boxes, and the farm beasts carved in smooth, white wood, and the cuckoo clocks, and the reflection of woman and boy was there between them and the things behind the show-window glass. The mother was wearing a pale wool sweater, and a rose-colored skirt, and on her feet were suede slippers such as a ballet dancer wears, and she stood there, chewing her gum reflectively. "Look at that darling little fawn," she said, but the boy was looking past the wooden animals to the other things that hung inside. He could see tomahawks, cardboard but painted silver so that they had the vigor of weapons, with Indian horses splashed in savage flight across their ersatz metal; he could see leather-thonged bows, and painted arrows, and the feathered head-dresses of Indians, and, beneath these, the world of music boxes abruptly died. "I'd like to buy myself a music box," said the mother, and she turned to go through the shop door, touching her own soft, light, un-Indian hair.

The German who owned the store stood just below the headdresses and the tomahawks, but so far removed from them that he seemed a figure cut from a newspaper tabloid and placed, as colorless as print, under their barbaric reality. He spoke English in a way the mother did not, and had she referred to this, he would doubtless have told her that he spoke a better English, for what was she but an American who had no right to the English tongue? He had been a POW in England, he said, as if this were a distinction to which she could never hope to attain.

"Gosh, those music boxes are cute!" the mother said, and then the boy asked her a question about his father's people.

"What kind of a headdress do you think my grandfather wore?" he said.

"Well, maybe on the reservation he didn't wear a head-dress," said the mother, but her mind was on the music boxes with the pretty Alpine scenes done on their lids. "Maybe your grandfather's grandfather, or somebody way back like that, wore a headdress. My husband, he's part American In-dian," she said in explanation to the storekeeper, and he looked at her with a bleak, jaundiced eye.

"These come from Munich," he said, and behind the counter he turned to take one down. He held it before them, the ivory-stemmed, many-colored feathers springing thickly from the headband of green leather, and the strings of beads and the raccoon tails swinging shoulder-length on either side. "The Indian was introduced to Germany by the German author, Karl May," he said, permitting the Indian no choice of nationality.

In the end, it was a music box in the shape of a drum and painted mauve, with a mountain chalet done in light and shadow on the cover, that the mother bought. When she lifted the lid of it to take the powder puff out of its circular mauve tray, intricate threads of music were plucked, as if by magic, from within. There were three tunes in it, and the "Blue Danube" was the one that played the longest, and when they were back in their own house in the American community, and the delicate skeins of the tune unwound beneath the powder puff, the mother waltzed slowly through the room, her eyes half closed, her soft hair floating like a young girl's from her shoulders as she danced. No matter how long she lived, she said to the boy, she would never like anything better than listening to the three small tunes the box contained.

"Maybe when you have time, you could look at the Roebuck catalogue and ask about the boy's-size rifle," the boy said tentatively when the "Blue Danube" was done.

"Oh, I wish you had some feeling for music, John, that's what I wish! All this business of shooting and killing, it makes me sick!" his mother said, her voice coming the long way back from enchantment to him. She moved to the table, and picked up the little mauve drum, and she turned the silver key tighter and tighter so that the music would play.

That was a Friday, and in the evening the sergeant neither the boy nor his mother had seen before walked into the house. He was a heavy, big-boned, slow-moving man who, perhaps because he did not raise his voice as did the other non-coms, or because his eyes, which were yellow as a cat's eyes, moved

from object to object in retarded motion, appeared to function in a condition of total repose. He came into the front
hall, and he leaned against the wall, smoking slowly, his rifle
hanging from his shoulder, his bag at his feet. He stood there,
immune to the uproar of the others, his eyes looking through
the kitchen doorway at the mother in a corn-colored sun dress,
making sandwiches at the table, but looking as impersonally
at her as he looked at the pictures on the wall or at the thin
boy in his dungarees.

"Ain't you coming along with us, son?" he said then, and
he stood with his pale eyes holding the boy's eyes motionless
while the stream of preparation moved around and past them
in the encumbered hall. "When I was your age, I used to go
hunting every Saturday night with my old man. You get some
kind of coat on you and come along," he said, and the boy
hesitated only an instant before turning quickly toward the
stairs. "I'll be waiting at the door for you," said the sergeant,
and he was there when the boy came back with his mottled
calf's-hide jacket on, and they went together down the dirt
path to the cars. The father's winterized jeep stood by the
curb, and the sergeant opened the door of it as if he had done
this many times before, and when the boy was in, he swung
his musette bag in over the front seat, and he climbed up,
carrying his rifle with him, his back and shoulders stooped
within the cramped interior, and he sat down on the rear
seat by the boy. "My old man used to call it going to the
other side of the moon," the sergeant said. He stretched his
heavy, slothful legs across the accumulation of paraphernalia
that already cluttered the floor, and his big shoulders pushed
against the Plexiglas of the rear window, the surface of which
had been rendered opaque by days or weeks, or months, it
may have been, of rain and dust and grime.

"My father tells me about a lot of things," the boy said.
"He says if my grandfather went hunting with us, well, he'd

put his ear to the ground to find out where the roebucks were feeding."

"That was the Indians' telephone," the sergeant said.

"He was a chief, and I guess he wore a headdress," said the boy. "I saw them in the German store today."

And then the father and the others, bearing their variegated equipment, came out of the house and down the path, and the boy's heart went bleak within him, for he knew what was to come. The father was trimly dressed and belted in his khaki, and his step was quick and light as he came toward the jeep. He laid the bag, and the binocular case, and the cigar box of ammunition on the motor's flat, square hood, and, his gun hanging from his shoulder, he leaned in to set these things in place. The muscles twitched in his copper-colored jaw as he worked, but, except for this, there was no sign that he had seen the sergeant and the boy.

"I'm taking this young man out hunting with us tonight," the sergeant said at last from the shadows of the rear seat.

"Only he isn't going hunting," the father said, and he did not lift his head. "You get on back to the house, John," he said. He worked in silence and proficiency, dark-skinned, intent, and, before the boy moved to go, the quality of the conflict altered, for the mother had come on her ballet-dancer slippers through the yard and across the dirt walk to the jeep.

"If I stayed home from the show to make them, maybe you could remember to take them with you," she said, standing incredibly clear-skinned and glossy-haired in the light that had no hint of evening in it, holding out to the father the paper of sandwiches he had left behind. Only when the father turned back from the open door did she see that the boy and the sergeant were seated in the jeep, and the look in her face turned sweet and slightly dazzled in the summery air. "Oh, excuse me! I didn't know there were people already in," she said politely.

"I can't say as he asked me to get in, but I always like a jeep," the sergeant said, and he lifted his hand slowly and took the fatigue cap off his head. "Only if I had a family, a fine little family like he's got, I think I'd buy me a regular car—"

"Oh, his family!" said the mother in derision, and she touched the ends of her soft hair.

"I keep a jeep because it suits me for hunting," said the father, and, having said this, he closed his mouth again.

"Oh, hunting!" the mother cried out; for whatever the time of year, each was possessed by his own complete desire: the mother for the father to dance with her at the Sergeants' Club, or to sit close to her in the darkness of a movie theatre, and the father's longing to move across the fields and through the woods in the twilight of morning or evening, and the boy's longing for the accouterments of man and his activity. "I don't recall having seen you or your wife around the community," the mother said, and smiled at the sergeant who sat in the shadows with the boy.

"Because I ain't got a wife," said the sergeant, stirring gently in his area of quiet. "I'm in barracks, and I tell you it's real lonesome there. I guess that's what led me to take your boy along hunting tonight—"

"Except he isn't going hunting," said the father. He was ready to leave now, and he straightened up, and he had no time to waste.

"Why shouldn't he go?" the mother cried out suddenly. "Why in the world shouldn't he go?" Her slim bare arm in the sleeveless yellow dress moved quickly, and she flung the wax-paper parcel in past the father onto the driver's seat. "If some gentleman comes along who's considerate enough to want to look out for John, why, I think it's simply wonderful! I'm certainly very grateful to the sergeant. You," she said, turning sharply on the father, "won't have to be bothered with him at all. And there's no reason why you should be, is there? You're only his father, and that's really nothing, is it? That's nothing at all when rabbits and deer and boar and things like that are running around asking to be shot. Even a wife's just nothing then," she said.

"Get out now, John," said the father, his voice as low as if he spoke in the quiet of the forest.

"You're hard on him, ain't you, Sarge?" said the other sergeant, but he shifted his heavy legs so that the boy could climb across.

"I'm hard on everybody. You can get out, too," the father said.

The boy and the mother went back into the house, walking a little apart from each other, and the boy went into the dining room, and he stood close to the window, watching the cars from there as, one by one, with the hunters and their paraphernalia in them, they drove away. And the boy remembered another time that could not have been too long ago, for the reality of it had not altered, an evening when he and the father had walked through the woods together, and the silence had parted before them like water parting before a swimmer's hand. The father had carried no gun that time, but had talked of the way the leaves turned with the wind, saying this meant rain would fall before the night was through.

Indian blood, said the father's voice, will tell you to move upwind, and will tell you not to stalk your enemy before a storm, for after rain he can read the record all too well. And then the silence broke, and a babble of bird tongues filled the forest, and there stood the tough-hided monster, the wild, reddish sow, with her forefeet spread, and her eyes of golden glass. "That's what the birds were talking about," the father whispered, and his hand touched the boy's shoulder, and they stood still.

"Anyway, I almost went hunting," the boy said now, but it may have been that he felt the quality of courage disintegrating in him, for he walked out of the dining room, and up the stairs.

The lights were lit in the windows of the houses of the American community, and in the windows of the German houses across the valley, but he had not slept yet when his mother called him to come and eat.

"I made some peanut-butter sandwiches," she said. They were there on a plate on the oilcloth of the kitchen table, and beside them stood two glasses of milk. She did not wind up the music box, but instead she took out a pack of cards, and she and the boy began playing slapjack as they sat there eating the sandwiches, with their hands slapping hard at the faces of the knaves whenever they played them out. After a little while they heard the front door open, and they turned their heads, and they saw the sergeant who was a stranger to them standing there. He had closed the door behind him, and he stood in the hall with the hunting equipment still slung from his shoulder, holding his fatigue cap in his hand. "Oh, Lord, I must have forgot to lock it!" the mother cried softly, and the cards fell from her hands.

"If you let me come in, I wouldn't stay long," the sergeant said in a low voice.

"Well, it's getting late for callers," the mother said, and the boy watched her shake her hair back like a lovely movie star.

"I wouldn't take up much of your time," said the sergeant, moving down the hall. "If I could sit down for just five minutes, I'd tell you what I been thinking about ever since I met you, and then I'd go away."

"My husband, he doesn't care for late callers," said the

mother, but she looked with singular pleasure at the sergeant, her chin lifted, her eyes half closed, as the boy had seen her look into the glass. "What kept you from going hunting with the rest of them?" she said.

"A woman," the sergeant said, and now he had ceased to move again, and he waited in the narrow hall. "If you asked me to sit down, I'd tell you about her," he said, speaking very humbly.

"There's an alarm clock on the kitchen dresser," the mother said, turning her head to look at it. "You can come in and sit down with John and me five minutes, and then you'll have to go."

"Thank you kindly, ma'am," said the sergeant. He began to move again, reaching dreamily, lazily, to lay his cap on the coat-rack shelf above his head, slipping the bag and the rifle from his shoulder and hanging them below the cap, moving carefully, deliberately. Then he came down the hall toward the woman and the boy who sat in the bright, square box of kitchen light. "This is like coming home," he said. He drew the third chair out from under the table, and he sat down and folded his arms in the khaki sleeves of his jacket on the oil-cloth cover, and he looked at the mother's face.

"Get him a Coke, John," said the mother. As she picked up the scattered playing cards to lay them straight, the sergeant kept his eyes on her narrow, white-skinned hands.

"I don't want to drink nothing. I just want to sit here dwelling on things," said the sergeant gently. But still, once the boy had opened the bottle and set it down before him, he lifted it and drank. "Thank you, son," he said, and he looked at the mother's face again. She was straightening the cards in her fingers, and petals of color lay warm under her eyes. "Sometimes a man'll go so blind he won't see the treasures he has right under his own roof," he said.

"Get the sergeant an ash tray, John. Maybe he'd like to smoke," the mother said.

"I don't want to smoke," the sergeant said, but still he took out a cigarette, and lit it, and then he broke the match in two, and dropped it into the ash tray the boy had put down on the cloth. "I wanted to know one thing. I wanted to know the name and the location of the German store in town where they got them Indian feathers. I want to buy them, that head-dress, for the boy." He took the cigarette from his mouth, and his yellow eyes were on the mother's face as he held it out to her across the oilcloth, and across the bits of peanut-butter sandwiches still left on the plate. "I lit it for you. You take it," he said in a low voice to her.

When the mother reached out for it, her hand was trembling, and her eyes were held by the sergeant's eyes as she put it in her mouth. She drew a deep breath of the smoke in, and then she turned her head and spoke to the boy, and her voice was trembling and light.

"You'd better go upstairs to bed, John. It's getting late," she said.

The boy waited a moment, still hoping she might say the store's name where the feathers might be bought, but she did not say it. She was looking in weakness and helplessness at the sergeant, and the boy went down the hall, his eyes on the sergeant's rifle on the coat rack, and he went up the stairs.

That was Friday night, and on Saturday the shabbily garbed offspring of the American Army of Occupation played their wild games in the yards and streets of the community. The heels of their cowboy boots were worn, but nailhead-studded holsters hung at their hips, and the imitation ivory revolvers these encased were bejeweled in emerald and ruby and topaz. Dogs raced behind the fences of the individual yards, yelping for freedom, and others ran with the children—boxers, and

wire-haired terriers, poodles, spaniels, dachshunds, or schaeferhunds, each dog in itself the emblem of the temperament of
the humans with which it lived. Little girls, wearing blue jeans
only a few sizes smaller than those their mothers wore, followed, the shifting center of agitation, pushing their burdened
doll coaches and whispering together, forever lingering on the
outskirts of the games the cowboys played.

The boy was out with these others in the tide of sun, ready
to lash or be lashed to the stake for burning, or to draw his
jewel-studded pistol from its holster and menace the girls from
ambush as they came. The mothers were down the hill at the
commissary, getting the weekend groceries in, and the fathers
were gone—they were off in the wilderness, hunting still, ex-
empted for a little longer from daily liability. The German
housemaids had ceased their work, and they leaned their
strong, bare arms on the window-sills, and, wooed by sunlight,
they called their own language out above the midwestern or
the southern sound of the children's voices, and the barking
of the dogs.

"Lise! Helga! Erika!" the maids called to one another, and
the German delivery men on the American milk truck that
had halted at the end of the lane called out: "Lise! Helga!
Erika!" in falsetto mimicry. The milk truck was khaki-colored
like an army truck, and its windows were barred like the windows of a prison van, but on the rear door of it was painted a
pink-legged stork, better than life-size, with its eye cocked,
half in sagacity, half in humor, and in its beak it held the four
ends of a folded diaper in which were borne bottles of milk
for the children of the American community. "Helga! Lise!
Erika!" called the male voices in mockery, and the men
jumped onto the truck and slammed the barred doors closed.
The motor throbbed, the gears changed slowly, and as the
truck jerked into motion, and the big wheels turned, a wild,
stricken cry was heard on the bright air, a cry so alien to the

medley of other sounds, so wounded in its anguish, that the
truck ground to a halt again, and the men jumped down.

The thing that had cried out in fierce reproach lived still. It
was a wire-haired terrier, part white, part black, which must,
a little while before, have tired of playing and flung itself
down, panting, in the truck's area of shade. And now, still
panting, it made its way across the lane, and its entrails followed, writhing with their own hot life as they whitened in
the dust. The first sharp note of terror had ceased, but a wail
of indescribable mourning came now from the bright-tongued,
dripping mouth, a long, outraged lament for all that was lost
forever, all that must be traded in for death with this breath
or the next because of one fatal instant of immobility.

The German maids were fixed like images of women in the
open windows in the sun, and the three men from the milk
truck stood mute before the spectacle, their hands fumbling
in their pockets for cigarettes, while the dog sought to sit on
the soiled, flattened rags of its hind legs, and could not, and
turned, snarling and snapping in frenzy, seeking to tear the
dusty strings of its own vitals away. Even the little girl whose
property he had once been watched tearless and in silence, as
the cowboys watched. But it was the children who knew what
there was to do. They held the dogs back by their collars,
striking the muzzles of boxers, or poodles, or schaeferhunds
when the high whining of curiosity whistled too loudly
through the eager snouts, and they spoke cautiously together,
as if in church, and then the boy turned to the men.

"If I got my father's pistol, would you shoot him so he'll
die?" he said.

For a moment the three Germans did not speak, and the
dog turned its head again and snapped at its own disembow-
eled and living substance, its eyes glazed sightless with pain.
Then the tallest man, wearing glasses, opened his mouth as if

he had an answer to give, but instead he straightened a cigarette out in his fingers, and put it between his lips. The driver of the truck smoothed his brass-bright hair back with the palm of his hand, and ran his tongue along his lip, and looked at the other men, but he too did not speak. The third man was dark, with a slender, sunburned neck and square brown hands, and he wore the anciently but snappily cut black breeches and the high military boots, now cracked with wear, that father or uncle or history had bequeathed to him. Having no military decorations to embellish what he wore, he had stuck two daisies, with a length of the coarse stalk and green buds, behind his ear.

"Okay, I'll shoot him," he said, his accent as good as an American's, and the boy turned swiftly, and ran through the sunlight toward the locked, silent cars that waited still at the far end of the street, swerved between the last two, and then raced through the gate of his front yard, and up the path, taking the corner to the back door fast.

The Walther pistol was kept in his mother's and father's room, on the top shelf on the clothes closet, strapped in a leather holster and concealed, for safety, under a pile of folded khaki handkerchiefs. He knew he could reach it by standing on a chair. Twice his father had taken it out before him and cleaned it, and showed him how to handle it. It would be loaded, for the father kept it loaded ever since burglars had broken into the house, but the magazine safety would be on, and no cartridge in the chamber yet. The boy stood on the straw seat of the chair and reached into the corner of the shelf for it, and he could feel the blood pounding in his eardrums as he touched the smooth leather of the belt and holster with his groping hands.

Then he was out again in the sunlit lane, and nothing had altered. The maids waited motionless at the windows still; the knot of children had not unraveled; the shadow cast by the halted truck, the Germans smoking their cigarettes, the residue of the dog's life staining the dust were all unchanged. The dog lay propped on its front legs, its wild tongue panting, its lips drawn back from its white teeth as if preparing to laugh aloud.

"You'll have to release the safety," the boy said as he took the pistol out of the stiff, tan, leather pocket that strapped it fast.

"Okay," said the dark-haired German in the knee-high boots.

When he cocked the pistol, the children did not move. It did not occur to any of them to turn their heads or go. The German held the pistol at arm's length and took careful aim while the cowboys stood, holding their own dogs by the collars as they watched, or holding to their scooter or bicycle handle bars, and the girls to their doll buggies in which their soft-skinned, life-size infants rode. And the terrier looked with his unhinged, frenzied eyes at the disaster which seemed scarcely to be his as it lay discarded in the dust behind him, and his bright, young mouth was still ready to laugh. The boy put his hands deep into the pockets of his blue jeans, and he closed his fingers tightly in his palms as he waited for the sound to come. But the German did not fire. Instead, he lowered the pistol, and he turned toward the boy.

"If the MPs come along, I'll get into trouble," he said, the cigarette jerking on his lip.

"But they won't see you. They're not around here," the boy said, and the German gestured with his chin toward the row of houses where the maids leaned eagerly from the kitchen windows in the sun.

"There's too many people watching. They'd all tell who done it when the MPs asked," he said, and he took the stub of the cigarette from his lip, and let it fall.

"But you've got to shoot him. You've got to do it," the boy said, his voice gone high.

"And if I don't get him the first time, then I'll have to shoot again," said the German, and he gave a short laugh. "That'll be giving the MPs two chances to hear. Or maybe the shot goes wild and hits the street, or hits a rock, and bounces back, and one of the kids gets hit instead."

When he lifted his hand to draw the back of it across the sunburned square of his forehead, the two daisies on their tough, green stalk fell from behind his ear into the dust, but he did not see them fall.

"That's right," said the tall German who wore glasses.

"It's *verboten* for any Cherman to have a firearm," the blond one said.

"Okay, then let me have the pistol," said the boy.

He held it in his right hand, at arm's length from him, and there was no color left in his face, but his arm, his hand, were steady as he aimed.

"Does he know how to shoot?" the tall German asked, looking anxiously through his glasses at the other children.

"Sure, he knows how to shoot. His grandfather was an Indian once," a cowboy said.

And then the blast of it came. The boy heard the snarl in the terrier's throat, and he lowered the pistol, and he saw that the dog lay on its side, and the panting had ceased, and the shape of laughter was stiffening on its mouth.

"You got him right between the eyes," said the dark-haired German, and he lit another cigarette, and stooped in his ancient military boots to see.

On Saturday evening, at suppertime, the doorbell rang, and the sergeant whose face they were beginning to know walked in as he had done the night before, and hung his cap on the clothes rack in the hall.

"You shouldn't have come back," the mother said, standing bare-limbed, her feet in gilded sandals, bare-armed, in a pink summer dress, holding to the kitchen table for support.

"I had to come back," said the sergeant. "I've been thinking about it all day."

"About what?" the mother whispered, and her eyes moved on his face.

"About last night," he said, standing big and indolent before her.

"I know, I know," whispered the mother, and the sound of her voice died.

And on Sunday evening he came back again, and, as had happened before, when they had eaten they had a game of slapjack, and then the mother sent the boy upstairs.

"The sergeant has to get to bed early too, so he'll be leaving any minute now," she said.

But on Sunday night it was different, for the hunters returned late from the woods, and the tumult of voices as they started their cars in the lane outside and called out to each other woke the boy from sleep. Once they had gone, he lay listening to his father's voice, speaking from the jeep, or from the hall, and he knew that at least one man had stayed with him. And then he heard the drag of bodies as the dead beasts were carried in, hearing even that intermission in their work when his father and the other man paused to open a bottle in the kitchen, and the sound of the sliding panel of the dresser as his father took the glasses out. Twice he heard the slamming of the refrigerator door, and then the whine of the spigot as they ran the water over the ice trays. After this interval, they came out into the hall again, his father and the other man, and, with his head raised from the pillow, the boy could identify each move they made. Now they were lashing the four feet of the roebuck together so that it might be hung in the cellar from a ceiling hook, and the boy heard the grunt of their breathing as they stooped, the scrape of their shoes on the stone of the cellar stairs as they bore the roebuck down. They made the journey twice, stopping to drink again in the kitchen after they had brought the second body in from the car and laid it on the floor. So it would be a boar and a roebuck, he thought, for two roebucks were not allowed one hunter. And suddenly he did not want to think of the lifted guns, and the animals panting out their lives, and he turned his face to the pillow to keep the sight away.

But still he lay listening, and after this work was done, and the door to the cellar closed, the men went again into the kitchen, and their voices murmured as they drank. It the end the other man went down the hall, and out the door, and the boy got from his bed, and moved in the darkness across the bare boards to the window. He watched the headlights brighten the lane a moment, and the last car go. Now only his father's jeep was left by the curb, and his father moved in the kitchen, and the boy heard the mother stirring in her room, she too having waited perhaps, listening, as he had listened, for the last hunter to go. He heard her seeking her slippers and dressing gown, and then she went softly down the stairs.

"Oh, my God, there's blood all over!" she said, not having reached the last step yet.

"All right," said the father, speaking from the distance of the kitchen to her standing on the stairs. "I'm a hunter, a good hunter," he said, his voice hard, and a little vain. "I'm also a good sergeant. I'll clean up any muck I've made."

"Who came back with you?" the mother said.

"A friend," said the father, and then there was a pause, perhaps as he lifted the glass from the table and drank again. "A friend who doesn't talk out of turn to other men's sons, and doesn't get lonely for other men's wives. Next time he comes, tell him to take his cap with him when he goes."

"Well, I'm sure I don't know what you're talking about," the mother said.

And now the father walked out of the kitchen, and into the hall, and his footsteps halted near the stairs.

"Don't be frightened. The killing's over," he said, and the mother gave a little cry.

"You're hurting me! You're hurting my arm!" she said in a low voice.

"Well, there's the blood on the floor. So maybe there won't be a next time. Maybe we finished him off," said the father, speaking savagely.

"You wouldn't have done that!" the mother cried out, speaking scarcely aloud.

"You'd better not look in the cellar," the father said, and the boy heard him jerk the sound of laughter out.

"Well, that sergeant," said the mother, and her voice was dimmer, farther now, and the boy knew she must have moved down the hall into the kitchen, and had perhaps sat down at the table where the sergeant had eaten with them, perhaps even taken the father's glass up in her hand. "He came back to get the name of the German store where the Indian head-dresses are. He wanted to buy John one. That's all he wanted," she said.

"An Indian headdress made in Germany!" said the father. "Did you tell him that having Indian blood in your veins doesn't mean wearing feathers pulled out of a German turkey's tail?"

"He just asked the name of the store, and then he left. He's going to buy it on Monday for John," said the mother, speaking softly, as if in grief, perhaps nursing the glass in her slender, white-skinned hand.

"Let him bring it here. I'll shoot him through the heart as he walks through the door," said the father, and the boy stood in the dark of the upstairs hall, listening to him speak. "Having Indian blood means the country comes to life for you, even this cursed, devil-ridden country, this country of barbarians," he said. "Not the people's faces, or their language, all right, not that, but my blood gives me what's in the grass and sky and trees. As long as men keep quiet, I can remember all the signs, and all the memories that aren't even mine, and not even my father's and grandfather's, but older than that. I can read the stars the way they did, and shoot just once, and kill with that one shot, because my blood remembers that they did." And, *Maybe she'll tell him,* the boy thought, standing in the upstairs hall; *maybe she'll tell him about the dog, and that I couldn't stop crying after she came up the hill. Maybe she'll tell him I kept on seeing him panting,* he thought, but the mother must have been thinking of other things, for she did not speak. "I got a boar and a roebuck this time. The others got zero," the father was saying, but saying it softly, without vanity. "They haven't got forest-sight."

The sound of it paused, and after a moment, the boy heard him set the bottle down on the table, and the water from the spigot running into the glass. "Nobody can take it away, nobody at all," he said. "I go out in the woods, and it's there, and there's nothing else, and the year, the country, and woman, even, they're wiped out. I'm a man alone, and I need to eat, and I'm going to kill in order to eat, and I shoot just once because I know distance, and light and dark, and my hunger's as steady as my eye. And then I come back to this!" He broke it off suddenly, and the laughter jerked out. "To a hall with a sergeant's cap hanging in it! Listen," he said, and his fingers may have closed on the mother's arm again, for she gave a little cry. "I am my father's son, and my son is my father's grandson, and whatever I have, it was given him, too.

When he goes hunting, my son, he'll go when he's ready for it, and not with a stranger, but with me. Get that straight," he said.

The boy listened in the dark of the upstairs hall, and he thought: *Maybe when the stain's gone from the dirt out there, I won't see him sitting up panting. Maybe when it starts raining, and there isn't any more dust on the road, I'll stop remembering.* In the kitchen, there was the sound of water gushing into the pail, and then this ceased, and the father walked out into the hall and set the pail down, and the scrubbing of the boards began. *Maybe this year he'll teach me how to read the stars,* he thought, *and I'll learn that, and maybe next year will be different, and I'll want a gun again.*

"Listen," the mother said from the kitchen. "I bought one of those music boxes. You know, the powder-puff kind. I'll play the 'Blue Danube' for you. It's the prettiest thing you've ever heard."

"All right. Play it," said the father, scrubbing the wood.

As the delicate threads of the tune unwound, the boy went back to his bed again, and he lay down without pulling the covers over him, and lay looking at the dark in the window that was richer and deeper than the bedroom dark. Every now and then the father would halt in his scrubbing of the hall, and the boy could hear the whisper of the mother's feet as she danced across the floor. Her hair would be floating free of her shoulders, and her pale silk dressing gown swinging around her, light and wide, and the boy felt a sense of peace laid like a cover over him. The door downstairs was closed against the night, and against any stranger who might come, and his mother danced, and, because of the whiskey she had drunk, her eyes would be heavy, like a dreamer's eyes.

"Kiss me, kiss me, John, kiss me," she said to the father, and the scrubbing in the hallway ceased.

"Fix me another drink," said the father after a moment, and his voice was not the same voice. "I'll waltz with you, baby, once I've got the barracks clean," he said.

A Disgrace to the Family

THIS was their first breakfast together, after five months of separation, and, because of what had happened, it was not easy for the father to find the right things to say. They sat in the morning sunlight, with two cups of coffee and a plate of sugared doughnuts before them, at one of the tables which stood on the covered asphalt walk outside the American coffee-shop door. The man was in a suntan uniform, with a gold leaf on each shoulder, a spare, weary-lidded man, with his jowls dyed ruddy, perhaps from the outdoor life he liked to lead or perhaps from a steady, if circumspect, intake of alcohol. He had removed his stiffly visored cap, with the brass insignia weighting it, and laid it on the chair that stood empty between him and the seated boy, and it could be seen that the color of youth was beginning to fade from his closely cut brown hair.

The boy had quite another air about him, a casual, poetic look, with the green eyes and the straight black hair which bespoke Irish blood. His skin was exceptionally white, his nose was short, and his delicate lips seemed drawn and pained, with what may have been for the moment nothing more than bodily fatigue. The gray flannel suit he wore, he had slept the night in, stretched out on the cushions of a first-class compartment bench in the Paris–Frankfurt train.

He and the man had carried their trays out from the cafeteria counter, and now the boy pulled his rumpled flannel jacket off and jerked the black silk shoestring tie from under the soiled white collar of his shirt, and tossed them both across the back of the chair on which the man's army cap rested in the shade.

"Well," said the man. He cleared his throat, keeping his eyes to himself until he had determined how much of censure and how much of love and welcome he should give. "Well, Tar, how does it feel to be fourteen? Only five teens to go before you're twenty," he said, committing himself to nothing yet.

He looked quickly across the cups, and the sugar basin, and the cream jug, and the plate of doughnuts, at the boy, not meeting the clear, fearless eyes, but letting his gaze glance off across the silky eyebrows which converged in a few vagrant hairs above the childish nose.

"I guess I feel sort of responsible," the boy said, and the man felt an abrupt sense of shock that these were the words the boy had chosen to say. At the sound of them, the man looked in discomfort across the well-tended triangle of thin spring grass to the varied and fluctuating tide of men and women, some in uniform, others not, which moved in the sunlight through the open portals of the Post Exchange. "Maybe something like making the grade of corporal when you've been a private for thirteen years," the boy said, not quite making a joke of army ratings, but still with a twist of humor, of irony to it. "How did it feel when you got to be a major?" he asked respectfully then.

He did not look at his father as he said it, but he spooned the sugar into his cup, and stirred it, and picked up a dough- nut in his travel-grimed fingers, and, before he took a bite of it, he looked shyly across the table at the man.

"Well, I can't say I remember feeling any added importance when it happened," the man said quietly, and his eyes went narrow as he looked away into the sun. But whatever he said, his mind was on the other thing, and how he would bring himself to speak of it.

His army friends—the bachelors, the couples, on the same post with him a hundred kilometers farther up the Hessian river—knew this much, but nothing beyond it: they knew that his son, the one child he had, was coming from an American boarding school in France to visit him for the first time in the Zone. "Hi, there!" they'd been saying for two weeks now, halting their cars on the country road and calling through the open windows of them to where he sat behind the new car's wheel. "What day's the boy getting in?" they'd say; or the affable couples, in tactful, casual pity for his eternal loneliness, might ask, "Let us know if there's anything in the way of rolling out the red carpet for him you'd like to have us do." And the man had felt his own rawboned, ruddy, blue-eyed face seek to break its mask of disappointment and bitterness, and give them the grin that they expected, for they had no way of knowing what depths the meeting held of complexity and pain. *In your language and mine,* he could not bring himself to say, *he's been court-martialed. He's been given a dishonorable discharge. He's been sent away.*

"Maybe after a certain age," he went on saying to the boy, who was dunking his second doughnut in the liquid in his cup, "let's say around forty, the pattern for responsibility or irresponsibility's already been set." *But try to keep the moral tone out of it, try to keep from alienating him with that,* he told himself quietly, and he took a swallow of coffee.

"Only you're not forty yet," the boy said, defending him from the unseen adversary of age; and, now that he had spoken out in loyalty, they looked, for a troubled, unexpected moment, with sudden emotion into each other's eyes.

The man may have said then that in a few more weeks he'd be forty, or he may have merely begun eating, with the memories coming to confuse him of the things they had done in other years together, before the name of honor had been impaired. And, as he ate, the fugitive hope came to his mind that now the boy was here with him they might go hunting together, as they had hunted in Maine one season when the boy could hardly lift a rifle; but almost at once the shadow fell across his heart again, as manifest as if someone had halted beside their table and stood in silence between them and the light of spring.

"The people look pretty grim here," the boy said, watching them coming and going through the tall, arched doorway of the Post Exchange.

"It's just possible that nobody gets much pleasure out of an occupation," the man said, eating. "Neither the occupiers nor the occupied. But that's something between you and me."

"After you've seen French faces for a long time, you feel the difference," the boy began saying, but this was the kind of thing the man did not want to hear said.

"Did you pick up much of the lingo over there?" he asked, clearing his throat of the sudden irritation in it.

"Quite a bit," said the boy, with a bite of doughnut big in his cheek. "I like it. I can read it pretty well."

"I thought I noticed a little difference—a kind of accent," the man said, perhaps believing it was like this they might come, cautious step by step, to the threshold of what had taken place. He looked at the thin bleached wooden spoon he held in his hand, his face baffled, looking perhaps blindly at it, and without warning he snapped it in his fingers and dropped the pieces on the asphalt under his feet. "We've got a two-hour drive to the house. We might as well get going," he said.

They walked beside each other, keeping a little apart, along the triangles of grass, past the Quartermaster's Clothing Store and the Beauty Shop and the While-U-Wait Shoe-Repair Salon, to the parking lot.

"As soon as I get home, I'll take this suit off," the boy said, and he might have been speaking of a regulation prison dress. "I'll change into dungarees as quick as I can. You know what I've done? Read all the old books all over again, and stenciled the names of the famous on my dungarees—Pathfinder and Deerslayer and Uncas . . ."

"Look, Tar," the man interrupted, perhaps believing for a deceptive moment that the boy was eight or nine years old again, and that nothing of speech or ease or comprehension had been laid away. "Tar," he said quickly, and in that instant it seemed to him that he would be able to go on with it, and then he heard the voice of the colonel's wife calling out as it had called across the Snack Bar to him the afternoon before. "Hi, there! You see that boy comes right over to us as soon as he gets in, hear now? My bunch of wild Indians wants to put him on their ball team!" she had warbled from the organized, tactful front of pity for one widowed officer's loneliness. "Except that he can't be accepted on equal terms with other kids," was the answer he hadn't given her. "He's forfeited his right to that, my son has," he hadn't said. And "Hi, there!" the voice of the colonel's wife called ever more distantly, ever more faintly, dying to silence at last in the Snack Bar a hundred kilometers away.

They had come to the curb where the long, gleaming cars were parked. The boy drew his open hand along the shining black hood of the impervious car.

"You know, I like her," the boy said, his voice gone cunning again, either with humor or irony. "I like her extra wheel base and her mechanical drive and her air heater," he said, and the man felt the sense of judgment falter in him, for surely it was only the uncovetous who could speak so lightly of a thing which women dreamed of in their beds at night, and which men would strive a lifetime to obtain.

And now the boy rode beside him in the fine new car, with

the music from its radio playing to them, and they did not speak their thoughts aloud as they watched the needle quivering higher and higher on the gold-faced dial. The *Autobahn* streamed swiftly under them, and the man drove with a certain pride at first, as if he, too, played some meaningful part in the car's accomplishment, and then he stopped the vanity of this, and he glanced sideways at the reflection of the boy in the windshield mirror, thinking, in sudden irritation, that the boy's hair had been let grow too long. But that was France for you, that was certainly France, he thought, impatient with himself for not having foreseen it; even within the normal, homelike surroundings of an American school, that was the kind of thing France could be counted on to do. And now that the boy's hair was as long as a poet's hair, it seemed to him even more like that of the boy's mother. Here was the blue-black, living hair that had been hers, and the greenish eyes, and the tender mouth, alive still and close, in the glass bay of the car beside him, although it was four years since she had died. And if France could be blamed for the length of the boy's hair, perhaps the other thing could be laid to that alien country, thought the father, and he cleared his throat, as if to begin the words of it at last. But he did not speak, for it was then, with the needle trembling at sixty, that the outlandish object raced across the *Autobahn* before them, and the tires screamed out as the father swerved the car.

"That was a close one," he said, and he sat back, his blood gone weak, behind the wheel. He had brought the car to a halt by the side of the highway, a distance beyond where the dog stood now, incongruous as a scarecrow in the right lane of the streamlined road. The dog's lean legs were propped apart on its outsized paws, spread wide in order to hold its carcass upright, and its bony, lantern-jawed skull was raised so that its nostrils might catch the scent or its eyes might search the faces of the riders who flicked past. The man and the boy turned in their seats to look, and through the back window of the car they saw him moving tentatively toward them, advancing with a cautious, crablike gait.

"He's looking for someone," said the man, and he added, "He's got the blood of a hunting dog in him. He can't walk straight."

"He's a big, thin puppy. He's scared," said the boy, and he opened the door of the car, and stepped down onto the strip of earth that hemmed the road. "Come on, old man, come on," the boy said, but the dog had halted.

It stood quite still now, perhaps ten yards behind the car, with one forefoot lifted, watching the boy with dark, white-rimmed, craven eyes. Its coat was mottled brown and gray, and through this shabby garment thrust the points and angles of its framework.

"He hasn't got a collar on," the boy said now.

"If you put him over a clothesline and beat him, the dust would come out of him like out of a door mat," the man said. His right arm, in the suntan sleeve, was stretched out along the back of the seat where the boy had ridden beside him, and his fingers tapped limberly, quickly, on the linen of the cover, the knuckles showing white beneath his ruddy skin. "What do you intend to do with him?" he said.

"Well, I'd like to take him home with us and feed him up," the boy said, and, turned in his seat, the man sat watching the boy move toward the dog across the concrete surface of the *Autobahn*, the slender boy figure, with his hair long on his neck, and one hand outstretched, and the thin fingers snapping in cajolement to the dog, which sidled slowly, unsteadily away. And, with each step he took in his bagging gray trousers, it seemed to the man that the boy moved further and further from the confines, and from the correction even, of the inflexible system of which he was himself a part.

He watched the curved, vulnerable body moving off through

the noontime sun, seeing it so clearly as the dead mother, come alive and tender and wooing again, that he feared if he watched it longer his own belief in the justice of the discipline which must be meted out would be drained forever from his will. Perhaps the boy had her love of poetry, too, and her singing voice, the man thought; and the words of a song she had sung, and that he had long forgotten, returned to him, and he sang the first lines of it, hardly aloud, as he sat alone in the car.

"Then put your head, darling, darling, darling,
Your darling black head my heart above,
Oh, mouth of honey, with the thyme for fragrance,
Who with heart in breast could deny you love?"

And then he closed his fingers tightly into his palm, as if throttling the sound of this, and, turned in the seat still, he watched the dog backing toward the edge of the *Autobahn,* and the boy moving after him with his wooing hand outstretched.

Then the dog whirled suddenly, the loose ears swinging like ribbons come undone, and it fled, in one long, unbroken streak of terror, its half tail clapped in panic between its sloping thighs. And this might have been the last they were to see of the dog—the sight of it skidding into the fern and brambles and brush—except it was perhaps even closer to starvation than its jagged hide betrayed. Just as it left the suave surface of the road, its claws danced sideways as if on ice and, in full flight still, it lurched and fell. The man watched the boy stoop down by the roadside, and pick the dog up, and bear it in his arms—the angular, unyielding head, the bony forelegs, threshing in rigid protest—back to the waiting car.

"I bet he isn't a year old yet," the boy said, breathing a little hard.

"I bet he's over a hundred," the father said grimly. "If they saw him in Spain they'd put blinders on him and send him into the bull ring and let him be gored."

But still the father got out, and he spread an army blanket over the linen covers of the big, softly cushioned seat, and the dog sat upright, as stiff as if shackled by *rigor mortis,* on the army blanket, its front legs braced, its bones thrusting like kindling through its dusty hide.

"He looks as though he'd been walking for a couple of months," the boy said. He had turned in his seat to look at the dog as the car began to move. The blade of its jaw and the pallid gums showed naked within the loose, speckled, hound-like lips, and it watched them with a regard that had gone already beyond human wariness, and beyond surrender, beyond man's valuation of cowardice even, obsessed as it was by the vision of eternal hunger which burned in the reddish caverns of its skull.

"He's probably walked from the Eastern Zone," the man said, and, driving, he could see in the dusky glass of the mirror tipped above the windshield how the sunlight glinted across the dog's narrow shoulders and across its chest and brow. And this glowing copper burnish on the hide, this, like the crab-wise gait, was part of the hunting dog's true heritage, the man knew, handed down untampered with, no matter what quantity of tamer blood had watered the veins of the generations that had intervened. "Put a scythe across his shoulder, and he'd do for the figure of Famine in a pageant depicting European culture," the man said bitterly.

"Well, you know, I might call him that. I might call him 'Famine,'" the boy said. He could not take his eyes from the dog that rode behind them, with the sunlight giving an auburn nimbus to the parched hair of its coat. There it rode, as stiff as a corpse on the gallows, swaying upright with the fluid, easy swaying of the car.

The house they reached an hour or more later stood to itself a little distance outside the American community. It was a worn white stucco house with a flat modern roof, and the terrace that fronted it overhung first the garage that was built into the slope of the wooded hill, and then the walled lane, and, last, the river valley. By the time they had come to it, the man's will seemed to have hardened, for he could not bring himself to say "Here we are, then," or "How do you like the looks of it?" but he drove the car at once, and with savagery even, into the garage beneath the terrace, and closed the double doors of it, so that anyone passing in the lane might not see it standing there and know that they had come. It was as final as if he had said to the curious countryside and to the Occupation forces on its soil that the bachelor friends, and the affable couples, and the colonel's wife, could stew a little longer in their pity, for this was not a homecoming. It had a sterner, more official name.

"Take the bags," the man said sharply, speaking German, and the wizened, bent *Hausmeister*, in his starched white jacket, lifted the boy's two worn, scuffed bags and carried them up the cemented garden steps in deceptive, obsequious alacrity. In the entrance hall, the *Hausmeister* set them down on the clean china tiles while he closed the door, with its burden of clouded bull's-eyed panes and iron fretwork, behind the man in his uniform and the boy in his shirt sleeves and the dog with the bones wearing through its threadbare hide.

When the *Hausmeister* had stooped and picked up the bags again, and borne them away up the polished oak stairs, the man and the boy and the dog stood alone in the silence of the hallway. "Of course, you know, Tar, I've had a letter from the school, sparing no details," was the way the court-martial proceedings began, without benefit of judge or jury. And then the man turned to lead the way into the library of this house which bore the temporary name of home. "You know, the school won't take you back," the man said, once they stood in the room.

To himself he thought, *I need a drink, a stiff drink, or I need to go hunting before I can go through with it. I need to establish myself before him;* and it came to him then that the longing to take the boy hunting had never left his mind.

"You know the charges," he went on saying, and the boy said in a low voice that he knew. He stood there in his soiled, rumpled shirt, the collar of it open, the gray, bagging trousers hanging precariously, it seemed, on the worn leather belt at his hip bones; and the man felt his own hostility rising like a tide within him at the sight of the gentle, brooding look which did not falter in the boy's grave face. In the presence of the antlered deer heads, and the tusked boar heads which looked, with glazed golden eyes, down from the walls, and in the shadow of the towering, national pieces which furnished the room—the massive bookcases, cabinets, sideboards, designed by greater-than-life-sized men, it must have been, in order to contain the outsized German tomes, the super beer mugs, the mighty busts of statesmen and composers—the boy appeared even more frail, more vulnerable, than in the sunlight on the *Autobahn,* and the man ran his finger in irritation inside the collar of his suntan shirt, and undid the button at the neck, and tossed his khaki tie away.

"Look. Before we talk about it I want to get my dog something to eat," the boy said. "You know, the good-officer-taking-care-of-his-men kind of thing. *Proveditor, provedore,*" he said, the ring of irony or mockery nearly as audible as laughter in the lightly spoken words. It was when the boy turned to go, and the carcass of the dog turned on its rigid, rust-colored legs, perhaps not to follow him so much as to try for liberty again, that the man saw the boy as lost to the code to which he himself gave fealty, saw him corrupted by some foreign knowledge, some covert access to poetry or beauty, or to love, which made them strangers because it made light of all the rest.

Once the boy and the dog were gone from the room, the man went to the heaviest of the cabinets on the summit of whose accumulated niches and recesses and shelves a mammoth bust of Bismarck stood, its blind bronze gaze not circumscribed by the library walls, but fixed in rebuke, it seemed, upon an eternal Germany which lay, unaltered and unalterable, beyond. The man took his key ring out and selected a key from among the others on it, and when he stooped to open one of the three richly carved doors which formed the cabinet's base, he saw that fresh scratches defaced the wood around the lock. He opened the cabinet door, and took the half-empty bottle of whiskey out, and before he poured the first drink into the silver goblet which hung, bottom up, over the cork, he set the bottle upright on the library table and satisfied himself that the liquid still stood at the nearly imperceptible pencil mark he had made on the label the night before. And, once assured that the *Hausmeister* had not yet found the way to manipulate the lock, he took the first drink, and then the second, quickly down. And *My son expelled*, he thought, as, for the third time, he poured the silver goblet full. *Expelled from decency, from honor, from confidence, yours, mine, or anybody's. You face a firing squad for the equivalent of that.*

After a moment, he corked the bottle again, and covered the cork of it with the upturned silver cup, and when he leaned over to put it in its place, the heat of his shame for what his son had done poured out of his heart and into the muscles of his lean, bare neck, and he knew that he could never face the women and men of his own kind until the boy in his soiled, casual clothes, with his grave, brooding eyes and his ironic tongue was gone again, and his going been explained away.

"The cook say lunch finished now," the *Hausmeister* said,

trying his English out as he stood in the doorway of the library, and the man spun as if he had been caught in the act of murder in broad daylight in the sun-filled room.

"*Ready* . . . not finished!" he shouted aloud, aware that his mouth had gone suddenly dry and that his hands were trembling as he drew his palms in agitation back across his hair.

The shame burned there still, like a sunstroke searing his flesh, as he and the boy began eating lunch together, one at either end of the long table, with the *Hausmeister* in his white jacket serving them quietly, obsequiously. But in the middle of the meal the boy laughed outright.

"I can't help thinking it's funny to have hamburger and canned spaghetti served by a butler," he said.

"I suppose you expected lobster and caviar. I'm afraid I forgot to order it," the man said, and now, drinking the cold beer down, he believed it was some external heat which rendered the air impossible to breathe, and he bade the *Hausmeister* lower the jalousies at the south windows which opened upon the terrace and the sight of the countryside beyond its ivied balustrade.

"Excuse me for saying that. I'm glad to be here," the boy said quietly.

Once the blinds had stemmed the tide of light and heat, and the *Hausmeister* had gone softly down the stairs to the kitchen on the floor below, it seemed to the man that the secret he and the boy shared was closed safely away with them in the cryptlike dimness of the dining room, and that he must keep it here even though it meant that one of them must be done to death in fury and furtiveness, stamped violently and silently from life or else throttled soundlessly into extinction so that no outcry would be made, no passer-by would know. He did not raise his eyes to look the length of the table at the boy, but instead he watched his own limber fingers turning the horn-handled knife that lay beside his empty plate.

"So sixty thousand francs," the man said now, his fingers playing with the knife. "Sixty thousand francs taken out of other boys' rooms at night, stolen out of their pockets, their letters, their desks."

"Yes," said the boy, speaking gravely, but still with a certain dignity and ease. "That's over two hundred dollars. There were some boys there who had too much money to spend, and others who didn't have enough, so it made it a temptation."

"But you didn't need it!" the man cried out, with nothing but grief left in his voice, and at the unequivocal condemnation of these words the clarity and the look of fearlessness ebbed swiftly out of the boy's face.

"No, I didn't need it," he said, his voice coming quiet and far from the other end of the table. "But the boy who took it thought I did."

"The boy who took it—" the man began saying, and his heart moved with hope for an instant, and then he tossed the horn-handled knife impatiently away. "Oh, the one who wanted it for lobster and caviar, you mean?" he said. He had got to his feet, and now he stood, swaying a little, feeling hot and perplexed with ill temper in the close air of the room. "Where's your starving dog?" he said, but this was not what he had intended saying, and he left without hearing the answer the boy had started to give.

In the basement kitchen, the dog had eaten what the boy had put before him, his body arched as if he stood in a high wind, his tail blown forward between his quivering hindquarters, his lean jaws jerking the mouthfuls of raw meat down. But, even though fed, he gave no sign of recognition when the boy went to him, but he sat erect on the folded army blanket, hungering still, and watching for escape. And now, in the boy's room, he did not surrender to the softness of the rug on the floor or the boy's hand stroking his skull. He merely waited, the red coals of his eyes not extinguished, for all their fire was invisible now, but cannily veiled, while the man and the boy, in their separate rooms, seemed to sleep the hours of the afternoon away. But they did not sleep deeply, for, in the broken bits and pieces of their dreams, each told the other the strange but credible story of his life, in which the only experience they shared—except for that of sharing the same family name—was that of remembering the same woman, and of shedding upon her long-dead and long-unheeding breast, one his drunken, and the other his adolescent, tears.

Now twilight had come, and the man opened the library door and ventured out on the terrace, believing that no one would perceive him standing high above the valley in the dusk. He stood watching the evening move up the quiet trough of the country below him, the bluish spume of it fluxing into darkness as it reached the poplars and willows on the sloping riverbanks, and engulfed the river which lay between this delicately wooded hill and the roofs of the medieval town. He felt soothed and nearly at peace and he told himself now that if he and the boy could be left long enough to themselves, if they could keep away from their countrymen, the look of an identical honor might become apparent exactly, whether the eye that acknowledged it were that of to them, unaltered by darkness even, and the contour known warrior or poet, or the hand that felt its quality were bare or gloved or weaponless or closed upon a gun. The thought of hunting had begun to possess him again, when the boy's voice spoke out behind him on the terrace, saying the lines of a poem that he had once known well. The boy's voice recited:

> "Now with the coming in of the spring the days will
> stretch a bit,
> And after the Feast of Brigid I shall hoist my flag
> and go—"

"Where did you learn that poem?" the man said, a sense of sorrow for all that was dead and finished flooding his heart.

"It was written by an Irishman named Stephens. I've been reading his things," the boy said. "And I remember my mother singing it to me. I have a friend at school, a boy called Luc," he went on saying with a certain eagerness. "We've been reading a good many books together, for we seem to have the same taste in things. Perhaps we understand each other because his mother is French and the father and mother are divorced. I mean, Luc's partly foreign, the way I'm partly foreign," the boy said.

"You're what?" the man said in some surprise, but he felt no sense of outrage, as he would have felt at any other hour of the day.

"Well, my mother was Irish," said the boy.

"Irish-American," said the man.

"Well, at any rate, we came to a decision about ourselves. We've read quite a lot, and we've talked about a number of things," the boy said, and he came forward to the balustrade, his moccasins whispering on the gravel, and leaned on the stone of it, watching the tide of darkness rise. "We knew the school we were in was no good for us . . . no good for either of us," the boy said, "and we knew we had to get out of it and start getting our training for the kind of work we want to do."

"And what kind of work do you want to do?" said the man, hardly knowing the sound of his own voice.

"Well, my friend, this boy called Luc, he wants to be a doctor, a surgeon," the boy said. "He wants to go to the right school to prepare himself for that. Perhaps he feels himself French, because of his mother or perhaps the language comes easier to him now, but, anyway, he's found a French school in Paris where he wants to go."

"And his father's trying to make an American out of him?" said the man.

"Well, his father's a lawyer," the boy said. "He's got a big practice in Chicago. He's going back to Chicago soon, and he wants to take Luc with him. He wants Luc to study for the law. And Luc's afraid of his father, so he'll probably go. He'll give up what he wants to be, and he'll try to be a lawyer." There was silence for a moment before the boy added, "But he might just as well put a bullet through his head."

"And you . . . are you afraid of your father?" said the man, and he seemed to be speaking to a much younger child than the one who stood not far from him on the terrace in the dark.

"No, I am not afraid. I want to be a singer," said the boy. "And for that I want to go to Ireland. I want to take a trip to Ireland to find out about the people who were once my people. I mean, I want to find out about my mother's people. There were minstrels and poets and composers among them, and I know the names of the villages where they lived."

A *singer, a ballad singer*, thought the man, and for a moment he thought he would not be able to hold the rising laughter back. *My son, the only son I have, expelled from boarding school for theft, will now take up a singing career*, he could hear himself saying to the colonel and the colonel's wife. Or, *My son*, he might say; *you know, the thief—well, now he's a tenor. Can't keep up with the young people these days.*

He might say it to the affable couples or the bachelor friends, and then he knew he would start laughing, he would stand there, shaken with violent laughter before them, laughing painfully, uproariously and hideously, the sound of it like the braying of an ass.

And now the telephone bell rang inside the house, and the

man shouted out to the *Hausmeister* to say that he had not returned; and when he faced the darkness of the land again, he saw that a few delicate stars had come into the arch of sky above the hill on which the town and castle stood. Nine links of tawny light, like the lighted windows of a ferryboat moored at a pier or the lighted windows of a train abruptly halted in the countryside, shone now between the castle and the river, and these, the man said when the boy's voice counted them aloud, were the lighted windows of the Sergeants' Club. In a moment the sound of the Saturday-night dance music came sweetly across the water and land to the height at which the man and boy stood on the brink of darkness, the far strains of it rising and swelling and fading, then rising and fading again, with the gentle fanning of the springtime air.

"I've been thinking of military academy for you, Tar," the man said, and he looked across the dark, wide cradle of the valley to the lights where the sergeants danced with women in their arms. "I know enough people, so, in spite of what's happened, I could fix it up. I could get you in military academy. I'm sure of that."

"Except I wouldn't agree to go," the boy said, speaking quietly.

"Well, take the army. Consider it," the man said, striving for patience. "There's enough you can hear said against it, and against the military brain, the military code. But, I tell you, it gives you definitions. Good ones, too . . . perhaps not good enough for the poets," he said, and once he had said it, he did not like the taste of venom it left on his tongue.

"And so, if I went to military school, I could be a sergeant instead of a poet, couldn't I?" the boy said, and through its mockery, the pulse of the music came lightly, rhythmically, like the give and take of a dancing woman's breath.

Could they have fought a duel, each for his own assessment of honor, they would have given definition to their conflict, thought the man, but he knew there was no equal ground for any man or boy to meet on other than the terrain of their own separate determination, and no weapons authorized save each his own bleak, unbending will. But it came to the man that if they turned in early, while the sergeants' music still rose and faded in the warm spring night, then they could be off an hour or more before sunrise, each with his gun, and get in the twilight hunting both of the Sunday morning and the Sunday evening, and whatever happened, either by choice or accident, between them would fall into its destined, chronological place.

"What do you say we get up early and go hunting tomorrow?" the man said, saying it casually, as if the thought of it had come to him for the first time then.

"Okay," said the boy, but there had been an instant of hesitation in it. "Okay. I could take my dog along and try him out," he said.

Before he went to bed the boy ran on his moccasined feet down the stone steps to the basement where he and the *Hausmeister* had closed the dog away. When he had unlocked the laundry door and switched on the light, he saw the folded blanket and the tin dish of water on the floor beside it and the iron-barred window, as they had left it, standing open, on the lane. Except that the dog was gone, nothing had altered, and on the iron bars which were planted deep in the stone frame of the window, and placed scarcely far enough apart for a man's hand to pass, the boy found the wisps of auburn hair attesting that it was through here the dog had fought his savage, desperate way.

This might have been the last they were to see of him. The man said as much that night when the boy came up the stairs again. "When they're foot-loose like that, you can't do anything with them," he said, dismissing mongrels, as if they were poets and singers, from the society of upright men. And he believed it still the next morning when they set out in the early cold.

It was four o'clock of a day raw enough for November, and they had flight jackets on, and their trousers tucked into combat boots, and beaked canvas caps, which had been scarlet once, but which were soiled by wear and weather, pulled down on their heads. Two Mauser rifles were rolled on the floor of the car behind them, and as the man drove out of the garage below the terrace, the headlights flooded across the stones of the lane wall and turned the ivy leaves as emerald green as if seen by the light of day.

They came into mist as soon as they descended to the river road, and the man drove slowly, with the drifting phantoms of vapor writhing and twisting like the damned before them on the opaque screen established by the headlights' glare. But once they had moved out of the valley and into farming country, the mist drew off between the rising hillocks, and the man knew that the wraiths of it would follow the passage of water now, and that in the dawn it would trace the streams, and hang like breath above the springs and marshes, following water, as smoke will mark the covert presence of fire under grass and under forest leaves.

"We ought to see boar, at least," the man said, as he drove with the boy beside him, and then he spoke of the personal and unrewarded honor of the hunt, of the obligation to deer and boars and roebucks, and even foxes, in relation to the cycle of their lives. "The rules are there, but you don't get put in the guardhouse if you don't observe them," he was saying. "Every time, every hunt, it's a choice you make for yourself. Either you shoot the doe with her fawn or else you don't shoot her, although they're pillagers, every one of them. Pigs will root a potato field out overnight; they'll ruin the crops of a whole region, and deer the same. But even with pigs you make your own decision if the pig has young."

"I don't think I'll shoot at all," the boy said, and he gave a jerk of laughter. "I've forgotten everything you taught me up in Maine."

"Keep the wind in mind," the man said, driving quickly. "Don't take for granted the way it's blowing. It often turns tricky at the end of night."

The air was clear, but dark still, as they came through the sleeping villages, past the silent, beam-lashed houses whose theatrical façades swung for an instant chalk-white into the flood of the headlights, the geraniums in the window boxes colored briefly and vividly with light. They could smell cattle now, the odor coming from the courtyards, strong and fresh, through the partially lowered windows of the car; and then this was gone and the scent of the pine woods spread about them like the waters of a wide still lake, as the houses dropped away. Trees pressed close upon one another to the edge of the road, their trunks seen corrugated, their branches intricately meshed, but the channeled lights of the car revealed nothing of the fleet, furtive life which trembled in the forest's heart.

"I remember something about boar charging the hunter, don't I?" the boy said.

"He'll charge you if he's nicked and can still run," the man said, taking the corners fast. "Only he's got to know where you are, so it's up to you to stay downwind. You aren't afraid?" he asked.

"No, I'm not afraid, but I'd like to be good at it," the boy said, his voice earnest, humble. "I'd like to be quick and certain at hunting, the way I know I am about swimming or hockey—"

Or slipping into other boys' rooms at night, without a hitch, without anyone knowing who it was until they found the money in your bag—the man went savagely on with it, but he did not say these words aloud.

"The uncertainty's the good part of it," he said instead,

swinging the car along the narrowing road. "There's never any clue given, and no way of knowing until the end whether you've won or whether you haven't, because you never know when or how or from what direction the quarry will come. And there're times when you can't even know what the quarry will be, and what you carry home dead isn't what you set out to kill," he heard himself saying, and he felt a chill of premonition enter his heart.

They had driven due north for half an hour or more when the man said, "In ten minutes we turn off the road," and instantly the headlights picked out a shape which stood foraging in the gutter of still another village street, its thin back curved, its tail drawn close between its legs. Even before the boy's hand had closed on his arm, the man slackened the speed of the car, and, as they approached, the beast in the gutter raised its craven head, and they saw the two fierce blazing points of red which were its eyes.

"That's my dog. That's Famine," the boy said quietly, and just beyond where it stood, the man halted the car.

"You aren't going to do it all over again—" the man began saying, but the seat beside him was already empty and the door hung open above the manure-clogged cobbles of the street. But this time when he returned, the boy was not bearing the dog in his arms, but it walked beside him, the boy's hand holding its head upright by his grip upon the slack skin of its neck.

"He's got a bone," said the boy, and the dog looked in unmanned apology at them, a broad, flat, filth-encrusted bone fixed in its jaws.

"He's been excavating for dinosaurs," the man said grimly, and when the boy opened the back door of the car, they saw the dusty remnant of the dog's tail quiver an instant, as if the heart within the boneyard of the breast were moved by the memory of something akin to welcome which they had conceded it once when the sun was up, and taken away again when darkness fell.

The motor turned softly as the man took the bellied concave glass flask from the inside pocket of his jacket and unscrewed the metal thimble from its mouth, and poured the thimble full. While he drank, the boy stooped to lift the dog in through the open door, and the dog did not relinquish the bone between its jaws, but merely endured as its unyielding legs, its knobbled spine, its whole stiff, unmanageable carcass, were hoisted to the seat.

"For Pete's sake, shut the door! The air's as cold as Christmas!" the man said. He filled the metal thimble to the brim again, and held it an instant between forefinger and thumb before he placed it to his lips. "Here's a drink to the dead, the poor dead game we're going to carry back with us," he said, trying to make it humorous, and he drank the whiskey down.

The boy had closed the back door of the car, and now he came to the front, and he put one foot in the combat boot inside to take his place beside the man who sat with the top of the flask poured full again.

"Well, sixty thousand francs," the man said quietly, as if musing on it, saying it as casually as if he spoke of the time of day. And with one foot on the cobbles and the other in the car, the boy seemed to falter, and then he stepped up and sat down on the cushioned seat and pulled the door closed. "Sixty thousand francs. You damned thief. You damned thief," the man repeated softly, and in the light from the dashboard he saw the boy's face drained of blood.

"You damned drunk," the boy said through his teeth.

"That's a good one!" the man said, beginning to laugh. As he screwed the empty cap back on the flask again, he held his anger in. "What were you going to do with all that money? May I ask what your plans were?" he said.

"I don't have to answer you," the boy said, his voice

squeezed tight within his throat. "We're different kinds of people. We don't use the same kind of words."

"Oh, my lines don't scan, is that it?" the man cried out, and he flung the car into gear in fury, and the back tires spun on the cobbles an instant before they gripped the road. "I'm only an officer in the army! Is that what's the matter with me? I can't sing 'Dark Rosaleen' or 'The Wearin' of the Green,' so you have nothing in common with me! I can't go along with the Irish, is that it?" he shouted aloud.

"You leave the Irish alone," the boy's strange pained voice said in the careening car.

They did not speak again until they had reached their destination, and then they were on foot in the fields, the rifles loaded, the binoculars around their necks, and no bond of speech or love to link them. They were two men walking in hostility, with only the safety catches on their weapons between them and what they had set out to do. Neither the chill rolling country nor the forest ahead had visible boundary or shape yet, but the first was known by the presence of stars, and the second by their absence, the fields and marshes established unmistakably by the mere vastness and stillness of the air which opened wide above. The man led the way, and the boy came behind him, with the dog held in leash by an end of rope which the boy had retrieved from a pocket of the car.

All through the autumn and winter the man had come here with the forester, and he could have taken the direction in his sleep, but because of the drink in his veins he felt another dimension in the familiar substance of the landscape, as palpable as the drop of a precipice or the cold proximity of stone. He moistened his finger for the feel of the wind in the dark, and he and the boy moved on against it, keeping first to the paths between the newly planted fields, and then to the sucking ruts of the wagon road, crossing open country toward the waiting wood. And twice as they advanced through this last brief interval of night, the man seemed to hear the whisper of flight ahead, and he halted, and the boy behind him halted, but if game were there, the dog gave no sign that he had caught its scent.

Later, the stars began to alter. Their color deepened, and they hung isolate and golden and singularly proportioned, the sculptured depth of each seeming to cast a shadow behind it in the lighting sky. And presently the first cold ashen look of morning came behind the forest, giving outline to the assemblage of trees. Now the stars were gone, and the man halted again, and lifted his glasses and slowly, inch by inch, he searched the slowly emerging, mist-threaded sweep of land. And then, without warning, the flickering of life was there, hardly discernible on the rise of furrowed ground, caught once in the glasses, then lost, then caught again, and instantly his hand stood still.

There, on the slope above the area of swamp, was the distant, frantically dancing thing, invisible to the naked eye still, and not of a color with the dawn, as deer or roebuck at this season would have been, but stump-black, and nearly slipping the grasp of vision, a darker, faster-scintillating shadow in ceaseless motion, as both light and shadow of a long-outdated silent film will dance in ceaseless motion on the screen.

"There's a pig up there. It looks like a big one," the man said. As he lowered the glasses, he felt the high, breathless pressure of suspense stifling his heart. He had turned his head slightly and he spoke under his breath, but he might have been blinded to the sight of the boy standing close behind him in the twilight, for nothing was left of past or present except a wild pig which rooted for sustenance two hundred yards away. "We'll have to move in closer before we can get a shot," the man said, and he slipped the rifle from his shoulder, and, with thumb and forefinger, he set the safety catch free. At once they were moving again, but no longer toward the forest, but wading, parallel to it now, through the soft, dawn-bleached marsh grasses, breasting the static lagoons of mist, and then coming clear of them into the channels of translucent air.

The man halted again in the suck of the marsh, and the boy halted behind him, and the man raised his rifle to his shoulder and set the hair trigger, while his eye sought the boar again in the sight fixed to the rifle. And there was the shape of it, grotesque, nearly neckless, sharply defined, and still struggling in frenzy, as if held captive in the gray lens of the sight. "Rooting potatoes out," the man said, and then his shot splintered the absolute quiet of the fields and the marshes, the reverberation returning, like an answering salvo, from the far dark hollow of the trees.

"You hit him," the boy said in a low voice.

"Yes, but that's all. He's running," the man said.

He lowered the rifle, hearing the pig's outraged clamor before his eye quite saw it go. Had the wind borne it the intelligence of where they stood in the wetness of the swamp, it would have swung toward them—snout, twisted tusks and yellowed fangs—in shocked fury, the man knew. He had seen it happen more than once before. It would have given them both, and the dog, the full measure of the fierce, tough-hided power still vested in its flesh. But now it fled like the possessed, galloping, squat, black and bull-like, toward the far refuge of the wood, and the man raised the Mauser again to cover the narrow flanks, the small, speeding, lighter-colored hoofs. Afterward he could not explain to himself what had occurred.

He knew this much: the pig was racing neck and neck with its own annihilation, and then he heard the boy's voice speak to the dog before boy and dog went quickly past him, the dog gasping and crying and choking in its passion as it pulled on the rope. And perhaps, if the hair trigger had not been set or if his finger had stopped in time, the thing would not have happened. But as he shot, he saw the pig plunge down through the vapors of mist, emerge in crystal air, and, as the reverberation of the gunfire died, plunge into mist again. The dog was gone, the boy lay on the grasses, and all sound and motion ceased upon the dawn-bleached land.

"I've shot my son," the man said, but he did not believe it, even when he had said the words aloud. He dropped his gun to the ground and took the hunting cap from his head, and he ran his finger inside the collar of his shirt, his throat reaching for air. Then he walked across the palely lighting marsh to where the boy lay, and he fell on his knees beside him, and his heart had turned to fire in him. "Do not die," he said to the pure white face, as if this order given by an army officer's tongue might have meaning to a poet as well. "Do not die," he said, and he lifted the boy to remove his arms from the sleeves of the jacket that he wore.

With the boy's head fallen, as if in sleep, against his breast, he found the gushing mouth of blood in the right shoulder, and he laid the boy carefully down upon the grasses again. His hands had turned weak as a woman's hands, and they were shaking like a woman's, and he strove to steady their trembling as he took the glass flask from his jacket and unscrewed its top. Then he raised the boy's head on his arm again, and he let the liquid fall, drop by drop, against the barrier of the boy's white teeth. But when he pressed his whiskey-soaked handkerchief upon the wound, the boy whimpered and roused, and looked into his face.

"Where's my dog?" the boy said, and he turned his head toward the comfort of the man's breast and cried.

"I'll find him," the man said. "I swear I'll find him for you." He was trembling still as he lifted the boy in his arms, and walked, carrying him, across the mysteriously brightening land . . .

"Someone else took the money," was the first thing the boy had said when he lay on the back seat of the car. "I wouldn't be saying this now, or ever, if I wasn't shot."

"Stop talking now!" the man had cried out, driving fast toward help through the early day. "For God's sake, stop talking, Tar! You can say it another time to me."

"No, I have to say it now," the boy had said, perhaps thinking there would be just this brief final moment allowed, and the man had known then that the boy, too, believed that he would die. "I had to cover up for somebody else. His father would have been through with him. I thought you wouldn't believe it about me. I told him it would be all right because you wouldn't believe it, no matter what the school wrote to you. I thought you knew I couldn't be bothered doing anything like that," the boy's far voice had said.

"So it was Luc, the one whose father's a Chicago lawyer?" the man had cried out. "He thought you needed it to get to Ireland," he said, with the pain of contrition closing in a vise upon his heart.

"Well, that's my business," was all the boy had said.

Afterward, perhaps three weeks or a month afterward, when the evil, tusked head of the boar was mounted, and hung with the roebuck skulls and horns, and the deer antlers, and the lesser boar heads, on the library walls, the man liked telling his bachelor friends, or the colonel and his wife, or the various others, the story of how the boar was slain. Once the bullet was out, and the boy lay sleeping in the army infirmary bed, the man had gone back to the country again, and, in the light of midday, the recounting of it went, he and the forester had retrieved the rifles, and found and followed the trail of the boar's feet through the mud of the marshland, but the boy's dog was not there. They found the bright, stained grasses where the pig must have floundered a moment in defeat, and the marks of its stampede where it had struggled upright and gone on again, the cloven hoofprints brimming with the liquid of diluted blood. And they had followed the dark, impermeable drops of its bleeding through the forest, the trail of them like the beads of a broken necklace scattered alike on the dead and the living leaves.

After two hours of it in the heat, with no sound but the crash of their boots through the labyrinth, and no sign of the life they sought through the complex weaving of the branches, they lost the trail, and that might have been all there was to the story, if the dog's voice, savage and guttural with menace, had not spoken through the trees. First they perceived the jagged hindquarters, with the copper burnish on the hide, and then the narrow shoulders, and then the emaciated neck, with the end of rope around it still. It stood with its back to them, frozen, one shabby forefoot lifted, and even when it heard them coming, it did not turn its head. Trapped in the underbrush before it, stood the wounded boar, as tall as a calf, it had seemed to the man as he lifted his gun, with its monstrous tusked head lowered, fixing the dog with its evil yellow eyes.

"So for one day I had a first-rate hunting dog," the man would end the story. For, once they had got back to the forester's house, the man and the forester bearing the body of the pig between them, the dog had taken fright at the sight of a woman in peasant dress on a bicycle, and had set off, with his sideways gait, down the country road.

The man and his army friends would sit on the terrace of a summer evening, and while the music playing in the Sergeants' Club came across the valley to them, he would fill the highball glasses up again. And as the *Hausmeister* in his starched jacket passed the canapés from chair to chair, the colonel's wife might ask, "And the boy? How's he getting along in Ireland?"

"He's doing fine, just fine," the man would answer, and he'd take the post cards out. "Here's one I got today, sent from Claremorris, in County Mayo," he'd say, and he'd show the picture of the country to them. "That's where his mother's people always lived," he'd say.

The Soldier Ran Away

THE colonel's son was twelve the winter he started to make the pipe rack for his father. He was a handsome, dark-eyed boy, with a voice as high and clear as a choirboy's, and a quickness, a nimbleness, about him that was in his mind as well as in his flesh. He had a skill for carpentry and mechanics in his fingers, and he could shoot game as expertly as any man his father hunted with. In the cellar of the house in which they were billeted in Germany, he and his father had set up a carpenter's bench, and there, underneath the strong stone house, they worked in the evenings or on half days or holidays.

"Look, Jeff, the idea is this," the colonel would say, and, quickly, expertly, he would sketch the plan of the bookshelf, or the oval tray, or the wren house. The boy would come close to study what he drew, and they would talk of the quality of wood and of the forests of home. "Someday we'll build a shack in the wilderness, a real log cabin, with timber we've cut down ourselves," the father would say, speaking of America as if it were a strange, far country that they had still to discover together.

Every morning a staff car would come along under the tall, ancient chestnut trees that lined the avenue, and the boy would stand in the window and watch the man dressed so trimly as a colonel go down the gravel of the path to wait on the sidewalk until the driver had slipped from under the wheel and opened the car door. For he was a doctor, and this was the routine. At a quarter past eight he would leave for the army hospital, playing the role six days of every week, and two Sundays out of every month. The rest of the time he was a man in a khaki shirt, with the collar open, who worked at the carpenter's bench with his son, or took him hunting in the German hills, or stretched out his legs at leisure while he read of the other, wider forest lands of home.

It was winter, and the mother had taken the boy's sister off for a two-week visit to Swiss and Austrian skiing places, leaving the men with the German maid who came at half past seven and left again at half past three. If the beds were aired and made, the food bought, cooked, the house cleaned, it was accomplished while the men were away. For, in spite of the wisdom in his eyes, the boy was a schoolboy, and after his father had gone off in the morning, he would take his bicycle out and throw one leg in the blue jeans over its saddle, and, his 'coon cap on his head, speed down the wintry, tree-lined avenue. This was their life, the male life wholly separate from the female life, and it might have continued in this coupled intimacy had not the boy thought of making the pipe rack for his father's birthday, which was a week away. He would take the tools he needed, and the wood, and the diagram, up to the attic, he decided, and work on it there in the evenings in secrecy.

"The attic's so big not even our eight trunks take up any room," he told the two friends who cycled home from school with him, and he took them up to see it. It was a cold, bleak place at this time of year, but the boy believed that if he left the door open at the foot of the stairs, the steam-heated air would move up the stairwell. "Here's my Gulf Stream," he said to his friends in his high, musical voice, as they mounted in the current of heat. "We could set the tennis table up in the middle of it," he said, and the friend named Bob Spanner spoke of putting ropes and bars and rings up on the strong wooden beams and making a gymnasium of it.

Two tilted skylights in the solid, sloping roof let in the light of day, and, standing under one of these, the friend called Malcolm Price pointed to a row of carnival masks that hung the length of one great beam. "You'll have company up here," he said, looking at the green poll parrot's face, and the devil's mask, brick red, and crowned with blunt black horns. On the other side of the parrot hung the gray cat's face, with one ear broken and its sharp, white whiskers bent, and then came two great headpieces in papier-mâché. One was a tusked boar and the other a sly, white-breasted fox, to be worn like helmets, with the throat fur molded with artistry.

"I used to collect masks once," Jeff said, as if dismissing the far time of his youth.

"We could have a square dance up here," Bob Spanner said, and he started calling: "The ladies to the center with the right hand around!"

But when Jeff came up to work after supper, the sound of the other boys' voices and the calls of the square dances were there no longer. There was only the sound of his own steps as he carried a small table up and placed it under one of the two yellow bulbs of light. The wood that he would need, and the tools, he laid on the nearest trunk top, and then he spread open the drawing of the pipe rack, and as he stood studying it there was only his own breathing on the quiet air.

That was the first night, and it could not be said that the suspicion came to him at once, but at the end of the first half hour the beginning of it was there. There was nothing the senses could identify, but every now and then he would lift his eyes from his work and look at the row of masks in uneasiness. "You fox, you devil," he would not say aloud, "you are making me nervous." But on the second night he was so much aware of the undefinable presence that at one instant he swung around from the table, and the wood he was working with fell from his hand. But there was no stir of other life in the cold and silence of the attic.

"When you're ready to start in working in the shop again," said the colonel, one evening of that long week, "I have an idea. I thought of making a Lazy Susan for the dining room before the womenfolk get back."

"Sure," said the boy. "Sure, but I've got homework to do," and he saw the eagerness fade quickly from his father's face. Then he turned his head, as if in guilt, and started up the stairs.

He passed the bedroom floor, where the mother so often sat in her own room at her desk in the evening, writing letters home. But now her room was empty and his sister's room was empty, and he mounted swiftly, softly, in his ancient sneakers, to the floor above. His own room was there, and the extra bathroom, and the spare room; and the attic was even higher in the cold. And when he opened the door at the foot of the stairs, he heard the sound of surreptitious flight above, and he stopped motionless, his heart and blood as quiet as if turned to stone.

It was his hand that first recovered the power of action, and he raised it and turned the electric switch, and instantly the light fell across the steep flight of stairs. But except for this one movement of his hand, all else was halted in him, and he could not put one foot before the other and move up the stair well, and he could not turn and go.

There is someone up there, he thought. *There has always*

been someone. All the time I've been working on the pipe rack, someone's been watching me. But now there was absolute silence in the attic, and he backed away, hardly knowing that he moved until he came abruptly against the banister rail.

"Dad!" he called out, but from the warm, bright world below came only the far sound of American voices and American laughter from the radio, and he knew that his father was in another country, and that his own voice, calling, could not be heard. *And if I ran and asked him to come up,* he thought, *he would see the pipe rack;* and he held his breath in his teeth, and returned to the open door and mounted into the cold. In the shadows hung the carnival masks, their faces as varied as those of living men and women, but no other sign of flesh and blood was there.

In the morning he questioned his father. "Do you remember the squirrel that used to climb up the vine to the balcony?" the boy asked as his father buttoned his olive drab tunic over in the hall. "I used to put out nuts for him," he said. "Do you think he might have moved into the attic for the winter?"

"I think he'd be showing a lot of sense if he did," said his father, and he glanced at the time on his wrist before he went out the door.

But when the boy went up to his work in the attic that night, he stopped suddenly beside the table, his eyes held by the masks. Now he knew it was not the squirrel he had heard take flight between the trunks, for the order of the masks had altered. Where the poll parrot's head had hung, the fox grinned slyly now, and the parrot hung between the cat's head and the devil's mask.

The boy looked only for a moment, and then he drew his eyes away and put them on his work, seeking to let no sign betray him. He would keep his attention on the wood, the tools, his hands as active and unshaken as if he worked without the knowledge that a stranger watched him from the obscurity. After a while, he was even able to bring himself to whistle softly, not looking toward the row of masks, but working carefully as he studied the drawing underneath his hand.

Who was it that watched him, he asked the silence. He would be a German, he thought; perhaps one of those Germans who wandered from place to place, as he had seen them wandering in the two years he had been in Germany. He would be a stocky, putty-faced man, with a look of bitterness around his mouth, he thought; and, as he worked, the wood, the tools, connived with the shrewdness of the living to foil him, as if knowing this was the first thing he had set out to do alone. In the making of the tray and the wren house and the other jobs of wood and paint, the father, too, had leaned above the table, his patience making more than the drawing clear. But now the boy's hands stumbled in uncertainty. Time was passing, and the pipe rack was no more than pieces of a puzzle he could not set straight.

He worked for an hour and a half, seeking not to believe that, without his father, he could not do this first thing of his own. Then he went in weariness down the stairs and switched the light off and locked the attic door. He locked it against a wandering German who had no other place to sleep, he thought, before he himself fell asleep; and all the next day, in the big, light classroom, he could see the stranger clearly.

He thought of how the German must climb the vines to the sloping roof at dark. In rain, or snow, or through fog, or in brilliant, icy weather, the man would keep to the chimney sweep's footholds across the roof until he reached the skylight, and then he would pry the window up and drop, soft as a cat, onto the trunk below. The boy could see the German's face, down to the dogged misery of its features, and he did not like the sight of it. But it was the knowledge that the pipe rack was not nearly done, and his father's birthday three days away, that finally took him in the evening up the attic stairs.

This time a shaft of cold cut sharp as a blade across the air, and the boy looked quickly to the roof, and he saw that the skylight window above the carnival masks stood partly open. He knew that he must cross the floor, and step, as if casually, on the trunk top, and reach up and draw it closed. And then he glanced at the wood and the tools lying on his table, and he did not go. For he saw that the pieces of the pipe rack no longer lay undecipherable, as he had left them the night before. The grooves into which the shelves must fit had been expertly cut in the harp-shaped wall piece, and when the boy lifted the delicately turned shelves, he saw that the tedious job of beveling the inner edges had been accomplished. Now they would fit into the wall piece with certainty and logic. There was only the shaping of the open circles of the pipe rests to be done, and one of these had been begun, but not completed; and after that the varnishing. And then the boy looked slowly up from these things he held, knowing, before he saw him, that a man had come out of the shadows of the attic and was standing, silent, there.

He was a young man with a long ruddy face and a light thatch of hair, and he was dressed as any German would have been dressed, his trousers and jacket not matching, his shirt GI khaki; but in his strong, rigid back, his healthy flesh, there was recorded no long and bitter history of misery. He did not speak. He waited, his small, deeply set blue eyes watching the boy with a troubled, concentrated gaze.

"Who are you?" the boy said. "What are you doing here?"

"Trying to get warm," the young man said, the voice hoarse, the speech American. "The night air don't have such a salutary effect on my breathing apparatus." The voice had a sad, vain attempt at humor in it. "You come up the stairs tonight before I could close the French window on the sun terrace." The young man rubbed his upper arms with his open palms. He was big-boned, with a spine and neck straight as a rod, and when he turned to step up on the trunk, the boy could see that the jacket was tight across his back, and tight in the armpits. Out of precaution, he wore no shoes, and the socks that had been khaki were washed nearly colorless and were lacy with holes. When he had closed the skylight, he dropped soft as a cat from the trunk and looked at the boy again. "Your folks, they army or civilian?" he said, and it was important to him, the answer that would come.

"Army," the boy said.

"The brass?" the man said.

"All right, the brass," the boy said quietly.

"You'll laugh, but I picked out these palatial quarters because of the company," the man said, as he jerked his chin at the masks. "That fox! I seen first cousins of his in Pennsylvania." His concentrated gaze was fixed on the boy. "Before you started coming up here at night, I had them heads for company. I had my spiritual communion with them. I'd talk to the poll parrot about my trip to sea. It was okay, except the boat was going the wrong direction," he said, and the wind cried suddenly underneath the eaves. "I'd take that cat's head down, and I'd tell it what happened to cats back home if they went around catching songbirds," he said. " 'Keep to field mice,' I'd tell it. But that wild pig there, he belongs to this side of the water, so I just left him be."

"And the devil?" the boy said.

"Oh, that devil!" the man said, and he rubbed one rawboned hand over the short strands of his blond hair. "It used to get me. I couldn't stand it grinning at me, so I moved it so I could get some sleep at night." And now the wind cried louder and sleet lashed across the skylights. "Look, I made a mistake; all right, I made a mistake," he said. "I got out of the army, and I should of stayed in."

"Well, everybody makes a mistake sometime in his life," the boy said in his clear, high voice of hope. "I was doing everything wrong with this pipe rack, and you straightened it out."

"The evenings was long up here until you started coming up," the man said. "I done something like it in the winter at home, so I thought I'd try my hand. Look, I'm just like anybody else. I came over here in the army six months ago. Back home," he said, "my folks got a farm thirty-two miles from Scranton, P A. Before I came over here, I'd never been farther away from home than Scranton."

"I've heard Pennsylvania's nice. I've heard the country around there's very nice," the boy said courteously.

"It's the prettiest place in the world," the man said. "If I'd of stayed in the army, I'd of got back there in the end. But now I got a hard time ahead if they catch up with me. I made a bad mistake, and I'll get court-martialed for what I done."

"What is it you've done?" the boy said, and his eyes were filled with adult wisdom as he waited for the man to speak.

"I been AWOL two months now," the man said finally in a low voice. "When I got over here, I got so I couldn't think of nothing but getting out of the army and getting rid of the uniform, so's I could get back to where I figured I had the right to be. I got friends here, German friends, and they help me out. Every day I go and eat with them. But I got to get myself straightened out now. I can't go on like this," he said, and the storm pounded loudly on the roof and the wind cried through the eaves.

"Well, you could go back to the army and tell them what you just told me."

"I'm afraid to go back," the man said, "and I'm afraid to

stay away. I'm nineteen years old, so I figure maybe I got fifty years ahead of me, living like this. Seems like it's getting colder in here, or maybe it's because I got a cold on my chest," and he tried to button the thin jacket over his big bones. "Somebody's got to help me," he said, with no sound of drama or appeal in it. "Somebody's got to help me out of this."

"I'll help you," the boy said. He laid the delicately beveled pipe shelf flat and pushed the other tools aside.

"What's your dad's rank?" the man asked in a low voice, and as the boy began measuring and marking the unpainted wood, the man reached out to hold it steady with his hand.

"Well, he's a colonel," the boy said, not looking up from the thing that he was doing, for the first time speaking of rank as if it required some apology. "I want to cut four holes in each shelf, you know, like the diagram, for the pipes to hang from."

"A colonel," the man repeated. "So I been living in a colonel's quarters!" he said, and he jerked the laughter through his lips. "Officers, they got brass instead of blood in their veins. He'd turn me in, for sure."

"He's not an MP. He's a doctor," the boy said in rebuke. He had picked up the trim electric jigsaw, and now he saw the blade of it was gone.

"That's what I stepped out to tell you," the man said, his face gone sober in apology. "I broke the blade last night, trying to get the first hole done. You'll have to put another one in."

"Only I don't have any more," the boy said, a sense of desolation spreading in him. "We've written home for more, but they haven't come yet."

"I can get you one in a German store tomorrow," the man said.

"The German blades don't fit my jigsaw," said the boy.

"Look!" cried the man, and his voice had come alive with

eagerness now. "I got a German friend. He's got a toolshop. He'll let me take a jigsaw out. It won't cost you a cent!" he said.

"My father's birthday," the boy said then; "it's the day after tomorrow. I got to cut the holes tonight. Tomorrow there'll be the varnishing to do."

"I can get the jigsaw now! You wait!" said the man. "I'll be back in half an hour."

"There's a gale blowing outside," the boy said, but the inflexible neck, the rigid spine were there before him. "You better put a coat on," he said, watching the man lace up his shoes.

"I done without a coat so far," said the man, with such decision in his voice, his flesh, in the spring of his body to the trunk, that the boy could only stand and watch him go.

He drew himself up on the heels of his hands, his big legs swinging free, and, like a man forcing himself through the hatch of a submarine, he was suddenly released into the current of the streaming, rocking dark.

When he was gone, the boy looked at the watch strapped on his wrist, and saw that it marked half past eight. He jumped up on the trunk to close the skylight, and a spray of sleet struck hard against his hands and mouth. Then he went down the stairs and closed the attic door. He ran down the next flights swiftly. The door to the library stood open, and he could see his father seated, reading, his legs stretched out. The boy stepped softly across the threshold, and he stood hesitant a moment before he spoke.

"I wanted to ask you a question," he said, and his father looked up at the boy from his far, clear island of lamplight. "Did you ever want to leave the army—I mean, illegally? Did you ever want to go AWOL—I mean, when you were young?"

The father closed his book upon his finger that marked the page. "I wanted to be a doctor in the backwoods," he said.

"Perhaps I always wanted to go AWOL for that. But out of cowardice, routine, whatever you call it, I stayed where I was. But, you know, Jeff, on a night like this, with the wind howling outside, I'd like to be the renegade, the timber wolf, with his tail between his haunches. Listen to this," he said, and he opened the book again. " 'Picture him with his blond hair and his blue eyes, six-feet-three on his snowshoes or in his moccasins, traveling, over rough country with a hundred pounds of supplies and equipment on his back,' " the father read, his voice quick with excitement. " 'He is fifty miles from the nearest settlement and he'll be many miles farther before he swings around south again . . . he finds his way through country no white man has ever seen before, locating his range by a pocket compass, counting his paces, sweeping the forest with his keen blue eyes, sorting out pine from the rest of the timber, studying the soil to judge what lies out of sight (white pine in sandy soil, jack pine and Norway pine in heavier soil), his memory recording this country like a camera. He knows the forest like a Chippewa and he carries whole countries in his mind. Whole countries without a footprint in them, except his own,' " the father read, and then halted abruptly. "I've got to stop reading stuff like this," he said.

"Well, if a soldier does go—if he takes off—then what do they do to him?" the boy asked quietly.

"A soldier?" said the father. For a moment it seemed to be a strange word to him, and then he came back to reality. "Well, if a soldier goes away with the intent to stay away, and is apprehended rather than returning voluntarily to military control, the sentence could be dishonorable discharge after several years of hard labor," the father said. "Is it wartime or peacetime you're thinking of?"

"It's now," said the boy soberly.

"If the offense were one of AWOL only, and not actual desertion," the father said, "the sentence could be of hard labor and time of confinement. But there might be extenuating circumstances."

"But what if he only wanted to go home?" the boy said. "What if that was the reason why he ran away?"

"Well, if you're talking about desertion, and if the soldier is found guilty of desertion, then that's the end of it," said the father, and he gave a yawn. "Whether you do it for murder, or love, or out of loneliness doesn't matter materially in the end. You might as well rule the motive out, as long as the result is the same."

"That's a bad rule," the boy said.

"What do you mean?"

"Any rule that doesn't consider the reasons for doing a thing must be a bad rule," the boy said, and he stood looking at his father with his grave eyes.

"Well, good or bad, discipline has to be consistent," said the father, but now it was the colonel speaking, and the boy knew there was nothing more to say. "An army couldn't exist on a basis of compromise," the colonel said, and then he went back to the book, and, with the altering look in his face, he escaped into timber country, into conflict that had no concern with man's conflict with man, but with man versus beast and versus element.

The boy crossed the hall to the dining room then, and went through it to the kitchen, switching the lights on as he passed through the doors. He set water in a saucepan on the white-enameled, modern stove. He took a jar of soluble coffee from the dresser shelf and placed it, with a cup and saucer, on the breakfast tray. He filled the sugar bowl and laid the tongs across it, and then he sought the silver spoon he liked the best, with an edelweiss and a chamois head in intricate relief upon it, and put it beside the cup. When the water in the saucepan boiled, he poured it into a metal jug, and set the jug, in its drift of steam, in the middle of the tray.

As he did these things, the boy thought of the man who was out in the storm now, and who had lived two months in the attic over their heads. Any night, he thought, he could have opened the attic door and come down and stolen the things he needed—money and clothes and passports—and gone away. But, instead, the man had talked to the parrot and spoken of songbirds to the cat's white-whiskered mask.

The boy picked the tray up carefully, and he came through the dining room with it. From the hall he could see his father reading in his zone of lamplight still, so lost in trailless country that he did not turn his head. But as the boy began to mount the stairs, the father's voice called out suddenly.

"What about getting to bed, Jeff? The women will be coming home tomorrow night, and you don't want to look tired out."

"I'm going to bed," he said. "I've just got some homework to finish first." He was safe now; he had reached the landing, and he kept on climbing toward the attic stairs.

The man came back late. It was half past nine when the boy heard him at the skylight, and he came in as if pounded and discarded by a winter sea. He took out the saw from where he had carried it inside his jacket, and then he pulled off his shoes and peeled the drenched jacket away, but nothing could stop the shaking of his bones. The boy fixed the coffee in the cup, and made him drink it down.

"I'm afraid it's not very hot now," the boy said.

"It seems hot all right to me," the man said, and the boy went down to his own room and took his sheep-lined jacket from the wardrobe, and put it around the man's shoulders, but still the deep, terrible shuddering did not cease. "When I get warm, I'll be okay," the man said. "I'll get the pipe rests cut all right; I'll get them done." The boy went down the stairs again and brought up the two wool blankets from his bed. "We got two nights left," the man said. He sat on the edge of the trunk with the blankets held around him, his strong, flat neck and his spine unbending still. "Working together, we'll get it done," he said, the words shaking in his mouth.

The boy did not know at what moment of the night, or the early morning, it may have been, that the pipe rack was completed. It was not finished when he went down to bed, but when he went up at eight in the morning, it was already varnished a deep mahogany, and it stood, as if in a gift shop window, on the work table to dry.

At first the boy believed that the man was out already, and then he heard him murmuring and he moved across the trunks to where he lay. He was there behind the farthest trunk, bedded down on a mattress of newspapers, with the blankets from the boy's bed that had covered him now tossed away. His eyes were closed as if in sleep, but if this was sleep, it was a state of being so violent that the sleeper himself cried out in protest against it. The boy knelt on the trunk top in his sneakers and blue jeans, and reached down to touch the restless, burning hand.

"A fox'll thieve and kill. I seen him doing it," the man murmured, viewing, it seemed, the endlessly unwinding reel of memory. "A fox'll leave a ring of chicken feathers, and you'll find them in the moonlight. I seen it. Or else you'll find the hind leg of a fawn. Take him!" the man cried out, and from the beam above, the needle-nosed fox smiled slyly, viciously, down on them. "Take him!" the man cried out, his closed eyes fighting for sight. "Take him instead of me! He lied, thieved, killed," he said, his bright, congested face flung wildly from side to side. And then he grew calmer for an instant. "I can swim," he said, with a certain shrewdness in his voice. "I can swim," he whispered. "I can swim," and the boy's heart was stricken in him as he went down the stairs.

Afterward he told himself that he should have squeezed an orange before going to school, and taken the juice up to the man and made him drink. And when he came home from school at lunchtime and found the man's nostrils fanning rapidly for air, he should have done more, far more, than merely get the two aspirin tablets and the glass of water down his throat.

When the boy came home again at half past three, the house was quiet, and he made a pot of tea in the kitchen and carried it, with lemon and sugar, up the stairs. The man slept even more uneasily now, and his flesh was fire to the touch, and the boy's hand trembled as he fed the spoonfuls of liquid into the parched mouth. At five-thirty the staff car brought the colonel down the avenue of chestnut trees, and the boy was there to let him in, and then he stood in silence before him.

"What's up?" said the father, putting his cap on the rack.

"I have a friend," the boy said, forcing the panic out of his voice.

"You mean Bob Spanner, Malcolm Price?" his father said.

"No, it's another friend," the boy said. "He might be going to die."

"Well, I suppose his mother and father have called a doctor in?"

"No," said the boy. "He comes from Pennsylvania. He hasn't anyone in Germany."

"You mean he's over here alone?" the father said, and now he walked toward the library with his arm around his son's thin shoulders.

"Well, he got to be alone," the boy said. "He didn't want to. He didn't start out that way." And then, suddenly, he wheeled and cried out, "Will you give me your word? Will you give me your word about him?"

"My word?" said his father, stopping short in true surprise.

"Your word that you'll be on his side," the boy said, and they faced each other on the threshold of the library.

"But what side is he on?" said the father then. "Don't I have the right to know that?"

"He's my friend, that's all. He's on the same side I'm on," the boy said, and he felt the weakness of crying beginning in him.

"All right. I'll give you my word, Jeff," the father said.

The colonel was a strong man, but even for a strong man it was not easy to lift the violent dreamer who fought the poll parrot and the cat and the Pennsylvania fox. The colonel bore him by the shoulders, and the boy took him underneath the knees, and they raised him across the trunks as he cried out in his delirium.

"He'll have to have oxygen," the colonel said, once they had got him on the spare-room bed. The boy fetched the doctor's bag and the night wear from his father's room below, and, having examined the clogged, whistling lungs and listened to the racing heart, the colonel gave the penicillin shot. "Pneumonia. We'll have to get him to the hospital," he said.

"The hospital? You mean the army hospital?" the boy said.

"Well, yes," said the father, his hand already on the door. "I see he hasn't any papers on him, but he's American, isn't he?"

"Yes, he's American," the boy said, and he stood looking at the man whose head tossed on the pillow, fighting for something as commonplace as breath. "But you can't take him to the hospital. If you did that, they'd know."

"Know what?" said the father, with the stethoscope hooked around his neck still.

"That he's a soldier. That he hasn't any right to be here," the boy said.

"So that's it. So he's your soldier," the father said, after a moment, and then he went out of the room, and he did not close the door behind him, but went on down the stairs. The boy heard him descend the first flight and cross the bedroom

hall, and then go down the second flight. Then he heard him
dialing in the entrance hall.

"This is Colonel Wheeler," he heard his father say, the voice
not loud. "Give me Emergency," he said, and the ill man cried
out as if in protest. "Colonel Wheeler," the quiet, authorita-
tive voice said, and it went on, saying: "I want you to get me
an ambulance here as quickly as you can." He spelled out the
German name of the street, calling it quietly, letter by letter.
"I'll need two containers of oxygen, and make it fast," he said.

The boy had come down the stairs, running swiftly, and, as
the colonel put the telephone arm back in its place, he stood
slender, almost frail-looking, in his cowboy shirt, before him
in the hall.

"You can't do that. You can't turn him in. You could put
him in a German hospital," he said.

"Look, Jeff," said the colonel. "I've done what I said I'd do.
I've taken his side without asking any questions about him.
I'm giving him a chance to fight for his life, and maybe that's
all he has the right to ask of anyone."

"But he's not asking anything!" the boy cried out, trying to
say, and not quite saying: *This is something between me and
you!*

"Look, Jeff," the colonel said again. "A pilot fumbles a
landing, and he's had it. A fighter miscalculates a punch, and
he's down for the count. If you make a mistake—well, somehow you've got to take the rap."

"He's taking the rap!" the boy said, and he tried to keep his
voice from trembling. "He's been taking it for two months,
and he's taking it upstairs now."

"An army, Jeff—any army—wouldn't get very far on that
kind of reasoning," the colonel began saying. "An army—" he
said, but he could not find the rest of what he wanted to say
because of the look in the boy's strangely adult eyes.

"If that's the kind of army it is, then I don't believe in it," the boy said. "It's not any kind of army," he said in his high, clear, almost dedicated voice, and the color went out of the colonel's face, and he turned and walked into the library and closed the door.

Going up the stairs, the boy sensed the desolation, as if, in the silence of the library, the forests of their pioneering life together, the long, running trails of their adventuring, were, tree by tall tree, and valley by valley, to be destroyed. If these trees fell, he knew the mysterious horizon which had always lain ahead would dwindle to the horizon of all men's lives. If these valleys were laid waste, there would be no male wilderness to be conquered as men together, sharing the burden and the hardships as they had shared the dream.

Tomorrow my father will be forty-three, the boy thought. *He is too old now. He cannot understand.*

It seemed to him that he stood a long time by the ill man's bed, hearing only the throttled rhythm of his drowning, and then the far wail of the siren spiraled, threadlike, coming nearer, ever nearer, the sound of it filled with such grief that the boy put his hands over his ears as the ambulance stopped beneath the chestnut trees. The doorbell did not ring, for the colonel had already known, and opened the door. And then the boy heard their voices—his father's voice and the medical sergeant's voice—and the steps of the others—the stretcher-bearers—as they came toward the stairs.

"A pneumonia case," the father was saying. "I've given him penicillin, and I want to get him on oxygen right away. A soldier," he was saying as he and the others crossed the bedroom hall, and the boy stood erect by the soldier's bed, his hands closed into fists. "A young kid who'd been AWOL, and who must have seen my name outside on the door and came in to give himself up," the father was saying as they started up the second flight.

"How'll we check him in, sir?" the medical sergeant said.

"I don't know his name. We didn't get that far," said the father. "Give him mine. Call him 'Wheeler' until he comes around. I'm responsible for him. I'll ride up with you and take care of the formalities."

"Yes, sir," the medical sergeant said, and now they came through the door together.

"He came here wanting to turn himself in, trying to find the right authority, and I found him suffering from exposure," said the father, and he and the boy might have stood there alone in the lighted room, the trees of their wilderness tall around them, the horizon opening wide and far.

French Harvest

A country, like a person, is not an easy thing to return to once you have left it; for if you demand pride of yourself as well as of others, you have no patience with the duplicity of sentiment. I did not come back to France to walk the streets of Le Havre, or Lyon, or Paris with my heart gone fluid with recognition; not this year or any year would I do it, for I had come back to find the living, not the dead. If you believed some of the living who talked to you, the Resistance had been forgotten, and the men who had survived it forgotten, as well as those who had not survived. Some of them who had survived needed arms and legs, having lost their own, and some of them needed pensions, but no one had got around to that yet. Everything belonged to the new race of people, the black marketeers, with their full, pink cheeks and their bloated limbs and the diamonds on the fingers of their plump, clean hands.

There were only a few among the living who remembered still. There were the families who kept the flowers eternally fresh in the vases that hung at the Place de la Concorde by the *métro* stairs—there where the names of their sons were inscribed and the dates when they had met their death. And there were others. There was the wife, it may have been, who kept the ivy green in the little jar fixed at the height of a man's heart on the apartment house wall, with the legend engraved on the slab of stone above it saying that here Louis Vaillant, a *gardien de la paix*, had lost his life on August 19, 1944, after having attacked a German tank and destroyed it with a hand grenade.

The rest of the people talked of wheat—of the wheat that America had sent, or the wheat that Russia had sent—and whether it was white wheat or red wheat was of no importance, they said. What mattered was that it be made into bread to fill their children's bellies, and no questions would be asked as to the soil in which it grew. There was a little woman who used to sit behind the wicket in a post office in Montmartre, and she was sitting there still, with the colored pages of stamps laid out like the map of a foreign country before her. When she recognized my face she said:

"Where is the American wheat? What did our government do with the wheat you sent?"

And the man who stood in the line behind me, leaned over my shoulder to speak. "Is it true that the official our government sent to Washington to negotiate for wheat looked up the wrong word in the dictionary and asked for corn instead?" he said. "Is that why our bread turned yellow overnight?"

Or, in the bake shop, a man might take up a length of bread from the shelf, and the feel of it in his hands would cause the rage to rise in his throat and throttle him anew.

"You bakers! You're bandits, the lot of you!" he would cry out. "You give us this stuff like an iron bar and call it bread!

And you bake white bread to eat at your own tables, and to sell to those who can pay the price for it! That's where our flour's gone!" he would shout.

And the baker would smile a little as he took the frail green tickets and the money, and no matter how many people waiting in line for bread had heard the accusation flung at him, there would be no sign of anger in his face. It may have been that he had heard it said so many times a day or during the week or month that the bread ration had been cut that the accusation no longer mattered to him. Or it may have been that he—like those who waited in line in bleak and still, unexhausted patience—knew that the words the man had shouted out were true.

If you believed others who talked to you, times had been better under the Occupation, and there had never been any conquerors to speak of except the Americans who had come raping and pillaging and desecrating across France's soil. The gas chambers had been forgotten, and the deportation trains, with the travelers who had ridden upright in the boxcars, all forgotten. There were many among the living who remembered nothing of the armies that had lingered on their territory except the GIs who had climbed one night onto the Jeanne d'Arc statue which stands at the Place des Pyramides and straddled in drunken triumph her gilded horse, riding like liberators behind her armored figure, aping even the gesture of the lifted sword; or remembered those other GIs who had removed the swinging doors of the ladies' rooms in restaurants, because of the *"dames"* stenciled on them, and had borne them through the streets of Paris on summer evenings, roaring their shameless songs aloud.

"It might have been better if the Germans had won in the end," the shopkeepers and hairdressers and hotelkeepers could find it in their hearts to say to you now. "When they were here, at least we had discipline, order."

"Look," I said quickly to the hotelkeeper, "I'm going out into the country and talk to other people. I'm not going to sit here and listen to it being said to me any more."

"*Quand même*," said the hotelkeeper, making out the bill, "there was one thing about the Germans: whatever they did in other countries, there was nothing to complain about what they did to our hotel rooms—never a broken window, never a scratch on the furniture . . ."

As soon as you saw the fields and the forests, however, you believed in France again. As the bus moved past the rippling meadows and the leafy groves, it was clear why this vision of beauty, of profligate foliage and rich earth, had turned the blood of the conquerors hot with love. How the pulse of the Germans must have quickened to swooning as they took possession of this country, they with their scrupulously counted and labeled timber, and their highways lined by milestones as cold as those that mark men's graves instead of by the tall lovely bodies of living trees. If you accepted as testimony the full green and golden fields, you would have believed that France was a flourishing country still, and the potato crop and the rye and wheat crop abundant. In spite of the talk of want, and in spite of the drought, when you looked from the bus windows, you believed in the fabulous richness of the earth that stretches forever between the châteaux and the rivers of France, growing food enough and to spare to satisfy the hunger of its people, growing such grapes for wine as does the earth of no other country, perhaps because of the blood of Frenchmen that has been shed there generation after generation.

The house to which I went stood outside the village, a small unturreted château approached by tree-lined lanes leading from the highroad and the broad, deep stream. I had not seen it since before the war, but, however you approached it, it was still a place of freshness and of ineffable charm, with its stone painted white, its shutters gray, pleasing and flattering you whichever way you turned your head. Pastures unfolded toward it from the stream where the poplars trembled delicately in every leaf, and as I came up the short-cropped meadow in the afternoon, there was no sound except that of the skylarks' singing and of the cattle's lips pulling at what remained of the grass. I carried a rucksack on my shoulders, and in the pocket of my skirt was the key to the front door and a letter from French friends saying they were going to stay in the south a little longer, and that I could live in peace there until they came back. I crossed the lane that ran along the garden wall and opened the white door by the carriage gate. Nothing had changed in the courtyard, and the lizards flicked quickly before me between the stones; and nothing had changed in the gardens, except that the grass had not been cut, and moss had grown across the faces of the statues that stood beside the fountain in which water no longer played. Inside the house, too, nothing had changed, except that the signs of any personal life were gone, and, visible still but a little faded, the word *Kommandantur* remained on one of the bedroom doors.

When I awoke the first morning, I lay in quiet a moment, looking around the room that was filled with light. There were yellow rag rugs on the waxed floor, and a single white shelf, with paper backed, variously colored French novels standing the length of it, ran along one palely tinted wall and halted at the clean, white wooden chimney piece. At the two long windows hung yellow curtains, as transparent as glass, which must have lent a look of sunlight to the room even had there been none. On the table by the bed the candlestick stood where I had put it the night before, the candle burned low in it and icicles of wax dripping static from its fluted brass.

"Today I must call the village electrician," I said, but I did not move. Beyond the windows was the music of cowbells, and the voices of rooks as they congregated as thick as thieves in the tall trees of the forest behind the house. I shall stay here a long time, I thought, and in the fields and along the roads and in the cafés I shall hear another kind of talk. I shall forget the strikes, I thought, and the look in the women's faces when they say to you: *What do you do when your husband brings you home eight thousand francs at the end of the month? What do you do with eight thousand francs when butter's a thousand francs the kilo? I'd light the fire with what he brings home if I had any coal to shovel on after* . . . "I shall forget the sound of the hotelkeeper's words and the hairdresser's words," I said to myself, "for there will be men here among the living whose memories will be all of a piece, not broken and scattered through the years."

But as I lay watching the curtains stir at the windows like softly drifting veils of sun, I did not know the names or the faces of these other men, and I did not know the electrician would be one. I telephoned the electrician before noon, and when he heard it was for the little château outside the village, his voice went wary across the wire.

"So you are the friend who was there before? So you have come back again?" he said.

"Yes, I've come back," I said. "But it's been a long time."

"Not a very long time," said the electrician's voice, speaking carefully, warily.

He said he would not send a workman but would come himself, and, within the hour, he pushed his bicycle through the door that stood open in the wall. He was a youngish man, and he carried his tool bag slung over his shoulder on a leather strap. As he stood his bicycle up near the courtyard gate, his eyes looked darkly, sharply at me. He had a gray cap pulled down on his head, and the roses left on the vine above the kitchen window touched the stuff of it as he turned toward where I stood. His jacket had once been navy blue, perhaps, but now it was faded, and there were patches of other cloth at the elbows; his trousers were GI khaki, which someone had turned up at the ankles for him—a Frenchman's legs are some- times shorter than an American's—and he wore rope-soled shoes. He came across the garden, and shifting his tool bag on his shoulder, touched his soiled gray cap in greeting as he stopped before me in the sunlight.

"The lights," I said at once. "I didn't know they'd be off. I found the meter last night, but I couldn't do anything with it."

But he did not seem to be thinking of the lights at all; it may even have been that he had not heard what I said. He had thrown back his head, and I could see that his cheekbones were high in his long, narrow face. His nostrils were pinched and colorless, as if from hunger or suffering, but it did not seem possible that he could be a hungry man. He stood look- ing up at the delicately turned stone of the cornice above the château doorway, and under the visor of his cap his thick, black eyebrows met across his nose.

"There used to be a bat's nest there," he said, and he jerked the line of his bony jaw toward the cornice. "A handful of baby bats up there one spring. That was when the Boche was here." And then he looked back at my face again. "You're not the woman I expected to see," he said, and except for the cold, quiet condemnation in his voice of the other woman who had been here, it might have been said in apology.

The electric meter was in the vaulted cellar where the wine had once been kept, but now the wine was gone, and the stone shelves and the iron racks stood empty. We could see them as I carried the lighted candle down into the well-like quiet of dark and damp. When we stood on the earth floor at last, the electrician took the candle from me.

"I turned the switches and looked at the fuses last night," I said, but I was thinking of the other woman now, and trying to see her as he must see her as I watched the side of his face. He had lifted the candle so that its light reached higher, and, for a moment, he did not speak. He stood in his old faded jacket, studying the meter, and then he slung his tool bag off his shoulder.

"She was a foreigner, too," he said, "so that's why your voice was like hers when you called. I thought she'd decided enough time had passed, that enough people like her had slipped out of the jails and nothing said. That's why I didn't send a workman. I wanted to deal with her myself," he said.

He stooped to take the tools from his bag, and as he worked, I held the candle for him, and his shadow stood taller than a man's upon the wine cellar wall.

"And if I had been that woman, then what had I done?" I said, and I held the candle higher in the darkness as I waited for his answer.

"Slept with them here, eaten at table with them here," said the electrician grimly. "The day of the liberation, the mayor and I and two Americans came in to get her," the electrician said as he worked, "but she had neutral papers on her, so we couldn't lock her up. She was a neutral—she slept with them and ate with them and drank French wine with them, that's all." And then he said another thing to me, saying it so clearly and simply that the voices of the hairdressers and the shopkeepers could not be heard speaking any longer, would perhaps never be heard to speak again. "The Boche gave his soul to the French a long time ago," he said, and he worked with the twisted bits of wire, "and now every generation of them tries to buy it back in blood. I said to the Boche when he was

here: 'They can't be bought back, the things you want, the
things you keep groping for in the dark.' 'What things are
you talking about?' the Boche used to say in fury to me, and
I'd answer: 'Your soul, and your honor, and your courage.
Whenever you won, you lost all three.'"

Suddenly the light sprang up in the bulb that hung in the
wine cellar, for the electrician had fixed the fuses at last. And
now the talk of the Germans ceased for a little while, and the
talk of wheat began again; it was to be heard that morning
by the bread wagon that stopped before the village church,
there in the mouths of the women as they counted their
bread tickets and their money out across the wagon shafts. "If
the harvest is good, the ration may be better next month,"
they said, and they looked at the face of the bread woman for
some sign of hope, as if she, who dealt in a measure with
officials, would know far better than they themselves, who
merely worked the soil, how good the crop might be.

I went into the roadside café with the flute-shaped bread
under my arm, and the café owner told me that the wage the
harvest workers were paid was six hundred francs a day now,
and from behind the counter where he stood he sold me a
bottle of red wine. In back of him, over the mirror, hung the
fly-specked yellowing likenesses, with their countries' flags
crossed above them, of Roosevelt and Churchill and Stalin
and De Gaulle. Men had left their jobs in the factories or
had closed the doors of their little shops for the month or the
six weeks that the harvesting would last, the café owner said
to me; and when the grain was in, he said, the same men
would move down to the wine-growing parts of the country,
even taking their families with them, for women and children
were paid well, too, to do the *vendange* there.

"Besides the pay, they give them a meal a day and a place
to sleep," the café owner said across the two glasses of wine

we drank. He had a sharp little face, as quick as a fox's, but when his mouth closed on his words, the shrewdness went from it, and it was set, like the electrician's, in a look of actual pain. Owing to the drought, 1947 would be a year famed for its wine, he said, and a good wine year was an omen. "It has always come as a warning to Frenchmen not to forget their soil. The warning was given in 1929, before the beginning of our corruption," he said, "and none of us heeded it. Everywhere you went in the ten years following that, you saw how the country had been abandoned. In the south, you'd travel for kilometers through hills of plagued and abandoned vine. Even before the war, we had forgotten how to grow wheat," he said, and in the shuttered darkness of the empty café, he took another swallow of red wine, and he drew the back of his hand along under his mustaches. "Now that we're bankrupt, we'll learn to be humbler, and we'll learn to grow wheat again," he said. As he talked, the prosperity of France seemed to lie just ahead, no further away than next year or the year after that, and, for a moment, there seemed no further cause for fear.

The second night as I lay in bed in the darkened house, I felt the moonlight like a presence in the garden, and because of it I could not sleep. I lay watching the panel of the open window at which the curtains had ceased to stir, and in which the light stood milky as dawn, and I thought of the armies that had passed along the highroad beyond the pasture and the stream, and the men who had turned off the highway to come here and sleep—first the Germans advancing, and then the Germans in retreat, and then the Americans coming. I thought of how the sound of their feet must have been on the stones of the courtyard and across the waxed floors of these rooms; and it was then, in the bright, calm silence, that I heard the voices speaking in the lane beyond the garden wall.

"Heil Hitler! Geht's gut?" the first voice said, and the other answered:

"Heil Hitler! Wie die Erde dürstet!"

For a moment, I did not believe in the voices. I got quietly from bed, and crossed barefooted to the window. I stood a little to one side of the brilliance, looking down across the garden and the lane. The moon could not be seen, and the clear, cold light of it seemed to rise as evenly as water from the garden paths and from the soft deep grasses of the orchard; it mounted the whitened stones of the wall and poured out across the lane and the short-cropped pastureland. The alleys of trees that led away to the stream were no longer conduits of darkness, for the leaves were lacquered with light, and the trunks themselves and the boughs were lambent and as smooth as sculptured stone. And then I saw the two men standing just beyond the garden wall in the moonlit lane. Their heads were bare, and, in the warmth of the night, their shirt sleeves were rolled up from their forearms. They must have called out at first at a little distance from each other, for now that they stood close I could hear the murmur of their talk, but I could not hear the words they said. But even with the sight of them below me in the countryside washed marvelously clear with light, I still did not believe in the language they had spoken, or in the greeting they had given. I did not believe that a voice had said in German in the hot European night: *The earth is thirsting*, or *How parched the earth is*, or *The earth is parched for rain*. It was because of the memory of the armies that had passed by these walls that I had seemed to hear men's voices greet the dead, I thought; or it was an echo of other years that the stones returned now, and I waited by the window. In a little while, the two men moved off through the moonlight together, and I could hear the sound of their boots like the steps of living men upon the thirsting soil.

And *ne l'oubliez pas*—don't you forget it—they were living men, the café owner said when I told him of it; and that was their native tongue they spoke, and those certainly the words they said. I met him the next afternoon by the pump as he set out to look for fodder for the rabbits he kept behind his house, and when he saw me, he set down the wheelbarrow handles and shook my hand. Here in the open, he seemed a tougher, more muscular man than he had before, and his eyes were quick and brown. He wore a beret low on his brow, and his eyebrows and the hair in his ears and the mustaches on his lip were as bright and dry as fire springing across his face. In the seams of his strong, short neck, nailheads of dirt had been driven, and they studded as well the nostrils of his pointed nose.

"If you go as far as the farmer's market place, you'll see them—the German prisoners," he said, and you knew from the sound of his words that his memory had not split in two. His jacket was black alpaca, polished high, with the faded ribbon of the *Croix de guerre* fixed in the left lapel. As we walked out of the little cobbled square where the single, ancient dark-leafed tree and the pump beside it made an oasis of shade and damp in the desert of the stones and streets, you could see that his gray and black-striped trousers—like those that a diplomat of another era might have worn—were patched across the seat. Along the walls of the country lanes were posters, some showing a fat bag of grain and some a richly burdened spray of wheat, with legends saying: *Deliver your wheat—ALL of your wheat! Deliver it NOW to give your country bread!* "We lost too many in both wars, and so now we need help in the fields," the café owner said. "Dead men can't work the soil. They only fertilize it," he said, and the wheel of the barrow he pushed before him cried aloud as it turned in the ruts of the road.

Now the wheat had been cut; it lay in field after field on either side as we followed the wagon roads, with the wagon tracks carved deep in the hard-baked soil. And now the men worked at binding it into sheafs, scattered groups of them to be seen as far as the eye could reach, their backs bent under the solid weight of sunshine. Above them, flapping black above the burning golden world, the crows flew, cawing singly, hovering like vultures above a plagued and dying continent. For the first time in the memory of the country people, said the café owner as we walked, horses had dropped dead in the fields before the plow this summer. He said that last week a man who had come from the mountains had told him that even the glaciers were shrinking slowly in their beds, their substance pouring from them like a man's blood running dry. This year the rivers of France had become too shallow to move the shipping from one port to another so that now throughout the country you saw the canal boats lying idle between the locks. Coal could not be moved from one place to another, he said, and potatoes lay rotting where they were. And he spoke of another thing: of the sugar that went by truck, at night, clandestinely into Germany, and, as he talked, the iron wheel of the barrow he pushed cried out as if in pain.

We had come in sight of the farmer's market place when the first German prisoner, his strong, tanned torso bare, came down the wagon road toward us, walking slowly along the wheel ruts. He carried a spraying machine strapped to his naked back, and, as he approached, it could be seen that he was a handsome dark-eyed boy not twenty yet, with thick black curls and a rosy face. Over his torso and his cheeks and hair, and over the canvas trousers and the broken shoes on his feet, a delicate film of white had been cast by the spray, but, for a moment, it seemed that he had in some profligate gesture of irony been powdered with the flour that no Frenchman could buy. When we passed near to one another on the road, the German boy smiled a little hesitantly at us, and then he shyly turned his finely powdered, ignorant face away. The café owner, still pushing the wheelbarrow, jerked his chin in his direction, but his eyes did not falter; no word was uttered in greeting, and in silence we passed by.

"There're twenty of them working at the farmer's wholesale market place," the café owner said as we followed the wagon trail where it led beneath the apple trees. Now and again, we stopped for a little to pull at the vines that clung to the roadside rocks, and we piled onto the barrow these winding garlands of dusty green. The rabbits' hearts would shrivel in their breasts at the sight of it, I thought, for the leaves of the vine were dry to the touch, and the sap had hardened in its veins. "They must have taken that one out of the classroom to put the uniform on him," the café owner said, and for the first time the sound of bitterness was in his voice. "He's a child, but child or not, there's no reason for any of us to pass the time of day with him. *Bon jours* didn't come so easy in 1944. You couldn't hear them very well above the gunfire executing hostages," he said, and his hands pulled fiercely at the vine.

Now we could see the rest of the prisoners, the far line of them working like men on a chain gang, with their naked backs bowed over the fallen wheat. There, against a backdrop of yellowing birches, the far line of bowed enemy figures harvested the grain for France this year as they had foraged the same grain in the years of the Occupation that were scarcely past. There they bowed in labor above this coveted soil, as if giving aid to the stricken or the dead, their toil mingling now with the toil of Frenchmen in singular, silent union, as their blood had, through generations, never ceased to mingle in violence with French blood. And *wie die Erde dürstet!* said the memory of the prisoner's voice, speaking softly across the land.

"They've lived here three years or more as Frenchmen live," I said. I was looking for pimpernel flowers among the tall weeds we had broken, for, even though faded, they might bring death to the rabbits who waited in their cages, their fleetness and nimbleness subdued behind the wire to a crouched, trembling expectancy.

"Next month the prisoners will be repatriated," the café owner said. He stood looking away at the far, bowed line of them, his mustaches burning across the side of his foxlike face and a tuft of fiery down springing from his ear. "They will go back having learned one thing. They will have learned that the story they were always told of France's soil being richer than that of their own country is true, and they will remember it, and they will not sleep easy until they can return—but not to return as prisoners," he said, and as he stooped to pick up the handles of the wheelbarrow again, the look of shrewdness had gone from his face, and only the look of grief was there.

From here it was not far to the farmer's market place. It lay just ahead, basking in peace in the embrace of a winding, low stone wall. The road that we followed led to the gates of the farm and through them, and there five black Great Danes, as large as deer, perceived our coming and leaped upright before their thatch-roofed kennels, their shining flanks quivering. They bayed and slobbered in outrage, and strained at the ends of their chains as we passed them by. The main buildings of the farm formed a fortress in themselves within the outer wall, and the bridge we crossed to the three-sided courtyard may have been a drawbridge once, but now ducks lay in the shade that it cast into the dust-filled moat below. The courtyard that opened before us was as clean as a freshly swept room, and the wall of strong, gabled buildings held it fast. On either side, as one entered, stood the watering troughs for the livestock, with the miracle of water lying untroubled in their mossy depths and pink-tiled roofs standing over them to keep them from the sun. Here, by the shaded pump, the café owner set down the legs of the wheelbarrow; he turned and looked with satisfaction around the orderly place.

The first building to the left was that which housed the sheep, and the upper halves of the handsome oak doors stood open so that as we approached we saw the multitudinous faces of the flock within. They lifted their heads and looked at us, as silent as spectators in a motion-picture theatre, their small chins shifting as they chewed, their weak, pale eyes fixed on the screen of sunlight on which we had appeared. Next to the sheep, in the same unbroken block, came the dairy, with the tall, clean milk cans visible, standing in shining pillars in the partial dark. Beyond that, the barn, with no pile of manure before its doors, made the angle of the corner; and next to the barn was the farmhouse itself, adjoining it, so that in winter the warmth from the cattle might lean against it in a strong, fragrant wall. The farmhouse ran the full width of the courtyard, flanked on both sides by its auxiliary buildings. Only the lace curtains and the pots of geraniums at the barred windows of the lower floor distinguished it from the other buildings, for it was like them in height, and the pink tiles of its gabled roof were the same, and its substance the same grayish stone. And there was another difference: the lofts beneath the eaves of the other buildings could be seen to be packed with fodder of alfalfa and dark clover heads, for the loft doors stood open, while under the eaves of the farmhouse was the honeycomb of the pigeon-cote, and the high façade of its circular openings murmured with their voices, and the lime-hung ledges were aflutter with quick-winged pigeon life.

On the other flank of the farmhouse lay the stables, and

in the shaft of sunlight that fell across the open doorway, the great tasseled fetlocks and the hoofs of the work horses could be seen as they stamped at flies in the stable's shade. Then came the poultry houses and runs, as finely equipped as aviaries; and next to them the well-stocked wood house, and the lofty wagon shed, in which the farm implements and the vehicles were arranged. Everything was in order in the shed as well: the plowshares scraped clean of the earth through which they had traveled, and the planks of the ancient farm carts scrubbed white as fresh, sawed timber; but in this country where, in eight years, little had been produced for the use of its own people and little replaced, the iron-bound wheels of the wagons were warped to another shape from use.

The farmer's wife came out the door to greet us, a blondish-haired woman, still under forty, who wore a dark-flowered, long-sleeved apron, and black cotton stockings on her well-turned legs, and black felt bedroom slippers on her feet. She said *bon jour*, but there was no look of pleasure in her flushed, amber-eyed face, and she gave us each in turn a damp, limp hand.

"So things are not going well?" asked the café owner, and she shook her head. "A little water wouldn't hurt any, would it?" said the café owner, with what might have been taken for humor.

"If it came now, it would come too late," said the farmer's wife.

"Not too late for the autumn sowing," the café owner said. A piece of blond hair had come down across the woman's perspiring brow and cheek, and she set it back with the fingers of one hand. Her husband was out in the fields with the workers, she told us, and the café owner said we had not come to call, but that we were out after rabbit fodder and had just happened to pass by. "Next month you'll be twenty workers short," he added.

"We're going to have trouble getting the planting done without them," the farmer's wife said. "First they stop the rain with their atomic bomb, and then they tell us we have to send the German prisoners away." A black and white puppy, bowlegged and as soft as suet, came out the door from under her skirts. The agitation of his outsized tail unbalanced him, and he fell down the one step and onto the cobbles of the courtyard, still wagging his tail as he fell. "They keep everything clean. They've been disciplined. We'll never find anything like that here," she said, and she stooped to pick up the soft, fat puppy, turned him over, and set him upright on his paws.

"What kind of men are they?" I asked her. She looked at me slowly for a moment, her fingers setting the pins straight in her hair.

"There're two kinds that I know of," she said. "There're the old ones and the young."

"And what do they talk about?" I said, and the farmer's wife looked at me slowly for another moment.

"The old ones talk of going home," she said, considering it. "The young ones talk of Hitler. They say if we had a dictator, we'd be better off in France." She turned her amber, heavily lidded eyes toward the café owner. "Maybe they're right. You hear so many people saying it that maybe there's some truth in it. Maybe we need a dictator to straighten the country out," she said.

The café owner looked out over the courtyard, and over the bridge, and over the dusty wagon road that led away beyond it, his eyes seeking beyond the apple trees to the parched fields, seeking far across the thirsting earth of France.

"No," he said. "Our needs are simpler than that. Do not let them confuse you. We need wheat, we need grain, we need rain."

Perhaps it was not until the very last days of the harvest that the women of the village believed in the failure of the wheat. They knew of the frost that had blighted it when the crop was young, and they saw the cabbage plants mounting like palm trees, row after row of them in the fields; they saw the leaves of the potato plants turned to scorched paper by the sun; but in spite of the signs their faith in the wheat had not yet left them. It was with them still on the Saturday night when the village fete began. The carousel and the shooting gallery and the nougat booths had come in their motorized caravans the day before, the train of them as shabby as a convoy of gypsies coming up the road. Even the dance pavilion was brought on a caravan, one that had been a Paris bus, they said, perhaps twenty years before; and owing to the length of the boards and the poles lashed to its trailer, it took the curves slowly, and its motor died twice as it came up the hill. On Friday evening, the caravans drew up beside the commons that lay between the mayor's house and the church, and, as darkness moved across the country, the thin blue threads of smoke from the caravan kitchens faded, and the separate glow of their fires could be seen in the still night air. The troupers dined late, and they did not begin to drive their stakes into the ground until the moon rose, and then the planks and the beams and the grim paraphernalia of festivity were unloaded from the vans. The frame of the shooting-gallery scene, and the fortune-telling wheel, and the tiers of the prize-winning booths were lifted out, and from the road you could see the horses of the merry-go-round with their forelegs arched and the curved-neck swans as they lay, sculptured to singular fantasy and beauty by the moonlight, in static flight upon the dew-wet grass.

And then, on Saturday night, the dancing began to the sound of the accordions, and the young men of the countryside came into the dim yellow light of the tent, wearing suits and shoes so new that it seemed they had never been worn before. There were those who had brought their wives in pale silk short dresses with them, and they paid for their strips of tickets at the entrance and guided their wives carefully in their arms as they moved across the boards. The others chose partners from the row of girls seated in chairs along the canvas wall. Above the collars of their shirts, the backs of the young men's necks were red from the seasons of sun, and the black of the soil was in their nails still as they held the women close to them. The sweat shone on their faces, and the pavilion shook with the weight of their steps as they danced in the heat and tumult on the crowded floor. And "a little water wouldn't hurt any," the men might say to each other in greeting, thinking of the fields still. It was only later when they had drunk well at the café that the dancing grew wilder, and they began to think of love.

"You have to dance until five o'clock in the morning," said the electrician, and we danced together. He was dressed elegantly now, in a dark green suit, with his thick hair back in a cowlick from his brow. "On the two nights of the fete, you have to dance until five in the morning," he said, and he danced quickly and well in his narrow, pointed brown shoes, with his shoulders hunched a little. "During four years there were no fetes, and we didn't dance," he said, "so now there are four years out of our lives that we have to make up for."

In between dances the measure of the accordions ceased in the tent, and then the music of the carousel could be heard as it turned outside in the breathless night. The men would go under the canvas flap and cross to the café to drink again, and the girls would sit down on the chairs and wipe their faces, and talk and laugh among themselves as they waited for the melodious breathing of the accordions to begin again, and for the men to return and take them in their arms.

"Let's go to the café and have a glass," said the electrician.

Outside, the merry-go-round was turning, its jeweled canopy overhead and its glass panels glittering with light. Above the sound of its pianola playing, one could hear the clear high "ping" from the shooting gallery as a clay pipe or a bird went down. And on the revolving white horses and the swans of the carousel, young lovers rode with their arms about each other, and others, on the plush-covered seats of the ornamented sleighs, kissed gently, mouth to mouth. As we passed the illuminated booths, the women in their white aprons cried out:

"Nougat! Nougat! Nougat from Montélimar!"

We had come beyond the ambit of light when the electrician said: "The population of France is on the increase now. Perhaps that's because of the village fetes—" and in the darkness I could not see him smiling, and I knew, for the first time, that the moonlight was not there.

What was to happen did not come at once. The door of the café stood open; men stood drinking and men sat drinking at the tables, some with their Sunday hats on still, but in their vests and shirt sleeves, having taken off their jackets in the heat. The air was filled with the smoke of their tobacco, with the tumult of their arguments, and we edged our way between them to where the café owner stood. He was at his place behind the counter, serving drinks, watching the packed tables, and rinsing the glasses in the tub of water set beneath the *zinc*. He turned his head quickly, sharply, as he worked, alert to the speech of the living in the café, and harking as well, it might be, to the dead. He wiped his palms dry quickly on his apron, and shook our hands. He spoke in a low voice.

"The radio says rain," he said, as he lifted bottles and poured drinks. He said he would take a cognac with us, and we drank together. The talk of the men grew louder at the tables, but the café owner stood like a deaf man before us, no longer listening to them speak. For outside lay the dark, ex-

hausted earth, stricken by drought and spent by the contests
in which it had been the promised trophy, and the café owner
turned his head toward the doorway now where the earth lay
burdened with its uneasy dead. "The radio says rain," he
said again, and then suddenly he jerked his head up, and the
lights in the café faltered an instant as the sound of thunder
split the dark. "Hush!" he said, and the room went quiet.
Wie die Erde dürstet, wie die Erde dürstet, whispered the
memory of the prisoner's voice across the silence, and then,
above the music of the merry-go-round and the accordions in
the dance pavilion, we could hear it coming like a great sea
roaring in across the trees.

Army of Occupation

THERE was a train which left the Gare de l'Est at twenty-
five minutes past nine every night, but it was not a French
train. The guards at the platform gates were American MPs,
and the ticketmen were GIs. They looked at the French girls
who had come this far to kiss goodbye the men who were
going back, and they passed their judgments and their com-
ments on them. They watched the women and men who
stood clasped together in a final embrace—Frenchwomen,
and men of the American Army of Occupation going back
for another stretch in Germany after a furlough spent in Paris
in pursuit of love. The train known as the Duty Train, the
"Main Seiner," made its thirteen-and-a-quarter-hour run between the two rivers of two countries. The German sleeping
cars and the third-class carriages renounced their former nationality in defeat and became links coupling together the

disparate states of America, and the sad, wild, longing outcry —no longer recognizable as singing—of the men of these states could be heard in the crowded corridors and the compartments even before the train pulled away. Even while the gates were sliding closed between the Frenchwomen and the last, racing uniformed men with the weight of their duffel bags balanced on their shoulders as they ran, the drunken speeches to Michigan or California or Maine were roared out through the open windows, and then the trainman's sharp, lingering whistle blew, and the lanterns swung, and the Duty Train pulled out into the dark.

It was a man's train, and yet a few scattered women used to ride on it—American women: Wacs, or Army nurses going back to duty, or War Department employees going where they had to go. Among these few women who went through the gates one cold February night, there was a slender, pretty girl in uniform, with the patch of a war correspondent on the right sleeve of her overcoat, and the letters "US" stitched on the left. She carried her Val-Pak easily in one gloved hand, and her hair was brushed out from under her army cap, glossy and soft and nearly black. As she passed beneath the platform lights, the men at the windows called out to her and whistled, but in spite of the rouge on her mouth and the shortness of her skirt, there was a look of modesty, of shyness and vulnerability about her, so that she seemed at once different from the other women hurrying by. Perhaps it was merely that she was alone, while the others hastened in twos or threes up the crowded, tenebrous platform, half running on their high, bold heels, with their breath showing white on the air before them as they talked or laughed aloud. Or perhaps merely that she walked with her head a little lowered, while the others did not, or else that the things that passed through her mind were different. She did not look toward the men, and she did not seem to hear them calling out.

When she came to the third-class carriage on which the letter "B" hung black on a square, white sign, she swung her Val-Pak up the high steps through the door. Although there were still six minutes before the train would go, the outcry had already begun in the packed, cold cars, and the girl made her way, a little hesitant, a little shy, past the soldiers blocking the corridor. "Roll me over / In the clover," wailed the voices in grief from behind the closed compartment doors, and far ahead, in almost unbearable sorrow, other voices cried out "Reminds me of / The one I love" in drunken, unmelodious complaint.

"Compartment 5, Seat 29," the girl said half aloud, holding her ticket in her hand. And then she had found the number, and she put her hand on the sliding door of Compartment 5 and pulled it back.

There were three soldiers sitting inside on the long, wooden seats, and one of them, a sergeant, who was in the corner at the right of the door, must have just ceased singing, for his mouth hung open still. He held an uncorked bottle of cognac in one hand, and he looked up at the girl standing in the doorway, and then he threw back his head and bayed the wolf call long and wild and loud.

The soldier who sat across from him got slowly, carefully to his feet. "Take a glance, gentlemen, at what they're passing around with the coffee and leecures tonight," he said, and he reached out and took the Val-Pak from the girl's hand. He was a big, pink-skinned young man with heavy, sloping shoulders, and his reddish hair was cropped close upon his broad, round skull. "They take away Montmartre, but they give us a war correspondent," he said, and as he raised her bag to jam it onto the rack, he lost his balance and caught at the handle of the door. "What paper you representing?" he said.

The girl stood in the doorway still, troubled and young, with her dark hair soft around her face. She looked at the sergeant, who sat holding the bottle of cognac between his spread knees, and at the soldier standing beside her, whose eyes had begun at the patch on her shoulder and moved slowly, unsteadily down to her sheer stockings and her brown tie-shoes. Beyond them, there was a third soldier. He was sitting by the window and had not turned his head, and now, as the Duty Train slipped into motion, she saw the platform lights flash in accelerating rhythm past his ear and the cap he wore pushed low upon his forehead.

"I'm free-lancing," she said. She did not say, *I'm going to Germany to see him. He's showing them how to publish papers over there.*

"Have a seat," said the big soldier, swaying toward her. "You've never had it as good as this before. Everywhere else in the train they're packed in eight or ten to a compartment. You never had it so good anywhere you've ever been," he said.

"She's afraid. The poor little thing's afraid," said the sergeant. He sat looking up at her, his pale, soiled hands closed on the cognac bottle that hung between his knees. "She's afraid of you and me and this here bottle."

"No," said the girl quickly, "I'm not afraid." She stepped inside, and because of the cold in the corridor she pulled the door shut behind her, and at once the sound of the singing was closed away, fainter and sadder, and she stepped past the two men and sat down on the same side as the sergeant, but at a distance from him. The two soldiers looked at her ankles and legs as she took her coat off; they watched her take off her fur-lined, good leather gloves, and fold them and put them into the brown leather bag that had hung from her shoulder by a strap. Then the sergeant raised the bottle of cognac to his mouth, his lips funneling moist and red around the bottle's greenish glass. When he had drunk, he handed the bottle across to the big soldier with the reddish hair. He sat down again on the opposite seat, and raised the bottle to his mouth, and as he drank he swayed with the swaying of the train.

"I see you're married," the sergeant said to the girl. He sat looking down the length of the bench at her, and he jerked his chin in the direction of her hand. His chin was deeply cleft, and a thread of cognac that ran through the cleft and the stubble shone yellow in the compartment's naked light. "I see you got a ring on your finger," he said. The cuffs of his shirt hung loose below the sleeves of his blouse, and as he looked at her he fumbled a moment at the undone buttons at his wrists.

"Yes, I am. I'm married," the girl said.

The soldier had lowered the bottle now, and he wiped the mouth of it with the inside of his hand. "Have a drink," he said, and he shifted down on the bench a little to hold the bottle out to her.

"No, thanks," said the girl.

"She's a lady," said the sergeant. He gave a sad, loud guffaw of laughter and slapped his thigh.

For the first time, the soldier sitting by the window turned his head and looked at them. "There's enough of them that ain't ladies traveling on this here train tonight," he said in a slow, stubborn voice. His face hung narrow and pale between monumental ears, the features of it nearly poetic in their melancholy. "There's two sleeping-car loads of French war brides traveling right along here with us tonight," he said, and perhaps he should have been speaking of plowing one crop or the other under, or of getting the silos full, instead of talking like this to strangers about women. "I don't envy them none that's getting them dames," he said.

"French war brides lying down in sleeping berths while American war correspondents have to sit up all night. That's rough. That sure is rough," said the sergeant, and the boy from the farm pushed his cap down lower on his brows and turned his face to the dark of the window again.

The big soldier handed the bottle of cognac back to the sergeant, and then he slid farther along on the boards of the seat until he was sitting opposite the girl. "I got a bottle of Martell in my coat there that nobody's ever touched," he said. He leaned forward, his arms leaning on his thick, broad legs, his knees coming close to the girl's knees. "If that's what's keeping you from drinking, I'll get the new bottle out. You won't have to drink after anyone else. It's as pure as the driven snow," he said.

"It's not that," the girl said. She put her soft hair back from her shoulders, talking a little loud above the steady roaring of the train. "I just don't like the taste of it—not straight." For an instant, she saw the booths of the Third Avenue bar where they'd gone in the one winter they had had together, gone six nights a week in the early hours of the morning, after the paper had been put to bed. "My husband's a newspaperman," she heard herself saying, and now that she spoke of him, the tumult and outcry had seemed to cease in the train so that these strangers might listen, the cursing and crying and moaning for another country to come to a halt so that these others might hear more clearly the inimitable sound of love. "So we used to keep funny hours," she said, "and on the way home from work we'd stop in for a drink, at one or two o'clock in the morning, or whenever it happened to be. He needed something strong, and he'd take it straight, but I could never manage to get it down." She could see him in his old blue jacket sitting across a table from her, the first taste of the drink taking the weariness from his face, and giving the gentleness back to his mouth and eyes. "I haven't seen him in eight months," she said. "I've been around newspapers all my life, but I couldn't get over. I simply couldn't get them to send me over." *In thirteen hours now, a little less than thirteen,* she thought, glancing at the watch on her wrist. The distant voices in the train had begun to sing again, and she listened to the faint, far, nostalgic music as she sat smiling blindly at the soldier's swaying face.

The sergeant had been watching her, and now he put the cork back into the bottle of cognac, and pressed it down with the cushion of his thumb. Then he propped the bottle upright in the corner, against the wooden paneling, and he slid unsteadily along the boards until he had come close to the girl. "We're good guys. We're all right guys," he said, and it might have been that the words she had spoken had touched some troubled springhead of emotion in him. "You just got to try and understand us." His tunic was open, and his big, soiled hands were fumbling in his pockets, and after a moment he brought a piece of paper out. "I got this to show the army. I got this to show them I wasn't off somewhere getting drunk, like they might think I was," he said, and his black-rimmed fingers held the creased bit of paper out to her, and she took it in her hand.

There was an English doctor's name and address in Somerset printed out at the top of it, and under this the simple, explicit statement of fact was made: "This is to certify that John Henley White, born January the fifteenth, 1947, died of pulmonary pneumonia on February the nineteenth, 1947, and that his father, Sgt. Harry White, of the United States Army, was present at his funeral. Here witness my Hand and Seal . . ."

Behind the sergeant, the cognac bottle had toppled over, and it rolled back and forth on the wooden seat with the motion of the train. As he reached back for it, he kept his eyes on the girl. She looked slowly up from the words that were written on the piece of paper.

"Surprises you, uh?" he said. He took the cork out of the bottle with his teeth, his head tipped sidewise to do it, and still he did not take his eyes from her, and he waited a moment before beginning to drink. "Surprises you to find out I had a son, don't it?" he said. He was almost smiling, as if relishing the wiliness of some trick he had played.

The girl folded the paper where it had been folded before, and he looked at her fingers as she gave it back to him.

"The nineteenth of February. I'm sorry," the girl said in a low voice.

"Sure. Four days ago," said the sergeant. A dribble of cognac was running down his chin. He put the doctor's certificate away in his inside pocket, and he passed the bottle of cognac to the soldier on the other seat. "He was five weeks old, John Henley White. My wife's an English girl, married her two years ago over there when we were stationed in Somerset," he said. "That's where I come from now. She sent me the telegram last week and I flew over. I took one of them big planes, not any of these here little French crates but the big, four-motor jobs you read about in the papers always cracking up." His heavy lips hung open, bright and moist, and his eyes, with a slight glaze on them now, were fixed on her face. "I bet I gave you a surprise. I bet you'd never have taken me for a married man," he said.

"Look," said the big soldier, and he leaned toward the sergeant from the opposite bench. "Does it occur to you that the lady is bored with all this kind of talk? Does it occur to you that beauty incarnate doesn't give a snap of her dainty fingers for your relatives?" He handed the bottle back to the sergeant, and the sergeant lifted it and threw back his head and drank what cognac remained in the bottom of it, and then he dropped the empty bottle on the floor and kicked it under the seat. "You got to make yourself interesting to a lady," the big soldier said. "Tell her about your travels, the countries you been to, the kind of things you seen." He stopped talking, and he sat there looking at the girl, his big, square-boned knees in the khaki cloth almost touching her knees. "In the past three days I've been in Paris, I spent two hundred thousand francs, and I don't regret a penny of it. Not for what I got," he said.

The little farm boy by the window, with the cap tipped low on his brows, turned away from the rushing darkness of the night outside and looked at them bleakly, almost reproachfully, again. "I don't envy you what you got in Paris. I don't envy nobody anything he's got," he said. "I could of had exactly the same as anybody else. I could of had a French war bride traveling right along with me on this here train tonight. I could of been taking her to Bremerhaven the way the rest of them are going, if I'd of been sucker enough to marry her."

The sergeant gave a yipe of laughter. "You sound as if you turned kinda choosy just when you hadn't ought," he said, and he slapped his thigh, and guffawed high and loud.

"I found out too much just in time," said the farm boy, speaking slowly, stubbornly. He looked at them in something like hesitation a moment, as if there were more to say and as if he were about to say it, and then he turned back to the fleeing darkness, to the memory of the fields of home, the valleys and hills and the snowbound roads of home to which his longing gave substance in the foreign night. "Roll me over / In the clover," came the faint, sad chorus of crying down the corridor, and the farm boy rubbed his hand quickly on the pane. "Well, what do you know, it's snowing," he said. The big soldier stood up from his place opposite the girl and began making his way unsteadily toward the corner by the door where the two swaying khaki overcoats hung. "I bet there's a lot of that laying around home now," said the farm boy by the window.

"A lot of what?" said the sergeant, holding his loud, high laughter in.

"Why, snow," said the little soldier, as if surprised that it fell in this foreign country. "Real, winter snow. I bet they're out coasting at home tonight."

The big soldier had reached the overcoats, and he stood there swaying and groping in the pockets of one of them. In a moment he brought out the fresh bottle. "This time you're going to start it off," he said to the girl. He sat down facing her again, and he held the bottle between his knees as he uncorked it. "You're going to have first go at this one, just to sweeten it for the rest of us." He held the bottle toward her. He had spread his big legs wide, one on each side of her silk-clad legs now, ready to close in on them in flagrant embrace.

"No," said the girl. "I'm tired. I want to try to get some sleep."

"Man," said the sergeant, "she just don't like Martell. You can tell that the way she's looking at it. She don't like your brand nohow, boy, so you might as well take it away." He slid back up the seat until he was in the corner by the door where his overcoat hung above him, and he reached up and pulled a bottle out of a pocket. "The brandy of kings," he said with a roar of laughter. "Good old Courvoisier," he said, caressing the bottle in his black-nailed hands.

"You see," the girl began in a quiet voice once his wild, high laughing had ceased, "it's after half past ten at night."

The big soldier opposite her was smiling, his heavy, sloping shoulders hunched forward, and he held the bottle of Martell toward her still. "You'd better try some of this before you drop into the arms of Morpheus," he said.

"No," said the girl again, and, with her coat around her, she moved down the boards of the seat and settled herself by the window. Just across from her now, the little farm boy was asleep with his narrow, tired face against the glass. "I'll take this end," she said, making it sound natural and right above the steady, mechanical rhythm of the train. "You two will have all the room you need up there." But the sergeant's arm had reached out and gone suddenly around her. He brought it tight around her neck, with the back of his soiled hand pressing her throat, and his knuckles forcing hard against her jawbone and her chin.

"Not until I get what I want," he said. She could taste his breath on the little space of air between them as he forced her head and her soft, glossy hair back hard against the side of his face. "I want to get some of that rouge off your mouth. I've been wanting to ever since you walked through that door," he said.

"Would that I might leap to the lady's defense," said the big soldier, "but you outrank me, Sergeant, you outrank me." He had shifted down closer to the farm boy so as to sit nearly opposite to her still, and his legs in their khaki were stretched out now as if in longing toward her. "You take what you're entitled to, Sergeant," he said, and he lifted the bottle of Martell and took a long, deep drink. "You take it first. I'll take what's left."

The girl's heart beat swiftly in impatience and outrage a moment while the back of the sergeant's hand forced up her chin. She was thinking fiercely, *They can't do anything, not a single thing. In a little while he'll walk down the platform, looking in every window for me. . . .*

"Stop being fools," she said in a low, unshaken voice, and she twisted within the crook of the sergeant's arm, and with her two hands she lifted the weight and the abomination of his flesh, and flung his arm away. His will, and his tough physical power, seemed suddenly to have ebbed in weariness, or hopelessness, or in the remembrance of some half-forgotten grief, and his hand, with the sleeve unbuttoned at the wrist, fell soiled and empty on the wooden seat.

"What I need is a drink," he said.

It was then, as he lifted the bottle of Courvoisier to drink, that the compartment door was jerked suddenly back, and a tall, young, blue-eyed corporal stepped in. He wore a battle jacket, with three years of overseas stripes on his sleeves, and his hair was black, and it fell loosely across his forehead, soft and untractable, as if it had just been washed that afternoon. He closed the door behind him, and he stood with his handsome young head lifted, holding to the handle of it still, his grave eyes looking straight toward the corner where the girl sat with her legs drawn up under her and her coat around her in the cold.

"I saw you in the station when you came through the gate," he said. "I thought maybe you had a sleeping berth, and then I just saw you now through the compartment window as I came down the corridor." He did not seem to see the others sitting in the compartment with her, or the sergeant's legs stretched out like a barrier across the aisle. "I've got a seat in the car next door," he said. "I mean a seat with upholstery—second class. You'd be better off in there, if you'd like to take it," he said.

"And you?" said the girl, speaking quickly to him.

"I'll switch with you," he said.

The big soldier had been drinking from his bottle of Martell, and now he wiped his mouth with the side of his hand and held out the bottle to the corporal. "Oh, young Lochinvar, take a drink of this," he said.

But the corporal had not seemed to hear him speak. He was looking straight at the girl as he stepped across the sergeant's outstretched legs. "I'm so sick of looking at Frenchwomen," he said, and he sat down on the wooden seat beside her, sitting sidewise so as to look into her face. "You're American. You're wonderful," he said.

"Take it somewhere else," said the sergeant, who slumped on the bench behind him, but the corporal might have been a deaf man for all that he knew the sergeant was there.

"I haven't been home for eighteen months," said the corporal, his voice eager, his blue eyes in their short, thick fringes of black lashes fixed on her eyes, his ears deaf to everything except what she might say. "Eighteen months is a long time to be away from where you want to be."

Behind him, in the corner, the sergeant straightened up, and slapped his thigh, and roared aloud. "It's rough, it sure is rough them treating you like that," he said, and he lifted the bottle of Courvoisier and drank again.

"I want you to have my seat in the other car," said the corporal. With his long, narrow fingers he combed the loose hair back off his brow. "You're beautiful. You're like all the girls at home who don't come over."

As if the single word "home" had sounded clear as a clarion call above the rushing tumult of the train, the farm boy by the window roused from sleep and raised his head. "You on your way to Bremerhaven?" he asked in his slow, stubborn, perplexed voice. He sat looking across at them, and at the light, in bewilderment a moment, blindly fingering the stuff of his uniform as if it were not khaki but denim or corduroy, perhaps, that he had expected to find there. "You on your way home, too?" he said. But the corporal had not seemed to hear him.

"I haven't anything against the French," said the corporal, looking at the girl still. "But the women aren't like you. Your skin is different, and your hair, and the sound of your voice is different."

"You'd better watch out, Corporal," said the big soldier, and he grinned at them from the other bench. "She's got French blood in her. She's got a drop or two of English, too."

"No," said the corporal, and although he heard the sound of words at last, he did not turn his head from the sight of her. "They don't make them like that over here. They don't know how," he said.

"There're plenty of them there French ones on the train

tonight," said the farm boy by the window. "War brides. French war brides," he said, looking at the corporal. "Some fellas don't seem to give a whoop and a holler what they get hold of. Maybe they don't know something I found out just in time about the French," he said.

"Isolationist, are you?" said the big soldier, and he lowered the bottle of Martell.

"Sure," said the farm boy in his slow, stubborn voice. He turned his face back to the darkness of the night. "That's the word I was looking for," he said, and he drifted bleakly into sleep again.

The sergeant had got unsteadily up from his place by the door, and with one hand he held to the baggage rack above him for stability while he took the two or three steps down the compartment to where the corporal sat beside the girl. "I guess ladies and gentlemen don't drink the way the rest of us do?" he said, and he stood there swaying above them. His tunic hung open still, and in the hand that swung by his side he held the half-empty bottle of Courvoisier.

"Sure, I drink," said the corporal, glancing up at him. "I've been drinking for two days in Paris. I don't want to drink any more." He shook the hair back off his forehead, and then his blue eyes looked eagerly, earnestly, through their smudged fringe of lashes at the girl. "I've got a house at home, a house of my own," he said. "My uncle left it to me. I've rented it to a family. They pay me a hundred and twenty-five dollars a month, and I'll get more when the OPA controls are off. But I don't want to live there. I'm just telling you about it so that you'll know. What I want to do is to go up to Alaska," he said, his voice grave, eager, young. "I want to open up some kind of an inn, something with cabins, or maybe bungalows, in the woods around it, up on the Alaskan highway. I've been getting estimates on the price of land up there, and building's cheap once you get your ground cleared. Do you think you'd like Alaska?" he said. "It would be for about three months of the year, the season up there, say the fifteenth of June to the fifteenth of September, and I'd build something really good, something picturesque. Do you think you'd like to take a chance on it?" he said.

The sergeant made another unsteady step, and now he stood between the girl and the corporal, a swaying barrier, holding with one hand still to the baggage rack above his head.

"Perhaps we could talk about it tomorrow," the girl said, and she touched the corporal's sleeve an instant. "I'm tired. If you meant what you said about the seat in the other car, I'd like to take it—"

The sergeant's head swung like a bell between them now, his moist lips open. "You get out of here," he said to the corporal. "Get out quick."

"No," said the corporal. He looked up in almost childlike credence and trust at the sergeant. "I'm twenty-three," he said, and he put the hair back off his forehead. "I swear I've been looking for twenty years for her. I never thought I'd find her overseas." He turned back to the girl again, and he went on, saying, "I'm from Oregon, but that doesn't mean I want to spend my life there. I'd want the woman who married me to have as much say about that as I have myself. But I'd like you to think about Alaska. I'd like you to keep it in mind." He put his hand in his blouse now, and he felt in the inner pocket of it. "I've got some photographs I could show you— just small ones, but they'd give you an idea," he said. "There're trees there that take your breath away, bigger than in California even, and when you get up high enough, it's glacier country."

The sergeant swung, seemingly without muscle or bone, like a hanged man between them. "Go on. Get out of here. Get out," he said.

"Sure," said the big soldier on the other side. "You be a good boy and run along back to Oregon."

"You'd better go," said the girl in a soft voice to the corporal. "You go, and I'll go with you." She had gathered her coat closely around her, and she slid her legs carefully, cautiously down.

"Yes," said the corporal, but he did not get up from the bench. He sat there looking at her. "My God, you're beautiful. I love you. I respect you," he said.

The sergeant held with one hand to the baggage rack still, and although he had scarcely seemed to move, he raised the nearly empty bottle he held in his other hand, and he brought it down, vicious and hard, on the side of the corporal's head. For an instant the corporal's underlip quivered like a child's, but he did not fall at once; he even sought to rise to his feet, with a look of surprise and sickness on his face. And then his eyes closed, and he sloped sidewise, huddled within himself, and the sergeant lurched aside to let him slip to the compartment floor. When he was down, lying full-length as if in sleep, the sergeant leaned over him in silence and hit him again, this time across the forehead where the loose hair fell upon his brow, and what was left of the cognac ran out of the mouth of the bottle and splashed across the front of the corporal's blouse and stained the campaign ribbons on his breast. The girl sat gripping her coat around her with her trembling hands, and her teeth were shaking in her head.

"Let's kick the guts out of Oregon for interfering where he wasn't wanted," said the big soldier. He tried to get up from his seat, but he couldn't stand any longer. Beyond him, the farm boy slept in peace against the cold, dark window glass.

The bottle of Courvoisier had dropped from the sergeant's hand with the force of the last blow he had given, and now he stooped down, grunting, his soiled fingers groping for the bottle as it rolled back and forth across the compartment floor. When he had got hold of it again, he raised the emptied bottle above the corporal's head.

"Don't touch him! Don't you dare to hit him again!" the girl cried out. She had jumped to her feet, she had flung herself forward as if to save from annihilation the actual flesh and bone of all that remained of decency. *There're other people on this train, like people you know, like people you see in the street,* she was thinking in panic. *There're Wacs, and brothers, and sons, and husbands . . . there're people singing.* She could hear their voices, far, unheeding, calling out in nostalgia, as the Germans had called out before them, to a loitering, blond-headed woman named "Lili Marlene." *People who understand words, if I can get to them, if I can say the words to them,* but her legs shook under her as she walked. She had got past the big soldier, who sprawled in stupor on the bench now; she was making her way past the body of the corporal. The sergeant stood upright, his legs straddling the fallen man, the empty bottle hanging from his fingers, swaying, half smiling, before the compartment door. "Get out of my way!" she cried out in fury to him. "Get out of my way!" And he did not speak, but, half smiling still as she flung by him, he lifted his hand and stroked her soft, dark hair.

Outside in the cold of the corridor she began to run past the closed compartment doors, the drawn curtains, the masked lights, running fast, with the tears falling down her face, toward the sound of the sad, sweet, distant voices in the rushing train.

A *Puzzled Race*

THERE was nothing of the bureaucrat, nothing of the acquiescent man, or the bending reed in him, although he walked out of a building that housed government offices with an ease that signified he was familiar with the territory. He was gray-haired, and neither tall nor short, not old or young, with a quality as solid as stone about him, and a vigorous step. The air felt foolishly tender and light on his cheek as it might to a man newly in love, and the delicate leaves of the trees before him, the floating heavens, seemed too ethereal to be a part of Germany. Behind him was the vast, familiar honeycomb of the offices of the United States High Commission, and, as he started down the steps, he thought of his age, and a network of lines diffused in humor around his eyes. *I'm too old to feel this pull at the heart,* he thought, but in spite of the accumulated years of his life—nearly fifty now—and of the political climate of this particular year, the spring all about him seemed almost lovelier than any spring he could recall. It had not been lent this poignancy because of any wild, new attachment either to woman or country, he knew as he waited for the uniformed driver to bring his car up to the curb. His wife was his established love, and he needed no other, and America was his country. No surge of nameless emotion could persuade him now that Germany was better than he had believed merely because its outer texture was transformed by May.

"Home first, and then to the airport," he said to the back of the driver's head as he got in the car and closed the door; the same head, the same set of the cap, the same flushed cartilage of the ear, he had spoken his directions to for two years or more. *And this perhaps the last day I'll ride behind him*, it occurred to him, and he lowered the window glass and looked out in silence on the vineyards they were passing. The vines hung like emerald necklaces on the high, tilted slopes above the swiftly flowing waters of the Rhine. Perhaps he felt this sudden tenderness for the landscape of Germany because he might not see it just like this again, for in a few hours he would be leaving it, and, if he returned, he knew this defense-less moment of its rebirth in spring would be forgotten as the Ice Saints of May came shivering in. He had come to know it as a country in which one iron season followed upon another, because of the iron faces, the iron intentions, the bland, iron aplomb. But as he settled back on the deep cushions of the seat, it seemed to him for just this brief instant that he too had laid down his arms, and that Washington could do exactly as it wished with him. *Just for this second, as I look out*, he thought, *I do not care*.

Within a quarter of an hour, they had reached the housing project, and they drove past the rows of two-story apartment buildings that zigzagged, bright with stucco and nickel and plate glass, among the apple and pear trees of the farming country whose fields and orchards had followed the river here before. This was the American enclave, with an unfinished look to it still, but the circular flower beds before the Post Exchange and before the Coffee Shop were planted with pur-ple and white hyacinths, and grass was beginning to grow at last on the stretches of tan mud around the commissary and the gas station and the dry-cleaning plant. *One strip of newly broken land along the Rhine seeking with desperation to emulate America*, the man reflected, *but failing because the reason for America was not there*. Except for the bicycles, the kiddie cars, the tricycles of U.S. make, that lay discarded on sidewalks and cement-bound lawns, it was still Germany; and except for the children coming home from school, bands of them in blue jeans and cowboy boots, even a group of Cub Scouts in shirts and caps of blue and gold. From the car, he could hear the children's voices, midwestern, tough, and, at the same time, vulnerable and shrill, stirring in him the memory of other springs.

America, he thought, his arm cradled in the car's brocaded sling, *this time you're going to show me a grim face.*

Beyond the apartment houses were four geometrically angled-and-roofed houses, built closer to the river and given an aura of seclusion in indication of the higher rating of the men who lived in them. The car had entered the drive of the first of these, and the man saw the boy waiting on the path that led to the whitestone step and the clouded glass of the front door.

"We should leave at four. I'll have my bag ready by then," he said to the back of the driver's head, and he moved forward on the seat. "Get them to fix you a meal in the kitchen before we go. You'll get back late." The car had stopped, and the man got out, and closed the car door behind him, and he started walking toward the boy. "Isn't it getting too hot for the 'coon skin cap?" he said.

Even before the car had stopped, the boy in his blue jeans and red flannel shirt had begun coming over the flat slabs of the pavings that marked the path. And now, head lowered, he turned on his black and white sneakers and fitted himself against the man, his left shoulder pressing, thin and forlorn, into the hard bones of his ribs. He put his hand on the boy's right shoulder, feeling the brittle, inverted cup within his palm, and the sharp wing of the shoulder blade.

"Can I go to the airport with you?" the boy asked, not looking up. He was watching his own feet and the man's, lengthening his step to walk as the man walked toward the smooth, white step and the ultramodern door.

"It would be better if you stayed here," the man said.

"Mother doesn't want to leave Vinnie while she's coughing still. You'd better stay with them."

"I'm going to have lots of trouble with my arithmetic," the boy said. "Are you sure you have to go?"

"Yes, I have to go," said the man, and he looked down at the silvery, brown-tipped hairs of the raccoon cap, and the oval of leather that formed the crown. "They want me to answer some questions," he said.

"How many days will it take?" the boy asked, and now he hung back a little, prolonging the moment before they must go up the step.

"I hope it won't be more than a week," the man said, walking slower too. The striped raccoon tail hung the length of the hollow of the boy's thin neck, and when he raised his hand quickly to look at the man, the tail swung, fat as a caterpillar, to one side.

"What kind of questions will they ask you?" the boy said, scrutinizing the man's face now.

"Oh, about people," said the man, and he looked down into the long-lashed eyes below him. The brows were as black as his own brows, but delicate and silky, and the eyes were clear and gentle and a translucent blue. "Just about people I used to know."

They had come so close to the scrubbed white step that had they moved forward they would have mounted it, and opened the door, and gone into the house together, but the man lingered too, as if reluctant to let this moment go. He felt the perishable bones of the boy's shoulder in his palm, and he thought of the process that turned the softness of a boy's substance to that of a man, the toughening, the hardening, the growing suspicion of one another, and the final dying of belief, until citizen suspected citizen, and friend looked warily at friend. *When does it begin? How does it happen?*

the man thought, looking down into his son's face. *When do men begin doubting each other, and fear to look into each other's eyes?*

"Why can't you answer the questions from here?" the boy asked, his head tilted back, holding stubbornly to the idea that the man might still not have to go.

"I answered them from here," the man said. "They want me to say it over again, out loud."

"Because they didn't believe you?" the boy said, his eye gone a little shrewd.

"Perhaps some of them didn't," said the man. Looking at his watch, he thought: *I must get my things together, get the papers straightened out, the last things said to Mary before I go.* And then he saw the look in the boy's face, and he turned abruptly, and drew him with him down the stone path, their backs turned on the house. "I don't want you to worry about it," he said, his hand holding the boy's shoulder hard. "It's going to be all right. Last night I found a book about Daniel Boone on the floor beside your bed. It must have fallen off when you went to sleep. I picked it up and I read it straight through to the end. Maybe you haven't come to the part where they didn't believe the answers Boone gave."

"I'm at the part where his son gets killed by the Indians," the boy said, walking close to the man.

"Well, you'll read the rest," said the man. "You'll read about how, at one time in his life, his fellow citizens couldn't agree about him, so there was nothing for it but to have a trial." He and the boy had left the angularly paved path, and crossed the drive, and they stopped at the edge of the field that, generation after generation, before the Americans had come, had been plowed by German plowshares, drawn by German horses, driven by German hands. But now the field waited, as if in bewilderment, neither pasture nor orchard, garden nor lawn, and certainly not fallow land. "Look," said the man. Through the ancient trees that leaned, lovely with May, at the end of the field, could be seen the swiftly passing Rhine, and great, handsome barges rode the current, so heavily loaded that only their cabins, as pretty as cottages, with geraniums blooming in their window boxes, and children playing at their doors, rose above the waterline. Yet, however heavy the cargo that they bore, they sped along with singular festivity, as if to the pace of music rippling fast across the water and the air. "There goes a barge flying the Belgian flag," the man said, and, standing with his son in the delicate, spring light, he suddenly saw the words as clearly as if they were written out across the mud and grass. "Men who in private had questioned Boone's loyalty now doubted it in public," went the grievous legend, and he looked away from it to the pennants of bright, flapping clothes that hung, drying, on the barges' decks. "They were cruel, and they were unjust, but they were very natural, these grave suspicions of Boone's loyalty," the words went on. "Americans were a puzzled race in those years . . . There was nothing for it but a formal trial. That Boone ever really contemplated treason is a ridiculous idea, disproved by all his years of faithful service," went the tape recorder of his memory. "It was not the last time that he was to feel the ingratitude of his friends, but it was the first and perhaps the bitterest . . ." Watching the barges go, the man said: "I'd like to take that book on the plane tonight."

"Sure, you can take it," said the boy, but his mind was on something else now. "If you got on that barge then you wouldn't have to go to Washington. You could go to Belgium instead."

"Except that isn't where they're expecting me," the man said.

When they turned to go, the words that he had not said aloud moved with them, and the man watched them pass, like subtitles on a movie screen, across the macadam of the drive.

"In a week, they're going to have the kite-flying contest like last year," the boy said in a low voice as they went up the path.

"I'll try hard to be back for it," the man said. "I'll do everything I can."

"But in the end," the boy said suddenly when they reached the step; "I mean, this thing about Daniel Boone. Did they believe him in the end?"

"Yes," said the man. "Of course they believed him." He could not say to the silvery hairs of the cap that moved below him: *They acquitted him, but something was altered in him, something they hadn't the power to condemn or clear. Boone went to Spanish territory, to Louisiana, in the end, and became a Spanish magistrate. He didn't want to give up his American citizenship and become a Spaniard. But he did. It meant becoming a respected man, and making a living for his family again.* "They had a trial, and he was acquitted of the charges. You wouldn't be wearing a raccoon cap today if he hadn't been acquitted. Boone wore that cap for half a century before Crockett came along." He pulled the plump, striped tail as they went up the step together. "*In later years,*" the words moved in silence across the frosted glass of the door, "*his children often repeated Boone's stories and his opinions, but to this episode they seem never to have referred.*" "I'll be back in a week, and I'll bring you a kite, and we'll fly it, and perhaps we'll win like last year," the man said. He was thinking of his wife upstairs as he walked into the hall.

Fire in the Vineyards

THE house to which the mother and the children had come to live in for a little while was ornamental enough to bear the name of château, and it stood on sloping ground among the vineyards of southern France, two miles or more out of the fishing town. It was an Englishman's property, a place on which wine was grown, and bottled, and sold to restaurants, or else for export, or to individuals who came in their own cars for it, knowing the value of its name. But now the Englishman was dead, and his wife had gone to Cornwall to visit her people for the summer, leaving the house to the mother and children until the vintage time would come. So it was theirs, but it was no more than a fragment of possession, the mother knew, this temporary title they had been given. They were allowed access to the château's material residue, to the garden hedged by tapering cypress trees, to the stagnant lily ponds, and the crumbling walls on which scaled salamanders moved quicker than light.

But the essence that kept the place from dereliction was not theirs. Father and son, down to the third generation now of men and their women, it was the beat of the peasants' hearts that could be heard in the somnolent quiet, and the movement of their life in the cellar chambers, and the murmur of their voices through the heat as they worked among the vines. Men and their wives and their children labored together, tending the vineyards and the orchards, picking the grapes and pressing them when the right season came. They filled the vast, ancient kegs, and bottled, and corked, and labeled the wine, and pruned the vine in late December. In August, they gathered green almonds and dried them for winter eating, and they plucked the olives from among the trembling silvery leaves, and crushed them under the horse-drawn, granite cylinder to oil that ran, slower than honey, into the great stone jars.

All summer the peasants would be at their work of washing the wine bottles clean, and filling them from the giant casks that stood in the dark cellars at the back of the château, transforming the ritual of the seasons into commerce as the retired English army officer had disciplined them to do. Whenever the mother and the children passed the open door, the peasants would look up and say *bon jour*, and roar the words out about the weather, their voices continuously amazed, although, now that it was summer, the weather scarcely altered. The sun was as unremitting as the grinding whispers of the cicadas in the trees, and when it set, the cicada voices died with its light, and an uneasy silence fell upon the evening air. But the peasants spoke neither of sunshine nor rain, but of the wind, like fishermen. One day the *mistral* might be blowing, and that was good wine-bottling weather, for it wiped the foreground and the rocky skyline clean. It blew in from the northwest, across the Gulf of Lion, cold and arrogant and alien as it strode across the beaches and the flowering cliffs. But it was not alien, for it was there, hammering the coastline, for two hundred days of every year. After it had gone on its way, a fitful, pleasant breeze, with the taste of salt in it, might cavort in off the Mediterranean waters, and then the heat would close down again in suffocation on the prostrate land.

"It's good for the vine, the drought!" the peasants would say, their voices as loud as if they called across a long distance to the mother, for theirs was the vocabulary of the vine, and, because she was American, it must seem to them that hers would be of war and the atom bomb, and they were not sure that they could make her hear. Let the springs go dry in the rock, and the goats tethered in the fields cry out with thirst; let artichokes hang like blackened skulls on their ashen stalks, and it did not matter, their dedication protested, for such things meant that the vine would flourish as in no common year. "It will be a good crop!" they would roar out of the damp, cool caverns where they worked, knowing that drought is the climate in which the vine draws body and power from the diathermic soil.

On another day, the peasants might try to speak to her of the thing that stood between them.

"You're American, but you've been to England?" they would say. "If you talk to the English, they'll tell you they've had enough, the way we French have had enough." They would stand in the shadows of the cellar rooms, their faces masked by the obscurity, saying: "You are American. You live so far away that you are not afraid of war the way we French and the English are afraid."

At that time of the year there were the customary number of English travelers, red-kneed, big-wristed, young men in khaki shorts and dusty boots, with the Union Jack spread like a declaration of their neutrality across the knapsacks on their backs. In hobnailed boots, they tramped the southern roads between the vineyards and the olive groves, their backs bent under the weight of their portable stoves and their utensils, under their books and their shabby clothes, because of their poverty and their determination, already aged, dogged men. Or there were the other English who rode, two by two, erect on motorcycles, with their tin pots and pans strapped to the canvas rolls behind them; or the English families who traveled in cars of such dilapidated distinction that there was no need for the "G B" above the numbers of the license plates to indicate from where they came.

They had a look of earnest shabbiness about them, these

English, thought the mother as she walked with her three children along the port of the fishing village, with the Mediterranean lapping at the stones. They had none of the assurance of the German tourists, for the Germans, with so much to answer for in every European country, now carried their heads higher than any other visitors, in order not to hang them low in shame. The English looked as poor as beggars as they passed the Germans sitting in the cafés, and their motorcycles were enough to make you split your sides with laughter as they stood parked along the waterfront beside the shining American cars.

"You are American," the fishermen would say to her as she and the children bought the fresh sardines from the baskets lined with seaweed laid on the harbor stones. On the delicately tinted wall of the wharfside café would be written in strong black lettering, as it was written on the gas-station roof at the entrance to the town: "Amis, Go Home," or "*Les Américains en Amérique!*" "You are American," they would say, the rejection so impersonal that there was no venom left in it. And their silence added: *You are not afraid of what may happen the way we are afraid.*

"I can tell the difference between the English and the French," said Fife, who was eight that summer. The mother and the children walked up through the parched fields, carrying the fish, and the lengths of bread, and the fresh fruit in their rucksacks, and the children would look at the words lettered faintly on the garden walls, "U.S. Go Home," and then they would look away. "The English get the reddest on beach," Fife said. He wore blue jeans, and American sneakers, and his voice sounded high and clear above the rasping of the cicadas in the almond and the olive trees.

"I can tell Frenchwomen because their hair is rusty," said Candy, who was ten. "I can't tell the difference between any of the men yet. Wherever they come from, they all turn around and stare," she said.

"Frenchmen's hips are higher up, nearer their armpits," said the girl named Claude. "Englishmen have theirs nearer their knees." She was slender, and tanned, with the small, grave face that had been hers at three years old no different now that she was twelve, except it was borne higher on her lengthening bones. "There are several other differences," she said, with dignity.

"Frenchwomen kiss louder than other women do," Candy went on with it, and her wheat-colored braids swung forward in the sunlight as she made the explosive sound of their embrace on the back of her own brown hand.

"Americans kiss very, very silently," said Fife. "In the movies I've seen of Americans kissing, they never make a sound."

"Oh, it's hot, it's much too hot!" Candy cried out in sudden impatience. "I'm too tired to go any further, and there's a cicada caught in my hair!"

And then one day, as the *mistral* blew, the forest fire began to burn. It was just past noon, at the hour when all life and all activity attenuated toward food and sleep, that the siren wailed its prolonged warning from the fishing town below. The peasants stood in their doorways, shading their eyes against the midday light, and the American children stood up by the château's lily ponds, where they had set their boats afloat in the high wind, their hearts chilled by the sustained, unearthly cry.

"It could be a drowning or it could be a fire," one of the younger peasants said, and an older one who stood near him, his grim face shaded by his copper-skinned hand, said:

"It could be for twelve o'clock. Sometimes they blow their whistle a half hour off."

It may have been that they were all blinded by the mere

presence of the meridional noon, for it was a minute, perhaps longer, before they saw the smoke through the blowing tracery of the olive trees. The mother and children followed the peasants out onto the wagon road to watch the smoke now billowing in creamy fury across the wooded hill. It took them another long moment to see that a wheat field had gone first, and then an orchard, and that the fire had charred fig, and olive, and cypress trees across the shallow valley, and was climbing fast to higher land. As they watched, the *mistral* unfurled the flames in sudden, flapping banners above the scrub and the writhing treetops, waving them ever higher in its strong relentless hand.

"This isn't the time of day for a forest fire," said the older peasant as the vertical note of the siren began its wailing fall. "The *pompiers* are fathers of families like anybody else. They've got the right to eat their lunch in peace," he said.

"Even if Monsieur Mistral laid down now," said the younger peasant, speaking of the wind as if it were a man, "you'd still have the birds and the rabbits carrying the fire on them. A wild pig will carry fire twenty–thirty kilometers a day, from the sparks caught in his fur as he runs before it. If there's no more than just one cicada flying with his wings lit, you can't say the forest fire's out."

Again the cry of the siren rose, and in the blinding dazzlement of afternoon, the deeper, hotter texture of the flames sprang in dark-plumed triumph above the land. And now a rust-colored jeep, its warning signal gasping in puny alarm, could be seen moving up the valley road, with a fire engine following behind.

"That's the fire chief," said the older peasant, not saying it to the mother or the children, but to the implacable wind.

"He's known Monsieur Mistral thirty years," the younger peasant said.

From where they stood, neither jeep nor fire engine seemed

larger or better equipped for action than a child's mechanical toy. The two minutely laboring vehicles proceeded up the bleached, walled road, passed the charred area the fire had left behind it, bypassed the fire itself, as if their destination lay still farther, and, at a break in the slumbering wall, turned off the road and into the tilted fields. There they rocked ludicrously upward, not toward the fire, but still higher, and when they halted, the firemen in their light-blue shirts scattered like confetti across the faded pigment of the grass. But they were men, with the ruse of men in their heads and in the white rope of the hose they carried, and so they could outwit the mindless torrent of liquid flame that poured across the thirsting hill.

It was more than an hour before the strong, flapping flames fell, tattered, from the black masts of the trees, and the smoke thinned out to mist which the *mistral* swept away. By evening, there was only the smell of fire left in the nostrils, and the eye saw the dark scar left on the wooded land, like the shadow of a cloud cast on sunny water, or on a field of yellow grain.

But that was not the end of it, for the story of how the fire had begun was still to be recounted, and whether it was truth or rumor, or who had told it first, nobody knew. But it was told in every shop and café of the fishing village, and repeated even by the fishermen as they mended their nets along the harbor, and by the peasants as they washed the bottles in the cellars on the north side of the house. It was this: that an American soldier, on furlough from Paris or Orléans, had driven that morning into the village in his fine, big car and parked it under the sign that said no parking was allowed. The soldier had drunk three *pastis* on a café terrace in the sun, the story went, or drunk half a bottle of cognac, and then refused to pay. When the café proprietor said he would call the police, the soldier had said: "France never did nothing but

sit on a corner holding a tin cup out, and we're sick of dropping the dollars in"; or said: "France died a couple of cen-
turies ago"; or said: "There's eighteen cafés in this town, and
there's one church. That's all any Christian needs to know."
Then the soldier had walked unsteadily across the cobbles of
the port, and raced his car through the narrow streets of the
fishing village, and out the pastoral valley road, mistaking it
for the coastal road, because by that time he couldn't read
the signposts any more. And, driving crazily between the
long, low, orchard walls, he must have flung his cigarette
away, and the paper-dry field of wheat went first, and then the
orchard, and it was even said that two milk-giving goats had
perished. A farmer coming home had heard them bleating in
the flames.

It was no longer said that there had been a forest fire near
the fishing town, and that the *pompiers* had extinguished it,
for now another element had come alive in it. Whether or
not there was an American soldier who had drunk too many
pastis in the sun no longer mattered, and the name of the café
where he had sat was of no consequence, nor the words he
might have said. Whoever he was, he had been endowed now
with political distinction, and as he reeled across the stones he
became the figurehead for whom the slogans were written out
in letters taller than the orchard trees. Fife stood in his black
rodeo shirt, and his black rodeo trousers, on the quayside, his
hands thrust in his jewel-studded pockets, his eyes fixed on
nothing, perhaps seeking to see the soldier, with the cigarette
on his lip, making his way like a blind man to his car.

"I don't believe it was an American that did it," Fife said.

Claude had carried the fishnet that afternoon, and there
was a hermit crab caught in the meshes of it, and she watched
with gravity his small, evil, almost human face, his outsized
thumbs, his irritation. Her feet were bare, and there were

viscous ribbons of seaweed between her toes. The muscles tightened in her long, brown, slender legs as she crouched down.

"Sometimes soldiers in foreign countries get lonely," she said, watching the crab, "and then they take too much to drink."

"But even if a soldier was lonely," Fife said, and he looked out over the moored boats riding quietly, "and even in a foreign country, I bet he wouldn't forget the things he learned about fires when he was a Scout."

"Oh, Fife," said Claude, "then you grow up, you smoke, and you drink, and your memory fails you!"

She held the hermit crab on the palm of her open hand now, and Candy squatted beside her, her braids bleached white as cotton by the sun.

"Does every hermit crab live with an anemone?" Candy asked the mother, but it was Claude who answered.

"They live in discarded mollusc shells," she said almost in rebuke, "in association with annelid worms or sea anemones. But whether they're parasites or just flowers the hermit crab wears as ornament, nobody really knows."

But Candy was lost to them now in other conjecturings, her head turned from them. There were two lovers sitting on the moss-grown landing steps beyond, the water rising and falling in slow, unceasing motion just below their naked entwined feet. Their clothes were poor, their flesh was smooth and dark, and bronzed still darker on their throats and forearms, and they shared one cigarette between them, the girl taking it in her narrow fingers from her own mouth once she had drawn a deep breath in, and then placing it in the boy's pale, handsome mouth. When the cigarette was done, she put her hand on the back of his sun-blackened neck, and drew his face to her face, and kissed him long and sweetly in the golden light. These were the two that Candy watched, her

thin, brown arms around her drawn-up knees, her nose a little
wrinkled; and when she had watched them from this side for
a space of time, she moved in her faded shorts to the other
side, and squatted down again, her eyes quizzical, her toes
spread on the stones, and she watched the sight of love for a
little while from there.

"You Americans, you've got a country all to yourselves as
big as Europe," one of the fishermen had begun saying to the
mother, his blue eyes as cold as metal on her. He stood barefoot, broad-shouldered, in his singlet, a man of fifty maybe,
with his blue cotton trousers rolled below his knees. In one
hand he held the soft lifeless body of an octopus, its long,
rose-colored legs, which could no longer reach and writhe, like
the delicate roots of some exotic plant he had taken from the
sea. "You've got so much territory, you Americans," he said,
"that one side of a hill burning, it isn't the same as it is to a
Frenchman or an Englishman. In America, you've got so
much of everything, you can afford to blow some of it up in
those atom bomb experiments, so what's it to you, a hill burning, or an acre of forest trees wiped out?"

"I don't believe the story about the American," Fife said,
and he looked out past the semaphore at the harbor entrance
to the cliffs that built up from the sea.

A few days after that, the summer was suddenly done, and
the stony hills, the long-eroded cliffs, the sapless vegetation,
took on another, more heterogeneous look. There were shadows cast, and the wine cellars, with their ancient barrels taller
than a man, loomed strangely in the evening. The château
tower, its windows thickly webbed by spiders and sibilant with
the stirring of many dying insects' wings, was a place to turn
from when the night had come. Once the peasants had closed
the heavy cellar doors, and left for their houses down the cart
road where the vineyards sloped away, the mother would
make the shutters of the windows fast, moving from one

hushed room to another while the children slept. Downstairs, there were branched candelabra on the walls the length of the quiet salon, with crystal lozenges, blackened by time, hanging like trembling tears beneath the pear-shaped bulbs. By their uncertain light, she could see her own figure, slender and tall in the long, blue dress, cross quickly toward the mirror in its massive, gilded frame, and she halted there, and looked behind her, as if in fear, before she faced her own eyes in the glass. It seemed to her then that the shadows in the long room had come alive with the movement of many people, people from different countries, and all of them empty-handed, shabbily dressed, and some of them gaunt with hunger, and the words that they whispered like the final dying of insects' wings were: *Peace, peace, peace, for God's sake, peace. We have had enough of war.*

"Yes, peace," the mother said aloud to her own reflection, not allowing her eyes to look away. "What are we doing in uniform in every European country? What are we doing here?"

Outside in the water-lily ponds she could hear the throbbing of the frogs, as rhythmic as breathing, and she turned from the mirror and walked to the handsome, spindle-legged desk, with its brass-encrusted drawer handles, and she sat down to write. Whenever the frog voices abruptly ceased, as if at a signal, she knew it was because a white owl had swooped down through the moonlight to a plane-tree branch above the stagnant water, and that the frogs would be silent in caution until he flew away. It happened every night, and every night she thought that this time it might not be the white owl drifting down on his spread wings, but the movement of a great many people gathering outside that had brought the deep, clonking music to a pause.

"Dearest man," she began to write in almost overwhelming tenderness, "I think the children and I should meet you somewhere else. There doesn't seem much point in you coming so far to join us here." She did not add: *Perhaps somewhere more neutral; but where in Europe can we turn?* "The *mistral* is blowing colder and colder two days out of three," she wrote, "so I think we should plan on another place for your time off. I'm going to start packing tomorrow morning. Send us a telegram, and we'll meet you wherever you say. Perhaps Switzerland?" she suggested. She would wait until his arms were around her before saying: *I too, I too, am afraid of what may happen this year, or next, without us knowing that it is taking place. The wrong voices are speaking out for us in our country, and we cannot be heard—we, you and I, and Claude and Candy and Fife, we have been silenced. You could not possibly come here.* "We could meet you in Davos," she put at the end of the letter, and the frog chorus ceased outside as the owl swept down, or the people of other countries gathered outside the windows, and she addressed the envelope quickly to the U.S. Army colonel's name and his outfit in Frankfurt, Germany.